THE DANC

Ishani Kar-Purkayastha works in Lou ͜ ᴜᴜᴜᴄ ʜealth.
In 2010, she won the *Lancet Wakley Prize* for her essay, *An Epidemic of Loneliness*. She has also written a short story, *The Sky is Always Yours*, to be published in an anthology of British Asian writing, *Too Asian, Not Asian Enough*. This is her first novel.

the Dancing Boy

Ishani Kar-Purkayastha

HarperCollins *Publishers* India
a joint venture with

New Delhi

First published in India in 2011 by
HarperCollins *Publishers* India
a joint venture with
The India Today Group

Copyright © Ishani Kar-Purkayastha 2011

ISBN: 978-93-5029-124-5

2 4 6 8 10 9 7 5 3 1

Ishani Kar-Purkayastha asserts the moral right
to be identified as the author of this work

HarperCollins *Publishers*
A-53, Sector 57, NOIDA 201301, India
77-85 Fulham Palace Road, London W6 8JB, United Kingdom
Hazelton Lanes, 55 Avenue Road, Suite 2900, Toronto, Ontario M5R 3L2
and 1995 Markham Road, Scarborough, Ontario M1B 5M8, Canada
25 Ryde Road, Pymble, Sydney, NSW 2073, Australia
31 View Road, Glenfield, Auckland 10, New Zealand
10 East 53rd Street, New York NY 10022, USA

Typeset in Dante MT Std 11/13.7
InoSoft Systems

Printed and bound at
Manipal Technologies Ltd., Manipal

For ma and babu

The Beginning

Calcutta, 1998

The woman who would have been my grandmother used to say that when souls have unfinished business in the world of the living, they wander, trapped between realities, sometimes for ever.

It is always those who have loved the most – riddled by this most unbearable of nostalgias – who return time and again, to nestle amongst those whom they held close, amongst those who might slowly be forgetting, permitting time its victories.

Yet, there are places, situations that exist beyond the boundaries of time. There are bonds, affections that may never be forgotten. Like ours. Because we were not just close. Moyna and Moyur. Moyur and Moyna. We were not just close. Once upon a time, we were almost the same.

❀

The long hospital corridor winding down to the maternity wing was silent except for the creaking of tired wheels. Shiuli lay semi-recumbent on the stretcher, clutching her belly as the porters pushed her along and a nurse chattered incessant words of distraction. Shiuli called out and the strained rattle of her voice echoed down the hall, bouncing along the old whitewashed walls that stretched towards the immense high ceilings of colonial times.

'Bolo, Shiuli. What is it?'

'You are here, aren't you?'

Moyur nodded, mute, guilty of a thousand desertions.

'And the others?'

'Coming... behind.'

Moyur glanced back at the family. They were all there, following as best they could. But for once he wished that they might pause, might leave him be. For once, he wished that Shiuli wanted him more, and them less. If never in love, then at least in moments of crises past, they had come together. Or rather, she had come to him and led him from the precipice. He wanted his turn.

Moyur inhaled. The clinical fragrance of phenyl soothed him, somewhat.

In the examination room, the lady doctor was waiting.

'Husband?' she asked.

'Yes,' Moyur replied.

She glanced at Shiuli, who nodded her assent, and signalled Moyur to one side.

We seem to be struggling. But I don't feel distressed, not like the last time. Lines are set up, pumping fluid into Shiuli's veins. They give her medicine for the pain, medicine to soothe her nerves. Nothing touches me. I am warm, safe in my cocoon. It is different this time, there is no sadness. I know they want me.

Eventually, the doctor paused in her examination. She looked at them in turn, first Shiuli and then Moyur.

'Mrs Mitra, Mr Mitra. We will have to operate. Immediately.'

The doctor bent down till she was level with Shiuli. 'There is no room for delay, Mrs Mitra. Shall I get the OT ready?'

Before Shiuli could reply, Moyur interjected, 'Aren't you going to get a second opinion?'

'Mr Mitra, there isn't time. One of my senior colleagues will also be in attendance. We will be operating together. He is on his way.'

Moyur lunged at the doctor, clutching her hand within his folded palms. 'Please, doctor didi, save them. Save them.'

'Moyur, they know what is best.' Shiuli turned to the doctor. 'Didi, can you please give me a minute with my husband?'

'Of course. I'll get theatre ready.' The doctor left the room, shutting the door loosely behind her.

'Shiuli, Shiuli.'

'Shh, Moyur.'

'Shiuli, it will be fine. We have to be brave.'

For a moment, the room fell silent with the fraught unity of desperate situations.

'Promise me, Moyur, if I don't survive this...' Shiuli's voice fractured. In its place lay half a sob, half an unmentionable possibility. 'I don't want her ever to know that her mother died.' She rubbed her eyes against the anchol of her sari. 'You can marry again, Moyur. You can be happy. All of you. Promise?'

Moyur didn't reply. For the first time in so many years of marriage, Moyur clung to his wife, wishing he could tell her he loved her, wishing the truth would slip like an accident from his tongue. But he couldn't.

'Give me your word, Moyur. She must never know,' Shiuli insisted.

Moyur shook his head. 'You will be fine, Shiuli. Doctor didi said it is a routine operation. She sees these sorts of cases all the time.'

'Do you promise, Moyur? Do you promise?' Shiuli's eyes pressed him.

Eventually, Moyur gave in.

The time-worn hinges of the door announced the return of the surgical team, this time dressed in theatre blues. They guided the stretcher through the door.

'Shiuli, we'll be waiting here for you.'

A flurry of sound followed the trolley – the footfalls of theatre operatives and nurses, the indecipherable codes they shouted urgently at each other, the haunting symphony of battling alarms.

❀

As we recede, I look back down the corridor. The bleakness of night descends upon Moyur. The family has gathered around him. A toothless ayah lounges against the wall. Dull yellow light sways across the blemished cement floor as a solitary low-watt bulb suspended by a long iron chain rocks with the lazy tick of a pendulum. Anxieties chance upon this emptiness to invade Moyur's mind. No one else hears. No one else knows that there was not just Moyur, but there was always Moyna as well.

But maybe the time has come for me, Moyna, to find my own world, my second chance. As I wait for the doctors to try and save me, I decide that whatever happens the time has certainly come for me to tell Moyur's story.

Part I
1987

Dance for me, my peacock dance,
Dance the dance they tried to steal.

Dance for me, my peacock dance,
The dance we danced before we lived.

Dance for me, my peacock dance,
The dance we danced before we breathed.

How beautiful the male peacock is as he dances, electric blue plumage erect, burning brightly in the monsoon sky.

1

As the monsoon clouds erupted, ma erupted through the door into Moyur's room. 'Chhi chhichi, Nimai, just see what your son is up to. You must teach him the meaning of discipline or he will never stop all this.'

Moyur let go of the sari but the lissom silk, caught in a warm draught, billowed up in front of him, unwilling to leave his fingers. Delighted, he took a step forward, hopeful of one last illicit feel as the fabric wafted to the floor. 'Ma, I am only practising so I can work in the shop. You always scold me.'

Ma ignored him. She snatched the sari from where it had come to rest, draped around his petulant ankles, and unleashed upon it a frenzy of folding. 'Nimai, Nimai, are you listening? Ever since we got rid of that maid, whatever her name is, things have gone from bad to worse. Who knows what curse she put on him? You never can tell with these people.'

Moyur watched his mother mechanically rebuking the beautiful sari. She never wore the many silks she owned, leaving them to languish while choosing to dress as she had that day in an over-starched ochre taanth arranged stiffly around her, adding inelegant layers to her voluptuous midriff.

The grunts and shouts of boys playing football bounced in through the open window. The park lay adjacent to the house and Moyur's bedroom overlooked the pitch. There would be much tussling and an unnecessary excess of diving and sliding into the cool, freshly forming mud. All of a sudden, Moyur regretted his earlier decision. He could have been there, playing, drenched in the monsoon.

The last few weeks had been unbearable: another relentless summer of viscous days and feverish nights; of skies ripe with clouds poised to erupt. Whenever he could, Moyur had been outside because the rain did not just soak his clothes, it quenched his heart and the dry summer soul, infusing it with life. And he, like the rest of the city, scurried about, pretending to run from cover to cover while secretly dashing for a feel of the softest, sweetest raindrops in the world.

Bapu appeared at the door. 'What is the problem now? I am already late.'

'What late? This is why he has turned out like this. Always putting your business first,' ma retorted. 'Is it more important to you than your one and only son's future?' Ma's eyes, inky black, flashed between the sari and bapu's hesitant frame.

'Why are you getting so agitated, Kakuli?' Bapu's voice was flat as always. 'He is only playing, na?'

'Is this what you call playing? What fate gave me such a husband on top of the son?' Ma slapped the back of her hand against her forehead, as she often did when deriding destiny. 'Enough is enough. Idle mind is devil's workshop. Really, these days it seems you are always playing.' She tucked the loose end of her sari into her petticoat and stood before Moyur. Bapu, who was slightly to one side, an unwilling participant, directed his gaze wearily between the two adversaries. He sighed. 'All right, let me take him to the shop.'

These were the words Moyur had been longing for, but before he could say anything, ma, who had grown even more incensed, replied, 'Are you out of your mind or what? You want to take him to the sari shop with you – is there nothing in that head of yours?'

Bapu did not respond. He glared at ma; then, in a barely audible voice, he instructed Moyur to follow him. As they headed downstairs, ma called out in a more subdued voice, 'At least don't let him near the saris.'

Bapu grabbed Moyur's hand and bundled him through the front door. They opened up their matching green and black striped umbrellas and walked to the bus stop, bapu muttering under his breath, 'What does that woman expect? Put food on her plate, entertain you – what else am I supposed to do with you? The shop won't run itself, will it?' Moyur followed him as invisibly as he could. He reckoned bapu didn't want an answer to that last question and he worried that any trespass into his monologue might lead to an inadvertent change of plan.

It was not the first time he was going to the shop; bapu often took him along to help in the run-up to pujo, when everyone in the city bought saris and the shelves were emptied as soon as they were filled.

Moyur's main job was to bring tea for the customers from the cha-wala. If they looked like they were going to spend a lot of money, bapu, or more often his right-hand man, Joba kaku, would send Moyur to the stall around the corner to bring them a bottle of cold Mazaa or Thums Up. Shopping in Calcutta must have been a tiring, dehydrating endeavour. It always seemed that way because Moyur was kept occupied from morning to evening ferrying tea and bottles of cold drink between bapu's sari shop and the corner stall.

Well, that is a small lie. Sometimes Moyur dithered along the way. Sometimes he stopped to pet the stray dogs or banter with the rickshaw-walas. On good days, the cha-wala gave him a free cup of tea because he was such a good customer. The cha-wala was an old gentleman, his hand trembled each time he lifted the battered steel kettle in which he carried his concoction. He only had one kettle. The newer guys had two: sweetened and unsweetened. But he only had the strength for one. Nobody complained. In any case, the demand for unsweetened tea had only just been invented.

The tea and chatter broke up the to-ing and fro-ing. If ma had known, she would have been happy. The less time he spent in the shop, the happier she was. After all, Moyur was her only son and as much her father's grandson as bapu's son. So, another small lie, but this is the last one: Moyur did not have that many bottles to carry because the ladies who came to their shop were the sort who were either too sophisticated to accept complimentary cold drinks from shopkeepers or too hot and bothered from their exertions to drink tea. Moyur spent most of his time standing in the shadow of the doorway, just out of sight, watching bapu as he threw open sari after sari with a quick upward flick of his wrists, in front of a congregation of marvelling eyes. Moyur loved watching the colours reveal themselves, the endless variety of design from the cheapest machine block prints to the most expensive intricate hand-woven embroidery. He loved the glimpses of tentative excitement before prices were named, hearing the oohs and aahs, the deliberations and the smiles. Most of all, he longed to touch those beautiful pieces of fabric and wrap himself in their expanse. But, at twelve, he was far too young to be entrusted with the handling of saris. Moyur had to serve his time as the boy who fetched the drinks.

That day, however, the first day of the monsoon, business was slow on account of the downpour. Without customers, the shop seemed deeper than usual – a long corridor stretching away from the predictable bustle of the road into dark recesses full of undiscovered pleasures and palpitations. The red cement floor, normally covered in street dust brought in by the stampede of slippers, had a fresh sheen. The stools remained stacked and the white cloth covering the raised white display platform was uncreased. All day, the glass doors that stretched along the length and breadth of the back wall remained shut, saris subdued in pristine piles.

It was not till afternoon that Mr Rajagopalan arrived, laden with goods. The large jute bags he carried were overflowing with fabrics that announced themselves in a cacophony of colour and jostling cellophane packets. He placed his red and blue striped carriers on the white platform and folded his hands.

'Nomoshkar, Mr Mitra.'

Bapu strode to the front of the shop. 'Oh-ho, Mr Rajagopalan, I had completely forgotten about our appointment. Have you come straight from Madras?'

'No, no, don't worry. Appointment is not till next week but I arrived in Calcutta early, so I thought, why don't I come and see if Mr Mitra is free. Then maybe I can absolve myself of my business today itself.'

'Very good.'

'Will that be of convenience to yourself, sir?'

'Yes, yes, you have come on a fortunate day. The shop is empty. It looks like the shop has been awaiting your arrival only.' They both laughed.

Bapu gestured towards Moyur.

Moyur, who had been sitting cross-legged in one corner of the platform, unravelled his legs and walked self-consciously towards them. Bapu turned to Mr Rajagopalan. 'This is my only son, Moyur. He wants to do an MBA, then take over my business one day, isn't it, Moyur?'

Moyur stared, mouth slightly ajar, at the sizeable visitor. Mr Rajagopalan's forehead was covered in a fine film of sweat that re-formed every few seconds despite the continual efforts of his soggy handkerchief.

Mr Rajagopalan nodded. 'Yes, well, lot to learn, lot to learn. In which class you are studying, Moyur?'

'Class six, St James' Boys School, A.J.C. Bose Road, Calcutta 14.'

Mr Rajagopalan guffawed and ruffled Moyur's hair. 'Very good, very good. Attention to detail from such a young age bodes well for the future.'

The look of pride that spread across bapu's face caught Moyur off guard. 'Moyur, why don't you get our guest something to drink? What would you like? Tea? Something cold?'

'One hot tea with milk.' Mr Rajagopalan ran his thick fingers through Moyur's hair again before spreading himself across two stools. 'And two sugars in that. No dieting for me.'

By the time Moyur returned, Mr Rajagopalan, bapu and Joba kaku were deep in conversation. Joba kaku was an expert buyer. Although bapu made the final decisions, he often deferred to Joba kaku's knowledge of market prices.

The contents of Mr Rajagopalan's bags had been laid out on the platform in front of the glass cabinets. Not wanting to draw attention to himself, Moyur placed the earthenware cup delicately on the stool next to Mr Rajagopalan and retreated to his corner.

'So what about these benarasis, Mr Rajagopalan?' bapu asked. 'They are very beautiful. How much are you charging for this one?' He pointed to a deep red benarasi onto which thousands of tiny flowers had been embroidered in gold zari. Yet more leaves and flowers adorned the anchol.

'This one, sir, I won't lie to you. At the outset, let me tell you that this sari is more expensive than the rest, but the reason is that the threading is so fine. Even on the closest inspection of these flowers, I will challenge you, sir, to tell me that you can see the stitches. As for the anchol, just imagine how beautiful it will look swishing across somebody's back.'

'Okay, okay. How much?'

'I will not insult you, sir, by asking one price then haggling for another. Thirteen thousand rupees – final price!' he announced with a flourish. At which both bapu and Joba kaku exclaimed. The bargaining went on until they came to the black bomkai.

From within his bag, Mr Rajagopalan withdrew three pairs of sunglasses. Putting one on himself, he advised bapu and Joba kaku to put on a pair each as well. 'You will see why.' Then, suddenly noticing Moyur, he threw a pair towards him before bapu could protest. 'Even your youth cannot protect you from this,' he said, rocking his head from side to side.

Delighted, Moyur donned his sunglasses.

'This bomkai I have recovered with much endurance, Mr Mitra. As you will see, it is not like anything I have ever brought you in the history of our humble acquaintance.'

Bapu looked bemused but he humoured his guest.

'It is a piece that I have found through recommendation of one of my dearest friends, freshly departed from this earth, may his soul be in peace. There is a village in Orissa, not far from Berhampur. Are you familiar with the area at all?'

'You must forgive my ignorance. I have never had the good fortune to travel that way.'

'No, no. No question of forgiveness is arising. Anyway, it is a small place. They have not even seen motor cars there. You know,' he continued, throwing his right hand across his chest, 'the day I arrived, the whole village was pushing my car along the road.'

'Why?'

'You ask me why?' He shook his head. 'This is the big question, isn't it, sir?' Mr Rajagopalan looked wistfully at bapu.

'So?'

After a suitable pause, Mr Rajagopalan started again. 'I say it is the central government. Why should they care about a village in Orissa? Those village roads are not suitable for cars. It only went so far. Then dead. Hundred per cent dead. It is a miracle we could start it up again. Anyway, that is not why I am telling you this. The people there are not just layabouts. They came to greet me. And they took me to Padma's house. Have you heard of Padma? Padma Senapati?'

Bapu shook his head.

'He is a rising star of India. His saris are everywhere – Bombay, Delhi, Madras, even foreign. Only Calcutta is yet to catch up. Now he is so busy with orders that the whole village has become his factory and he is the guru. It just so happened that the day I arrived, he was busy doing what he loves most – embroidering. The village people, keen though they are, they are simple – I cannot blame them for it. They did not warn me that the master was at work so, as I walked in, my unsuspecting eyes were dazzled into momentary blindness by the brilliance of his stitching.' Mr Rajagopalan raised both hands to shield his eyes as though at imminent risk of being blinded again. 'I am not going to make the same mistake with you. Now that you have your sunglasses on,' he said, pausing to allow them to prepare themselves, 'let me take it out.'

Bapu, Joba kaku and Mr Rajagopalan sat in a triangle, Mr Rajagopalan at the pinnacle, revelling in the attention he was commanding. Moyur, still perched on the outskirts, inched towards the trio, clutching his sunglasses to his eyes.

Mr Rajagopalan unwrapped the sari very slowly from its brown paper cover. At first sight, Joba kaku gasped. The whole room brightened. Golden constellations danced upon an expanse of raw, blue-black silk. Demi-gods cavorted divinely along the length of the anchol. Moyur stopped breathing. They all did. For it was the most spectacular sari any of them had ever laid eyes on, but they were not allowed to feast for long before Mr Rajagopalan began folding it away. 'You shouldn't look upon it too much at one go. You will get a headache.'

They watched in seduced silence as Mr Rajagopalan reverently folded the sari and tenderly nudged it back into its packet. Once he had put it away and retrieved the sunglasses, he asked, 'So, Mr Mitra, what do you think?'

Bapu nodded his vigorous agreement. 'It is too beautiful, Mr Rajagopalan. You have outdone yourself. But how can one wear such a precious thing?'

To which Mr Rajagopalan replied, 'Precisely. A thing of such magnificence is to be beheld in small doses only.'

Bapu did not reply immediately. Mr Rajagopalan persevered in filling the gap. 'May I be so bold, sir, as to suggest that perhaps your wife… what with pujo around the corner…'

Perhaps residual guilt from the morning played a part in swaying bapu into buying that bomkai for ma. Perhaps it was Mr Rajagopalan's gentle cajoling. Whatever the reason, Kakuli Mitra became the proud owner of the most exquisite bomkai that was ever exchanged at the Bengal Silk House.

❀

Ma was born in Calcutta, and with her first breaths she inhaled the dusty, humid air of Maryland Nursing Home on C.I.T. Road, in the heart of the city. She was born to Mou and Debashis Mondal, a dedicated housewife and her successful engineer husband. They were, by all accounts, an affluent family with a three-storey house in Lake Gardens, the upcoming posh new development for middle-class Bengalis. In fact, the only mistake her spirit had perhaps made in choosing that family was their lower-caste surname, Mondal. Our grandmother used to say that there is a way to know how far the spirit of a newborn has travelled. Maybe it was all confabulation (dimma loved to tell stories), but she said it with such assuredness that it was hard to doubt her. The further a spirit travels from its previous surroundings, she said, the more the baby cries on its first night in its new world – from bewilderment, perhaps, who knows? But the fact is that ma did not just cry, she howled, on and on through the night, with screams so piercing they sliced through the city, all the way to the ears of Pandit Chatterjee, who would one day be appointed to fix up her marriage. Innocently, she had given the pandit a searing headache and years later he returned the favour, equally innocently.

Ma and bapu were married at a very young age. Younger even than the norm for two such people hailing from their backgrounds. For ma, who had spent her entire life in Calcutta, getting married at eighteen was virtually a scandal amongst her friends. Ma's voice was voluptuous, and though she never announced her grudges within the family, most of the neighbourhood was well aware of the misfortunes fate had dealt her.

Bapu turned a deaf ear. Who, after all, was he to stand in the way of ma's one true pastime? She often boasted about how talented she had been as a young girl; how heads would turn as she walked back home from school in the late afternoon; her stunning dance recitals and nightingale-like voice, so melodious that even the most troublesome wailing baby was instantly silenced. And what had become of her since the wretched day that she was married? Fate had stolen from her all her talents, all her beauty in one fell swoop. All she had been left to console herself with were her conversations with the other women of the para as they hollered to each other across the network of balconies that split the skies: juicy bits of gossip about everything conceivable, in particular their husbands, the sexual deviances of the maids, the marriageability of the unmarried and, of course, the injustices of fate.

Bapu, in contrast, hailed from the Sunderbans. His capital lay in his name, Mitra, the Kshatriya name complimenting ma's aspirations towards a higher caste, and in a modest confidence in his lineage that buffered him against both a sense of inadequacy and any burning ambition to prove himself. His desires began and ended with a decent job and a steady income. He had acquired his wife through the endeavours of two over-zealous families, and although he did not completely understand her, he never felt this to be a particular impediment to marital harmony. She had borne him a son, albeit a slightly odd son, of whose character he was somewhat uncertain. But who was he to complain? On the whole, bapu was satisfied with his life. Fate had held his hand as he crossed the gulf from the Sunderbans to Calcutta and, with a little financial assistance from his in-laws, even given him his own little business.

❄

Mr Rajagopalan departed with three empty bags. Apart from the black bomkai, bapu bought fifty-seven saris from Mr Rajagopalan and placed orders for three hundred more, to be delivered in time for Durga Pujo.

Bapu and Moyur closed shop at six that evening. Bapu was keen to get home: the rain hadn't stopped for a second and the shop lay disappointingly empty.

The 201 back to Salt Lake was heaving with the office crowd. The best place to stand was at the front of the bus, just behind the driver, where the ladies' seats were. Bapu squashed himself against the other passengers clustered there, and Moyur stood in the little hiatus between bapu and the ladies. The dirty glass windows of the bus had been pulled up to keep the water out, so bapu and Moyur sweltered in the pungent interior. By the time they got off, their clothes were damp from collective sweat and dirty rain.

Ma was standing on the balcony, watching the road. As soon as she caught sight of them, she rushed downstairs to open the door.

'You two are completely wet. Go quickly, Moyur. Have a bath or you'll catch a cold.'

'Yes, ma.'

Over his head, she looked questioningly at bapu. 'How was your day?'

'Tell your mother, Moyur. How was it? We had a gala time, tai na?'

'Good, good.' She kissed the top of Moyur's head. 'You know I don't like being angry with you, but why do you do such naughty things?'

'Sorry, ma.'

'Tomorrow, why don't you go and play football in the park? Tinku and Bapta came looking for you. They need you on the team tomorrow. They said it's BB versus BC. Important game.'

That cheered him up. Tinku and Bapta were his best friends, apart from Jonali. They also went to St James' Boys School, A.J.C. Bose Road, Calcutta14, and in some ways they were better time-pass friends than Jonali. Still, Jonali was special.

'Can I go and see them?'

'Not now. Go wash up and then eat something.'

As Moyur climbed the stairs, he catalogued in his head the fifty-seven saris that bapu had bought from Mr Rajagopalan.

2

Chakum, chukum, chakum, chukum.

Lunchtime, the following Monday. Ma had already left the table. Moyur glanced at the clock. It was almost two. He bundled the last handful of rice and dal into his mouth. Lily mashi, the cook-cum-general-take-carer of daily life, waited with a look of long suffering. She peppered her watch with forays back into the kitchen where she created mini commotions of clashing steel crockery to make her point: she had things to be getting on with. Moyur's plate was almost clean but he licked his fingers with contrived diligence. Their stand-off had become a daily ritual.

Lily mashi had been with the family for over five years. When she first arrived, her blouses had been too loose for her, the fabric of her petticoats bunched up around her slight hips, but as time passed it became quickly apparent that Lily mashi had a knack for cooking. Not only could she prepare the staples of household cuisine to perfection, she also picked up a multitude of recipes for snacks, which she experimented lavishly on herself before unleashing on the rest of the family. As a result, she had, over the past few years, grown perfectly into her hand-me-down blouses and wide petticoats.

Moyur lifted the plate to his face and ran his tongue across it – side to side, up and down.

'Eeeesh! Why don't you lick all the plates in that uncivilized way? Then there'd be no need to wash the dishes. Save me a job.'

He put down his plate. 'First class, Lily mashi.' His chair screeched across the mosaic tiles as he stood up.

'Do you have to make such a godforsaken noise?' she retaliated but his compliment had placated her and she couldn't quite suppress a smile.

Moyur stuck his belly out and stroked it as he made his retreat.

'Go wash your hands, rinse your mouth.'

Moyur obliged, accelerating towards the sink as she spoke. He shook his wet hands, scattering drops of water across the floor and on the recently painted walls.

'Change out of your uniform,' she shouted after him as he made his getaway, but he was not in the mood to listen. On the bus ride home, one of the older boys had passed a whisper across three rows of eager ears to Jonali, making her blush and the messengers erupt with laughter. He had been sitting across the aisle with Bapta and Tinku, absorbed in a discussion about their upcoming football tournament.

'Jojo, what is it? What did they say?' Moyur had asked, standing up.

This only prompted a further round of cackling.

Jonali straightened herself and, with an air of magnificent superiority, declared, 'Nothing, childish nonsense.'

Moyur turned to face the row of boys behind her. 'What did you say? Go on, tell me.'

He was met with conspiracy. He stared hard at them but it made no difference to a situation that was not that rare on the school bus. It was, after all, the only place, other than the annual sports day, where the girls from Pratt and the boys from St James' were within inches of each other.

Moyur had to sit back down. The straggles of silliness were subsiding and Jonali was resolute. Even when they got off the bus, she refused him the details. Now, that was not fair. Not when he told her everything; besides, he needed to know, he just did.

For once, it was Moyur who arrived first on his balcony. He was restless. 'Jojo, Jojo, are you coming?'

Jonali lived next door, and if they had been a foot or two closer, they might have been able to jump from one balcony to the other. The door to Jonali's bedroom lay at right angles to Moyur's balcony, and when she left it open he could see straight inside. He had seen her combing her hair, doing her homework. He had never seen anything interesting though – the door was always closed then, like it was now. Jonali opened it a fraction and stuck her hand out to signal five minutes.

Moyur slumped onto the warm floor and peered through the railings. In the distance, a bus rattled as it wound around Salt Lake. Their para was one of the oldest neighbourhoods in this Calcutta suburb, with its sun-bleached assortment of higgledy-piggledy houses on narrow pock-marked streets that once upon a time had been avenues.

'Hi, Moyur.' Jonali's bedroom door creaked open and she emerged on her balcony and immediately flopped into position, arms and legs folding gracefully into place. Her thick, shoulder-length black hair was disciplined into its usual plait. They sat for a few minutes in silence, surveying the streets below. Nothing ever happened in the middle of the afternoon. Sometimes a cow would amble past, swishing its tail to ward off the harem of flies buzzing around its behind.

'So, are you going to tell me?' Moyur started.

'Tell you what?'

Moyur gestured towards the road and Jonali rolled her eyes.

'You're still after that?'

'Yes,' he said, feeling a little wronged by her pretended maturity.

'It was nothing.'

'But I want to know.'

Jonali sighed. 'Ritesh said, do I want to go with him to the park tonight.'

'Is that all?'

Jonali nodded.

Moyur considered the significance of the message. 'Why does he want you to go to the park?' he asked finally.

Jonali shrugged. 'Who knows?'

They returned to their thoughts, Moyur almost satisfied but feeling like he shouldn't be. Across the road, an old banyan tree had taken over the entire corner plot of land, its giant branches yawning across the sky. Underneath its canopy a few saleswomen had gathered. They sat on their haunches, gossiping and arranging baskets of steel crockery.

'Where do you think they live, Moyur?' Jonali asked finally.

'Those women?'

'Do you think they are married?'

'Definitely.'

Jonali sighed. 'I don't ever want to get married, Moyur. See how sad they look.'

The women were dressed in bright saris with sequins that shimmered in the splinters of sunlight filtering through the leaves.

'I think they look beautiful.'

Jonali giggled. 'You toh think everything is beautiful. Silly.'

Moyur didn't reply. He continued to study the women, who were talking and laughing with an adult poise he wished he had.

'Why don't you come over, Moyur?' Jonali asked. 'Ma has gone to Gariahat. Shikha didi is out.'

Moyur turned to face Jonali, enticed by this last piece of information.

'Really? Where?'

'Pujor bajar. They won't be back for hours.'

All of a sudden, the bland afternoon tingled with opportunity, her invitation triggering a cinema of clandestine pleasures in his head.

'Let me check on ma.' Moyur stood up. He hesitated. 'Are you sure it's fine?'

'I am telling you na.'

'Okay, I'm coming.'

Moyur tiptoed into ma's bedroom. Ma was lying on her side, facing away from the door. Her breathing was slow and reassuringly regular. He watched her for three minutes, timing it with his digital wristwatch. Then, convinced of her sleep, he left.

It took barely a minute to walk the few paces between the two houses and as he approached, he heard her chappals slapping against the stairs. Jonali opened the door, breathless, smiling with anticipation.

'We can borrow some of ma's stuff as well today,' she reported.

'Where's Riya?'

'She and kakimoni have gone to kakimoni's mother's place. The house is empty.'

'No way!'

Jonali grinned. This rarely happened. There was always someone around. And they were all so nosy. If they ever shut the door, someone or the other would come knocking at once.

With unnecessary stealth, they walked into Jonali's room. On the floor she had laid out a decoy – Snakes and Ladders, the counters dotted randomly in various stances of mid-play, the die carefully splayed, one on the board and one on the floor.

On the bed, Jonali had displayed four saris, all of which he recognized, except one.

'Can I try the pink one?'

She nodded. 'Maybe you can show me how to put it on this time, Moyur. You are so good at it.'

'No problem. I'll teach you.' Moyur struggled to draw himself away from the saris on the bed. 'Let me just put mine on first, so that I remember.'

Moyur picked up the pink georgette and began rolling it between his thumb and index finger, savouring the flimsiness of the fabric. Caught in its soft fluidity, he moved his arms reflexively into position, one on his hip, the other rotating above his head, indulgently tracing the shape of his daydream.

'Moyur,' Jonali snapped, 'will you teach me or not?'

Guiltily, he focused on his friend. 'Sorry. Of course I'll teach you. In fact, by the end of the day you'll be a pro. Just let me put on mine first. For practice's sake.'

Jonali rolled her eyes but said nothing further.

Moyur turned away from Jonali and picked up the matching pink blouse. They were roughly the same size, Jonali and he, so the blouse fit him perfectly except for the small pouches where Jonali's breasts would have been. Had he been by himself, he would have stuffed it with rags, but he couldn't bring himself to do this with Jonali watching. Instead, he carried on with the rest of the routine, putting on the pink petticoat and then the sari, acutely aware of Jonali's unrelenting gaze.

When he finished, she clapped. 'Bah bah, Moyur. You put me to shame. I should be the rajkumar and you should be the rajkumari.'

'We can't play that any more.'

'No? Why not?'

Moyur observed Jonali's blossoming body a little enviously and then turned to look at himself in the full-length mirror behind the door of the almirah.

'Do you have any lipstick?'

'Why can't we play?' she persisted as she held out some lipstick and kajol that she had smuggled from Meena pishi's dresser, a slight pout dancing on her lips as she did so.

'Accha baba, we can play if you want to,' Moyur replied, 'but you can't wear a sari and also be a rajkumar.'

'Why not? It's our game, our rules,' she said, handing him some bangles.

He conceded. As quickly as he could, Moyur dabbed kajol on the inner rims of his lower eyelids. With red kumkum he drew a teep on his forehead and applied the bright lipstick.

Then he turned to his accomplice. She had already put on her petticoat and blouse. Ruefully, he noted again how she fit her blouse, her small breasts snugly filling the pockets that sat redundant against his own spare chest.

'Come and stand here, and listen to everything I say.'

Jonali nodded.

'You start on the left hand side of your body, okay? You take one end of the sari and tuck it into the petticoat. Then you take the rest of the fabric and wrap it around your body as many times as it will go until you get to the anchol. You have to drape the anchol over your left shoulder. Got it?'

Jonali concentrated on his every instruction.

As he wrapped the sari around her, he let the back of his hand brush against her left breast, hoping she wouldn't notice. He was overwhelmed by a desire to compare them with his own attempts at makeshift bosoms.

Immediately, she stiffened and a flush spread across her cheeks. Moyur stepped back.

'Do you want to do it yourself, bit by bit?'

Jonali shook her head.

For the remainder of the lesson, they both kept their eyes trained on the fabric and the various manipulations it was undergoing.

'Okay. Well, next, you have to make the pleats. You take this fabric at the front and you start folding.' Moyur guided the pleats expertly along his fingers. 'You have to hold them now, Jojo.' When they were ready, accordion like, he handed them over to Jonali. 'Hold them tight,' he instructed, dropping to his heels. 'Holding?'

'Yes,' Jonali replied.

He tugged the bottom of each pleat to bring it level with the rest. 'Okay, now tuck them into your petticoat.'

As the swathe of red fabric became her sari, Jonali hijacked the commentary. 'Then you tuck the back in, and pin the anchol to your blouse. Done.'

'Yes. That last pinning is optional.'

Jonali admired herself in the mirror.

Moyur gazed at her reflection. 'You look beautiful,' he whispered.

'You are just saying that. You think everything is beautiful.'

'No.' Moyur inched closer to the dresser. 'Do you want to try to put the sari on yourself?' he asked. He wanted her to move so he could carry on applying his make-up. But she didn't. She loitered in front of the mirror.

'You're such an odd boy,' she said.

Moyur sat down on the edge of the bed and waited for her to carry on, but she continued her musings in private. Moyur stuck his tongue out and licked a bead of sweat that had gathered along his upper lip. He tugged at the pleats of his sari, arranging them obsessively so that they fell perfectly, one on top of the other.

'Moyur, do you want to see my breasts?' Jonali said suddenly. Before he could reply, she added, 'You know, only for a minute, and you can't touch, but...'

Moyur held his breath. Lately, his voice had been as temperamental as the Calcutta power supply. Afraid of his tone and of appearing too keen, Moyur constructed responses in his head with which he might gracefully accept without appearing foolish or bad. Between his legs he felt a swell of nervous excitement that perplexed him. Eventually, he replied, 'Okay.'

'Really?'

'Yes.'

'Fine. You won't tell anybody.'

Moyur shook his head.

'Not even Tinku.'

'God promise.'

They looked at each other for a few seconds. An inconvenient suspicion that this was wrong niggled at Moyur's conscience. He let it niggle.

'Sit there and don't get up,' Jonali instructed. 'Whatever you do, don't get up. And no touching.'

Jonali turned away from Moyur, which gave him the opportunity to steal furtive glances at her back – elbows on either side, working industriously to undo the hooks the tailor had sewn on, the guardians of her modesty. When she had finished she walked towards him, stopping a few feet away; the thin fabric of the sari still covered her chest. Clutching the anchol with her right hand, she leaned forward. 'Give me your watch. I am going to time it.'

Moyur hesitated. It was a cherished birthday present. He had taken ma from shop to shop in search of the perfect dial. Still, there were bigger things at stake now. Worst case scenario: he wouldn't get it back. His eyes drifted to the flimsy frontier between him and Jonali's breasts. He undid his watch strap and handed it over, keeping his arms as far away from her body as he could manage. Jonali took the watch and studied it. As she caught the rhythm of the second count, her head started bobbing gently in time with it, then her lips. 37, 38, 39. It seemed an eternity to Moyur, waiting on the bed, eyes riveted to the designated spot. 51, 52, 53.

'Okay. Time starts now!'

She dropped the anchol. With a great sense of purpose, Moyur focused on those two mounds of flesh; up and down they went in a gentle undulation. From his seated position, he leaned to the left and then to the right to get side views; he bent down to get a view from below. Her nipples were bigger than his, richer in colour and with stubby ends. He deliberated asking for a feel but before he could decide, the minute was up.

'Time's up,' she said, doing up her blouse. She did not turn away this time, watching him as she refastened the hooks, beguiled by his abject fascination.

'So, what do you think?'

Moyur felt the colour rise to his cheeks. He sidled further back onto the bed and began folding the other blouses that were laid out by his side.

Disappointed by his lack of appreciation, Jonali slammed the almirah door shut. 'That's the last time I am ever showing you anything.'

The two sat in silence, Moyur on the bed and Jonali on the chair, both contemplating.

After some time, Moyur asked, 'Why did you say I was odd?'

Jonali was not the type of girl to remain annoyed for very long. It was a weakness Moyur knew only too well and he quickly drew her back into the conversation.

'You know,' she said, 'how you like to dress up as a girl. Other boys hate that kind of stuff.'

'I don't just like dressing up. I like other things too.'

'Like?'

'Like being a shopkeeper.'

'Yes, but that is only because of the saris. Anyone can see that.'

'I like football. I like arm-wrestling. In fact, I am the champion arm-wrestler of this para.'

Jonali giggled. 'Impossible. What, you even beat Tinku?'

'Arrey Tinku, Bapta, Bittu. All of them. They are insects compared to me.'

'I don't believe you.'

'Fine. Don't believe me. Ask Tinku next time you see him.'

'No. Why don't we have a match now? Then I might just believe you.'

Moyur shook his head. 'No chance.'

'Why?'

'You'll get hurt.'

'No, I won't. Don't be like that.'

They bartered a while but in the end Jonali had her way.

Moyur crept out of Jonali's room and tiptoed across to the dining table. He picked up a chair and was about to sneak back when Jonali came to the door and started giggling. 'Nobody is going to see you, silly. Why are you walking so quietly?'

She stepped into the living room and started marching up and down.

'What are you doing?'

'Marching, like a prince.' She put on a gruff voice. 'Listen, all you citizens of Lanka, I am your rajkumar. I have come to find a wife. Bring me your daughters and sisters.' Pointing at Moyur, she continued, 'Who is that beautiful damsel over there? The one in the gorgeous pink.'

Moyur pranced across to her, carrying the chair in one arm. 'What kind of prince are you that lets his would-be princess do all the donkey work?'

'Ooh. Rajkumari, are you angry with your prince?' Jonali strode up to him. 'Okay, baba, sorry. Okay? No more monkeying around. Promise. Cross my heart, hope to die, stick a needle in my eye.' She crossed herself a few times and followed him into the bedroom.

Moyur put the chair down, and rolled out a maadur on the floor, so that they could sit without spoiling their saris. Moyur knelt on the mat, delicately tucking his anchol out of the way. Jonali followed suit. They put their elbows down on the chair and gripped each other's fists. The bangles they wore crashed against each other.

'At the count of three. One, two, three, go.'

Their arms lurched from side to side. Jonali proved to be one of Moyur's stronger opponents. As the battle climaxed, Moyur caught sight of himself in the mirror, in his pink sari, facing Jonali, undisturbed by the world around them. Dark kajol-framed eyes looked back at him, full of a longing that belonged to somebody else – a flicker of a soul that wasn't his. It was a distraction that cost him dearly. The next moment, his hand came crashing down, the weight of Jonali's triumph squarely upon it.

'I win, I win,' Jonali screamed, jumping up.

'No. That isn't fair. Rematch. I wasn't concentrating.'

'So how is that my fault? I won fair and simple. Anyway, I can't play again. My hand is hurting.'

Moyur turned away from Jonali and looked at himself again. The kajol-framed eyes that gazed back at him were his.

And they were also mine. Like an eclipse, riveting, ephemeral, one world traverses another. In a moment we will slip past.

He turned back and caught Jonali gazing at him.

'You look lovely, Moyur.'

Do I look lovely? I want to ask.

'You won't tell anyone, will you?'

She shook her head. 'And you?'

'No way.'

Neither will I, I say, but they can't hear me.

❋

As the afternoon went past, the first sounds of re-awakening wafted in from outside: dogs barking, the creeng-creeng of bicycle bells, the metallic drone of shutters being reluctantly rolled up.

'I'd better go now.'

But Jonali asked him to stay. He remembered that she had just shown him something – something special. So it was the least he could do; he stayed, for a few minutes. He would have stayed longer but the quiet winding down of their play was thrust into panic by the sound of a key turning in the lock.

'Jojo, Shikha, are you home?'

Startled, they looked at the clock. Quarter past five. Ma hadn't even started calling for Moyur yet.

'Oh, god. She said she wouldn't be back till seven.'

Moyur jumped up. His legs were trembling. He pulled at the sari. His fingers fumbled. Why had he secured it so well? Desperately, he rubbed the kumkum off his forehead with his spit and rubbed his lips on the inside of his T-shirt. Jonali fled to the living room to stall her mother.

'Why are you dressed up like this, Jojo? Are you alone? Who taught you to wear all this lipstick and nonsense?'

'Ma, you are back early. Did you buy anything?'

Moyur wrenched the bangles off his arm and they clattered to the floor.

Footsteps moved towards the bedroom.

'Let me see what shopping you have done.' He heard Jonali's attempt to rustle through the bags.

'Who is it? What are you up to, Jojo?' Then she saw him. 'Oh, Moyur. It's you.'

'Hello, Meena pishi.'

In turn, she clocked the unfolded sari on the floor, Jonali's clothes in a pile at the foot of the bed, his anxious efforts at concealment.

'Moyur, your mother is looking for you. Please go home. I will talk to her later.'

Moyur looked from her face, quietly simmering with rage, to Jonali's, crumpled in fear.

'Meena pishi, it was my idea. We were playing rajkumar-rajkumari.'

'Yes, I can see that for myself. You children are getting ahead of yourselves. Now get out.'

Moyur stumbled past Meena pishi and Jonali. Tears rose to his eyes, faster than he could wipe them away.

Out in the street, Tinku and Bapta were standing beneath his balcony, shouting for him.

'There he is. Where have you been? The match is at half-time. Are you coming or what?'

'He is crying. Why are you crying?' asked Tinku.

'Chhi chhi, why are you crying, khoka?' Bapta parroted.

'I'm not playing today.'

'Not playing?' Bapta sneered. 'What, your girlfriend told you she doesn't love you? Or she won't let you touch her down there?'

Without hesitation, Moyur punched Bapta on his shoulder. Bapta stumbled backwards.

'Chootiya. What did you hit me for?' Bapta swung his right arm to hit him back but Moyur ducked just in time. He barged into Bapta with his shoulder, almost knocking him to the ground. 'Stupid,' Moyur jeered, 'can't even fight properly.'

'Stop it, both of you. Stop it,' Tinku was yelling.

By now, ma had appeared on the balcony and started her wailing.

Bapta took another swipe and this time his fist landed on Moyur's nose. Blood trickled down his face. Ram kaku from the corner shop came running over and stepped in between them.

'What are you doing? Fighting like dogs. Have you no shame or respect for your families?'

Moyur wiped the blood from his face with his T-shirt. 'He started it by saying dirty things.'

'Aren't you ashamed of yourself? You still have the audacity to speak?' Ram kaku was revelling in his one-time eminence as moral arbiter. Moyur walked away.

Ma was already at the front door.

'What is going on, Moyur? Won't you even let me sleep in peace any more?'

Moyur brushed past her and went into the house. Tears and blood were slowly congealing down his face.

In the bathroom, he splashed himself with warm water. Ma was outside, banging on the door, demanding an explanation. He ignored her. In the mirror, he saw himself again. Another Moyur he had never seen before, with kajol smearing into tears smearing into lipstick smearing into blood.

3

The next morning, Moyur woke up to a house subdued by scandal. Through the sporadic rise and fall of the curtain in the doorway, he saw ma sitting at the dining table, her hair uncharacteristically tangled, her face riddled with distress.

Moyur's nose still hurt. The doctor had said there was nothing to worry about. 'These things fix themselves,' he had said with a lack of concern that Moyur had hoped would work in his favour but, as the threat to his health diminished, the consequences of his actions grew proportionately more formidable. So much so that bapu had to intervene.

Late into the night they had sat, on opposite sides of the dining table. Lily mashi had gone to sleep and ma was lying down, claiming she could not bear to look at her son. Of course, both Moyur and bapu knew ma was awake, silently listening to everything they said.

Moyur insisted they had been playing rajkumar-rajkumari. 'Look at Ram-Lokkhon on the television,' he told bapu. 'We were only copying.' Moyur could see bapu relenting. After all, in ancient times, princes would anoint their eyes with kajol and decorate their foreheads with chandan, and all the actors in the recent serialized versions of the great epics embellished their glances and movements with strokes of paint and the sparkle of jewels.

'Was that all?' bapu asked.

'Yes, bapu. I promise.'

'And the fight?'

'Bapta was saying filthy things about Jojo.'

Bapu inhaled deeply. Moyur had only seen him do that once before, many years ago, when Joba kaku had phoned bapu just before moving to the city; it meant that bapu thought something was serious. 'You were protecting...' Then he stopped and reconsidered. 'Moyur, neither of you are going to be children for much longer.'

'Yes, bapu.' He was ready not to be a child; he had been ready for a long time.

'As you grow older, you will understand that there are set ways to behave. You might not agree but what society expects, society usually gets.'

'Yes, bapu.' Moyur was not sure what bapu was talking about but he pretended, because from bapu's tone of voice it seemed like something Moyur should know.

'Take me, for instance,' bapu continued. 'I have complied and in return I have contentment. It is the clever thing to do.' Bapu stood up suddenly. It seemed an odd place to end the conversation. He pushed his chair back, walked over to Moyur and tenderly brushed away a stray lock of hair from his forehead. Then he bent down and whispered, 'But baba, you might have to be braver than we were.'

Unfortunately, ma believed neither in history nor in television serials, and the following morning, she continued, undeterred. What would Meena think? Would she ever speak to her again? For all his understanding and riddled talk of bravery and cleverness, when it came to confronting ma, bapu was a useless ally. And Moyur remained at a loss about how to tackle ma.

He replayed the scenes from the previous afternoon: Jonali and he playing together, the door handle turning, the frantic undoing of saris, Meena pishi's face distorted with anger. And then the run-in with Bapta, the fighting. Afterwards, the kajol-stained tears and lips as red as blood. Was it from the fighting? Had he been biting his lips? Moyur collapsed into the mattress; he couldn't remember how it had happened. He knew he had been there but as he tried to recount the steps, he found only impressions without the details of his wrongdoing.

Exhausted, Moyur lay in bed and closed his eyes. Tears welled up inside him and dribbled down his cheeks but he did not move. To step outside his bedroom at that moment would be to admit defeat. Instead, he meditated on sleep, on lullabies. Ghum parani mashi pishi, moder ghore esho... It was the song ma used to sing, and when she did she would stroke his forehead, her fingers heavy with affection.

Ma loved Moyur.

But that morning, ma was angry.

So I decide to sing him those lullabies. I am sure I will sound like ma. Indistinguishable, because wouldn't I have been her daughter? I open my mouth. Nothing comes out. I still my mind and try again. Moyur is waiting, anguished. But there is no sound in me, and I realize I have no voice; I have only my heart and it is pounding.

On the bed where he lies, his heart is also beating, fast and furious.

It is our hearts that always rhyme.

Moyur jolted upright in bed, his back stiff. This was not the time. One, two, three, four, five, six, seven, eight. He counted out loud, raising his voice over the beat in his head, breathless for it to subside. He reached a hundred, and two hundred and three hundred. His mind raced ahead of the beat, running from it. Until finally the music retreated. Safely away, Moyur turned back, and for a second there was an ache in his eyes.

He must wish for me. I am sure he does, but as I watch him recover, I feel great distances gather between us.

One day, we will be together again.

❋

Ma was still sitting alone, her head resting heavily upon her left hand. Her lips were parted, her eyes fixed and unseeing. Moyur felt a churning in his gut. Just a word from ma, even a harsh word, would be enough to dispel the hollowness that clawed at him.

Moyur pulled the blue mosquito net from under the mattress and stepped out of bed as noisily as he could. 'Ma?' She didn't reply. 'Ma?' He took three steps into the dining room. This time a little more bravely, he said, 'Ma.'

Abruptly, she pushed her chair back, stood up and disappeared into her room. She didn't even look at him.

Lily mashi was standing in the doorway between the kitchen and the dining room. Even she turned away, choosing to wipe down the spotless table instead.

Moyur spun round and went back to his room. He climbed into bed and cried.

❋

Later that morning, a sliver of normality crept into the grieving. Ma went into Moyur's room. He had been lying with his head buried into the pillow, muttering and dribbling into its surrogate comfort. She sat beside him and quietly put her hand on his head. Under her breath, she recited pleas to Durga – to look after her son, to bring him in line, to rid him of his oddities.

'Why do you do these things, baba?'

Moyur shrugged.

'Promise me you will stop.'

Moyur did not move.

'Promise me,' she repeated.

He nodded.

'On my life?'

Moyur lay still. That was too risky.

Ma sighed. They had reached their stalemate for the time being.

The negotiation between ma and Lily mashi about what to cook took place an hour behind schedule. In keeping with her daily ritual, ma doled out instructions to the ladies who wiped the floor and washed the clothes, but she laboured her words and punctuated her sentences with long wistful glances into the distance. Moyur and ma ate lunch together. Lily mashi's boredom was a little less apparent, her eyes and ears trained on ma's every utterance.

Afterwards, both ma and Lily mashi gravitated towards their naps. Ma took hold of Moyur's hand; a compulsory afternoon nap was going to be part of the new regime. Moyur was relieved, at least this once. Keen to prove his reformation, he sidled up to ma, clutched her hand and pre-empted her steps. As they lay down side by side, ma put her arm around Moyur and drew him into the warm curve of her body. Moyur relaxed into her, wondering if this meant that he had been forgiven. He wondered if Jonali was all right, if she was similarly being cradled by Meena pishi.

Moyur drifted awake to the sound of conversation. The heaviness of the afternoon had passed and the evening felt cool and dark against his skin.

'Let her come,' ma was saying. 'Have we got any snacks ready?'

'Tea, biscuit, muri,' Lily mashi replied.

'Can you make something else?'

Lily mashi kissed her teeth disapprovingly. Nonetheless, she headed back to the kitchen. Ma rearranged her sari and massaged the remaining traces of sleep away from her face.

'How much more hot water will you land me in?' She was speaking more to herself than to Moyur.

Moyur didn't know the answer. He tried to stay still but his body betrayed him, twitching nervously. Ma sighed. She moved to the other side of the bed and propelled herself up from the shifting softness of the aged mattress. Through half-open eyes, Moyur watched her walk to the dining table and sit down. The harsh white tube light flickered unflatteringly on her face.

As Ma drained her tea cup, the doorbell rang. Lily mashi's footsteps crossed the hallway into the balcony and she hollered down, 'Ke? Who is it?'

From the briskness of Lily mashi's walk, it was immediately clear who it was.

Moyur slipped out of bed and hid behind the doorway. Ma lifted herself wearily from her seat. 'Lily, are those pakoras ready yet?'

'Coming.'

Ma opened the front door. 'Meena. Come in, come in.'

Meena pishi began her onslaught before she had even crossed the threshold. 'Kakuli, of others I might have expected it, but you! I always thought, she is a woman with self-respect. Not the kind of woman who will let her son behave like an animal on heat.' Meena pishi took off her brown leather sandals and placed them roughly at the end of a row of shoes, upsetting their symmetry.

Moyur perched on one leg, one eye positioned in a critical gap between the door frame and the curtain.

'Why don't we sit and talk?' Ma's voice was tight. She kept wringing her fingers as Meena pishi laboured towards the brown rexin settee. It made Moyur nervous.

However, as Meena pishi launched into her list of accusations, it became quickly apparent that she had conjectured scenarios above and beyond anything Moyur and Jonali had done or even imagined. Moyur thought guiltily of Jonali's breasts, but Meena pishi did not allude to them. There was nothing but supposition, allegations of romance and misadventure but without any substance.

As reality sank in, ma's back straightened and her voice, when she eventually replied, betrayed her relief. The charges Meena pishi levelled at him were not the ones Moyur had been expecting. Nor could they have been the ones ma was expecting because he had overheard enough of her conferences with bapu to know exactly what worries lay at the forefront of their minds. Instead, the accusation ma faced must have seemed to her a blessing, because an errant thirteen-year-old boy, albeit sexually precocious, was infinitely preferable to an abnormal one.

'Meena, I am so ashamed of this whole mess. I have talked to Moyur and he has seen the error of his ways. Of that, you can be assured. Although, from what he says, they were only playing rajkumar-rajkumari…'

Before she could finish, Meena pishi interrupted, 'And you believed him. How you can be so gullible, god only knows. Can't you see he is lying? How many other thirteen-year-olds do you know who play rajkumar-rajkumari?' She laid particular emphasis on the word 'play'. 'If I hadn't got back in time, god knows what this would have led to.'

'Meena, are you sure you are not adding meaning where there is no meaning?'

'You were not there, Kakuli, to see their guilty faces. Maybe it is not so important for you to be cautious. After all, your son will be fine, but nobody wants a girl whose reputation is tarnished. And she will never marry into your household, will she?'

Meena pishi had raised her voice, and through the open street-facing windows she would have been easily heard by inquisitive third parties, of whom there was never any dearth.

Ma replied with great control, 'No, Meena, of course not. We would not expect a Brahmin family to enter into relations with us. You have nothing to fear on that front.'

'In this day and age, people's heads are filled with ideas that are well above and beyond their station.'

Ma stood up. 'Meena, please, enough is enough.' Moyur retreated a little further into the corridor, away from the curtain.

'Oof. Careful.' He bumped into Lily mashi, who had just arrived with a tray. She looked quizzically at Moyur. 'Ki? Big problem you have created? And you were just about to make another mess.' She elbowed Moyur out of the way. 'Let me see.' She studied the two women and, deciding the moment was ripe for her to intervene, entered the fray with a soothing tray of snacks.

'Tea, biscuit and pakora with Maggi sauce,' she announced.

'Very good, Lily,' ma said. She gestured towards the tea. 'Please.'

Meena pishi was not the kind of person to bypass tea and pakoras on account of the outrage she had suffered. She promptly reached across the table to where Lily mashi was unloading the tray. 'Kakuli, it is possible that I have gone too far. But you are fortunate to have a son. You will never know the worries a daughter brings. How much longer are they going to be children? You tell me.'

Ma picked up her tea, a little appeased. 'Just remember, one hand cannot clap by itself.'

Lily mashi looked towards the curtain where Moyur was hiding, her eyebrow arched in his direction. Moyur felt a slow, cocky smile rise to his lips. Yes, that would teach her to tut disapprovingly at his misadventures. Ma was on his side.

In a much more conciliatory tone, Meena pishi resumed, 'Kakuli, you may be right. Perhaps I overreacted. Jojo said the same thing – that they were playing. I suppose they are like brother and sister.'

Ma exhaled and swirled the tea around in her cup. 'I am glad you are coming to your senses, Meena. There is nothing going on.'

'I am the first to pray that you are right. But in the meantime, maybe it would be best if we get a second opinion.'

Ma raised her eyebrows.

'I am going to ask the advice of an astrologer for Jonali,' Meena pishi explained. 'What with the filth you see in the movies these days, I need to be sure she will not do anything... you know, impulsive. Also, whether her marriage prospects are at any risk of being damaged. Maybe you can do the same for Moyur. If the coast is clear for them both, there is no need for either of us to worry.'

This was a plan ma had no hesitation in agreeing to. It was also a plan that suited Moyur. More than anything, he wanted the restrictions that had been placed upon his friendship with Jonali to be removed. Having agreed on a strategy and reached a tentative resolution, oiled by a plateful of Lily mashi's pakoras, the two women parted.

❋

For ma and bapu, the difficulty was going to be finding a suitable astrologer. Moyur's destiny was a confusing mesh of planets that had tested even the most practised astrologers of the day. For reasons unbeknown to Meena pishi or indeed anyone else outside the family, except perhaps Jonali, ma and bapu had already consulted widely, hoping to somehow rationalize Moyur's peculiarities, but there was no accounting for the deviances of his personality. Every astrologer went away shaking his head. So it was after a great deal of research, recommendations from the extended family and much consideration, that they settled on Pallavi Devi, agreeing to pay not only her hefty fee but also her first-class travel from Lucknow.

Moyur liked her the moment she arrived. She was a modern-looking woman with short, boy-cut hair. Despite its length, there was a giveaway curliness to it. In the middle of her forehead sat a giant maroon teep. She had completed her ensemble with dark brown lipstick, although, with a journey behind her, it had faded into more of a stain than a colour.

'Don't worry, Kakuli, Nimai.' She looked at Moyur. 'And this must be Moyur. Very nice to meet you all.'

'We are honoured, we are honoured,' bapu replied.

'Shall I leave these here?' she asked, taking off her sandals.

'Yes, yes. Please come in, you must be hungry after your long trip. It was smooth, I hope?'

It was lucky that Pallavi Devi's initial refreshment was undertaken with such enthusiasm. She was respectfully coerced into polishing off a five-course meal, downed with several glasses of lemon shorbot. As it turned out, it was the only time that Pallavi Devi would eat at the house.

After her meal, Pallavi Devi casually asked ma for the scroll on which Moyur's horoscope had been drawn. It was well worn, having been untied and retied more often than any other scroll of similar age. Ma warned Pallavi Devi of the problems they had previously faced. But she clucked soothingly. 'How difficult can it be? Twelve houses, nine planets. There are only so many permutations and combinations possible and, believe me, I have seen them all.' With these words, Pallavi Devi retreated to her room.

That was the last they saw of her for forty-eight hours. Engrossed in its challenge, she studied Moyur's horoscope without food, without sleep. No one dared disturb her. Every hour or so, ma or bapu laid an ear against her door, perhaps hoping to eavesdrop on her thoughts. But there were no clues and the round-the-clock vigil proved redundant because when Pallavi Devi was finally ready, she flung open her door and urgently summoned the family to her room.

'Moyur, Mrs Mitra, Mr Mitra – I have, as you have seen, spent many hours studying your son's past, present, future. I have given great consideration to your concerns and tried to explain his abnormal behaviour. I have come across many peculiar horoscopes in my time and you must excuse me for drawing these comparisons, but I have read the horoscopes of hijras and homosexuals, murderers and dacoits. You can be assured that Moyur is none of these.'

Ma muttered a prayer. No one spoke out loud. Moyur looked intently at Pallavi Devi, willing her to present him with a solution to his life.

She continued, 'What I cannot say is what, in fact, he is.'

At this, ma let out a wail. 'Hai, hai re. What have we given birth to, Nimai? Even Pallavi Devi cannot fathom his birth chart.'

Ma dropped to her knees. Bapu bent down and put his arm around her. 'Calm down, Kakuli, please.'

Pallavi Devi looked solemnly at them both, avoiding Moyur. 'Your husband is right. There is no other choice. Simply, you must be prepared. I can only tell you this – sometimes the outcome can be greater than the sum total of planetary interactions.' Pallavi Devi crouched down till she was facing ma. 'Mrs Mitra, you must be strong.'

Ma was weeping now. 'What is the solution, Pallavi Devi? You are our last remaining hope.'

Pallavi Devi let out a sigh. She looked at Moyur, and in her gaze he felt a surge of compassion. 'Love him. That is the only way. I am sorry, truly sorry.'

Pallavi Devi left in a rush, refusing to accept any payment from ma and bapu. Moyur remained as he had been before her arrival – unfathomable.

For a few days following Pallavi Devi's departure, ma fell into a state of indifference. She would wake up late, half dress and sit in front of the television all day. Her balcony-chatter with the neighbours came to an abrupt halt. Sometimes she would put food in her mouth, sometimes she would glaze over the pages of a magazine. But she did completely abandon her attempts to rescue Moyur. Until the Saturday that Meena pishi came to enquire after her and the outcome of the consultation with the astrologer.

Ma had never mentioned Moyur's oddities to anybody outside the family. She was a gossip but Moyur's aberrances were too great, and she was fearful of bringing the chastisement of the para upon their heads. Nor did she want Meena pishi to think that he was sexually precocious and further jeopardize the relationship between the two families. With Durga Pujo a few weeks away, the time had come to be rid of malingering resentments.

So when Meena pishi sent word through Shikha didi of her intention to call upon ma, she put on a clean sari, dabbed some eau de cologne on her pulse points, combed her hair and arranged it in a bun. The telltale dust of freshly sprinkled talcum powder remained on her décolletage and neck.

Ma sent Lily mashi to the corner shop to purchase some mishti. After all, she was going to give Meena pishi the good news that there was no threat to Jonali's chastity on her son's part, and any good news must be accompanied by sweet treats for the mouth.

4

Almost three weeks after the day Meena pishi caught them, Jonali returned to her balcony to wait for Moyur. She rushed out as soon as her mother gave her the good news, desperate to bring an end to the undeserved curfew. There was so much to say. They hadn't even been allowed to travel together to school; Jonali's mother had taken it upon herself to hand-deliver her daughter to and from the school gates, suffering a combination of peak-time buses and rickshaws to do so. If only her mother had known the truth: Moyur was just not that kind of boy, and Jonali, well, she was destined for other things. For education and standing on her own two feet, so that if she ever were to find herself widowed like her mother, she would never have to approach anybody with embarrassed, outstretched palms.

Since the death of her father, Jonali and her mother had depended upon the goodwill of Jonali's kaku and kakimoni. They all lived in the same big house; they all ate together – Jonali, her mother, kakimoni, her little cousin Riya and their housekeeper, Shikha didi. Kaku was a marine engineer, travelling the world, sending back packets of cash to kakimoni. Kakimoni was the one who decided how much would be spent and on what. She was the one who paid for the food, the electricity, the gas. She was the one who paid for Jonali's tuition fees, and the one who handed her mother a small brown envelope at the beginning of every month – a package so discreet that everyone knew exactly what was in it.

Kaku and kakimoni were generous and well-off; there was no problem, not really, not in the grand scheme of things. But sometimes, just sometimes, in the little scheme of things, an inopportune furrowed forehead or a few meaningless titters – 'Oh, has she outgrown her uniform again?' 'School tiffin is getting so costly these days,' – would become so meaningful that the grand scheme of things would be rendered irrelevant.

The household carried on. But in Jonali's mind there was no question about what she needed to do, for her own future or her mother's. And in her plan of self-sufficiency there was no room for the inarticulate electric tingles of adolescence. So it was just as well, she supposed, that Moyur was not that kind of boy.

Nonetheless, when Moyur arrived on his balcony, Jonali felt her heart skip a beat.

'Everything okay?' he asked.

Jonali nodded. 'You?'

He shrugged. She knew that shrug.

'Moyur, I didn't tell anybody.' She watched his shoulders relax.

'I know. You never do.' He shot her a tentative grin.

'But I don't think we can do it again. Ma is getting suspicious.'

'Why? What did she say?'

'About the kumkum and the kajol... it doesn't matter. Overall, she thought we were... you know.'

'Yes, yes, I know,' Moyur said quickly. 'How silly of them.' His discomfort was obvious, and to Jonali it was the first indication that perhaps the conclusions her mother had jumped to were not too far off the mark.

'Have you made friends with Bapta?' Jonali asked. 'I heard about your fight from Shikha didi. Ram kaku told her.'

'Nah. He is an idiot. I don't want to set my eyes on him again.'

'Really? And Tinku?'

Moyur shrugged.

'I'm going to audition for the part of Durga tomorrow, for the para play this year,' Jonali said, changing the subject.

'Oh, good luck. You'll easily be the best.' As an afterthought, Moyur added, 'Of the girls.'

'They have roles for boys too, you know. You could play Mahishasura.'

Moyur shook his head. 'No, I don't want to be in any stupid para theatre. They are all poorly managed.'

'Nothing is ever good enough for you.'

'I meant, for my taste. Not that they're bad productions.'

'Suit yourself.'

Jonali turned towards the shimmering pink horizon. The sun was on its way down and the dusky silhouettes of coconut trees glided over barren rooftops. The maids had already gathered up the day's washing. A neon advertisement for Raju men's undergarments flashed at them from afar. It was the tallest board in Ultadanga, at the fringes of the main city, and the only one that could be seen from their house in Salt Lake.

Jonali was about to further persuade Moyur into auditioning when she stopped. He was somewhere else, a great distance from the time they were sitting in together. Rather than retrieve him, Jonali took the opportunity to study him, the shape of his body, with his lean charismatic limbs compactly folded out of the way, the soft mop of black hair that framed his caramel skin and full maroon lips. Her eyes travelled further up till she reached his eyes, only to find them waiting for her. Their eyes locked. Jonali felt her gaze entangling in his. The world fell away and she was there with Moyur, marooned in an enchanted interlude until a passing flock of homebound sparrows rudely interrupted them.

Moyur drew himself together. 'I better go now,' he said, looking away. 'There is a match tonight. East Bengal–Mohun Bagan.'

Jonali wrinkled her nose in distaste. 'Do you have to go?'

'The match is going to start any minute.'

'But this is our first meeting after sooo long,' she said, trying to sound casual.

Moyur stood, inert, his arms dangling by his sides, wearing the expression of a school boy caught on the verge of mischief. 'Yes, but it's East Bengal.'

'So what?'

'And Mohun Bagan.'

'It's always East Bengal and Mohun Bagan,' Jonali complained.

Moyur had nothing more to say in his defence, so he simply stood. Jonali watched him for a while. Then, annoyed, she said, 'Go.'

Moyur offered her a lopsided smile before hurrying off to the television. Jonali stayed on the balcony.

The allegations that had been levelled at their relationship had caught her off guard, setting in motion a train of ideas and barely mentionable feelings that she had never before thought possible. A part of her wanted things to go back to normal; a part of her didn't.

Jonali sat a little longer in the empty evening. She had a desk full of homework to complete but her mind wandered away from her ambitions, flitting far from her education, from her standing-on-her-own-two-feet-ing and providing for her mother, to the endless enticements of the big world.

A group of men, rickshaw-walas, food vendors and street sweepers, had gathered around a transistor radio placed on a makeshift pedestal outside Ram kaku's shop. A few minutes into the game, a cheer arose and the huddle burst into a display of celebratory jumping and back-slapping. Jonali sighed at the simplicity of their pleasures. Not so long ago she too had been uncomplicated.

It was not just the friendship between Moyur and Jonali that had to mend; ma and Meena pishi were also accustomed to being close friends and confidantes. In many ways, the reinstatement of one relationship oiled the wheels of the other. Although much of their lives was shared across balconies, there were some occasions when this just wasn't enough.

On one of the handful of sky-blue mornings remaining before the start of Durga Pujo, Moyur, on ma's instructions, donned a pair of freshly ironed shorts and a checked shirt in order to pay a 'proper' visit to their next-door neighbours.

Almost as soon as they had rung the bell, Jonali, ever on the lookout, opened the door.

'Hello, Jojo,' ma said, 'where is Shikha?'

'Eating. Come upstairs, Kakuli mashi. Hello, Moyur,' she added with a shy grin.

Jonali yo-yo'd up and down the stairs, trying politely to keep pace with ma, whose hips had started playing up again.

On the first floor landing, the shoe rack spilled slippers onto the floor. Moyur took off his Bata chappals and positioned them against a tiny bit of unused wall. The Saturday morning smells of luchi and aloor dom seemed doubly delicious because school was now out for pujo. Technicolour sound from their television crackled proudly through the front room. Meena pishi came into view. 'Come, come. Shikha has made breakfast. You must be hungry.'

'You shouldn't have gone to so much trouble, Meena. Next time we will have to think not once but three times before popping over.'

'What nonsense. It's hardly anything.'

Jonali's kakimoni nodded and smiled from her seat at the dining table. 'I was too hungry,' she mumbled through a mouthful, 'couldn't wait any longer.'

'Of course. Please eat in peace,' ma replied.

Jonali, who had momentarily disappeared, emerged from the bedroom with an ochre sari in her hands, her waddling five-year-old cousin Riya in tow.

'Let's see, let's see!' Ma leaned forward to get a better look. 'Lovely choice. How is your routine, Jojo? Have you been practising? You want to show your Kakuli mashi?'

Jonali tilted her head till it almost touched her shoulder, bashfully signalling yes. It had been a long time since she was the centre of attention. Meena pishi did not believe in putting fancy ideas into her daughter's head. She never celebrated Jonali's successes, and the many prizes Jonali had won for her academic achievements lay neglected in bottom drawers. She did not even celebrate Jonali's birthday, claiming it was bad luck to make undue fuss over a daughter, lest the attentions of the evil eye be drawn to her future. Such precautions were obviously unnecessary for sons, and no doubt Meena pishi would not have spared any effort had she been lucky enough to have one.

Of course, there were ways to give luck a helping hand.
Ma had known how.

❋

Every morning following their wedding, ma had risen before
dawn. She had plucked the finest leaves from the family tulsi
plant and set them afloat in a pitcher of milk and molasses.
Ma had offered the drink to the rising sun and prayed as his
chariots rose in the eastern sky. Received wisdom was that if
the mother-to-be consumed this concoction, the birth of a son
was guaranteed.

But what do you do if your daughter is determined?

Like I was?

How hard do you have to wish before you wish her away?

❋

The ritual for conceiving a son had been given to ma as a wedding
present, but she had never shared it, and never would. This was
just one of her inconsistencies: the way she both coveted Moyur
and disregarded him, sometimes sobbing for hours without
reason; the way she never let him dance yet cherished Jonali's
performances.

'Jojo, you are growing into such a pretty young girl,' ma said,
reaching forward to squeeze Jonali's cheeks gently.

'Kakuli, don't spoil her. Putting ideas into her head. She is a
handful as it is.'

'She will make a beautiful Durga,' ma continued unabated.
'Look at her eyes, big and oval just like Ma Durga. Jojo, why
don't you show us your dance? It will be good practice. Moyur,
come sit next to me.'

Moyur collapsed onto a corner of the divan.

'Moyur, do you want something to drink? Thums Up?' It was the first thing Meena pishi had said to him since that ill-fated afternoon and her words, though not unkind, prompted Moyur to recoil further into himself.

'No, I am fine,' he muttered.

'Shondesh? Shikha, bring him a shondesh.'

'No, I don't want one.'

Nothing in Meena pishi's tone or manner conveyed any allusion to their last encounter.

'Let him be,' ma said impatiently. 'He will be fine in a minute. Come on, Jojo. Let's start.'

With that, Jonali pressed play on the cassette-player and the music began. At first, Moyur pretended not to look, training his eyes on the dirty white ceiling fan as it laboured against the sticky heat, but soon the enactment of Mahalaya overwhelmed the little room, sweeping up the audience, Moyur included, into the folds of its panoramic myth.

Across three worlds, Jonali pursued Mahishasura. Wherever the demon walked, the ground shuddered with fear; wherever he breathed, the air rumbled with evil. Waters had bloodied and the orchards of heaven started to rot. Gods and goddesses had tried and failed to defeat Mahishasura. So they turned to Durga, the ten-armed goddess with one weapon for each of her hands.

As the story of their encounter reached its climax, the heavy anklets Jonali had tied on became a furious orchestra of brass bells; her feet hit the floor with the rising tempo of war. The universe quaked and fragmented into a million pieces; thunder and lightning, confused and terrified, crashed into each other; the skies melted from the heat of clashing weapons. Cardboard spear held aloft, she pirouetted from one side of the room to the other and, with one final lunge, thrust her weapon forward into Mahishasura's heart. Then stillness.

Jonali looked at her spectators for approval.

'Bah, Jojo. That was wonderful. Perfect,' ma volunteered the first comment.

Meena pishi, ma, kakimoni, Riya and Shikha didi were all clapping.

'I just hope that Tinku does his part properly. Even yesterday he forgot where he was supposed to stand,' Meena pishi said, flushed with pride at ma's commendation.

Jonali was alive with excitement. Braving the watchful eyes of the older generation, she asked directly, 'Moyur, was it good?'

'Fanta,' he mumbled.

❃

Moyur always felt ashamed of his behaviour that day. It was the first and only time that Moyur envied Jonali for this glut of attention, because it never happened again. But that day he was jealous of the praise that was lavished on her. He was convinced he could have done it better. After all, he was the one who, year after year, woke up at half past four in the morning to watch the state broadcast of the story of Mahalaya. He knew the movements by heart. He would have made a beautiful Ma Durga.

Or maybe I would have made a beautiful Ma Durga, dressed in a sari like hundreds of other girls across Calcutta, with ten bejewelled cardboard arms attached to my back, slaying demons in a myth.

5

A week later, the goddess finally arrived, in a fanfare of beating drums and skies thick with the aroma of incense. Every neighbourhood had its own effigies of Durga and her four children. Pujo committees around the city vied for the honour of being crowned the para with the most beautiful idols, the most spectacular lighting or the most elaborate pandal.

Moyur and Jonali lived along the main thoroughfare leading up to their para pandal, and every year, by a stroke of extreme good fortune, it fell upon them to oblige the goddess and the para pujo committee by allowing the decoration of their houses with garlands of flashing red and yellow tooni-lights. It also meant that neither Moyur nor Jonali had any need for the printed timetable outlining the when and what and how of the five-day festival. Every smell, every sound inevitably found them as they loitered on their balconies or ran from house to pandal, pandal to house.

These were free and easy times with no need for stillness or the curbing of random impulses. The one and only requirement was to greet the goddess. She was, after all, a guest. And to greet her in the newest possible clothes. Those who could afford it, chose freshly purchased garments; those who could not,

laundered and pressed their freshly acquired hand-me-downs.
But everyone was clean and well-turned-out with a sheen in their
attire and a skip in their sandals that could not be explained by
washing and ironing alone.

On each of the five days, as per ma's decree, Moyur took
particular care over his morning preparations. But on oshtomi,
arguably the most important day of all, he doubled his efforts.
Having saved the best of his new clothes for that day, Moyur
showered, sprinkled himself generously with lavender-scented
talcum powder and put on his new khaki shorts and red 'Hero
No. 1' T-shirt. Then bapu and Moyur strolled down to the pandal,
arriving just in time for the third round of pushpanjoli. Ma had
been there all morning, helping with the pujo preparations, but
bapu was not one to hurry on his day off. Life had taught him
to work hard, but he also understood very well how not to.

Bapu didn't talk about his misfortunes much but once or
twice he had let slip that his family had weathered their fair
share. Before partition, they had been wealthy, landed, but
that was in East Bengal. Forced by circumstance, bapu's father
had taken up a post in the West Bengal Forest Department –
from a landlord to a mid-ranking officer in the machinery of
a communist government. Still, old habits die hard and even
though bapu could not have long experienced the opulence of
his father's generation, having done most of his growing up in
a modest household, he was nonetheless able to enjoy simply
existing without the crises of pride or ambition that might affect
those of more humble blood.

Bapu and Moyur jostled alongside maybe a hundred or so
of their neighbours, waiting for pushpanjoli in unruly rows at
the foot of the raised bamboo altar on which Ma Durga and
her children were installed. This year the pujo committee had
decided on a red and yellow colour scheme. With the exception

of a few disobedient canes that protruded at odd angles from the cloth canopy, most of the scaffolding was concealed. Priests and devotees had filled the altar with fruit and flowers; mounds of incense lay next to piles of earthen lamps, garlands of marigolds and ghots full of water from the Ganga.

The head priest, who had been conducting the pujo for as long as anyone could remember, sat in front of the fire, his pot belly spilling over his white cotton dhoti, a few strands of well-oiled hair masquerading as a tika on his otherwise shaven head. He was the one who summoned life into the clay images and the one who performed the main rituals on each of the pujo days. He also departed with the biggest hauls of saris, mishti and jewellery, piled high on the back of his speeding moped: his Vespa.

Strangely, Jonali was nowhere to be seen. Meena pishi was standing at the edge of the altar with a daala of flowers. Spotting them in the crowd, she reached over and deposited a generous helping of flowers into bapu's cupped hands, which bapu divvied up between the two of them.

'Bhalo accho toh? I hope you are well, Nimai da, Moyur,' Meena pishi greeted them before continuing her rounds of empty palms, dropping in each an offering-sized quota of flowers for the goddess.

When she finished, the priest began the anjoli. 'Put your hands together and repeat after me. Esho sho chondono…' He would pause after every line and wait for the devotees to murmur the mantra after him. Moyur could never keep up. The words were too long and unfamiliar. To be honest, not many people could: there was always a subdued indistinctness to the pious murmurings except when they came to the last syllable of each couplet, which the crowd would pronounce together and then hurl the flowers at Ma Durga's feet with pent-up devotion.

After pushpanjoli, Moyur scanned the gathering. Tinku and Bapta were sitting together with a few other boys from the BB-block football team. Pintu swung back and forth on his metal folding chair. Bittu, standing next to him, was focused on Tinku's plate. Moyur hesitated. Before he could decide which way to go, Tinku caught sight of him and hollered, 'Hey, Moyur, come over. Why you are standing by yourself?'

'I have just given pushpanjoli without eating all morning. I have to find some food now.'

'I have food. Look. A whole plate. Come and share.' Tinku raised a plate, woven together with shaal leaves, on it the remnants of his feast.

'Where did you get it?'

'There's a guy just behind the park. Will I take you?'

'No, no. You don't have to. I'll get it and come back,' Moyur insisted.

'Thik bolchhish? You won't disappear?'

'Na, I won't.' Moyur couldn't help smiling. He hadn't spoken to any of them since that day outside Jonali's house. But Tinku was a good friend, a peace maker and, most importantly, co-starrer in Jonali's dance routine, which was due to premiere that evening. 'I'll be back in two minutes.'

By the time Moyur returned with his plate, Bapta, to his relief, had left.

'He had to go back home for something. I don't know what,' Tinku volunteered an explanation.

'Shame.' Moyur seized the opportunity to lament his departure, to appear the bigger man.

'Yes, it is a shame,' Pintu agreed.

Moyur and Tinku ignored him.

'You two need to sort it out.' Tinku's tone was mildly reproachful.

'Sort what out? There's no issue,' Moyur retaliated.

Moyur ate his food in curt silence before Tinku piped up again: 'One of you has to make the first move.'

Moyur carried on chewing.

Pintu looked from one to the other. 'You were the one who hit him first so maybe you should make the first move.'

Moyur's neck started to prickle. He gulped down his half-chewed bolus of food. 'Do you know what he said? Did you hear?'

'Chhar toh.' Tinku put a hand on Moyur's shoulder. 'He doesn't know or he wouldn't have said that.'

'Well, tell him to shut his mouth when he doesn't even know the full story.'

Pintu stared at Moyur. He was safe for now, as long as Tinku was around.

Moyur concentrated on his luchi and cholar dal while Tinku and Pintu busied themselves with watching the arrivals and departures of the pandal. Bittu stared at Moyur's food.

'Khabi?' Moyur asked him.

'If you can spare some.'

Pintu swivelled to face them. 'How much more can you eat, fatty?' No one ever called Bittu by his name. He was officially known as fatty. Most of the time, though, he was good humoured about it because they still let him play on the football team, as the goalie. He was good at that. He would simply stand in front of the posts, and the ball would bounce off his substantial frame.

And, more to the point, he always gave as good as he got. He had just started his retaliation, teasing Tinku, branding him a nachnewaali, a dancing queen, when Moyur interrupted to ask about the rehearsals.

'I saw Jojo dancing last week. Are you managing to get to your place properly yet? Meena pishi was worrying.'

All three of them fell silent. Turning to his friend, Tinku replied, 'Haven't you heard?'

His posture and tone were measured. 'Heard what?' Moyur asked.

Tinku said nothing.

'Please tell me. What happened?'

'Jonali isn't dancing any more, Maya is.'

'What?'

Pintu and Bittu glanced at each other before looking at the ground.

'What? Why?' Moyur asked again.

Tinku couldn't give him a satisfactory explanation. None of them could. 'Ask Meena pishi. She's the one who told my mother, who told me. She said Jonali isn't well, that's all,' Tinku said.

'That can't be right. I saw her yesterday.'

The three boys stared blankly at Moyur. Tinku looked sorry and worried at the same time.

'Okay, I have to find out what is going on.' Moyur turned back towards his house. As he walked away, Pintu's voice stealthed up behind him. 'What type of shit Romeo are you? Don't even know what your own girlfriend is up to.'

Moyur let it pass. They could think what they wanted.

❁

The situation was so severe that Moyur decided to bypass the balcony and go straight to the front door. Shikha didi answered his knocking promptly but her brow was inauspiciously furrowed. Shikha didi had on occasion proved to be a more formidable killjoy than Meena pishi, and this time too she filled the entranceway with objections. But Moyur was slight and had the advantage of speed; he wriggled past her and ran up the stairs.

Jonali was reclining on the divan in the living room, following the events on the television screen with a well-feigned air of long suffering. She started at Moyur's voice.

'Jonali, what's going on? Why aren't you dancing? Why didn't you tell me? Who's stopping you? Is it Meena pishi?'

As Moyur's questions tumbled out, he noticed with relief that Jonali didn't look at all ill.

Jonali sat up and tucked her knees underneath her. A spare bedsheet was lying next to her; she hastened to wrap it around herself. 'I'm not well, Moyur. That's why,' Jonali said. 'Anyway, what are you doing here?'

'Not well? Why? Have you got a fever?'

She said nothing.

'Tummy upset?'

She shook her head.

'Headache?'

'No. Moyur, you won't understand. It's none of those. I'm just not well, that's all.'

'That can't be it. You've wanted to do this for how long?'

Moyur looked first at her and then at Shikha didi, who had stationed herself behind him, busybody and self-appointed chaperone. Shikha didi asked him to leave. She told him it wasn't the right time and that he wasn't old enough to understand.

'Old enough to understand what?' Moyur countered, getting irritated with Jonali's insipid mood and with Shikha didi's interference.

'Women's problems, Moyur,' Jonali said finally. 'Count yourself lucky.'

And then everything clicked.

Of course Moyur understood. Except, to him they weren't problems. They were secrets that made Jonali beautiful; they were the mysteries abounding in her body that he would never behold in his own, no matter how much he wished. And the enchantment was not his alone. From amidst legend there arose a temple, surging with the enchantment of millions, teeming with prayers that waxed and waned with the cycles of nature and her goddesses.

A great weight lifted from Moyur's heart. 'Jojo, I know what's wrong with you,' he said.

Jonali turned from him to plump the cushions she had been leaning against. 'Shikha didi, can you bring me a lemon shorbot, please. I am feeling so weak.'

Shikha didi was about to head to the kitchen when habit checked her. 'Moyur? Anything?' she asked.

'No, Shikha didi. I'm fine.' Moyur sat down on the divan. He waited till Shikha didi was out of earshot before launching into his reproach. 'Jojo, you are such a drama queen. I know exactly what's up and I know the solution too.'

Jonali perked up at last. She propped herself up on her elbows and, for the first time that morning, looked at him directly. 'Really? Solution? Come on then, let me hear it. This will be a good one. Thousands of years of stupid rules... and now *you* have the solution.' She was smugly defiant in her self-defeat. It riled him but also made him wary.

'Promise you'll listen. From beginning to end. No interrupting.'

'Oh! So now you're all promise this and promise that.' Despite herself, Jonali smiled.

'Please, Jojo.'

Moyur felt her eyes on him, cynical and expectant in equal measure, with everything to gain and everything to lose.

'Okay, okay, I promise. Now start.'

Moyur took a deep breath and told her the story of Sati who, torn between her father and her husband, immolated herself. Overcome with grief, Shiva took the lifeless body of his beloved wife in his arms and began the Tandava, a dance so terrible that Lord Vishnu was compelled to send his chakra to stay the destruction. But Shiva was unstoppable, his anger an impenetrable haze that would not lift until the realization came upon him that Sati's body had been cut. In fifty-one parts, her body fell from the heavens onto earth. Only then did Shiva stop.

Across the world, fifty-one temples stand, piecing together a sort of guard over her. Where her mouth fell she speaks, where her eyes fell she sees, and where her hands fell she touches. Where her womb fell she bleeds and the temple teems with prayers that wax and wane with the cycles of nature. Once a year, in Kamakhya, the waters of the temple turn red. Pilgrims come from afar, bringing cloth offerings to be soaked in the holy water and distributed with the blessings of the goddess. Because it is from the womb of a goddess that the universe was born.

As the story came to an end, Moyur's voice grew more elated. 'So you see.'

Jonali looked sceptical. 'See? What is there to see?'

'There is a whole temple, thousands of devotees who worship the goddess when she has women's problems. All you have to do is dance.'

To his amazement, Jonali started shivering. Her teeth chattered so she could barely speak.

'Jojo?'

He stared at her, completely at a loss, until she responded, 'Moyur, why are you telling me this nonsense?' The curtness in her tone took him aback.

'But Jojo... I...'

'For once in your life... What sort of world do you think we live in, Moyur? Of all people, you at least should know better.' Jonali got up and stalked away to her bedroom. She looked back at him and sneered, 'You toh are always off with the fairies.' Then she slammed the door shut.

Shikha didi, who had just returned with the shorbot, gawped at Moyur. 'What happened?' she asked.

'Nothing.'

'Have you upset Jonali?'

Moyur didn't reply. Instead, he walked into her, deliberately upsetting the shorbot, making it spill stickily across the floor. Then he left without a word.

Part II
_____
1990

6

Hot afternoons seeped into one another and childhood fell further and further away into the recesses of memory. Moyur and Jonali succumbed to exams. For Jonali, they were the gateway to her college education; for Moyur, a hurdle to be jumped on his way to the much anticipated apprenticeship at the family sari shop.

As the month of March trundled towards the final set of compulsory state-imposed school exams, their afternoon conferences dwindled to nothing. Jonali, a keen student, withdrew completely from all distractions to dedicate herself to her books. She encouraged Moyur to do the same, offering to study with him, pressing upon him her notes and techniques. If she could, Jonali would have volunteered to study on his behalf and take his exams for him, but Moyur's destiny lay elsewhere and he was not to be swayed by the reasonable intentions of others.

The truth is that Moyur had never wanted anything but to work at the Bengal Silk House, and although ma and bapu would have preferred he pursue the much vaunted route of higher education, further education, etc, they too were eventually persuaded that perhaps Moyur's time would be better spent learning the ins and outs of the business. Despite ma's coveted knowledge of how to give birth to a thousand sons, she had settled on just the one. So, by a fateful coincidence, it turned out that Moyur was the sole heir to the family shop.

Ma and bapu did not, however, excuse Moyur from his schoolwork and, like Tinku, Bapta, Pintu, Bittu and Jonali, that spring Moyur found himself confined to the drudgery of his bedroom-cum-study.

Every afternoon, as ma, exhausted from supervising the household chores, wound down for her afternoon nap, Moyur was dispatched to his desk. Along the wall beside him, shelves bulged with books meticulously wrapped in brown paper. History, biology, chemistry, literature – subjects and topics tumbled around Moyur's head willy-nilly as he tried to grasp them and pin them down into some sort of order.

By far the most beautifully preserved was his geography textbook: sparingly opened and thriftily read. But the time had come when he could avoid it no longer, and so Moyur began in earnest, swivelling back and forth on the two hind legs of his chair as he tried to absorb the contents of the pages. He conjured up impressions of tectonic plates and prairies, but Moyur's imagination was never completely under his control, and as he flitted from one chapter to the next, the plateaus and deltas began to fill with cut-outs of people: boys and girls escaping from their desks to wander through adventures, prettily clad avatars in butterfly hues, fluttering from dream to dream. He was there with Jonali and Tinku. There were others too – kids from the bus, from the playground.

And I am there. Standing alone in the corner, next to the krishnochura tree. No one notices me because I am still so little. But then my heart wavers. I think he has spotted me. Moyur is coming towards me. I cannot believe that I might also get to play. I grow bolder. My heart beats louder and I spin a cocoon of sound around the two of us. Moyur plummets towards me.

My Moyur.

Moyur let his arms etch the shapes of our dances. Snapshots of himself dressed in resplendent fabrics filled his view. From a corner of his flip-top desk, Moyur retrieved ma's bright orange-red lipstick, the one she kept looking for, and lathered his lips with colour. Then he resumed the rocking of his hips and torso, from stance to stance, his fingers arranging themselves into mudras.

Moyur moved like his namesake, the peacock, in lilting circles, framed in a halo of proud turquoise. Why would ma give him such a name if she hadn't wanted him to dance? For his part, Moyur had, over the last two or three years, managed to keep his dalliances well under cover, secreted within the inattentive lethargy of sleepy afternoons. But that day, rest had escaped ma and, unbeknownst to Moyur, she had been prowling, chasing her siesta from verandah to verandah while Moyur danced. Until he chanced upon ma's contorted face, squashed against the window, watching as he twirled in mid-dance.

Ma's stare burned into him, accusing him of unspeakable things. For a moment he stopped. Moyur stuck his fingers in his ears. One, two, three, four, he counted in his head. For ma's sake. For bapu's sake. But, though he tried, how could he evict the memory of that heartbeat from his head?

Dub-dub, dub-dub. It is how we began.

Outside, ma began rattling the door to his room. The fan spun on its axis. Ghot, ghot. Distractions climbed into Moyur's head like bedfellows and he forgot the string of numbers he was clinging to. He started shaking. He trembled with conflict and the effort of restraint, but the sound flooded through him and Moyur abandoned himself to the most precious of our desires, and danced.

Ma let out a shriek. 'Nimai! Nimai! Hai kopal! Come and see what your son is doing.' She banged her fist against the window frame. 'Why, god, are you punishing me? Haven't I suffered enough?' Her words stumbled into one another. 'Why?' She thumped her forehead.

At the conclusion of his dance, Moyur faced her. He had never before deliberately raised his voice at ma, accepting her judgements as if truth were only on her side, but at that moment Moyur was on fire. His ears were hot with indignation, his feet stung with the friction of the dance, and his voice contorted itself like a noose around her. 'If you don't want me, kill me,' he screamed. 'You know the secret of giving birth to a hundred boys, you dayni, you witch. Have another son, have another ninety-nine sons. Forget this dirty little hijra. Why don't you, ma? Why don't you?'

Not a word. Moyur started shaking again. 'Why? Answer me. Answer me. Answer me.' He collapsed on the floor. Ma fled.

She never gave us an answer. Moyur recovered slowly, dragging himself out of this condition that we find ourselves in – of pathological nostalgia. It is only in the peaceful emptiness of night and in the quiet solitude of afternoons when there is nobody else jostling for his attention that I can call to him. But should I?

The woman who would have been my grandmother used to say that when a soul has parted with someone very dear, it cannot leave. Well, Moyur was not just dear to me – we were almost the same.

In the chinks of silence that filter through the humdrum of everyday, he is the only one who reaches for me. I know I should resist. I try, but just imagine how I feel when he holds my hand. We are back where we were so many years ago, with stubby limbs bobbing in soft, warm liquid; eyes that are not yet open; faces that still cannot smile.

Later, Moyur went to find ma. She was sitting alone on her bed, staring into space. Bapu had gone back to work and Lily mashi flitted around ineffectually, sending worried glances in ma's direction every few seconds. Moyur took stock at the doorway. He hated aftermaths. He hated being the guilty party. He had tried telling ma before but she never listened. Before he could escape to his room, he was intercepted by Lily mashi.

'Moyur baba, please go and give her a cuddle. That's all she wants – it's not right to give your mother so much pain.' She nudged him towards ma, scrunching her eyes in encouragement. 'Mothers are the closest thing to god. Go.'

Moyur took a couple of steps in her direction. 'Ma?'

Ma didn't reply; she let her tears speak on her behalf.

'Ma, please don't.'

She shook her head. The tempo of her tears abated, enough to allow her to speak between gasps. 'Why, baba? Why do you do these things? Time and time again. Your exams start in ten days.'

'You know why. I told you before but you wouldn't listen.'

'Again that nonsense?'

Moyur blinked back tears of frustration. When he trusted himself to speak, he muttered, 'But it's true. I can't help it.'

Ma cut him off. 'Shut up and get out of my sight. I don't know where you get these ideas but I am sick of your rubbish. From now on, either you behave or you get out of my house. Understand?'

There are times, like these, when the pain is too much. I want to tell ma that it's not Moyur's fault that he is all I have. I am the one you should be angry with. But ma doesn't care what I have to say. She barely listens.

There is not much that I envy Moyur. How can I? He is my everything. Still, if I could somehow rummage in the swollen gutters of feeling around Moyur, forage through the debris of ma's scoldings and rejections, I would scavenge for myself an ember or two of the love with which she cannot help but poison even the sternest of her reproaches.

Moyur cast his eyes in ma's direction. She was unwavering. Suddenly, Moyur hated ma and her heart of wood and steel. Most of all, he was overcome by the realization that he could never be the perfect son. Without another word, Moyur slipped away.

He never again asked ma why she didn't have any more children. He never tried to explain to her why he danced. Instead, he persevered with his exam revisions, trying to avoid as sincerely as possible the invitations in his head.

Before long, the day came around for the publication of the board exam results. Unsurprisingly, Jonali was in the top fifty students in Calcutta. Moyur's results were decidedly mediocre in comparison – certainly not bad, but not quite the outcome parents wish for.

On the evening that the results were announced, Moyur reunited with his classmates to celebrate the end of an era. Their destinies scattered upon the soil of life haphazardly, some chancing upon a fertile patch; others, not so well fated, landed on barren futures. Moyur was delighted with his result because it was both a qualification and a disqualification – good enough to hold his head high but not quite enough to mandate progression to class eleven and twelve.

Moyur didn't get home till after midnight. Salt Lake always fell asleep before the rest of Calcutta, so the streets were quiet.

A drowsy moon hung in the polluted mists of the warm night sky. Moyur could hear the shrill call of the night watchman's whistle and the thok-thok of his stick hitting the ground, announcing his imminent arrival. Nobody had ever seen the night watchman arrive, however.

Groups of stray dogs cantered up to Moyur to investigate and soon disappeared, abducted by other abstractions. Moyur felt like the biggest man in the world that night. Every breath he took filled him with the urgency of life. For so long, Moyur had been waiting for this; finally, it felt as though destiny and his dissonant horoscope might just keep their promises.

Moyur let himself into the house. Bapu was already asleep. Ma was at the dining table, her head lolling on her chest. A steel plate with three rootis, some chorchori and a piece of fish lay waiting for Moyur under a netted dome.

'Ma,' Moyur whispered. There was no response. He put his arms around ma and hugged her as softly as he possibly could, gently absorbing her startle so that she drifted awake.

She stroked his head. 'Moyur baba, what time is it?'

'Late, ma, time for you to sleep.'

'You know I can't sleep when you are out on the streets. Jaak, did you enjoy yourself with your friends?'

'Oh, very much. We went to Outram Ghat – got a boat, had some food, chatted.'

'Good, good. All right. Have some food, then go to bed. I have to wake up in a few hours.'

'Okay, ma, but you should go to bed. No need to worry; I'm home now. I'll eat and then go to sleep.'

Moyur had already eaten a fancy dinner at the jazzy restaurant overlooking the Ganga. They had taken over most of the top floor, filled it with stories and exploits. There had been so much food and drink that they hadn't been able to finish it all.

'Come on, start,' ma insisted.

Seeing she was not about to move, he began tearing up the rooti.

'Who else was there?' ma asked.

He told her, reciting the names one by one, offering a little background on each so she might place them, but when he looked up from his plate, ma's head was back on her chest, her breathing heavy. He got up and took hold of her by the shoulders, and this time she relented.

By the time he returned to the table, the night had grown still deeper. Moyur moved his plate to the head of the table and stilled himself into the silence. Yesterdays faded and the future, a flurry of expectation, waited on him. It was a good moment.

7

Even in the relative calm of suburban Salt Lake, it is almost impossible to linger in bed once the sun has lifted its head above the parapet. The crows with their ugly, raucous symphonies, the barking strays and the heavy chug of diesel engines passing by unite in a conspiracy to frustrate any slumber.

Despite these unremarkable but persistent tribulations, Moyur somehow managed to cling to his sleep, determined to leave the spell of the previous night unbroken for as long as possible. But even he could not withstand the merciless arm-swing of the newspaper boys.

Day after day, they serviced each house with their pre-ordered dailies – tightly rolled missiles of paper that landed on balcony floors with remarkable precision, most of the time. Every so often there would be reported instances of overshooting and the resultant casualties. Yet nobody had ever met a victim. To be honest, they were the sort of alleged ineptitudes that most people might ignore or have a guffaw over. Moyur had never thought anything of them. That is, until that morning when the newspaper flew in through the open window, weaving its way through the metal grills to touch down exactly on his forehead.

Moyur sat up and fingered the emerging bruise. There could be no escape from a day that so doggedly clamoured for his attention. He stepped from the bed onto the relative cool of the mosaic tiles.

Breakfast was waiting on the table. Some soft chhana, milk, bananas, rice, dal. Bapu was already sucking the last few grains of rice from his fingers. His hair, still slightly wet, was combed flat against his scalp, plastered down by a thin film of coconut oil. Bapu usually wore a panjabi to work. He had quite a few of them, washed by the woman who came every morning, ironed and folded by the man in the thick varifocals who sat at the corner of the park, and put into his cupboard by Lily mashi. Before getting up, he looked at Moyur. 'So when are you coming with me to the shop? Next week?'

Moyur felt a twinge of disappointment. He had been hoping for a more prompt summons. Why wait – he was desperate to learn, to start, to show bapu that this was not a mistake. 'Bapu, I don't need any more holidays. Why don't I come with you tomorrow?'

'Very well, if that is what you want. Maybe today you can think again about finishing your class twelve. Education is vital, especially in this day and age. Not like when I was a boy.'

Moyur responded with an automatic nod.

Bapu sighed. 'Who am I to give you a lecture? You already know...' Yes, bapu had his ideas, but on the whole he never let them impinge upon the momentum of life.

Moyur's induction into working life was so smooth, he barely realized that he was learning. Joba kaku was entrusted with Moyur's initiation and the arrangement proved ideal.

Joba kaku was from bapu's village in the Sunderbans. By the time bapu's father joined the West Bengal Forest Department, Joba kaku's father had already passed away. Joba kaku's mother was given a position in bapu's quarters, cleaning and doing odd jobs around the house. Often, she would bring along Joba, the younger of her two sons, and on the days that bapu was not at school, the two of them would play together. Despite the differences in their age and situation, neither family discouraged their friendship, and bapu and Joba kaku remained close into adulthood, until bapu moved away. Bapu became a successful businessman, Joba kaku worked on his family's allotments, but they did not forget each other, and when Joba kaku's family fell upon hard times, bapu went out of his way to give him this job in Calcutta.

Joba kaku's was a family of farmers. One evening, his elder brother Pulin was out in the fields much later than he should have been. He had been behaving strangely for a few weeks, and that night he didn't come home. His half-eaten carcass was found in the field early next day. The word in the village was that Pulin sought his own death, for what man, woman or child of sound mind and intent would walk alone in the dark in this land of tigers, unarmed, without so much as a flare or a whistle to summon help.

It was a desolate day when nineteen-year-old Joba lit the cremation pyre of his twenty-two-year-old brother. Pulin's mangled body was barely disguised by the wreaths of wailing flowers.

The next morning, Joba cycled to the local phone booth and telephoned bapu.

Ever since, Joba kaku had been bapu's assistant through all the ups and downs of the business. By giving Joba kaku a livelihood in the city, bapu had not only rescued him from the curse of the Sunderbans, he had also put food on his plate and in the mouths of his brother's widow, his nephew and his mother. The money had paid for the little one's schooling and for the roofs over all their heads.

Since Joba kaku regarded Moyur as an extension of bapu, his affection for the father also encompassed the son. Joba kaku never once questioned Moyur's inexperience or his position in the hierarchy of the sari shop. They both silently acknowledged that in the end the shop would be Moyur's. But for now Joba kaku was his senior; it was from him, and not from bapu, that Moyur learned what little he needed to.

Moyur knew instinctively how to flick his wrist and how to let a sari unfurl, allowing the fabric to perfectly divulge its hues, its patterns, its enigma. So, when he actually came to do it in real life, he executed even his first attempt with the expertise of an old hand.

'Very good, Moyur baba. Very good,' Joba kaku said, brimming with approval. 'I can see you will become my boss very soon.'

Moyur tingled with pride. As he grew more confident, he would sometimes, accidentally on purpose, drape the sari a little further up his arm than strictly necessary, and all the little hairs on his arm would quiver with excitement. Peacock blue looked good against his skin. In fact, every shade of blue suited Moyur's complexion, but there were so many dyes – too many to remain in a rut of blue. Colours that he had never even imagined catapulted into existence. There were many names for the colours – pistachio, peanut, ranga-mati red, magenta, shocking pink, cream, off-white, silver, mint – but no matter how many names they devised, the subtleties of shade outwitted them. And Moyur was only too happy to accept defeat at the hands of colour.

The following pujo turned out to be one of the busiest the shop had ever seen. Word of the owner's son's prodigious talent for finding the right sari spread through the households of Calcutta. And he was so young.

Moyur was someone who uncannily chose the perfect sari, the one that had been simmering in the depths of the buyer's imagination. A nascent daydream would become, with a flick of his wrist, a splendid reality. And oh, how he could talk, with that beguiling smile of his, floating around the shop, summoning from its recesses yet more irresistible pieces, the very threads that embellished them laced with seduction.

With the affectionate exactitude of a librarian, Moyur logged in his mind the particulars of every single sari that was held in stock and with each sale, with each new delivery, the register would be updated with the detail of the fabric, the colour, the weave, the style. Each and every one was tagged and, with digital precision, Moyur could match a customer's vague requests to the saris with which they walked out of the shop.

In the following months, not once did a customer leave empty-handed. Bapu paid Moyur a decent wage for his work, his initial reservations disappearing rapidly under bundles of hundred-rupee notes.

❀

Ma's reservations, on the other hand, were a lot more resilient, and whenever circumstances arose that might be schemed and connived into an opportunity to lure Moyur away from the shop, she managed to do so, in an unarguably reasonable way, usually with requests for cash that only Moyur could be entrusted with. It struck all three of them, Moyur, bapu and Joba kaku, how frequently ma seemed to have these urgent requests, all of which were to ensure the timely procurement of household supplies. In fact, what struck them most was how they had previously failed to realize the precarious nature of managing household stocks of kerosene, gas, flour, rice, oil and other sundry items.

So when ma sent a request for some funds, due to a sudden unexpected delivery of surplus gas cylinders, Moyur was promptly dispatched home with bulging pockets and a box of sweets from Gupta Brothers in case of sudden guests. It was, after all, only two days after Holi and the scorching blue days did nothing to deter the unpredictable deluge of visitors.

Multi-coloured sweat dripped from Moyur's brow as he made his way from the bus stop. Magenta tarmac melted onto his shoes. Everywhere, hotchpotches of colour glistened: on lampposts and letter boxes, on unsuspecting cows and bemused strays. The youngsters had played Holi like mad, dousing everyone and everything in a riot of pigment. By the time Tinku and Bapta came to pick Moyur up, they were smothered in clouds of red and green. Only their eyes remained recognizable, laughing under conspiratorial, caked lashes.

It was the one day in the year when, under the guise of wholesome festivity, the boys could let their hands wander freely amongst the young women of the para, and it was the one day in the year when the elders could not protest any duplicity in their intent. It was not something Moyur ever did. Especially not to Jonali.

He had seen her, of course. First thing, when he and ma visited Meena pishi. She had plaited her long hair away from her face and smudged kajol along her eyes. She wore an old buttercup-yellow chiffon sari, the thin fabric struggling to contain the exuberance of the body beneath. Moyur had dutifully traced a line of aabir on Jonali's arm and she had reciprocated by politely dabbing the red powder on his cheeks and forehead.

She had said that she was going out with Riya and a few of the girls from the para. He had hoped their paths might cross, away from the well-meaning eyes of ma and Meena pishi. But they hadn't, and the boys drifted away from the confines of the block. In an empty park beyond the reach of petty consequences, Bapta produced a bundle of ganja and rolled it into a joint. He had become a bit of a regular, often stoned, ever ready to be the supplier on special occasions.

Moyur took a drag. In the background, Bapta started singing. Tinku accompanied him, playing the tabla on his knee. Strains of a makeshift serenade and swirling gushes of intoxicant took Moyur back to a Jonali framed in soft smoke. He imagined her as a Bollywood heroine, peering at him from behind a mango tree; he would approach her, their fingers would touch, he would inhale her fragrance. They would draw closer together, their bodies almost touching. Except for the mango tree.

'Eyi, Moyur.' Tinku's hefty voice barged into his daydream.

'Ki holo?' Moyur followed Tinku's finger.

'Isn't that your girlfriend? Now you've had it.' Bapta and Tinku cackled in delight.

Moyur felt himself flush. He didn't want her to see him like this. What was she doing so far out, anyway? Tinku nudged him. 'Don't worry,' he said, 'just act normal.' But Tinku's ridiculous grin belied normal. Moyur grabbed Tinku's arm; there was no need to wave at her.

'Why are you spoiling our fun? You might not have the guts to do anything but I'm going after Rupa.' Bapta took a final drag on the joint before stamping it into the ground. To Moyur's dismay, he started walking towards the group of girls.

'Come on, hero.' Tinku took out some green powder from his pocket and wet it with his spit. 'To the battlefront!' He rubbed his hands together till they were covered in thick green paste and then wiped some on Moyur's palms.

Moyur lagged behind but Jonali had seen him. She was smiling and gesticulating at him with a fistful of powder. His heart skipped a beat. To the battlefront, he thought. And so it was, a barrage of wandering hands and nubile bodies, boys versus girls, clouds of red powder versus sticky green paste, clogged hair and eyelashes versus incriminating fingerprints on bare skin. Moyur didn't know what he was doing. He tried to be honourable but he could not always tell because it is hard to tell on a battlefield mired in colour and the smoke of the ganja plant.

He remembered laughter. Jonali's laughter on the battlefield.

❁

The clanging metal echoes of gas cylinders being unloaded brought him back to the present.

Ma was, as usual, watching the road in anticipation of his arrival. 'Baba, finally you are here,' she hollered from the balcony. 'I thought, today we are going to miss them for sure.'

'Na, ma. I can still hear them.'

Ma took the money from Moyur and sent Lily mashi to inform the gas men to deliver three cylinders to the house.

'Is your father expecting you back at the shop this afternoon?'

'I think so, ma.' Moyur hesitated. 'Unless you want me for something.'

Ma sighed and started rearranging the clothes that had been put out on the washing line to dry. 'Jojo dropped in this morning with some good news. She has got a place at Xavier's to do an honours degree,' she said. She sighed again. 'Anyway, at least eat something before you go back.'

Moyur made his excuses and left. Though his flair for business had won bapu over, ma, with her penchant for despair, would every so often indulge her disappointment that he had not continued his studies. Although Moyur bore her attempts to rescue him with good grace, he could not bear to be near ma alone when she was like this, consumed by his failure.

Left foot, right foot, left foot, right foot. Moyur concentrated on the road. It looked duller on the way back. He lit an emergency cigarette. How easily colour can seep out of the world. Left, right, left right.

❈

Moyur had almost reached the bus stop when he spotted Jonali at the top of the street. She was wearing a burnt-orange salwar kameez in the latest style, with three-quarter-length sleeves and side slits going all the way up the thigh.

'Moyur!' There was pleasure in her voice.

'Hey, how are you? I hear you have good news,' Moyur replied, hurrying towards her.

'Really? Who told you?'

He mock-frowned at her and, to his delight, she giggled.

'Well.' Jonali curled her tongue slowly in her mouth, relishing his attention. 'I got the highest mark in the year for our last assignment.' She smiled. 'And guess what?'

'What?' he asked on cue.

'I've got a place to study eco at Xavier's.'

Moyur felt a rush of bittersweet admiration. 'Jojo, you are unstoppable. You'll end up as a professor one day.'

'No chance,' she said, shaking her head. 'Ma said that after this degree, that's it. She didn't even want to wait this long.'

Moyur continued to look at her. 'Which way are you going?'

She nodded towards her house. 'You?'

'Back that way. But it's okay.' Moyur began to walk with her. 'So, wait that long for what?'

Jonali tilted her head and looked at him shyly. He wondered if she ever reciprocated his desires, even in the remotest, most outrageous of her fancies.

'For marriage, what else? You are sooo silly. You have no idea of the ways of the world, do you?'

Jonali's tone disappointed him. Yet he couldn't shrug from his mind the idea that she was also tormenting him. He wanted to indulge in the possibility of an inarticulate flirtation in her molten brown eyes. But each hope was haunted by the memories of their playtimes. Could he ever be anyone other than the boy she used to play dress-up with, the boy who had wanted to be the princess?

'Aren't you going to say something?' Jonali asked.

'Like what?'

Jonali giggled. 'Well, what good will a degree in economics be when I am performing my wifely duties?'

'What rubbish,' Moyur replied. 'Anyway, I thought you were against marriage.'

'I am,' she said, suddenly vehement. 'Dead against it. But ma is like a bulldozer.'

Moyur kicked a loose stone, sending it across the road. 'You can't stop studying. That would be stupid.'

'What do you care? You did.'

'I'm not as clever as you are.'

Jonali looked serious. 'Moyur, you didn't even try and you still got fifty per cent. I had to slug my guts out.'

'Jojo, you came in the top fifty in the entire city. We're not in the same league. In fact, I'm about ten leagues below you.'

Her voice elevated. 'No way. You're such a liar.' She tapped him on his shoulder in gentle rebuke.

'Ow, Jojo, that hurt.' He furrowed his brow at her and she laughed. The way she had laughed on the battlefield. The sleeve of her kameez rode up.

'Oh my god, Jojo, your arm!'

They both looked at the dirty green handprint on her arm and then at each other.

Moyur couldn't draw his eyes away from the mark. It was Tinku's nasty paint but the handprint on the inside of her arm, just above the elbow, was undeniably his. 'I'm so sorry,' he said.

'Don't worry, it'll wash off in a few days,' she said. Slowly, she drew the sleeve over the mark. 'I like it. Reminds me of you.'

Without thinking, Moyur put his hand on her back, but before he could finish his caress, she arched away from him and quickened her pace; she drew the shoulder bag she was carrying across the front of her body, clinging to it with both hands. A tinge of modesty accentuated the faded rouge on her cheeks.

'I should head to the shop.'

'You're going the wrong way,' Jonali said.

'I know.'

'See you later,' she said.

When? Moyur wanted to ask, but instead, he set off towards the shop. At the top of the street, he stopped to watch Jonali's hips sashaying in the opposite direction. He wondered if she would turn around like lovers do in movies, even though she wasn't his lover. Moyur scolded himself for entertaining such a childish thought. Yet he waited until she reached her end of the road. And then she looked; it was just a little look, over her shoulder, but it was enough. She must have thought him an idiot, still waiting, but she waved, a nonchalant sisterly gesture, which nevertheless filled Moyur with pleasure, and he bounded across the road towards the bus stop.

8

Park Street, neighbourhood of the well-heeled and well-educated, was overrun with posh boutiques and fancy restaurants; it was also home to Xavier's, where futures full of standing-on-your-own-two-feet-ing were built. And Jonali had the entry ticket. Months of diligence had paid off and the day had finally arrived.

The first time Jonali walked through those high gates it was to a magnificent drum roll, imaginary, but she was no less proud because of it.

Pale yellow buildings guarded the central playing field with its patchwork grass. Senior students dawdled on benches and stairwells, in the shade of the peepal trees that lined the fringes of the square. Their practised lounging impressed her. Jonali had already lived this scene, cherished it, rehearsed it in quiet snippets of time, whenever her mind could slip unnoticed into fanciful ruminations. In reality, the mid-summer colours were a little more faded and the grass more parched than she had imagined, but this just steeped it in the glamour of a profound history. Jonali inhaled deeply, breathing in the light-headed austerity of the college. Soon, she would belong.

On the way to registration, bearers interrupted her at every turn to point her in the right direction. 'Madam, this way.' 'Madam, up-i-shtairs.' 'Madam, fareesht laift.' Along the wall, a line of ex-principals, all Jesuit fathers, all from the tough love school of education. Smiles and sternness hand in hand. How apt.

The registration room on the first floor was easily recognizable by the mass of first-year students that spilled out from it. Jonali scanned the crowd. A couple of the girls from her old school had been awarded places at St Xavier's, but she did not particularly know them. They were society girls, veterans of the party circuit. She did not move in their circles nor they in hers. Her best friend had gone to Delhi to study medicine, leaving her alone in Calcutta.

Except Moyur. But where was Moyur? Where were their shared afternoons? If only Moyur had listened to her. They could have delayed this.

So many times, before the class ten exams, she had offered to help him but all he wanted to do was run the sari shop. Whenever she brought up the subject of education, he had quickly diverted the conversation, his eyes, so soulful yet so secretive, open only to one life, full of embroidered patterns and dancing dervishes. He had changed so much in the last few years. They all had. But he had changed the most. He had grown tall and athletic, with graceful limbs and a feminine turn of beauty that might look unnatural on any other young man, but in Moyur's case merely accentuated the drama about him.

The reality of the big world had aged Moyur. Standing-on-his-own-two-feet-ing suited him, infusing him with poise, taking him far away into the world of ordering and accounting, stocks and business, yes-madaming and no-madaming.

Moyur was a grown-up and she was a college girl, and although there would always be only three months and twenty-two days between his birthday and hers, somehow their ages had fallen out of sync. And now he was drifting towards another life.

The registration line inched forward. It seemed that many of the students already knew each other. Jonali scanned the queue for fellow loners but there was none close at hand, so she settled on the two girls immediately behind her, who were deep in conversation but in a reassuringly superficial one. Jonali used the pretext of borrowing a pen to introduce herself, and the two girls, Mita and Deepa, were more than happy to include her in their band. It turned out that all three were doing the bachelor's degree in economics. The discussion, therefore, turned naturally to the state of the nation, the much touted eight per cent rate of growth and the laughable assertions of politicians.

Caught up in early acquaintance, the trio found themselves progressing rapidly to the front of the queue, where the registration officers were sitting in a formal line, behind a long wooden table. In the centre, a woman with wispy grey hair was hunched over wads of paper, thick with important information. To her right was a middle-aged man with an abundant moustache and sweat patches spreading from under his armpits almost halfway down each side of his shirt. On her other side, a rake-thin woman with severe bulging eyes sat with her head propped up against her palm. Jonali started calculating. She didn't want the severe one. Guiltily, she hoped to be spared the man. Was it bad to want to avoid people on the basis of appearance alone? Regardless, she was relieved when she found herself in front of the wispy-haired woman.

'Name?'

'Jonali Banerjee.'

The woman looked noisily through her list, flicking impatiently between sheets. Then she started again, this time adding an occasional despairing shake of her head. Jonali tried to peer over the table, anxious that her name should not have gone astray, but the woman held the papers at exactly the wrong angle. After the second attempt, she stopped. 'Your name is not here. You have handed in your registration form?'

'Yes, ma'am. Definitely.'

'By post?'

'No, ma'am. I delivered it to the office by hand, ma'am. I would never take such a chance.'

The man sitting to her right piped up, 'Ki holo abar? What is the problem?'

'Looks like her name is not on the list.'

'Did she hand in the form?'

'Yes, she is saying she brought it by hand.'

The man did not comment further. Mita and Deepa had already finished and waved to Jonali as they left.

'When did you bring your form?' the woman asked.

'About a month ago. The day after the results came out.'

The woman looked at the list again but her eyes, bored with a day spent reading through the same lines again and again, skirted indifferently across the letters.

'It looks to me like you are going to have to go to the college registration manager downstairs.'

'But madam, I have definitely completed all the documents.'

'Well, it does not...' The woman looked up at Jonali's face and stopped in mid-sentence. She softened and said more gently, 'It is probably a clerical error. Not your fault. But you know how difficult it is... thousands of students every year. One or two are bound to slip through the net, isn't it? I am sure the manager will be able to help you.' She paused to allow Jonali to register the lifeline she had given her. 'Room 117, Mr Bimol Mollick.'

'Thank you, madam.'

Before she had quite stood up, the woman shouted, 'Next.'

❀

Room 117. There was a sinister ring to that number. No bearers pointed her in the right direction, no friendly commotion greeted her. A huge wooden door, slightly ajar, allowed a glimpse of the desolate interior. Jonali tapped on the door. There was no answer. She chided herself for her excessive timidity and then tried again.

'Door is open.'

Jonali tiptoed into the room. There was a long window at the far end of the room, guarded by half-open, dusky green wooden blinds. The ceiling must have been at least fifteen feet high, and from it, suspended by long steel chains, dangled two standard-issue Godrej fans. Three desks, strewn with papers and pens, envelopes and ledgers, stood against three walls. Two of these were unoccupied; at the third desk sat a college official, industriously reading the *Anandabazar Patrika*. Jonali took slow, quiet steps towards him. Without looking up, the gentleman recited, 'Mrs Chandrika Ghoshal, finance officer and issuer of tuition-fee notices, is not available. At present she is on tiffin break. Mr Shankar Dey, course administrator and distributor of reading lists, is not available. At present, he is also taking lunch.'

Jonali waited for him to continue but he did not. In a remote corner of his desk was a nameplate which she tried to decipher, but a thick coat of dust rendered it useless. She looked up to catch the gentleman watching her, his lips gathered into a fledgling smile.

'I should really clean that sign. Nobody ever bothers to read these things any more. Too impatient. Not everybody is polite like you. So, like the rest of world, I too have started catering only to ill-mannered folks. It is a real tragedy.' He stood up and put the newspaper down with a flourish. He was surprisingly tall, most of his height stacked loosely in his bamboo-shoot legs. 'How can I be of service?'

'Actually, I am looking for Mr Bimol Mollick.'

'Yes, yes. That is me. How can I help?'

Jonali began with a character reference: she was a reliable girl and she did not want to be misjudged. Mr Mollick listened attentively, rubbing his temples as she spoke. Jonali then proceeded to an explanation of the mistake that had befallen her. Not her mistake but, unfairly her consequences. When she finished, Mr Mollick took his time to respond. First he tutted, then he sighed. Then he tutted some more. From his drawer, he retrieved a copy of the list that the registration officers had been looking at. 'Come, let us look at this together,' he said. He pulled up another chair and they sat together, examining the list line by line, heads almost touching, Jonali willing her name to appear. It did not.

Jonali started rifling through her bag in search of anything that might prove that she had registered. She found the letter offering her a place, the letter with the invitation to register and a copy of the college prospectus. The remainder of her bag was a frustrating hole full of empty wrappers, ancient receipts, bus tickets and creams. She felt a tear balancing precariously along the lower rim of her eye and she tried to blink it away, but Mr Mollick noticed before averting his gaze in a hurry.

'Miss Jonali Banerjee. It is improbable, I might say even impossible, that we have made this mistake. We have been processing students for decades, if not longer. Maybe if you rack your brains you will remember what happened. It must be that you didn't bring in the form. That is the only explanation.'

Jonali nodded. But the tear that had been lurking on the lower rim of her eye toppled down.

Mr Mollick hastened away from the scene of the judgement, walking towards the warm breeze that the open window offered him. 'Is there anything else?'

Jonali tried to speak but her words were consumed by a poorly concealed whimper. She rifled through her bag for her handkerchief but it had trapped itself under a copy of *Femina*. She wiped her nose on her sleeve.

'Please, madam, crying is not the solution. You always have the option of re-applying next year if, for some reason, you forgot this time.'

Jonali did not move. She opened and closed her mouth until a few words emerged to her rescue. 'Sir, is there anything that can be done? I promise I brought the form.'

Mr Mollick sighed heavily. 'I don't know... you people, what you think.' He lumbered back to his desk. 'I'll look for your form. What is the name again?'

'Banerjee, sir.'

'Good name?'

'Jonali.'

He scribbled it down on a scrap of paper, reciting the name to himself under his breath.

'When will you know, Mr Mollick? Can I come back this afternoon?'

'This afternoon?' He directed a contemplative gaze at the wall-mounted clock, then to his wristwatch and then, as a finale, the clock again. 'Miss Banerjee, I have other things to do.' When Jonali remained unmoving, he snapped, 'Okay, four-thirty on the dot.'

'Yes, Mr Mollick. Thank you so much. You are saving my life. I will be back exactly on time.'

As she pulled the door behind her, she heard Bimol Mollick surrender himself to a heavy sigh. She suspected that he was not the kind of man to pander to the perceived carelessness of others – except that she had not been careless.

✻

Jonali found Mita and Deepa in the canteen amongst a gaggle of fresh-faced bona fide students. There was a lot of polite conversation and unnecessary giggling going on, which the two girls graciously interrupted to introduce Jonali to the group. After the inevitable questions about which degree and what class, they went back to their prior discussions – timetables, sessions, professors and extra-curricular societies.

'You're very quiet, Jonali.' Mita wriggled into a space beside her. 'Is everything all right?' Mita spoke softly, but it just so happened that her words coincided with a gap in the rest of the conversation. Suddenly, all eyes were on Jonali. So Jonali told them. And they were shocked, outraged to hear of the blunder the college authorities had made, indignant at the injustices she was having to endure.

There was even suggestion of protest, from Rono. 'Damn those incompetent pen-pushers,' he pronounced and the others nodded. 'Bloody corrupt clerks... Wouldn't surprise me one bit if they just sold your place. This has to end,' Rono continued, his voice getting louder. The group murmured its approval. 'Revolution,' he cried, standing up abruptly. 'We must rise up against the institution.'

Immediately, he was shouted down by the others. 'Arrey, hero, calm down,' and 'Here is our revolutionary,' and 'Even looks a bit like Fidel,' which met with such laughter and approval that Rono, blushing yet good-humoured, became the first in the group to acquire a nickname.

Still, the consensus was that Jonali should attend classes, no matter what, until the problem was sorted. In theory, Jonali agreed with the plan, although she did not like the idea of doing something she was not supposed to, even though she should have been supposed to. There was too much at stake, and she did not want to jeopardize her career for the sake of making a point. She thought of Mr Mollick. He seemed like a man put upon by the world, but he had agreed to help her. So she told them she was due to see him that very afternoon to resolve the matter.

'Why don't you take Fidel with you?' one of the other boys asked and the group erupted into laughter again.

Rono smiled with well-affected benevolence. 'Perhaps you should refer to me as leader.'

Once the cackling died down, both Mita and Fidel offered to accompany Jonali on her mission, and although she politely declined their offers, they insisted. The others in the ensemble too pledged to stay with her, but as the afternoon wore on they left, one by one, to carry out various urgent, suddenly-remembered errands. Yes, there was a great deal of empathy, but there was also smugness. She made them feel better about their timetables and not-up-to-scratch professors because at least they weren't her. Poor thing.

Jonali, Mita and Fidel moved closer to the kitchen so they could order tea with greater efficiency. It emerged that all three shared a great affection for cha. 'The beverage of choice in times of struggle,' Rono offered weakly as he lifted his cup to his lips. The girls smiled. Jonali felt she had made some good friends, although her pleasure was tempered with the anxiety that it might be short-lived. She studied Rono. He did in fact bear a vague resemblance to Fidel, with a head full of curly hair and a squarish face that tapered down to a pointed chin adorned with a straggly goatee. He caught her looking at him and responded with a goofy smile.

As the designated time approached, Jonali found it harder and harder to remain involved in the conversation, even though it was dominated by her impending liaison. Her eyes wandered maniacally to and from the oil-stained clock above the kitchen entrance. With five minutes to go, she stood up.

'Do you want us to come with you?' Mita asked.

Jonali shook her head. 'No, please go home. You have already done so much. I will be fine.'

'Impossible. We will wait here for you and you can come back and tell us what happened with the good-for-nothing registration manager,' said Fidel.

'Really, I'll be fine. Don't wait for me. He seemed very helpful. It's probably going to turn out to be a minor hiccup.'

But Mita was already signalling for another round of tea.

Fidel grinned. 'How many revolutionaries do you know who go home in the middle of the revolution?'

Jonali could not argue with that. In fact, his espousal of the cause, even if it was a little playful, fuelled her desperation to be a student. 'Okay, I will see you back here.'

'Best of luck.'

Jonali made her way across the field. With each step, Mita and Fidel shrank, not just in their presence but also in their possibility. They saw her looking at them and waved. She signalled back.

The door to room 117 was as she had left it. She knocked and entered. Mr Mollick was standing beside the window, looking out into the forecourt of the college. Mrs Ghoshal and Mr Dey remained absent.

'Mr Mollick?'

He held his hand up without turning. 'Miss Jonali Banerjee. Yes.'

'Have you managed to find the source of the error, sir?'

Mr Mollick slowly twisted into the room, squinting as he tried to locate her expression in the relative darkness. 'Miss Banerjee, I have not managed to find your registration documents. Tomorrow I am going to ask at the principal's office.'

The impassive note in his voice did nothing to dispel her disquiet. She needed him to understand that she was different – not like the rich boys who couldn't care less if their places were forfeited. Fat wads of cash would pave their way into one or the other of the city's elite institutions. Perhaps they would endure a cursory telling-off for being so useless, followed by a celebratory feast to uphold the family's devil-may-care attitude towards life. But she was not the kind of person for whom second chances were a frivolous habit.

'Mr Mollick, sir, is there nothing else that can be done? Surely the documents must be somewhere. I delivered them by hand myself.' Even as she spoke, Jonali couldn't help but sense the infectious resignation of the city corrupt her aspirations.

Mr Mollick shook his head. 'I have looked already. This is a most serious case, Miss Banerjee. But let us see what we can uncover tomorrow.' He stepped away from the window and started stacking the papers on his desk in readiness to leave.

'Where are all the registration documents kept?'

Mr Mollick gestured towards the filing cabinets at the other end of the room.

'Maybe if I checked them too?'

Mr Mollick looked up sharply. 'I have checked, Miss Banerjee, with the greatest thoroughness.'

Jonali stared at her feet, unaccustomed to being impertinent. Fidel's playful chants of rebellion clamoured inside her head. Would they really share her strife? She decided she had to try again. 'Mr Mollick, sir, I am so sorry. I have accidentally offended you. I am sure you have searched meticulously.' She paused for a reaction but none was forthcoming. 'It's just that I have worked so hard to get this place.'

Mr Mollick embarked upon a vigorous re-organization of his desk, but with the giveaway haphazardness of a man pre-occupied with other matters. Jonali was about to speak again but Mr Mollick cut her short, 'Tomorrow, if I find nothing, you may have a look through the cabinet.'

Jonali felt a flutter in her throat but she thanked him for the opportunity.

'I am not supposed to allow this, Miss Banerjee. Do you understand? These are confidential files.'

'I will not say a word to anybody. I give you my word, sir.'

Mr Mollick reached for his bag. 'This time tomorrow, meet me here. I will supervise.'

He held the door open, stepped out behind her and then locked it. His hands were big and square, out of proportion with the rest of him. 'The bearers have their own key,' he said by way of explanation. 'Not that they ever clean in here. You saw the dust in that room.'

Standing side by side with Mr Mollick, Jonali noted for the first time the dry, acrid scent of his body: the faint odour of cigarette smoke; it was almost Moyur's smell – but not exactly. Perhaps they smoked different brands. Mr Mollick caught Jonali staring at his hands and quickly put them in his pockets. 'Bad habit – nail biting.'

'No, no. Not at all. I didn't even notice.'

Mr Mollick kept his hands firmly out of sight. 'Tomorrow, then. Hopefully, something will be sorted out.'

9

The next morning, Jonali congregated with everyone else in the large quadrangle at the heart of the college. Day one – the most crucial of days. The day for beginning as you mean to go on. But how could she? There were students thumbing through pristine textbooks, others debated over principles and theories. Jonali stared into her nervous future, fidgeting with an empty bag.

From nowhere, Fidel sidled up to her. 'For you,' he said, holding out a brown folder, not unlike the ones that had been handed out to all new students. 'Last night I xeroxed everything: timetable, reading list, rules and regulations. So you have no excuse.'

Jonali undid the tie. 'Thank you, this is so thoughtful of you.'

Fidel was beaming. 'Look at the first page.'

He had even copied out the welcome letter from the college, whitening out his name and replacing it with hers.

Jonali sighed. 'This is amazing, but...'

'Of course you'll get your place,' he said. 'This is just a stop-gap.'

Jonali leafed through the contents. He really had put everything in.

'Come on. First bell has just gone.'

Bell number one – five minutes before class: get moving.

Bell number two – class about to start: in your seats.

Mita appeared as they began to walk. 'There you are,' she addressed them both. 'Come, shall we head?' She put her arm through Fidel's, letting Jonali follow just behind. Jonali didn't mind. They had both come from the same school. It wasn't their fault she was alone. Every few steps, Fidel would throw a glance in her direction and she would force a smile on her lips. Just twenty-four hours ago, she had arrived with the world at her feet.

Jonali had already covered many of the topics that were scheduled for the term, because that is what high-fliers do. Jonali had prepared, so that she could answer any question the lecturer might throw her way, but what with one thing and another, she could not concentrate; her mind wandered off, flitting back and forth, up and down the staircase, into room 117, rifling through the cabinets in Mr Mollick's room.

Scenario 1: All the documents are in alphabetical order; she goes through the Bs: Bagchi, Banerjea, Banerjee, Barua, Basu. Her document is not where it should be. She panics. Her fingers stumble along the papers. She is conscious of Mr Mollick watching the door nervously, and then, all of a sudden, there it is, stuffed indecorously at the back of the Bs, almost into the Cs. She retrieves it and gently hands it over, gracious in her triumph.

Scenario 2: All the documents are in alphabetical order; she goes through the cabinet systematically. This is round two. Mr Mollick has already asked her once to hurry. She feels an annoying nick as the sharp corner of a sheet of paper slices into her finger. Round two is almost at an end. She is at the Zs, she is behind the Zs, in the back pocket where missing papers go, but there is nothing. She turns to Mr Mollick hopelessly. What now?

'You. What is your name?'

Fidel, who was sitting just behind Jonali, poked her in the back. The lecturer was looking directly at her. Jonali felt her voice tighten. She couldn't believe her misfortune – her time was up already. The class was silent.

Suddenly, Fidel spoke up, 'Miss, it is Rono Ghosh.'

The lecturer glared at them both. 'I was not asking you. Still, I suppose you will do. All right, Rono Ghosh, please explain to me the meaning of marginal utility.'

Fidel launched into a vehement explanation that satisfied the lecturer, and she shifted her attention to another pocket of the classroom. As soon as she could, Jonali turned to Fidel to mouth a thank you.

After lectures and lunch, after the gossip and pronouncements, once the rest of the group had disbanded and Mita and Fidel had waited as long as they could, Jonali found herself walking wearily towards room 117. Again.

No one at home knew of the mix-up, not her mother nor her aunt, not even Moyur. Moyur, co-keeper of secrets. But how could she tell him? Where would she find him? When? How do you make whispers strong enough to traverse these great gulfs? Suddenly her heart ached for that intimacy. It wasn't the same with these guys, Fidel and Mita. Moyur would have waited for her; he would have waited till the end of the world, if need be.

Well, once upon a time he would have.

Jonali found Mr Mollick gazing at the street, his hand on his forehead, massaging his temples.

'Please sit,' he said.

Mr Mollick picked up a green pitchboard file from his desk and tugged on one end of the string tied around it. They both put on a display of concentration as it unravelled. The file contained only three or four sheets of paper, which Mr Mollick removed, one by one, laying them to rest on the desk, side by side.

'Miss Banerjee, I have made a separate file for you, containing all the correspondence that has passed between you and this college. You can see for yourself.'

Jonali walked around to stand next to him. She scanned the documents: the application form, the photocopy of her exam results and the offer letter. The conclusion from this display was obvious but she couldn't help but hope that perhaps this was not the end; perhaps this was the prelude to Mr Mollick magicking her redemption from the inner recesses of the filing cabinet.

'Mr Mollick, did you find anything in the principal's office?'

He shook his head.

'So what should we do? Shall we look in your cabinet?'

The chair creaked as Mr Mollick sat down with abrupt heaviness, completely out of keeping with his slight frame. His blue-and-white checked shirt, so carefully starched and ironed in the morning, had succumbed to the warm humidity of the city and hung limply from his torso. 'Miss Banerjee, I have explored all avenues with a great deal of thoroughness. As for these cabinets – it is not in the rules of the college to allow members of the public to look through official documents; however, I am willing to make an exception in your case.'

'Thank you, Mr Mol—'

He held up his hand, cutting her sentence in half. 'With the proviso that not one word of this is breathed to any person outside this room. No one. Is that understood?'

'Of course, Mr Mollick, sir. I am unable to express how grateful I am.'

Mr Mollick stood up. 'I am standing outside to keep watch.'

He extracted a cigarette from his shirt pocket. A few lonesome matches rattled in the matchbox he was carrying around. He lit up and inhaled deeply as he walked up to the door, pulling it behind him. Fumes wafted through the slight gap he left, tickling Jonali with thoughts of Moyur and Mr Mollick. It was a schizoid smell that both panicked and relaxed her as she thrashed along the length and breadth of the filing cabinet.

Jonali searched for as long as she could keep herself persuaded that she might yet find the missing form. But twenty minutes into her excavation of the two-by-one feet drawer, she accepted defeat and closed it, shutting her hopes away.

Mr Mollick returned to his office to find Jonali on the floor, leaning against Mrs Ghoshal's desk.

'Found anything?'

'No.'

'Well, I did tell you.'

'I know, but...'

Mr Mollick walked over to her and knelt down. 'Miss Banerjee, I am sorry. I really am.' For the first time, Jonali detected a hint of genuine empathy. 'But what can a lowly clerk like me do? You tell me. If I try anything, I will lose my job – guaranteed.' When she didn't respond, he continued, 'Believe me, Miss Banerjee, if I could do anything I would. You seem like an excellent student.'

His momentary lapse into kindness punctured her composure. Jonali tried to wipe her tears away but they tumbled so copiously from her eyes that her hands could not keep up. In fact, they kept her so distracted that she barely noticed Mr Mollick's arm slip around her shoulder. Gradually, her crying abated as she succumbed to the familiar smell of cigarette-laced sweat and rested her head against his chest. 'Miss Banerjee, please don't worry any more. You will have a place this year – I give you my word.'

Jonali couldn't believe what she was hearing. 'Really?' she croaked.

'I promise.'

It was then, at that moment, that Jonali lifted her head and Mr Mollick lowered his. Perhaps it was by accident or by the vagaries of fate that their lips brushed against each other, and instead of simply sweeping past, they paused. Jonali looked at Mr Mollick and he looked back. Aghast, amazed – in equal measure.

A volley of approaching footsteps mobilized them.

'My god! My god! What have I done?' he exclaimed.

Without a word Jonali jumped up and exited room 117, leaving Mr Mollick stranded alone in a potential scandal, his arms caressing the space she had hastily vacated. Her heart thudded an uneven pattern of bruises inside her as she fled.

10

At the Bengal Silk House, business was at a low ebb. Slow afternoons were filled with 'Ek do teen' blaring pleasantly from the television in the all-purpose tele-communications shop next door. A large mustard-yellow sign announced its STD, ISD and PCO facilities in fluorescent letters. The owner, Piklu, a lazy, conniving so-and-so, had also managed to ram into the six-by-eight feet shop a grandiose photocopier and a fax machine that nobody had ever seen in action. The two private phone booths at the back had been fitted with flashing wall-mounted metres that announced both the number dialled and the duration of the call. Moyur had to admit that Piklu had done well for himself.

Piklu's perch at the entrance to his telephone-cum-fax-cum-xerox shop was just about visible from the entrance to the sari shop. Moyur seldom saw him move from there. Work constituted a never-ending stream of filmi hits and collecting money from ordinary people to use his do-it-yourself telephones. In quieter times, Moyur occasionally contemplated sneaking off to catch a glimpse of some silver-screen diva dancing a pretty illusion for the streets of India, but the opportunity had not yet presented itself. How do you go about ingratiating yourself to a lazy, conniving so-and-so, whose television you want to watch?

Moyur waited with growing despair until that day when, just as 'Ek do teen' shimmied to its conclusion, a woman's voice rang out from Piklu's shop in shrill protest.

Satisfied that Joba kaku's sleeping body, prostate across the display platforms, was enough of a deterrent for would-be pilferers, Moyur slunk out to investigate this opportune disruption.

A woman in a synthetic pink sari was leaning over Piklu, who remained resolutely stuck to his chair, his lazy flesh oozing through the ventilation holes in the plastic backrest. The woman seemed as determined to remain standing, obstructing his view of the television, as Piklu was to remain seated. Her sari was covered in motifs that glinted with a cheap chik-chik sheen in the afternoon sun.

'Piklu? What's going on? Why this screaming and shouting?' Moyur asked, manoeuvring himself into a suitable position so that he might steal glances at the screen.

Piklu grunted towards the woman in front of him. 'Why not ask this lowlife? Acting like I am her servant.'

Moyur studied the woman. She didn't look particularly well-to-do but she had the self-assurance of a wealthier counterpart. She was neither pretty nor ugly and had an ageless face; all her features were in the right place; her hair was jet black and rolled into an obedient bun; her teeth, though slightly paan-stained, were regularly spaced and did not huddle together in unruly clusters in her mouth. Sequinned glass bangles stretched from her wrists to her elbows on both arms and the teep on her forehead was just as flashy.

'Didi.' Moyur stepped in. 'Is something wrong? Maybe I can help?'

The woman hesitated. Until Piklu let slip into her pause a

conspicuous self-satisfied grunt. Immediately, she began twisting her face, first one way and then another, in manifold expressions of annoyance.

'Didi?'

'Okay, let me tell you. I am asking this moshai to give me, upfront, the cost of a telephone call. But he refuses. He is saying, first call and then we can talk about money. But this poor woman needs to pace herself. At least give me a rate. I can't do all this talkie-walkie, magic-machine business.' She finished with one hand on each hip, her lips pursed.

Moyur's immediate instinct was to side with her. Her altercation with Piklu confirmed his assessment of his next-door neighbour as an idle good-for-nothing.

Piklu observed them both glumly. 'Who asked you to come here and be the big hero?' he asked Moyur.

'Piklu dada. What does it matter to you? Few rupees here and there are nothing for a successful businessman, but for the rest of us...' Moyur glanced at the woman. She was about to say something. He quickly looked away. It was a fine line he was walking, and easy to cause offence. 'All she wants is the per-minute charge. You must know it, surely.'

Piklu glared at him.

Perhaps he had overdone it. 'Boss, why don't you help this lady with her request?' Piklu softened a little. 'Besides, first rule of business... customer is always right.' Moyur flashed them both a grin he hoped they would find at least a little charming.

Piklu cleared his throat. The woman jangled her bangles. Moyur coughed.

Piklu made to stand up, but he didn't. He leaned back in his chair and, from a drawer underneath his table, he withdrew a pristine book of tables. 'Rupee a minute,' Piklu announced without looking at either of them. He left the book on the table. Moyur smiled at the woman. She responded with a sort of grateful grimace before scuttling towards the phone.

Piklu turned to Moyur. 'You want to join me?' he asked, gesturing towards the television.

'Why not?' Moyur replied casually. *Bollywood Top Twenty* had started almost two hours earlier. Only the last two songs remained. They were the super hits of the season but elapsed all too quickly, in a flurry of choreographed flirtation, with heroes and heroines skipping through the most idyllic of cinemascapes, all set in Switzerland.

The woman in the pink chik-chik sari emerged from the phone booth just as the curtain fell on hit number one, stepping perfectly into its gentle anti-climax. Both Moyur and Piklu looked at her, but Piklu's eyes flew back to the television. Mechanically, he totted up her bill and called out the amount due. The woman handed him some money and thanked Moyur.

'Was it useful, didi?' Moyur asked her.

'Yes. Very,' she replied. 'My friend is visiting me next week and I had to know when the train is arriving.'

'Oh, where is your friend travelling from?'

'Siliguri. Have you been there?'

'Once, I think. Maybe on the way to Darjeeling.'

The woman grinned, baring those neat, slightly paan-stained teeth and smooth pink gums. 'Don't you love the toy train?'

Moyur shrugged.

She shook her head. 'You need to go there again. We used to wait all day for the chug-chug of the train and then we would chase it, running through the clouds till we were out of breath. The tourists always waved to us.' She smiled. 'We were little devils.'

Piklu turned up the volume on the television.

'I must get going,' the woman said abruptly.

'Yes, me too.' Moyur was intrigued. The charm of her reminiscences eclipsed Piklu and the lure of his serialized electric dramas. He followed the woman into the street and pointed out his shop to her. 'Actually,' he confessed, 'it's my father's shop.'

'Same thing, na?'

'Would you like to visit, didi?' Moyur asked suddenly. The woman hesitated: the invitation was both earnest and odd. So Moyur had to insist. It turned out, though, that the woman in the pink chik-chik sari was quite amenable to persuasion.

'Okay, just this once. Because you remind me of someone.'

'Who?' Moyur asked.

But she could not tell him who.

Back in the shop, Joba kaku was still asleep. His white cotton vest had slipped to one side and his dark, exposed nipple rocked up and down in time with his snores. Moyur dusted down a stool for the woman and offered her some water.

'You are so kind. I think I have given you enough trouble already.' But as she spoke, her eyes travelled the length and breadth of the sari shop, enlivened by the possibilities that lay behind the glass.

'Let me show you something.'

Moyur stepped on the platform and strode along it, peering occasionally into one or other of the cabinets. The pleasure in her face spurred him on. His mind computed busily the saris that would most excite her, the ones that would most suit her. This was not going to be a gentle cajole into a few purchases. This would be a grand spectacle and he would be the maestro behind the show.

Sari after sari tumbled enticingly from his fingers, turning the white platform into a fantasy of gold thread against maroon, plum, azure, magenta. Bright bundles of crepe and silk tempted her attentions. With each sari, Moyur volunteered a little of its pedigree: where it had travelled from, what it was called, details he normally offered only the most accomplished of clients.

Unlike his usual customers, the woman did not touch anything; instead, the more voluptuously a sari draped itself across the space between them, the more determinedly she withdrew her hands.

Until Moyur brought out the red Sambhalpuri silk. There she lost control. Throwing caution to notions of status, she caressed the sari while Moyur looked on. One day, he thought, she might remember the time she visited his sari shop with the same mesmeric tenderness with which she remembered her toy train.

Moyur and his guest exchanged saris for stories, forgetting the world around them. Not until Joba kaku interrupted with his post-siesta sinus routine did they notice or even consider that they might have whiled away an entire afternoon on a whim.

'I am just going to freshen up, Moyur baba,' Joba kaku noted flatly, and then he stood waiting, as if for approval or explanation from Moyur, his eyes on the woman all the while.

'Yes, yes, no problem.' Moyur scrambled to gather up the saris, which suddenly seemed too callously exposed. 'Please, go.'

Once he could no longer be seen, the woman intervened, whispering a loud admonishment, 'It's no good me coming here. I shouldn't have done it. I am not the type of woman who can afford your company.'

Moyur had begun the task of folding the saris systematically. 'Don't even mention such a thing, didi. You have honoured me

by coming to my shop. Don't pay attention to Joba kaku.' He
pulled a face to emphasize his point.

The woman allowed herself a nervous giggle before returning
her attention to the Sambhalpuri silk. She had not let go, despite
Joba kaku's intrusion. For the first time, Moyur noticed how
unattractive the synthetic finish of her sari was. It was not the
kind of sari they had in their stock.

'That red one is a gem,' Moyur announced, still folding.
Suddenly he dropped the sari he was holding and jumped down
beside her. 'Let me put it on you.'

Before she could open her mouth to refuse, Moyur had fixed
a black elastic band over her waist, tucked one end of the sari
into it and begun pleating the remainder of the fabric, levering
it around his fingers, twisting his hand back and forth expertly.
Within seconds, the woman was transformed and she gazed in
the full-length mirror, not quite believing her own reflection.

Moyur watched the tentative explorations of her fingers as
she let them run along the anchol and then draped it over her
head, becoming a hostage to her imagination. This was why he
loved his job: so he could trade in the currency of daydreams,
even though he could not have his own. But this woman was
different, scared to indulge, wary of siphoning off too much
from destiny. Like me, he thought.

As he stepped back, the woman tugged at the sari. 'Babu, I am
very grateful to you for giving this poor woman such honour,
but I cannot buy it.'

Joba kaku had not yet returned. The sound of gushing water
in the back yard reassured Moyur that he still had some time.

'Didi, give me whatever you can afford.'

The woman looked at the floor and then back at Moyur.
'Babu, you are a master salesman,' she clucked at him, a wistful

smile playing on her lips. 'I will pay the full price. But babu, I cannot pay it all in one lump sum...'

Moyur picked up her sentence where her proposal lost its confidence. 'You will pay in installments. Weekly installments. That is the perfect solution. Didi, you are a genius.'

The woman grinned. She reached into her blouse and from within the cove of her bosom withdrew two hundred-rupee notes. 'First installment. Keep the sari for me until a special occasion comes along. It is safer here.'

Moyur put the notes in his pocket and retreated briefly to the cashier's desk. From the top drawer he withdrew a hardbound exercise book. He flipped to the back and drew three columns: date, payment made and outstanding balance. He filled them in and showed the entry to the woman. Her eyes drifted over the wrong page. 'Yes, very good, babu. Tip-top.'

The woman got up to leave.

'So, when are you coming back?' he asked.

'As soon as the second installment is ready. It might be a little less or a little more, only god knows.'

'No problem, didi. I don't mind if you pay in smaller installments.'

She smiled at him. They both knew her installment was already small.

'One more thing,' she said as she stepped into the street, 'this poor woman's name is Boshonti.'

11

As term progressed, Jonali continued her clandestine attendances, always wary, but gradually surrendering to make-believe student life. Every so often, Fidel or Mita would resurrect the topic of her struggle against the college but their playful agitation mellowed after Jonali informed them of Mr Mollick's endeavours. In truth, it was astonishingly easy to slip under the radar. This was college, not school. There was no roll-call. Of course, it was not ideal, but at least she was getting an education. Besides, paperwork took time. She would face Mr Mollick again as soon as the time was right. If she waited long enough, he might even forget the little mishap.

'What are you thinking?'

'Hmm?'

Mita asked her again, 'Arrey, what – are – you – thinking?' She stopped between each word. 'Always in a world of your own.'

'Sorry,' said Jonali, casting guilty eyes away from her friend. It all seemed so unreal. How much time does it take, she wondered, for such unlikely accidents to fade into implausibility?

'Don't tease her,' Fidel protested. 'Jonali, we were just talking about the lecturers. That Mr Pal is rubbish. What do you think?'

'Yes,' Jonali agreed, although she could not place him. She smiled gratefully at Fidel. He was always rescuing her: he had taken to sitting next to her in class and dutifully shielded her from any questions the lecturer happened to aim in their general direction.

Mita shook her head. 'I mean, even I could do better than that Mr Pal.'

They proceeded into a round of complaints, each trying to outdo the other. Jonali tried to keep up, interjecting when she could, but she struggled. Her head, normally a bastion of graphs and text, was filled with irrepressible thoughts and anxieties. She would not have believed herself capable of such impropriety, yet she kept returning to the fleeting comfort she had felt in Mr Mollick's arms; the frisson; the kiss – her first – not quite what she had been expecting. Not like the ones in the English movies she had seen at New Empire. Lingering and dewy-lipped. She shook her head at the comparison.

What would her mother say? She would get her married off immediately. Girls who want to stand on their own two feet do not cavort with college officials.

'Miss Banerjee?'

Jonali started at the voice. The officious tone sent an unexpected rush of blood to her cheeks. Jonali turned to face Mr Mollick.

Seconds dripped stickily between them, rife with latent gaffes. Finally Jonali spoke.

'Yes?'

Fidel and Mita followed with their eyes the curt volley of words that ensued.

'Your documents, Miss Banerjee. All in order. Apologies again for any error on our part.'

'Thank you, Mr Mollick. I am very grateful.' That was it.

Mr Mollick turned and walked back across the field. The envelope he had handed her lay loosely in her lap. Jonali wondered what this had cost him.

'Aren't you going to open it and check everything?' Fidel asked. 'You can't trust the bullshitters in this place.'

Jonali lifted the flap cautiously and withdrew the papers: her letter of acceptance signed by the principal, her examination number, a timetable, a reading list and the fee invoice. Fidel's constant criticism of the college authorities grated on her already fragile conscience. Clearly, he was not always right. Keen to extricate herself from his stifling support, Jonali insisted she deposit the fees into her account immediately, and took leave of her friends. The bundle of hundred-rupee notes had been languishing at the bottom of her handbag for long enough.

As she retreated, she felt herself being watched, so she did not look back, not until she was a safe distance away. Fidel had returned to his tea. It wasn't his eyes that were following her. Jonali hastened towards the finance office. The sooner she dispensed with the formalities the better; the whole situation reeked and Jonali couldn't quite believe she would be allowed to get away with it so lightly.

But the clerk who collected her fees was so cursory in his examination of her paperwork that any untoward goings-on would easily have escaped notice. Jonali had nothing to worry about. She walked away from the finance office, relieved but a little uneasy that the con had been so simple; a slight punishment, however inappropriate, would have calmed her.

Unsure of where to go but not yet ready to return home, Jonali returned to the canteen and ordered a cup of tea. Mita and Fidel had left, and only a handful of hard-core freshers dotted the place. She watched them, envious of their carefree induction into college life. There was no duplicity in their presence here.

Jonali reached for her envelope again, her lifeline. Forged? She tipped the contents onto the bench. It was all still there: the letter of acceptance, her examination number, a timetable, a reading list and the fee invoice. The invoice had been rubberstamped by the finance office: *PAID*. Jonali fingered the ink. How many more rubberstamps on the road to legitimacy?

A skin had formed on the surface of Jonali's tea. She took a sip and lifted the skin out with her finger and licked it off: sweet and milky. Then she rearranged her papers, ready to put them back in. But when she peeled open the envelope, she realized she had missed something, a single square of paper that had wedged itself in somehow.

Jonali felt her heart rate pick up ever so slightly. She retrieved the note, an odd-looking thing, a sheet torn out of an exercise-book, folded in half, then half again.

There were just two words on the sheet, precisely centred, in block capitals. Two words that sent her spinning.

FORGIVE ME.

12

Note number one: FORGIVE ME.
Note number two: WILL YOU BE MINE?

Finally, Jonali was in a position to start her studies in earnest. St Xavier's was not cheap and her mother had taken pains to remind her how much her ambitions were costing her in borrowed money and swallowed pride. For Jonali, there was only one way to progress, one way to pass exams – with colours flying so high they would leave kaku and kakimoni out of breath and her mother with no need for justifications.

Then why was she running late?

This should never happen again, she told herself as she rushed towards her class. Never. The first bell had gone and the freshers' classes were held in the farthest part of the building, as far as the distance between bell number one and two. If you missed the first bell, you were in trouble.

In her favour, the crowds had dispersed promptly. The classrooms she passed en route every day were already full today, not filling. The chatter she passed was already composing itself into a hush. But as Jonali approached her own classroom, the noise grew thunderous. She heard Mita's voice, indistinct and impatient. Jonali walked through the door and fifty pairs of eyes gravitated towards her; some jumped, some sidled, but they all lingered uncomfortably. Most of all Mita's.

'So?' Mita asked.

Jonali looked around. They were all staring. Her first thought was Mr Mollick. Someone had found out.

'So?' Mita repeated.

'So, what?' Jonali asked.

'You mean you don't know who it is?'

'Mita, what are you talking about?' Jonali's voice grew suddenly loud as the rest of the class fell silent on cue. Jonali looked up nervously. One of the boys in the front row winked at her. A couple of girls smiled. With relief she noted that there was little menace on her classmates' faces.

Mita accompanied Jonali to her seat and flung open the cover of her desk. On top of Jonali's disciplined pile of books lay a bright red, heart-shaped envelope. Jonali looked up to see Mita grinning triumphantly.

Bell number two began its drone and Fidel sauntered in. 'Come and look at this, Rono,' Mita called out.

'What?'

'Nothing. It's nothing.' Jonali banged shut the lid on her desk. 'Enough.'

'Ooh. Such a mood. Why don't you read it, Jojo?'

There was an unsettling undertone to her cross-examination. Was it jealousy? If only Mita knew how little she cared for such distractions.

'Later,' Jonali said.

'Later?'

'Mita, why don't you leave her alone?' Fidel came to the rescue as usual.

Mita frowned at him. 'Fine.' Fortuitously, the lecturer arrived then and launched straight into the wonders of economics.

As hard as she tried, Jonali could not focus, the red envelope burning a hole in her attention. Quietly, she slit it open and slipped the note that escaped from it between the pages of her textbook. Mita scowled at her. Let her scowl, Jonali reasoned; there was nothing she could do about it.

Note number two:

DEAR JONALI,
I THINK ABOUT YOU ALL DAY. I DREAM ABOUT YOU ALL NIGHT.
WILL YOU BE MINE?
_ _ _ _ _

❄

It must have been the briefest love letter ever written, and was suitably unsigned, barring the five dashes at the bottom. Jonali raised her eyes to see Mita reading over her shoulder. Mita gave her an apologetic smirk. It made her feel a little guilty. To romance vicariously came with the territory of friendship, and love letters were to be huddled over, read and re-read together. To be honest, under normal circumstances Jonali would have thought nothing of it. By default, Mita would have been her confidante. But these were not normal circumstances.

Thankfully, there was no name. Jonali relaxed. She smiled tentatively at her friend. 'I wonder who it is,' she ventured.

Mita nodded. 'Don't worry,' she said. 'We will find out.'

But the immediate drama of Jonali's romance was soon lost in the whirlwind of their new lives. Theatre groups, debating societies, chess clubs, ballroom dancing and poetry recitals beckoned. Mita threw herself into rehearsals for the end-of-term play while Fidel had been spotted by the captain of the cricket team. So, while her friends rehearsed and practised their afternoons away, Jonali plotted and schemed. She spied on Mr Mollick because he was the only one who knew her truth; when she didn't see him she worried for his job and well-being, and when she did see him she wondered how long his promise would last. Her friends might have forgotten about her dramas but for how long? Long enough for her to be rubberstamped into legitimacy? Maybe, maybe not.

Either way, she could not take chances with the man who had perpetrated not one but two compromising notes against her. True, there had been nothing since, but she needed to remain vigilant, to seek clues in his demeanour, to observe him from afar so that she might always have the measure of him. And so Jonali interpreted his dress, his posture, his state of shavenness, the length of his hair, how many cigarettes he smoked. He never clocked her, and week after week passed without event. Except that he seemed to be growing wispier – if a man can be described as wispy – camouflaging himself against his cigarette smoke. Until one week, when Mr Mollick didn't show up.

At all.

Jonali continued her vigil but with each passing day, she found the vacuum harder and harder to bear. Every second ate her up and what little concentration she had managed to reinstate eroded into a hollow. Better to know, she advised herself, than to keep imagining. But Jonali didn't want to re-route Mr Mollick from doing whatever he was doing, in case she made things worse for them both. Except, how could they get worse? Jonali's imagination was killing her and she decided she had to find out.

The morning she chose was hot but with a cool breeze that flirted with her, gently whipping stray petals through her hair. Jonali walked to room 117. She took it as a good omen that the door was open wide. Inside, though, the office was as empty as ever, barring one woman – Mrs Ghoshal, she assumed, remembering Mr Mollick's recitation on that first day.

'Madam?'

'Yes,' Mrs Ghoshal replied without looking up.

'I am looking for Mr Mollick.'

'He is not here. Can I help you?'

Jonali hesitated. 'Madam, I need to speak to him specifically.'

Mrs Ghoshal looked up from her papers. She was wearing a pair of horn-rimmed glasses, which she removed and placed very deliberately on the table. 'Who are you?'

'Jonali Banerjee, madam. BSc Economics.'

'I see. Well, Bimol submitted his resignation about two weeks back. He is winding up with the packing. He took out the last box just now.'

'He's left?'

'Almost. You might be able to catch him outside if you run. I will be dealing with matters that fell under his jurisdiction, until a new appointment is made.'

'Thank you, madam.'

Bad things happen to people who don't stop bad things from happening to other people, especially those who have been so helpful. Jonali ran all the way to the front gate, where Mr Mollick was hoisting his boxes into a taxi.

'Mr Mollick.' She was out of breath. She had to stop him.

He turned to her and his eyes were sad. The ice-cream-wala who was lounging in the shade picked that moment to stretch his back and his ears slipped a little further in their direction. Jonali had told no one. Jonali intended to tell no one. She eyed the ice-cream-wala.

'I hear you are resigning, Mr Mollick.'

Mr Mollick said nothing. He looked haggard. There were shadows under his eyes.

'But you can't,' Jonali continued. 'Is it because of me?'

He stopped loading the car. 'No, of course not.'

'Then?'

Mr Mollick sighed. 'Personal reasons. I don't wish to have further discussion on this topic, Miss Banerjee.'

'What is it? Can I help?'

Mr Mollick shook his head. 'Family reasons,' he muttered, looking away.

He was so severely honourable that her heart ached. 'Mr Mollick, please don't worry about me.'

'It is nothing to do with you.'

'I don't believe you, Mr Mollick.'

'What?'

'I don't believe you.'

Mr Mollick cast his eyes around. 'This is not the right place to talk,' he said, shaking his head. 'Do you know the Princess restaurant in New Market?'

'No.'

'Kathleen's?'

'Yes.'

'It is just next door to Kathleen's. Same side of the street. Will you meet me there this afternoon? Four o'clock?'

'All right.'

Jonali and Mr Mollick walked away from each other. Jonali wanted to run back across the field. She felt sick.

❋

The Princess restaurant was darker than she had expected. The main room was a wide central aisle with tables flanking either side. The walls were covered in a dirty, burgundy velvet that sucked greedily at stray flecks of daylight. The clientele was predominantly male, probably due to the in-house bar. It was a pragmatic choice. She was unlikely to run into any well-meaning acquaintances in such a hovel.

Mr Mollick arrived just a few sips into her Thums Up. He was out of breath and the bottom of his shirt, normally tucked diffidently into his over-ironed trousers, had come loose and flapped around as he moved. 'Sorry I am late.' He looked around the surroundings apologetically. 'It was the only place I could think of. I don't usually go to fancy places. I heard about this one from a friend of mine, when he was having some romantic trials and tribulations a few months ago.'

Mr Mollick ordered a fresh round of cold drinks. 'Well, Miss Banerjee, I am not sure what to tell to you.' He paused. 'I have never before behaved so improperly.'

'It was an accident,' Jonali rushed to protest.

Mr Mollick lit a cigarette and breathed in a lungful of smoke. 'Not all accidents are one hundred per cent accidental, Miss Banerjee.'

This was the closest Jonali had ever been to an out-in-the-open, face-to-face declaration of love and it made her heart pound. She changed tack. 'But surely, Mr Mollick, there was no need to resign?'

Mr Mollick stabbed the bottom of his glass gently with his straw. 'Miss Banerjee, you are bright enough to understand that your documents are – how to put it – a little bent. It has made me wonder. Is it the documents that are bent, or is it me?'

Jonali looked straight at him, into his dangerously earnest eyes.

'And I kissed you,' he continued.

'An accident,' Jonali whispered.

Mr Mollick shrugged. 'I have taken my decision. Better leave now with good references than two months later with a kick in the rear side.' He sneaked a glance at Jonali. 'You are very beautiful, Miss Banerjee – that is for sure. But I am just a clerk reaching for the stars.' He sucked at his cigarette dolefully. 'If I were a college boy I would propose to you this instant, Miss Banerjee. But I am not and it is better for me to leave with my dignity intact.'

This was not quite what Jonali had envisaged.

Mr Mollick continued, 'You know, I almost went to college. I secured top marks in my class twelve exams. Very good student I was, and I even had an offer of a place to study – at Bidyashagor College. Bengali medium college but an excellent institution. But you know, you can never predict what happens in life. Out of the blue, my father died. We are not a rich family; somebody had to work and I was the eldest son. I had to take charge of the house, to earn the crusts for my mother, sister and little brother.' He sighed. 'Still, it is the way it had to be. I did nothing more than my duty as the eldest son. Who else would do it?'

'How old is your sister?' Jonali interrupted.

Mr Mollick slowly withdrew from his soliloquy to focus on her. 'She is like you. How old are you? Eighteen, nineteen? She is five years my junior and she is attending college. That I made sure of. It is so important to get a good education. Everyone should be standing on their own two feet. Especially girls.'

Jonali couldn't resist a smile. How funny that he had chosen those exact words. 'What is your sister studying?' she asked.

'Economics. At Bidyashagor College.'

'Oh.'

'So you see why I had to get a place for you.' He shook his head forcefully, dispelling the distance that had settled between them. 'Miss Banerjee, I do not know what magic you have been weaving but I have taken risks I cannot afford.' He looked at her sadly. 'You think I am a crook?'

'No, no.' This was her opening to allay his fears. 'I am really sorry I made you do this,' she said, 'and I, for one, will not breathe a word about this to anybody.'

Mr Mollick sniggered. 'If only it were so simple. Really, Miss Banerjee, I think it is best we forget this whole episode. I am a clerk and a crooked man. You are a college girl. If my sister fell in love with a clerk I would be upset. There is no future in it.'

Jonali couldn't help reaching across the table and taking his hand in hers. His palm was moist. 'I am so grateful to you, Mr Mollick. To me it doesn't matter whether you are a clerk or not. You are a wonderful human being.'

'Really?' The hope in his voice was painful.

'Yes.' Jonali gathered her next sentence cautiously. 'But Mr Mollick, I don't think I am in love with you. I mean, this is the first time that I have been like this, you know... and... I don't really know for sure. But I don't think so.'

Mr Mollick retracted his hands, nodding excessively as he did so. 'Well, Miss Banerjee, I think the best solution is a cooling-off period. Then we will both know. I mean, you will know. I already know but it is my duty to give you sound advice.' He drained the remnants of his Thums Up and raised his finger in the direction of a passing waiter. 'Okay, Miss Banerjee. Let us get going. Soon we will have all the answers.'

13

Boshonti's visits, though unpredictably distributed from week to week, were always precisely timed. Moyur spotted her approaching from across the road, her trademark sari blazing a picture into the afternoon, matching silver and jade bangles stacked wrist-to-elbow on each arm, her ornate teep in place.

Hurriedly, Moyur rearranged the shop for the fourth time that afternoon. Joba kaku was tucked into a cool corner, snoring softly into a faded red gamcha, and bapu had left in urgent pursuit of his Tuesday afternoon round of cards. Moyur carried out a final check on Joba kaku, then he turned.

'Hello, Boshonti didi.'

'Nomoshkar, Moyur babu.'

Moyur held out a stool for his guest. Boshonti smiled at him. 'You are too kind, Moyur babu. Very good, wise soul inside such a young man.'

There was something about the way she said it that caught him off-guard – a wistfulness that was completely out of character with her lime-green-and-black leopard-print sari.

'Why don't you come and sit?' Boshonti asked.

Moyur crossed his legs into an obedient bow at the edge of the display platform and offered her his attention. But, unexpectedly, he was overcome. By the insidious sadness of my insidious soul.

There are times when it seems that it is only me, only my memories that do not succumb to the shimmering deceptions of this infinite separation; times when I wonder, Moyur, do you remember me? I convince myself that you must. How else this longing? So instinctive, so tumultuous. I cannot believe that it is mine alone.

'I have the next payment,' Boshonti persisted, vying for his attention. 'This time it is good money to make up for last time. You want it now?'

He couldn't hear her. The sound – the dub-dub, dub-dub – of stolen dances grew vivid in Moyur's head, washing out the drone of reality, of traffic and the chattering of passers-by. Boshonti's words floundered in the space between them. Moyur struggled to fill his lungs with air. He clutched his legs to stop them moving. He counted in his head to try and make it stop. It would not.

Boshonti should have been terrified but she wasn't. The further away he pulled, the closer she moved to him, transfixed, staring into his pupils, scrutinizing his malady with such immense hope that she makes me lose my breath. I realize that she suspects me. I realize that there was once another little girl.

❋

Boshonti was born and raised in the village Ghum. Set against the upward curve of the mountain, it was one of the last outposts of human civilization – a place on the edge of reality, where clouds would opportunistically drift in and out through open windows, filling the homes with charmed vapours. Spirits would pass through the village on their way up the mountain to the threshold where the world of the living becomes the world of the free. The old women of the village told stories about how, in days gone by, at a time when there was no electricity or battery-operated lamps, all the working folk would file indoors before darkness fell across the slopes. They told stories of spirits resting in trees, crying out to passers-by for a dollop of rice or a nibble of fish, trapped by desires they could no longer satisfy. And every so often, there would be a tale of some poor mortal who had been possessed by a soul with unfinished business.

Some spirits stayed long enough to restore the equilibrium, to right injustices; others were simply too confused, too distraught to find their way up the mountain. And then there were those souls that wandered for eternity – the ones that became addicted to the hope of being mentioned by loved ones, clutching to fickle remembrances that through the ebbs and flows of time would inevitably end in the tragedy of closure.

But over the years the village had changed. As technology sneaked its way up the mountain, the spirits were displaced further up, towards the sky. By the time Boshonti was a young woman, they had become a rarity; except for that one time, six days after the birth of her half-formed daughter, when Boshonti herself was taken over. It was an inopportune moment because her body was newly empty and her soul was nothing but a carcass, having crumpled under the enormity of what she had just done.

Boshonti had to be rescued by the local witch doctor – a sinewy man with dusty skin, hardened by years of high-altitude living. His hair was tied into a wiry grey-and-black bun that sat proud at the crown of his head. He brought with him a jhata, which he infused with a tincture of potent herbs. With this, he could cure all manner of maladies and exorcize even the most resilient of soul-squatters. The witch doctor took Boshonti to a clearing at the heart of the village where, witnessed by a gathering of friends and relatives, he beat her with his jhata, landing uneven strokes across her back, her chest, her arms.

Her mother had been there. Later, she told Boshonti that there were moments when she could not bear to watch; it hurt her too much and she wanted to run up and stop it all – because that is what mothers are supposed to do. But she was restrained by the other villagers. It was for her own good, they said, and they all stood and watched the spectacle as Boshonti writhed on the ground. Now and again, the witch doctor would let out a screech and his eyes would roll in their sockets, blurring the boundary between doctor and patient.

By the time he finished, dusk had fallen, and little by little the audience trickled away. Even Boshonti's husband left. Only her mother remained. Boshonti later discovered that it was on that same night that her husband had washed his hands of her.

For the next few days, Boshonti stayed with her mother, who nursed her body back to full health.

A month later, Boshonti went back to her marital home. She did not see her husband; he was out. It was just as well. Boshonti packed all her belongings into a large plastic holdall and left for ever.

❁

As Boshonti's story swirled around him, Moyur's body slipped away from the world.

And suddenly I am overwhelmed. For it is as times like these, far from Jonali, from ma, bapu, far from the myriad distractions of the world, that the promise of us, Moyna, Moyur, Moyur, Moyna, becomes palpable.

As his mind drifts further, his ears pick up the methodical beat, dub-dub, dub-dub: the song of the beating heart. He only hears it in snippets. But I hear it all the time, day and night, in the part of our consciousness that is mine – the rhythm is relentless.

Moyur moves suddenly with excitement and his body sends a gentle ripple through the liquid that comes to shore on mine. It fills me with an absurd happiness, to be back here – with Moyur. Listening, in tandem, with ears that are almost the same. Dancing, intertwined with limbs that are almost the same.

Yes, I am addicted to the time before we were children.

Here we are safe. So long as we remain just so. So long as we do not venture into recesses where darkness may be waiting. Like I did.

I panic.

He has heard.

I withdraw from our memory and Moyur hurtles behind me. I have to let him return to the late afternoon lull. We will go back again some other time, when we succumb to nostalgia and we are brave.

As Moyur resurfaced, his mutters evolved to sighs that, though wordless, were infinitely more comprehensible, more human. He felt Boshonti stroking his arms tenderly with callused palms; under her breath she murmured sweet nothings.

Moyur stared into the black hinterland of Boshonti's eyes. He was riveted to them, but Moyur didn't see himself reflected in those dark, expressive pupils. He saw a girl, dancing away from him, disappearing into the depths of Boshonti's past. Our past. Boshonti was staring back at him, following the trail of some other mirage, mirrored in the blackness of his eyes.

They stayed like that, spellbound, immersed within a shared melancholy.

Until the sound of bapu's voice interrupted the gathering darkness in the shop.

'Ki re? Why haven't you put on the lights? Is there a power cut?' Bapu's voice also woke up Joba kaku. He jumped out of his sleep into an industrious cross-legged seated position. Bapu flicked on the light switch. There was still some sun outside but the front of the shop faced east. Bapu took stock of the scene. He walked slowly to his spot behind the cash counter. Joba kaku, who had seen Boshonti fleetingly once before, seemed more taken aback than bapu and observed her reappearance with flagrant curiosity.

'This is Boshonti,' Moyur said by way of explanation, 'a very good customer of mine.'

Bapu nodded vaguely. Joba kaku continued to inspect.

'Nomoshkar, mister boss, mister number two boss,' Boshonti said, greeting first bapu, then Joba kaku, instinctively clocking the hierarchy in the shop. 'Moyur babu has been very kind to me,' she continued, 'letting a poor woman make weekly payments.'

At this revelation, Moyur blushed. He had not mentioned this to bapu. He hastily pushed the ledger towards him. Bapu examined the writing and returned it with a brief nod of acknowledgement that, financially at least, everything was in order. Boshonti took this as her cue to leave. 'Okay, Moyur babu, I should go now.' She looked at bapu and offered another nomoshkar in his direction before departing from the shop.

Later that evening, as they made their way home, bapu asked Moyur more about Boshonti: who she was, where she had come from, what she did. Moyur could hear how sparse his responses were. He knew bapu was dissatisfied, especially as there was undeniably something unsettling about Boshonti's poverty.

14

By the time of Boshonti's next visit, the white sheet on the display platform was covered in a smudge of dirty footprints.

'Really, you must have this washed, babu,' Boshonti said, patting the sheet and sending up a mini-dust storm as evidence. 'Thank god I have a stool to sit on.'

Moyur nodded, embarrassed. 'I know, didi. But what to do? The dhopa has gone back to his village. He said he would be back last week but there is still no sign of him.' He proceeded to rub the stains with a wet cloth, but ended up smearing them further into the sheet.

'Leave it for now,' Boshonti chuckled.

Moyur rolled the rag into a ball and threw it into a corner. 'Something to drink, didi?' he asked. Boshonti declined.

Boshonti wasn't thirsty. In fact she felt too full: of things, fluids, feelings, secrets – she couldn't express what it was that she was full of but she couldn't bear the thought of putting anything more into herself. What she wanted to do, what she had been aching to do ever since that afternoon with Moyur weeks ago, was to purge herself of some of the remorse she had been carrying around, day after day, year after year.

She looked at Moyur. He was barely a man, young enough to be her son. The curly sky-grazing eyelashes that framed his eyes, the softness of his skin steeped him with such innocence that she could barely believe such profound sadness lingered within him. When he walked around the shop playing with his saris, the lord of the manor, the host, the magician – the undertones were barely perceptible. Yet Boshonti had her inklings because Boshonti had her past and, like Moyur, she had lived in one lifetime more lives than her years could accomodate.

Boshonti asked Moyur many questions that afternoon: questions about his childhood, his loves, his losses. When she did not get the answers she was seeking, Boshonti changed tack. She told Moyur about herself.

❀

Boshonti arrived in Calcutta in 1982. At first, she was taken in by a distant cousin of her mother's – a lovely woman who looked after her as well as her means would allow and helped her secure work as a maid in a cluster of houses in a nearby para. Having left her village in a desperate bid to escape her nightmares, Boshonti adapted well to the exhausting daily schedule of mopping floors and hand-washing clothes for five households. She would wake with the cockerels, drink a glass of water and head off at six in the morning to begin her rounds. By the time she returned in the evening, she was so tired she just about managed to share a meal with her aunt before falling into a deep, stark sleep.

For all her work, Boshonti earned a monthly wage of eight hundred rupees. It was adequate for her needs. She handed over half of it to her aunt for food and lodging. Of the remaining four hundred, she sent two-hundred-and-fifty back home every month to her mother; the rest she kept for herself in a little stash in her plastic holdall. In the first two years, Boshonti's mother came to Calcutta to visit her, but Boshonti never went back to her village – until the day she got a telegram informing her of her mother's illness.

The next morning, Boshonti booked a train ticket. Before she left, she gathered together all her savings and, from each of the families she worked for, asked for advance payment of a month's wages. Some gave her what she requested, others gave her more because she was a reliable worker, and they all assured her that they would be praying for her mother's speedy recovery.

When Boshonti arrived at her village, she found her mother had withered away, eaten into by a hacking cough. Untouched plates of slightly rotting food busied her doorstep and the stale smell merged with the sickly stench of her sputum. When she saw Boshonti, she mustered a smile with the little energy that remained in her decaying body.

The following morning, Boshonti and her mother went to Siliguri. They took the mid-morning bus and arrived at the town in four hours. For Boshonti's mother, every step was an effort; she made slow progress, leaning heavily on her daughter as they walked from bus to rickshaw, and from the rickshaw, up the steps, to the outpatient department of the state-run general hospital. There, in the waiting room, hordes of people queued. Some looked well and Boshonti wondered why they had come; others, like her mother, teetered on the cusp of death.

When eventually they were seen, the doctor diagnosed tuberculosis. He prescribed an armoury of drugs and a monthly schedule of check-ups to last six months. The monthly bill for the entire treatment would come to several times Boshonti's wages. Though thankful that she had been frugal in her habits over the last two years, Boshonti knew her savings would not be enough to meet six months' expenditure.

She contemplated asking her ex-husband for a loan, but he had taken a new wife, who had recently given birth to a son, and would almost certainly refuse her. Besides, she could not bear the thought of resurrecting him in her life. She had only one option – to go back to the city and beg her employers for more generous advances, hoping her impeccable work record would be enough to persuade them. So, shortly after her mother started her first month's course of medicine, Boshonti came back to Calcutta, determined to somehow save her mother's life

This time, however, she discovered that her employers, under the stress and strain of having no home help, had lost much of their goodwill towards her. They seemed to have forgotten her mother's illness and, more crucially, their promises of support.

Dejected, she shared her quandary with the other maids who worked in the para. They were sympathetic, some even offered her a portion of their wages to help with costs. Unfortunately, what Boshonti needed was substantial and no amount of well-meaning could turn coins into bank notes. As the first month of her mother's treatment drew to a close, Boshonti received another telegram. Her mother was improving slowly. She had been to see the doctor in Siliguri. That was all.

Between them, Boshonti and her mother had enough to cover the second month but what about the other four? Her preoccupation consumed her and as her worry grew, she shrank. She lost her ability to concentrate, leaving floors chaotically mopped and clothes unclean. Her employers rebuked her; she assured them it would never happen again, but it did.

The day Boshonti got fired from one of her jobs was a bleak day. She walked to a quiet corner of the street. In the shade of a krishnochura, she hugged her knees to her chest and rolled tightly into herself, rocking her body back and forth as she cried.

The assaults of the past few years resurfaced in her mind. And she felt small, ill-equipped against the world.

Later, when she was walking home, Boshonti was intercepted by an acquaintance of hers, a girl she knew in passing, also a maid. This girl asked her many questions about what was going on and how much money she needed and for how long – minutiae that seemed irrelevant to a bit of casual empathy. Boshonti answered faithfully, too tired to wonder why.

Before they got to the bifurcation in the road where they would split up, the girl stopped. She spoke haltingly. Between every clutch of words she paused. She examined Boshonti's face. She started again. It was a meticulously constructed train of thought with which she wooed Boshonti, so artful that when the proposal finally slipped from her mouth, it did not seem extraordinary at all. Boshonti did not respond immediately. She knew she should feel offended, insulted, maybe even furious. Instead, she felt numb.

It took a week for Boshonti to make the decision, but with the month drawing quickly to a close, it was imperative that she find some money. She contacted the girl and the two of them set off to Sonagachi, where Boshonti was introduced to the madam who would become her boss and guardian for the next few years.

❁

At this point, Boshonti paused. Moyur had been listening in complete silence, following her every word. He could have recited the story back to her verbatim. Everything fell into place: her dress, her demeanour, her money. He had never met anybody who worked in a brothel before.

'Are you going to say something?' she asked.

Moyur stood up. He looked around the room. Joba kaku was still fast asleep. He had been right, after all, to have his suspicions. Moyur didn't quite know what to say. He was not sure of his own reaction because there was neither aversion nor any sense of betrayal in his feeling towards her. Instead, he felt an inexplicable gratitude that she had shared with him a fragment of her life. After all, Moyur knew only too well the burden of keeping secrets. And he knew the true value of a trusted friend.

When Moyur did not speak, Boshonti assumed the worst. She got up from her stool, shaking. 'Moyur babu, I should not be telling you all this. Please forgive me.' She started towards the exit when Moyur jumped down from his platform and barricaded her path.

'Boshonti didi, please don't go. I am so sorry. I was just, you know, a little... I didn't know what to say.'

Boshonti tried to sidestep him but Moyur was quick to block her, pre-empting her moves to the right, then left. 'Let me go, Moyur babu. Your eyes have saved your mouth the trouble of explanation. I understand. Let me go.' She raised her voice a fraction. Joba kaku stirred in his sleep; Moyur fell to his knees.

'Please, Boshonti didi, don't go. I was just thinking, on god. I was just thinking.'

He wrapped his arms around her legs and she almost buckled under his affection. It made her laugh. 'Babu, do you want Boshonti to break something?'

Moyur nodded vehemently. 'I don't care, didi. Please sit or I won't let go.'

Boshonti shook her head, indignation melting into a fit of girlish giggles. 'You are something else. Let go! Or else, how can I sit?'

Moyur repositioned himself on his platform and Boshonti sat back down on her stool. When they had finally recomposed themselves, Moyur asked, 'What happened to your mother?'

'She is fine now. After six months the doctor said she made a full and complete recovery.'

'Does she know? About your...?'

Boshonti shook her head. 'Nor does my aunt. I don't live with her any more. You can't really, you know, once you start this life.'

Moyur nodded. 'Boshonti didi, is that why you are so sad?'

She did not answer his question. Instead, she asked him, 'And you?'

Around them, the afternoon was morphing into evening. In the background, Joba kaku's snores became more intermittent. The shopkeeper from Gupta Brothers, clad in a checked cotton lungi, stepped onto the pavement to gargle away the remnants of his siesta, spitting forcefully into the roadside gutter. He waved at Moyur.

'It is getting late,' Boshonti said. 'I'll be back soon. Maybe next week.'

Reluctantly, Moyur had to agree. 'You promise you will come back?'

'Yes,' she said, 'I promise.'

As Boshonti walked away, she smiled for the first time in years – a smile that was wild and light and innocent.

15

Finally, Friday. Two whole days of safety, away from college and, more importantly, away from Mita.

Just the day before, Fidel had been offered a place in the cricket team, an incredible achievement for a fresher. They had been so proud of him, even when he had curtailed a tea-drinking session to practise bowling.

'That's it,' Mita sighed. 'We'll be lucky to have ten minutes of his time again.'

The two girls watched their friend in action. Neither cared much for cricket beyond the obligatory patriotic obsession with the successes and failures of the national team.

'They're all the same, these boys,' Jonali quipped, 'mad after sport.'

Mita looked at her slyly.

'What?' Jonali protested.

'Not just sport though, is it? Some boys are also mad after Jonali.'

Jonali tried to summon a look of disapproval but she was far too embarrassed to deliver it effectively.

'Don't talk rubbish.'

'No?' Mita was incredulous. 'Who sent you the letter then, huh?'

Jonali shrugged. 'I don't know. I haven't heard anything since.'

'So you still don't know who it is?'

Jonali did not like the tone of voice Mita had adopted. 'No. And I don't care.'

'That's not what it looks like to me,' Mita remarked. 'Always looking out of the window. Early for class, hanging around afterwards with a novel.'

Jonali laughed, a little nervously.

Mita giggled. 'So you do know who it is.'

Jonali shook her head.

'Arrey, buddhu, five dashes at the bottom – it's a clue. Which boy do you know with five letters in their name?'

Mr Mollick's first name was Bimol. The first note had been from him; so, Jonali assumed, had the second.

Mita continued impatiently, 'Oh, god help you. This boy is lovestruck and god only knows which planet you are on. F I D E L – five letters.' She paused. 'Have you really not noticed? He can't keep his eyes off you.'

'No way.'

'Arrey baba, yes way. Very much yes way.'

Jonali looked away. 'Such an over-active imagination, Mita – you should start writing for Hindi serials.'

'So you don't believe me?'

Jonali shook her head. 'No, I don't think he does, Mita. Honestly, I would know.'

Mita stood up. 'Suit yourself. Anyway, I have to go to drama practice now.'

The two girls walked towards the college gates. Neither spoke till Mita broke the stand-off. 'He will be heartbroken, you know.'

'Who?'

'Again who? I just told you. Fidel. He told me himself, just two days ago and... And now I have to tell him you are not interested.' She paused. 'You're not interested, right?'

'No, I am sorry, Mita, but I am not interested.'

'Well, who is it then?'

'Nobody, really. Nobody.'

'Fine. I don't believe you but that's fine. I'll tell Fidel – break his heart on your behalf.' With that, Mita marched off, leaving her very conspicuously behind.

Twenty-four hours later, Mita had still been upset, accusing her of misleading her beloved Rono. How complicated their friendship had become.

So it was with great relief that Jonali walked back on Friday afternoon along the final stretch of road between the bus stop and her house, with two whole days in between to protect her from the mess that had befallen her.

'Jojo?'

Jonali turned; she knew that voice better than her own. 'Moyur, after so long?' Jonali exclaimed, trying to sniff away a rush of emotion.

'Jojo, what's up?'

She smiled weakly. 'Nothing, nothing much...What are you up to these days? I hear you are a first-class businessman.'

Moyur nodded. He hadn't seen Jonali for a few weeks and was once again startled by how beautiful she grew in between their impromptu meetings. He had not seen her like this before, both spent and alive from the struggle of daily commute. Public transport suited her well, adding a kind of unkempt curliness to her hair and the dirty lustre of pollution to her skin. Whatever troubles she was having, he would happily have volunteered to kiss them away.

'What are you looking at?'

'Just you. How ugly you are getting.' Moyur squeezed her on the side, just above her hip, and Jonali squealed.

'How dare you? As for you, well, what can I say.' She shielded her eyes with her hand. 'I can't even bear to look at you.'

'Is that a compliment?'

'As if.'

'Okay, fine. You win. Now how about some phuchka at CA market?'

Jonali dropped her hand.

Moyur grinned, pleased at how well he still knew her weaknesses. 'My treat,' he added to seal the deal.

'All right. I might just let you off,' Jonali replied. 'Come on.'

❈

Twilight stretched languidly across the evening, in no hurry to make room for night. The stars that lit Moyur's sky twinkled with promise, his optimism infecting Jonali. The sunset danced across his handsome face. If only he were normal, she thought to herself as they walked towards the market.

It seemed that all the courting couples (and hopefuls) in Salt Lake had descended upon CA market that evening. Gaggles of unattached girls perused the stalls or strolled along the main thoroughfare, allowing their eyes to wander – discreetly, of course – across the groups of unattached boys clustered around motorbikes and mopeds.

'Any of them catches your fancy?' Moyur asked Jonali.

'Don't be silly. What about you? Look,' she nudged him, 'she is pretty.'

Moyur sidestepped her question with a glance at the sky, which obligingly erupted into a spectacular firework display. 'Looks like Mohun Bagan have won.'

'There was a match?' Jonali exclaimed. 'And you aren't watching?'

Moyur grinned. 'You spoiled my plans. I was headed to the nearest TV set when you flounced into view.'

'Hmm.' Jonali pursed her lips and turned her attention to the whizzing rockets being catapulted into the sky, momentarily eclipsing the night in explosions of firecracker colour.

Moyur traced the outline of her face with his eyes, followed the arch of her neck; a gold locket glimmered enticingly just short of the swell of her breasts. Her pleasure delighted him. He grabbed her right hand and ushered her towards the neighbouring park. The metal gate clanged with the effort of opening and shutting in quick sequence. Flakes of cobalt paint and rust rubbed onto their hands. They leapt across resting cows and mooching dogs, until they reached a clearing.

Framed by the light of a myriad fireflies, they linked arms and, in the long forgotten playground of yesteryears, spun round and round in circles, going faster with each turn, feet stumbling over one another, breathless.

Finally they collapsed into a heap. Mindless of the coarse grass that scratched their skin, the scattered pads of cow dung and the mild inquisition of passers-by, they giggled like the old times.

When they managed to compose themselves, Moyur reached into his shirt pocket and took out a cigarette; the tip burned a bright orange conspiracy into the night.

Jonali sniffed the air. 'Which brand do you smoke, Moyur?'

'Wills.' He inhaled deeply. Then he pointed it in her direction. Jonali shook her head.

'Have you ever tried?' he asked.

She hesitated. 'Yes, once.'

'What, with your college friends?'

'Maybe. Anyway, I didn't like it. It's bad for you.'

Moyur narrowed his eyes. 'Who did you try it with? What's his name?'

'No one. Why the inquisition all of a sudden? I told you na, I didn't like it.'

Moyur shrugged and took another drag. 'Hey, look at this. Can any of your college friends blow rings?' Before she could reply, Moyur had started sucking on the cigarette intently. He contorted his lips into a ring and blew out in controlled bursts. Smoke escaped from his open mouth in ribbons, puffs, semi-circles. He insisted she watch. Then finally it came, a perfect ring, and he pointed at it excitedly.

Jonali clapped half-heartedly. 'Marvellous, Moyur. What a skill you have acquired.'

'Why don't you try? Or ask your college mate to try. See if he can do it.'

'I don't know who you are talking about,' Jonali muttered under her breath.

'Fine.' Moyur flicked the butt into the distance. He could see he had upset her but wasn't sure he was ready to make an outright apology. Instead, he softened his tone. 'So, are you going to tell me why you were so upset before?'

'It's nothing, Moyur. Hopefully it will be sorted out soon.'

'What's this? Since when have we kept secrets from each other?'

Jonali's face was downcast, so he wriggled down, sticking his face under hers, so she might see his plea. She shifted. 'It doesn't work like that, Moyur. You can't just turn up and expect things to be where we left them,' Jonali told him off gently. 'You seem to have forgotten me.'

'That's ridiculous.' He sat up.

'Is your new life so special?' Jonali asked.

Was it? There was excitement in his new life, in coming of age. He thought of his new friend. Well, acquaintance. He had an inkling that Boshonti would turn into more even than a friend. He looked forward to her visits. He cherished her company, draped in chik-chik saris and enough glass bangles to make him blush. But that wasn't betrayal. It wasn't the same as longing for the girl you loved, the girl who had no idea. Sometimes he got distracted. But that wasn't betrayal, was it? That wasn't forgetting.

'You're the same, Jojo,' he retaliated. 'All college this and college that...'

She shook her head.

'Okay, I'll be better. I promise. Please tell me.'

Jonali began tearing the grass in short, dry clumps from the ground.

'Will you tell me if things don't improve?' Moyur asked.

'I'll tell you, and you can come and rescue me. It's about time you behaved like a rajkumar.'

A sudden uproar from the streets interrupted them. A power cut had plunged the block into darkness. Only the faraway stalls were visible, lit up by hurricane lanterns. They were the ones too poor to illegally tap the overhead electric cables. The market building itself had a backup generator, which supplied make-do electricity to those shops that contributed to its upkeep. It yawned into life, the indelicate dhok-dhok of its antique engine struggling to keep pace with the appetites of the flashing neon displays and ceiling fans.

In the park, under cover of darkness, Moyur leaned forward to caress Jonali's arm but she had already started to stand up and his hand grazed the swishing hemline of her skirt.

In his head, countless proclamations tumbled forth, but all he said was, 'Definitely, Jojo, any time you want to talk about college, just let me know.'

Before they separated, Moyur made her promise to meet him again, the following week – same time, same place – and she agreed, reassured that when nobody else knew, Moyur would always know.

16

'Eyi ne, number one. Write it. Green, sixteen...'
  'Shade?'

Joba kaku tutted at Moyur's interruption. 'Green, Mysore. Sixteen thousand.'

Moyur wrote in the ledger: Bottle-green Mysore silk with zari work. Kolka print. Sixteen thousand.

They were working their way through the cabinets, checking stock in a routine that Joba kaku tolerated and Moyur adored.

'Last one in cabinet, Joba kaku. Change places.' Moyur stood up before Joba kaku had even managed to shut the door.

Joba kaku frowned. 'We have a lot to get through today, Moyur.'

Moyur smiled. They alternated roles: the sari inspector and the note taker. Whoever was in charge did it his way. 'Joba kaku, I don't tell you how to...'

'Yes, yes, okay. Come on.'

Moyur opened the door to the cabinet. It still delighted him, especially at times like this when there was no selling, just observing.

'Moyur baba, please. We have to help your bapu also.'

Moyur conceded. Bapu had insisted on making a start but sorting the back room was a big task. 'Okay. First one... Are you writing, Joba kaku?'

'Hmm. Tell.'

'Blue, like the midnight shoroth sky, embroidered motifs of jasmine and rose along the borders. Radha and Krishna dancing together on the anchol. The thread is the colour of sandalwood. Very rare. Madras. Thirteen thousand seven hundred.'

Joba kaku scribbled in the ledger, finishing his entry before Moyur had ended his commentary.

'You're not missing out anything?'

Joba kaku shook his head.

Moyur had seen Joba kaku's entries in the past. Still, he would remember the sari, with or without the ledger, to the last twirl of Radha's dance. They continued this way, periodically changing position, Joba with his curt descriptions, Moyur with his affectionate ones. Hours passed. The para slowed into afternoon and Piklu's *Bollywood Top Twenty* came on.

'Moyur baba, how many more? I haven't had lunch.'

'You go now, Joba kaku,' Moyur replied. 'I will manage. Can you bring me a kochuri?'

'Yes, yes. Are you sure I should go?'

'Please. Just go.'

'Accha. Let me ask your bapu what he wants to take for lunch.' Joba kaku massaged his legs as he stood up. 'They have died today.' With pointed slowness, he stepped down from the platform and made his way to the back room.

There was something endearing about his drama, Moyur thought, as he returned to his saris. There were only a few left. He especially loved the toshor...

'Moyur baba! Moyur baba!' Joba kaku came running out. 'Come quickly. Your bapu.'

Moyur jumped down. 'What is it? What?'

But Joba kaku had already rushed back.

In the back room, bapu was resting heavily on one of the boxes, sweating profusely, his face dark. 'Bapu? What's going on?' Moyur rushed to his side. 'Joba kaku, please get some water.'

Bapu glanced at Moyur.

'Bapu?'

'Baba, pain in my chest.' His speech was broken. 'Bad pain.'

'Oh, god. Oh, god. Bapu, don't worry. One second, I'll be back.' Moyur ran into the showroom and shouted for Joba kaku.

Joba kaku was hurrying towards them with a bottle of cold water.

'Sit with bapu. I think he's having a heart attack. I'm going to call for help,' Moyur said. Joba kaku nodded and rushed to his task. Moyur ran to the telephone shop next door. 'Piklu, Piklu, bapu is having a heart attack. Phone, please! We urgently need an ambulance.'

Piklu sprang out of his chair and picked up the receiver. 'The best one here in this locality is run by the Sharmas. I know them,' he said and started dialling before Moyur could say anything further. 'Hello, hello. Sharma babu? This is Mr Sanyal from the STD/ISD shop. Yes, please, we urgently need an ambulance. Heart attack. He is like my very own father.' Moyur couldn't make out what the man on the other end of the line was saying. 'Yes, immediately. Address is Bengal Silk House. You know it? Yes, next door to my place and just two shops down from Gupta Brothers.' He nodded, put the phone down and turned to Moyur. 'They will be here in five minutes. Go and get your bapu ready. Do you want me to come with you?'

'No, Piklu. You have done enough. How can I ever thank you?' Moyur reached inside his pocket to get some money out to pay him but Piklu pushed his hand away. 'Chhi chhi. Go quickly. What is this money nonsense between us? We are like brothers. Now, go.'

Moyur had barely returned to the shop when, to his relief, a white Maruti van with large red crosses painted on either side pulled up. He signalled to the driver and went to fetch bapu.

In the back room, bapu was looking a little more comfortable. 'Moyur, you're back.'

'Come on, the ambulance is here. Let's go.'

Bapu hesitated. 'The pain is going now. I feel better.'

'I can stay here,' Joba kaku said. 'It's no problem.'

Moyur walked over to bapu. He bent down and put his arm around his back. 'Come on, bapu. We have to go and see the doctor. This isn't the first time, is it? I have seen you before – you stop what you are doing and sit quietly. This is what happens, doesn't it?'

'Moyur, you are making a fuss. It has almost entirely gone.'

'The ambulance is waiting, bapu. Let's just go and have a check up.'

'Okay, but you are acting like what-not has happened.' They stood up, Moyur supporting bapu, propelling him ever so gently towards the door. They were almost outside when bapu stopped. 'What if they find something?'

Moyur had seen bapu in many moods but he had never before heard fear in his voice or felt uncertainty in his step. He had never seen in bapu's eyes the vivid acknowledgement of his own mortality, and it left Moyur uncertain how to conduct himself. Eventually, he answered, 'It will be nothing serious, bapu, I promise.' Bapu surrendered to Moyur's words, clinging to his hand, seeking reassurance in the unspoken pressure of his palm and the frequent glances in his direction.

When they got to the ambulance, the driver bundled a mask over bapu's face, indicating to Moyur to hold it in place, and turned on the oxygen cylinder. The original elastic that secured the mask had been replaced by two pieces of string that the driver tied behind bapu's head with practised skill. He twiddled the rotating knob on top of the grey canister until it clicked into life with a loud hiss. 'Breathe. In and out, in and out. Slowly,' the driver instructed. Then he walked round to the front and started the engine. Moyur got in the back with bapu and they set off.

The mid-morning traffic was unusually considerate and once on the Eastern Bypass, the kilometres flew past. It was a new road, aptly named, bypassing much of the city; it served as a thoroughfare for the well-heeled but also one that the not-so-well-to-dos might drive down on the odd occasion, suffering a diversion for the sake of trying out the smooth, speedy tarmac.

The banks of the bypass were hives of construction lined with apartment blocks, hospitals, hotels in various states of dress and undress and the black, sun-baked bodies of men and women hard at work. The hospital they were destined for was one of these: foundation to full-swing in less than two years.

By the time they got there, bapu's pain had completely subsided. The doctor who saw him asked a few questions, listened to his heart, examined his heart tracing, gave him a stern pep talk, wrote out a prescription and instructed bapu to make an appointment to see him in his chambers after two months.

It transpired that bapu had not had a heart attack; however, he had just experienced his first warning that his heart might go on to have an attack if he carried on abusing it the way he was – with copious amounts of fried food and sweets, not exercising and working too hard.

In the taxi back home, bapu, to Moyur's relief, regained some of his understated obstinacy. As soon as the taxi pulled out of the hospital compound he started off, 'Who does he think he is? Lecturing me on what I can and cannot eat? Stupid fellow.'

Moyur couldn't resist a smile. He thought of bapu's weakness for fried food: with every meal there had to be fried potatoes or fried aubergines or fried fish or fried something-or-the-other.

'It's for your own health, bapu.'

'What health? What good is health to me if I cannot enjoy every once in a while?'

It tickled Moyur to see bapu in a fit of dramatics more suited to ma. Nonetheless, he infinitely preferred this version of bapu to the scared man he had shepherded into the ambulance a handful of hours earlier. Moyur sidled across the back seat of the taxi and put his arms around bapu.

'I love you,' he said quietly. The words almost flew out on the gusts of breeze whooshing through the open windows of the taxi. But bapu had heard him and, as he pulled away, Moyur noticed his eyes glistening ever so slightly.

'Bapu, are you crying?'

'No, no,' bapu replied. 'It's the pollution.'

'Oh. Okay.'

'Moyur, I am very proud of you. You looked after your poor bapu so well.'

'Bapu, you have to stop eating fried food, you have to do some exercise. Then I'll be proud of you too.'

They both laughed.

'Okay, baba, I will try my best,' bapu said, wiping his eyes.

This was just as well, because ma made sure that each and every one of the doctor's recommendations was instituted with immediate effect. Occasionally, bapu would sneak off to the shops and buy himself a secret samosa or two, but on the whole he stuck to his regime quite well. More fortuitously, he delegated most of the running of the shop to Moyur.

17

The Bengal Silk House grew busy – there were always some enthusiasts who started their pujo shopping two or three months ahead of time, and it was vital for businesses to keep pace. As a result, with each passing week, the respite of the lazy afternoon lull grew progressively shorter until it finally disappeared.

Almost in tandem, over the weeks following his visit to the hospital, bapu's health slowly took a turn for the worse. On the doctor's advice, bapu dropped his working hours to two half-days a week. This suited him well, except for the times when he forced upon himself excessive amounts of packing or lifting. The spray the doctor had prescribed for bapu resolved his heart aches but did nothing to help him prove to himself that he was still vital. In the end, bapu had no choice but to take some time off. Anxiety was invading his appetite, invading his sleep and even his pastimes, to the point where he needed complete rest, away from the demands of work. Of course, with Durga Pujo around the corner, it was a most inconvenient time for bapu to be unwell. But who can say that there is ever a good time to be ill?

Boshonti continued to visit at regular intervals, often with money – usually in hundred-rupee installments – and occasionally with just a coconut or a couple of mangoes as a stop-gap till the next payment. Her visits did not go unnoticed. Joba kaku commented on her comings and goings and quizzed Moyur on her background: her occupation, her marital status, etc. Moyur met his questions with apathy and an expert reticence that Joba kaku had neither the energy nor wit to negotiate.

Lately, Joba kaku had been pensive. According to All India Radio, another man-eater had been wreaking havoc in his village. Only one mangled body had been found, but it turned out to be the body of his neighbour, a bachelor who had often stepped in as surrogate uncle to his dead brother's son while he, the real uncle, was away earning money for them all. The news hit Joba kaku hard, and for a few days he retreated into his own apprehensions, leaving the running of the shop entirely to Moyur. It was only when the radio reported that the tiger had been caught did Joba kaku slowly begin to recover from the disquiet that had taken over his waking hours.

For his part, Moyur was happy to take on responsibility for the shop. In the evenings, he was the one to check the stock, complete the balance sheets and set up for the next day. He was also the one to shut the shop after everyone left, the one to release the saris from their glass cabinets, to lay them against his skin, to allow himself the fantasies that he had only dared imagine as a child.

The final Tuesday before Durga Pujo saw a heaving afternoon; the evening was shaping up to be just as productive when a whimsical drizzle extinguished the anticipated pre-pujo trade. Both Joba kaku and Moyur were overworked. Seizing the opportunity, Joba kaku decided to leave a little early. He was going back to the Sunderbans for the holidays and he had some shopping of his own to get done. However, as was his habit, Joba kaku, torn between two duties, dithered over his departure.

'Okay then, Moyur baba, I will be going now. Are you one hundred per cent sure?'

'Joba kaku, please, enough of your fretting. I have been working here for how long now? How many times have I done this?'

In the street, most of the lights had come on, bar a few that would stay flickering all night. They had been like that for the last two months. Nothing ever got fixed in this place.

In days gone by, the people from the Municipal Corporation used to hose the streets down regularly. That was before the trade unions, before the incessant striking. Now, nobody did any work. Not a thing apart from political muscle-flexing, which was rampant throughout the city's workshops and factories. A few weeks ago, some party hoodlums had dropped in, demanding money for some rally or the other.

Well. Let them be. Let the dust settle on the streets. Let the exhaust fumes thicken the air, because when the sun set through the haze, it made for Moyur a magenta sky. And in the back room there was a tiny window through which its rays dropped into his corner. He could see the mirror without switching on the light. And he always looked like magic.

'Don't worry, Joba kaku. I won't be here long. I just want to do the books and write the order. The cutting I'll leave for tomorrow.'

'Very well. I will see you tomorrow then.'

As Moyur watched Joba kaku's retreating back, no wider than fifty centimetres, he felt a twinge of guilt for inflating Joba kaku's confidence in him with bravado, for making light of his well-intentioned concerns about Boshonti. For a while, Moyur carried on with his work as best he could. It was too early to shut down the shop. Not that he hadn't shut the shop early in the past – he had, on three or four occasions – but he usually preferred to wait a little longer, until the sun began to dip.

It was at times like these that the hands of the clock were at their most lethargic. Moyur lit a cigarette. He never smoked in front of Joba kaku or bapu, though they knew. Besides, he had been smoking the same pack of twenty for almost a month. It was a luxury, one he indulged in only when he was alone and restless.

Recently, Boshonti had taken to visiting him later in the day. Once or twice, she had arrived after Joba kaku left, and the two of them had sat and gossiped undisturbed, deep into the evening. So when Boshonti arrived that evening, about halfway into his vigil, Moyur was not completely surprised. In fact, a part of him had been pining for her company. Moyur did not know why he was so drawn to this woman. Perhaps it was just that she was comfortable to be around.

'Boshonti didi. Come, come. You are looking tired today.'

'Life is hard for poor Boshonti,' she replied with a wide smile. 'Never mind. Today I have brought something for you.'

'What is it?'

'I went to Kalighat yesterday and got some proshad for you.' Boshonti unravelled a packet from her anchol and tapped it gently against Moyur's forehead. She proceeded to open it and took out a pera. 'Open your mouth. Aaaah,' she said. Moyur obliged and she popped the sweet into his mouth happily.

'Do you often go to the Kali mandir?' Moyur asked. His words were indistinct as he chewed them up along with the mishti.

'Once every three weeks. Sometimes more frequently. Always on a Wednesday.' Boshonti laughed wryly. 'I have many sins to atone for. 'And you?'

'No, not much. No one in the family is a devotee of Ma Kali.'

'Strange. I thought most Bengalis were.'

'Many are. But how come you go? You're not Bengali.'

Boshonti stretched her arms above her head and yawned. 'You ask a lot of questions, Moyur babu. All question, no answer.'

Moyur took his time to respond. His heart was skipping with the thought of what he was about to do. Still, she had shared so much of her past. It was his turn.

Moyur pulled the rolling metal shutter down behind them, locking the world out of his shop. He loved the shop more at these quiet times than at any other. The lights in the showroom were switched on, a bevy of insects fluttered around the bulbs. The din of their beating wings filled the vacuum left by the departing chatter of the day's custom.

The saris had been folded away, chairs stacked, floor swept. Moyur led Boshonti through the narrow gap between the two back walls into the stock room at the back of the shop. The dying embers of sunset illuminated his corner. Hastily, he shoved the boxes out of the way. Everything else was kept in strict order, for maximum efficiency in snatched moments: his mother's bra, lipstick, kajol and the sari.

He set up a stool for Boshonti and instructed her to sit. Her presence was vital but he could barely concentrate on his guest any more.

Quickly, Moyur put on the bra. It was a nice size, neither too big nor too small. He tried to emulate his mother's breasts by lining the inside of the cups with folded underpants. Once he had plumped them up to his satisfaction, he put on the black sequined blouse over the bra and smoothed out any visible bumps. Strangely, Moyur's beard had never fully erupted and even after several days he would only have the faintest smattering of stubble. His cheeks still folded into dimples when he smiled and his eyes were soft and luminous. Moyur did not have a petticoat so he kept his trousers on and used it to tuck the sari into. He could very easily have been mistaken for a young woman. A blush spread to his cheeks. How he wished he had some earrings or a bangle.

Moyur stood in front of the mirror and smiled. It suited him. It really suited him. He angled his body away from the mirror to peer at himself from behind and then from the side. He lifted the turquoise anchol over his head and looked straight at his reflection. 'Moyur, Moyur, Moyur,' he recited his name out loud, but where he is, on the fringes of our identities, he loses his way sometimes between where 'Moyur' has a meaning and where we begin.

He moved his arms delicately above his head in the manner of silver-screen nymphets. On cue, his hips began rocking, his torso swayed. And Moyur danced – out of compulsion.

And I dance with him. In the red haze of our existence, we move as usual to the steady rhythm of our heartbeats. We take solace in the peace that surrounds us.

Already I know this will not last. I remember too often the arguments and anguishes of the world beyond. Did you not know, I want to say, that I am too young for reality? I have no defence. One word is all it takes, one moment of hesitation. I look at Moyur. He is undisturbed. Does he not remember their anxieties? Did he not hear when ma and bapu cried? I cannot believe their thoughts were just for me. So I ask her, again and again, do you not want me, ma? Do you not love me? I wait and wait for a reply but they never say a thing. Not ma nor bapu. And that is how I know.

Moyur is dancing now, on the edge of my shadow. I must slip away before he realizes because I cannot hurt him with my truth. It is my responsibility. He has the world to distract him. What do I have but the memories of being loved that I borrow from him? I am the one who instigates these guilty pleasures, these trips back to a time when I too had potential.

I am an addict.

❀

By the time Moyur recovered it was almost too dark to see. He would have to switch on the light soon and finish the day's work. Moyur looked at the mirror.

There in the golden-orange half-light he had become a splendid, euphoric being with kajol-rimmed almond eyes and lips as red as sindoor. Behind him, he saw in the mirror, the fleeting presence of another soul. She was just as splendid but quieter. She looked like him, she moved like him. And she wept. The girl child.

In her corner, Boshonti was watching, her eyes following his every quiver. In Moyur's mirror she caught a glimpse of the terror she thought she had left behind, the terror that had settled in her soul many years ago, forcing her out of the village. She found it again in Moyur's body, and it made her want to howl again, like she had done the first time, for the misery of her circumstance.

18

The peacock feathers with which the dhakis decorated their drums swayed in time with the beat. How energetically they played. With each round, they put on the greatest show on earth. How else do you serenade a goddess but to drum the sound of longing into the heart of a nation?

From her balcony, Jonali studied a street suddenly awash with new styles: racy low-backed blouses and barely-there muslin saris, tight churidars that clung to the leg and feet adorned with the sweet tinkle of anklets.

'Riya, are you ready?'

'Done. Let's go.'

Jonali returned indoors to make one final check. She loved her spacious black patiala salwar and cropped jade kurti. Her eyes were still painted, lips still glossed, hair in place. Riya looked cute in a loose red kurta and matching bows in her hair.

The two debutantes were quickly absorbed in a flock of other girls, promenading self-consciously up and down the streets surrounding the pandal that housed the clay effigies of Durga and her children.

Under the awning of the goddess, boys watched girls who watched boys. Of course, they were all watched by the elders, gossiping guardians of chastity. The priests were busy with the aroti and the more pious members of the community interrupted their other activities to give their full attention to the evening prayer. Fragrant smoke billowed from the smouldering coconut husk with which the head priest venerated the goddess. With his other hand he chimed a brass bell in vague time with the dhakis' beat. The assistant priest held aloft a bundle of incense and a five-wicked oil lamp, which he moved in fervent loops through the warm evening air. Tears moistened the eyes of those who had become immersed in devotion, of those who had become enraptured by the orchestra of light and sound, and those who suffered from a low tolerance of smoky environments. As the final incantations vibrated through the crowds, the men and women clasped their hands. Even those who had been preoccupied with the more frivolous pastimes the festival had to offer, interrupted their pursuits for a brief, respectful nomo.

For Jonali, caught between the competing demands of the festival, the evening prayer was an unequivocal intermission before recommencing on the rounds of the para.

It was not long before Jonali, Riya and a handful of the para's young girls bumped into Moyur, Tinku, Bapta and their accomplices. The touring of pandals was an annual ritual and the two groups found themselves coalescing for the evening to continue their expedition.

It turned out that any early bashfulness of the chance encounter dissipated in a flush of festivities as they walked from block to block, discussing the various exhibits they saw. For most, the highlight was the Jurassic pandal where Ma Durga and her children were ensconced within the cavernous belly of a cloth-and-bamboo dinosaur, but of course there were the dissenters, amongst them Jonali, who preferred the more traditional styles that some of the older blocks had continued with.

The lighting, on the other hand, was less contentious. There was nothing to argue over. Salt Lake was no match for the rest of Calcutta, where stills from the ancient epics flashed alongside topical news items and even replica movie scenes to make up the nightly fantasia of light. Inside Salt Lake, the visuals were restrained to modest cascades of fairy lights along the street fronts or multi-coloured spotlights for the krishnochura and coconut trees.

This was a minor consideration, however. There was, on the way from one block to the next, an abundance of amusements to satisfy all inclinations. Street-side food vendors, mehendi artists, balloon-sellers, craftsmen and women with their handiwork on display and paan-walas clustered around the pandals, working into the early hours of the morning, catering to the insatiable crowds.

Against this panorama of hustle-bustle, it was easy to slip away unnoticed. While the others busied themselves with feasting and haggling, Moyur placed his hand firmly on Jonali's wrist. He tugged her gently towards the quiet spot he had scoped out. In his head he frantically rehearsed what he would say to her, how he would broach the subject, the opening lines. Maybe he could begin with a compliment, but he had tried that before and she was impervious. Flashbacks of his dressing-up sessions cluttered his mind, and he was alternately overcome with doubt and hope that she knew him too well.

Didn't all the world's greatest love stories take root in childhood? In every movie he had ever seen, true love eventually triumphed. There had to be some truth in it, surely?

As they walked further away from the main thoroughfare, the street grew darker, almost anti-climactic in the shadow of the excitement. 'Moyur, where are we going?' Jonali quizzed him.

'Almost there.'

'Yes, but where?' she persisted.

They turned the corner and stopped just behind the curve of the park wall, diagonally opposite the spot where they had left the others.

'Here,' Moyur announced. He was slightly out of breath and noted with disappointment the annoyance spreading across Jonali's face.

'Why are we here, Moyur? I promised kakimoni I wouldn't leave Riya alone.'

Moyur looked at his feet. His courage was quickly draining away, his opening line growing more insubstantial by the second. 'We won't be long.' He struggled to think. 'Are you enjoying yourself?'

'Yes, I am. Are you?'

'Yes.'

'Okay, Moyur, why are we here? Really?'

'You only said earlier that we don't spend time any more,' he said finally but his voice had descended into a sulk.

Jonali sighed. Moyur felt her eyes on him. There had been occasions when he had convinced himself that the way she looked at him was loaded with more than mere platonic affection, but these moments were far outnumbered by times when he had felt that it was no more than pity. Moyur shifted from one foot to the other. In the shadowy light he could barely read the detail on her face, but he heard the familiar contours of her exasperation. It reminded him of the afternoons when he would run over to her. Often she had become the disenchanted bystander to his self-consumption, yet she had always managed to draw him out, to include herself in his secrets. His secrets became their secrets. Why did she not do that any more?

'We should go back na, Moyur?'

'Yes,' he replied.

Jonali started walking back, Moyur trailed after her. It was a much shorter distance on the way back. They had been gone no more than a handful of minutes and they slipped into the mêlée as inconspicuously as they had left it.

19

The next day was nobomi. Jonali's mother and kakimoni left early for the pandal. Jonali and Riya relaxed in the living room. Jonali was coating her toenails in sweeps of scarlet varnish and Riya lay on her tummy, observing her intently.

'Jojo didi, you are so good at applying nail polish. Will you do mine?'

Jonali did not divert her attention from the task at hand.

'Jojo didi!'

Jonali looked up. 'You are really driving me mad today. Why don't you do it yourself?'

'Because I always make a mess, Jojo didi, and you do it like an expert.'

'Are you sure kakimoni won't mind?'

'Don't be silly. I'm old enough now.'

Jonali studied her younger cousin. Adolesecence had crept up on her without the family really noticing. It was probably her roundness that was so misleading. Riya wasn't fat but she was still soft around the edges. Despite her erupting womanliness, Riya retained an air of childishness that was deceptive. Petulance suited her well, masquerading as a bit of harmless self-indulgence, something she would grow out of.

'Okay,' Jonali conceded, 'but let me finish mine.'

'Yes!' Riya bounced up and lunged affectionately towards Jonali, almost spilling the bottle of nail polish in the process. 'Oops, sorry. Jojo didi, do you have any other colours?'

'In the shoe box under my bed. Now stop disturbing me or I'll never finish in time for pushpanjoli.'

As Riya departed in search of the treasure chest of varnish, Jonali continued to anoint her toenails. Her mind drifted back to the events of the evening just passed. Moyur must have had something important to tell her. Otherwise why take her to a quiet corner like that? She had been so brusque; Riya was more than old enough to look after herself.

Because of her, he had withdrawn. In the shadowy light, she had barely been able to read the detail on his face but she had heard the familiar contours of his breath; it had reminded her of the afternoons when he would run over to her. Afternoons of rampant togetherness and, in that moment, standing awkwardly in the dark, the realization had slowly crept up on her that she was actually in love with Moyur. And then what?

Each time she remembered, regret sunk a little deeper and heavier into her – it was too late. Moyur had already retreated into the safety of grown-up charades.

'Jojo didi. Found it.' Riya returned with a tattered cardboard box bulging from the weight of nail polish. 'Some of these are so old; you should throw them away. I bet they're rotten.'

'Have you decided which colour you want?'

Riya rocked her head from side to side. She placed the box on the floor, squatted in front of it, lifted the bottles out one by one, inspected and then returned them, making the bottles clink conspicuously against their neighbours.

'Do you have to be so loud? You'll break them.'

Riya frowned at her cousin. 'Why are you such a crank pot today?'

'I'm not. Just pick one.'

Riya picked a shimmering orange shade. She sat down on a low stool and stuck her feet in Jonali's direction. Jonali was a good pedicurist. Before applying the polish she gave Riya a massage, pulling and pushing her toes, pummelling cream into her cracked heels.

'Perfect,' she said when she finished, admiring her own handiwork.

'Thank you, Jojo didi.' Riya leaned over to kiss her on the cheek. 'Accha, Jojo didi, have you got a boyfriend?' she asked as she sat down again.

'What?'

'Just asking.'

'Where did you get that idea?' Jonali frowned at her cousin.

'No?' Riya raised her eyebrows. 'Are you absolutely sure?'

Jonali gathered together her accoutrements, put them on top of the box and was about to leave Riya to her games when she remembered. She turned to Riya, who was grinning, a piece of paper flapping wildly in her hand. 'Found it. Found it.' She put on a silly makeshift male voice and read, 'Dear Jonali, I think about you all day. I dream about you all night. Will you be mine? Dash-dash-dash-dash-dash. Five dashes. Who is it, Jojo didi?'

Jonali lunged for the letter but Riya was too quick for her. 'Tell me. Tell me.'

'How dare you read my private letters?'

'How dare nothing. You shouldn't have left it there. What if my ma or your ma had found it? Then you would have been in real trouble.'

Jonali lowered her voice. 'Just give it back.'

'Not until you tell me who it is.'

'Give it back.'

'No.'

'Give it back,' she screamed finally. It worked. Riya handed it over at once, her smirk shattered.

'And don't ever touch anything of mine again.' Jonali stormed off to her room.

❈

It was not long before Jonali stepped out again to apologize to Riya. She was not sure what had come over her. Lately, her behaviour had become so erratic. Too much had happened in such a short time; her life was unnerving her.

Jonali found Riya in her bedroom, lying on her front, reading a magazine.

'Riya,' she said, waiting at the doorway, 'can I come in?'

Riya shrugged.

Jonali went in and perched on a corner of the bed. 'What are you reading?'

Riya held the magazine up so Jonali could see the cover, then put it back down and continued to read.

'I haven't seen that one. Are there any pictures of Salman?' Jonali asked.

Riya shrugged again.

Jonali advanced a little further up the bed. 'Riya, I'm sorry. I shouldn't have screamed at you.'

Riya lifted her eyes from the page to focus on Jonali's face. She was trying hard to reject her cousin's apology, but Jonali knew Riya's attempts at harshness would be foiled by her curiosity; soon she would be back on her side.

'So, are you going to tell me?' Riya demanded.

'There is nothing to tell, baba. My friend Mita, you remember her?' Riya nodded. 'Well, she thinks it is a boy called Rono. I don't know. In any case, I am not interested.'

'Rono? That's four letters.'

'His nickname is Fidel. Long story. But I am not interested in him.'

'God, Jojo didi. Your first romance and you didn't even tell me? This isn't fair.'

'One, it isn't a romance, and two, not a word to ma or kakimoni. Got it?'

'What do you take me for?' Riya returned to her magazine, cruising through the pages mindlessly before starting again. 'So, Jojo didi, who are you interested in then? Any college heart-throb?'

'No.'

'Really, no?'

Jonali felt herself get hot and flustered.

'Aha!' Riya pounced triumphantly on Jonali's discomfort. 'I knew it. Who is it? Bolte hobe kintu, you have to tell me .'

Jonali shook her head. 'It's no one. Now stop this nonsense.'

'It's not this Fidel character, is it?'

'No.'

'Someone else from college?'

'Not saying.'

'At least give me some names that I can torment you with.' Both girls laughed but Riya did not drop her inquisition.

'Tinku?'

'Not saying.'

'Bapta?'

'Are you going to get ready for pushpanjoli or not?'

'Bittu?'

Jonali looked up at the ceiling and shook her head. 'Come on.'

'Moyur?'

She said nothing. At the mention of Moyur, Jonali didn't trust herself to make any dismissive gestures with conviction. So she sat absolutely still, willing her cousin to move on to the next name. But Riya didn't.

'It's not Moyur, is it?' she asked again, shrivelling up her nose in distaste. When Jonali still didn't respond, Riya continued, shaking her head to emphasize her disapproval, 'Jojo didi, it can't be Moyur. He is just so... so... ughh.'

Jonali stood up and walked towards the door. 'Come on,' she said, 'enough of your nonsense for one day. We have to get ready to go to the pandal.'

20

The goddess visits only once a year and it is a long journey from Mount Kailash to Calcutta. So for those five days, the city belongs to her. Moyur and Boshonti were no exception. The question of their meeting could not arise until after pujo.

'Nomoshkar, Moyur babu. I have payment.' Boshonti raised her voice so that her words might also reach Joba kaku's ears and make some headway into his pungent suspicion.

As her acquaintance with Moyur progressed, Boshonti had gradually replaced her low sleeveless blouses for high-necked, high-backed, long-sleeved versions. The saris remained of the chik-chik variety, but she picked more sober colours for her appointments at the Bengal Silk House, to try and blend in with their more regular clientele.

Moyur, who had gone to retrieve the ledger, made his way back to her with delighted haste. He slammed the open book down on the platform in front of Boshonti. 'Look, with this money you have completed the schedule of payments. Congratulations.' Moyur beamed at his friend. 'You can have it now.'

'What?' Boshonti stuttered. 'Finished?'

'Yes, look.'

He pointed at the final entry with a flourish, to guide her away from any possible embarrassment. It still astounded him that she had trusted him so implicitly. In exchange, Moyur had thought nothing of embellishing the amounts she had paid, adding a ten here, a fifty there. Confident that she wouldn't uncover his deception, Moyur left the ledger with her while he went to the stock room to retrieve the sari. It was a succulent hibiscus red with delicate kolka motifs woven in with a dull gold thread. It was most definitely not a chik-chik number.

'Oh, Moyur babu, it is the most beautiful sari in this shop,' Boshonti exclaimed as he carefully unfolded the sari in front of her. 'What will the other girls say?'

'What other girls?' Joba kaku interjected, his ears trained on their conversation.

Moyur and Boshonti both looked at him, irritated at the intrusion.

'Where I live,' Boshonti replied.

'Oh, and where *do* you live, Boshonti?'

Before Boshonti could reply, Moyur stepped in. 'Joba kaku, has the order for Mr Sharma been written yet?'

'No.' Joba kaku's voice was sullen. 'That is next on my list of to-do items.'

'Isn't it quite urgent? It was supposed to have been done and dusted yesterday.'

Joba kaku did not respond nor did he direct any further questions at Boshonti.

'I'm sorry, didi,' Moyur whispered.

'Don't worry, Moyur babu,' she said, lowering her face.

He tried to claw his way back into their earlier conversation. 'So, didi, when are you going to wear it?'

Boshonti looked at the sari with longing, at Joba kaku's back hunched reluctantly over a sheaf of papers, and finally at Moyur.

'It's too pretty for me,' she said. 'This sari is for someone young and beautiful, not for an old crone like me.' She pushed the sari towards Moyur. 'How funny, my name is Boshonti – and just look at me.' She shook her head. 'Well, at least god has a sense of humour.'

'You look lovely to me,' Moyur said.

Boshonti attempted a smile but slipped into a grimace. 'And where will I wear it? People like me don't go to these sorts of functions.' She sighed. 'How foolish I have been.'

Moyur racked his brains to think of some way of rescuing her but Boshonti was on a roll. 'Moyur babu, you keep it. Keep the sari. Give it to somebody. Some pretty, young, function-going lady.'

Boshonti got up from her stool in readiness to leave. To his annoyance, Moyur noted that Joba kaku had suspended his work once again. Let him stare, Moyur thought. Let him have his fill.

Moyur jumped down from the platform. 'Boshonti didi, I have the perfect solution.' He leaned forward and spoke, almost into her ear, 'You have to wear it to my wedding. You must come and you must wear this very sari.'

Boshonti stopped. 'Me?' She fixated on a single thread that had come loose and picked at it. 'We don't go to weddings, Moyur babu.' She lowered her voice. 'See your number two boss – what he will say?'

'I don't care about him. You will come to mine. Or else I won't get married. End of story.'

Boshonti smiled. 'So, have you actually got a sweetheart to marry, Moyur babu?'

'Yes.'

'Oh?'

'Okay, not yet but I am trying. Maybe you can help. Give me some tips.'

'Maybe.' Boshonti laughed as Moyur wooed her back to her stool.

Once Moyur started speaking about Jonali, he found he could not stop. How do you compress the story of a lifetime into a few paragraphs? Boshonti asked him for details and he overwhelmed her. It was impossible not to, after seventeen years of side-by-side. Seventeen years of shared first times with the girl for whom love had been invented. He knew the way her hair bounced when she brushed it and the way it curled when she didn't. He knew the way she pursed her lips to blow on her tea and which finger she dipped into her cup to take out the skin. He knew the silent conversations she had with herself and the soundtracks to her daydreams. 'So Boshonti didi, tell me, what should I do?'

At the outset, Boshonti had declared herself an expert in the field of romance. She had heard a thousand love stories albeit only those that concluded in the arms of a prostitute. It was love all the same. 'I think,' she said to him, after much deliberating, 'that you love her enough. And where there is enough love, everything will turn out all right.' She paused. 'I will pray for you, Moyur babu. Next time I go to Kalighat, I will pray to Ma Kali to please let Moyur babu marry his sweetheart.'

'Yes, but Boshonti didi, what will happen?'

'I just told you.'

'Yes, but I want details.'

Boshonti shook her head. 'Babu, don't look at me like that with your moody-moody eyes. It will happen as the goddess wishes.'

'You said you are an expert.'

'I will pray for you, Moyur babu. With all my heart.'

Moyur stood up to put the ledger away. He couldn't help but wonder where, in the hierarchy of prayers, a prostitute's might rank. He returned to find Boshonti ready to go. 'Okay, Moyur babu, long day for me today.'

'Same time next week?'

'For what? There are no installments left.'

The pair hesitated, in need of a premise.

'Oh, I know!' Moyur offered, suddenly animated. 'You should buy another one. For your mother – she is now officially invited to my wedding also.'

Boshonti smiled in relief. 'Very good. But I have to go now. I will choose it next visit, okay?'

Before she left that evening, Boshonti invited Moyur to her house for dinner. After all, if you are going to be somebody's wedding guest, there must be a few lunches and dinners beforehand.

❈

As Moyur walked down the streets of the red-light district towards the address Boshonti had given him, he risked a few glances at the women who adorned the doorways with their fanfare of shiny saris and fake gold jewellery, lips painted in deep reds and flashing pinks, cheeks streaked with rouge. But beneath the off-beat frivolity of their get-ups, their stares were hard. Moyur stumbled on a pot-hole to an immediate murmur of amusement and a chorus of cheap bangles as they manoeuvred themselves to get a better look.

The parcel of sweets he was clutching suffered the strength of his anxiety and crumpled inwards. How much further? In places like these the doors did not have numbers – Boshonti said most people had no use for them. She had told him to look for the black door, but every door seemed black.

'Babu. Babu.'

Moyur stalled. 'Babu, come back.' Moyur turned around. He had left Boshonti a few doors behind. She looked so out of place that he was reassured at once. He began hurrying towards her but quickly checked his pace.

'Boshonti didi, it wasn't so easy to find your place.'

'Yes. Sorry.' Boshonti searched Moyur's face. Moyur looked down. He was suddenly embarrassed – both to be in such a place and by his reaction to it. He, of all people, should know better.

The two of them stood on the street for a few moments, entertaining an alleyway of pimps and prostitutes, and then Moyur looked up at her. 'Boshonti didi, aren't you going to invite me in?' His voice rang strange in his ears.

'Yes, of course.' She led him inside, past several rooms, directly into an open-air alcove with a few worn-out armchairs and a small plywood coffee table. A couple of cigarette stubs lay on the floor. Boshonti hurried to sweep them away. 'Sorry, Moyur babu. I cleaned up just this afternoon.' All around them, closed doors lined the walls. 'No one is here today,' she explained. She sniggered uncomfortably. 'It is day of cleansing because tomorrow everyone is going to the temple.'

'Are you going?'

'Of course. I go to Kalighat every third Wednesday.'

'And will you remember to pray for me?'

Boshonti relaxed. 'Yes, Moyur babu, I promise.'

Boshonti had prepared a feast of aloo bhaja, fish and dal. She served Moyur before she took her own meal, fussing over him as if he were a long-lost child.

The truth is that Boshonti did have a long-lost child – like me – and ever since that first afternoon, when she had cradled Moyur out of his trance, the dub-dub, dub-dub rhythm that pervaded our consciousness had also invaded hers. The memories that

Boshonti had tried to leave behind in her village were resurrected by her proximity to another great unwantedness.

Boshonti forgot her own rhythm and took up the rhythm of our dance. When the moment arrived, as she heard her own beat marry perfectly with mine, Boshonti plunged into her story. Her confession.

❁

Boshonti married her husband when she was only fifteen years old. It was a reasonable age. Her body had begun to blossom, and it was felt best to get her married to protect her from the wayward glances of unscrupulous men. The first year of her married life had been blissfully happy. Her husband was not a man of many means, but he was kind and only a handful of years older than her. So in the evenings, after work, when the rest of the village was silent, Boshonti and her husband would giggle together, they would make love, and they would hatch plans for the future – plans that would carry them out of their little village, through Bengal, across the Deccan plateau, maybe even as far as Bombay. They would have a house, a clutch of babies and a couple of regular stray dogs to feed the leftovers to – because there would always be leftovers.

Boshonti and her husband gave names to their imaginary children. Boshonti had a long list of girls' names. She worked on the plantation, and as she plucked tea leaves and dropped them into her basket, she would give each one a name – Payal, Juhi, Reena. Boshonti's husband had an equally lengthy list of names for boys – Nikhil, Shantanu, Jibon. In the evenings they would exchange notes. But as it happened, their conversations were unequal because, of the two of them, it was Boshonti's husband who enjoyed being heard the most, and Boshonti was happy to listen to him.

They were both delighted when Boshonti became pregnant. The seed in her belly was not just a new life, it also marked the germination of their first shared dream. Boshonti suffered morning sickness, she suffered night terrors and swollen ankles – all these inconveniences she bore with grace. She also continued to work on the tea garden as they could not afford to live without her wages. Boshonti's husband took on extra shifts as a security guard at the estate manager's house, and they successfully saved up some money for her scans and medicines.

Just over two months into her pregnancy, a big scandal erupted. It was in November, a month with a reputation for mishaps. One night, as the cold mountain mists thickened around the estate, a gang of dacoits took the opportunity to ransack the house. They stole thousands of rupees in cash and whatever paltry jewellery they could lay their hands on. The manager, a bachelor, did not have a great fondness for gold and gems, so they found nothing more than a simple chain and a couple of gold buttons locked away in his top drawer.

News of the robbery spread through the plantation within hours. The villages that clustered around the tea gardens and depended upon them for their livelihood were especially subdued, wary of the consequences that might befall them. Boshonti even more so, for it was her husband who had been one of the three security guards on duty when the burglary took place.

That day, Boshonti could not face her work. She waited all day for her husband to return. And when he finally did, despite the fading light of dusk, she noticed that his arms were covered in bruises. She did not ask him any questions. Instead, she put a plate of food in front of him. Boshonti's husband was starving, but in one terrible day he had been so tormented by his own failings and by the merciless questioning of the district police that when his wife put the plate of rice and dal in front of him, he could not bring himself to eat. He began to weep. Boshonti rocked her husband's head softly against her body, stroking his forehead with the soothing, callused assurance of her palms. When he eventually quietened, Boshonti arranged the food into convenient balls and popped them, one after the other, into his mouth. Finally, she led him to bed and applied a cold compress to his arms while he slept.

In the weeks that followed, the wages that Boshonti earned kept the family going. But Boshonti was expanding, and although her movements were not yet cumbersome, she knew she would not be able to carry on plucking leaves at the rate necessary to sustain them both. And what would happen then?

At first Boshonti's husband had tried to find work, but in small mountainside communities, reputations are tarnished with such ease and enthusiasm that they might never again be restored. He was faced with a string of refusals, with mockery and snipes. Day by day, he withdrew, and no matter how Boshonti tried to entice him back into the world where they had conspired together to create a future, he remained unresponsive, consumed by an inwardness she could not penetrate.

Until the day he suggested they consult a doctor. Relieved that her husband was finally taking an interest, Boshonti took out from under the mattress half the savings they had managed to put together before the tragedy had struck. The following morning, Boshonti and her husband caught an early bus to Siliguri and found the doctor they had been recommended. He examined her and, satisfied that everything was in order, sent her for a scan. There were tens of diagnostic centres to choose from, some less expensive, some more so; they went to the one the doctor had suggested. Boshonti could hardly contain her excitement. She had heard stories of the tiny hands and feet, the face that would flash up on the screen – the first sighting of their baby.

Boshonti had never come across a raised bed before. Their bed at home was a ritual of a mattress being rolled out daily on their single multipurpose floor. So she struggled a little to position herself and was not sure whether to sit or to lie down until the technician impatiently gave her some instructions. Then he covered Boshonti's belly with a wet gel and angled the probe against her abdomen. Immediately, the screen filled with the image of the baby.

The man pointed his wand first one way then the other. As he did so, he made an occasional cluck or whinny, which Boshonti strained to decipher. Five minutes later, he removed it from her belly. 'Everything is perfect. No problem.' Seeing her gratitude, he treated her to a brief smile. 'Any questions?'

Boshonti shook her head and was about to get up when her husband interjected: 'Is it a boy or a girl?'

The technician shook his head and began wiping the probe down with a well-worn piece of grey cloth. 'Have you read the sign?'

'No.'

'It is not allowed. By order of central government.'

Boshonti's husband persevered, 'Sir, is there no way around this little order?'

The man hesitated. Boshonti did not think her husband's request was unreasonable; she too was curious. And it had been so long since her husband had expressed an interest in anything that Boshonti felt she should encourage his request, so she added her voice to the conversation. 'It will not take long to find out, will it?'

The man shook his head.

'Will it hurt?' she asked.

Again he shook his head.

'We can pay an extra ten-fifteen rupees,' Boshonti's husband added, sensing the malleability of the technician's good intentions.

That was the final straw. Boshonti lay down again and with another wave of the probe he gave them the answer – they were going to have a baby girl.

With just an hour remaining until they were due to catch the bus to go back up the mountain, Boshonti's husband remembered an urgent errand that he had promised a friend. He left her at a roadside restaurant with a plate of samosas and a cup of tea. Intent on enjoying the day, Boshonti did not ask too many questions. She was content to while away the remainder of the afternoon dreaming of her baby girl. She went so far as to indulge the happy suspicion that his task might have something to do with finding work. After all, here in the town, reputations came and went like the ebb and flow of a dirty river. Integrity was nothing; money was everything. It might even be that he was plotting the first step of their path to Bombay.

But when her husband returned an hour later, Boshonti noted with disappointment that the zeal in his face had gone; in its place was the familiar lethargy of the last few weeks.

They were both quiet on the bus ride back to the village and when they got home, they fell asleep after a subdued dinner.

The next day Boshonti went to see her mother to deliver the good news that all was well with the baby. Her mother would be relieved. For all her attempts at reassurance, Boshonti knew her mother worried for her. After all, an unemployed husband did not bode well for any pregnancy.

Despite her misgivings, every few days, Boshonti's mother would spend an hour or so persuading her daughter (and herself) that this was a minor trial of their faith – the kind a couple might look back on twenty years later with a kind of bittersweet affection for the resilience of their bond. Boshonti's and her husband's horoscopes had been compared before the marriage ceremony and had been found to be in harmonious conjunction with each other. In fairness to the stars, up until the day of the burglary, Boshonti had been very happy. So her mother preferred to think of the downturn in her daughter's happiness as a transient glitch rather than a precedent for the rest of her life.

After the two women had finished exchanging news and drunk a few cups of tea, Boshonti left for work.

That evening when Boshonti returned home, she found to her amazement that her husband had cooked dinner. He had prepared rice, dal and even fried some potatoes. He had set their plates side by side with glasses full of water and a small brass bowl with salt and chillies as the centrepiece. They ate, as usual, under the light of their hurricane lamp. Boshonti lavished compliments on her husband.

After dinner, for the first time in their marriage, Boshonti's husband asked her for permission to speak. 'Boshonti, I have been thinking about our situation.'

'We will be fine,' Boshonti replied nervously. 'What happened in Siliguri?' The question had been fermenting inside her for over twenty-four hours.

He shook his head. 'Maybe there is an opening for me. Maybe not. We have to wait a few weeks to find out.'

By then she would be struggling to work. 'We don't have a few weeks,' she whispered. 'Can't he tell you any sooner?'

He shook his head. 'Useless bastard. I pleaded with him. I went down on my knees, Boshonti. The bastard was enjoying himself.' He scowled at the memory. 'I begged him, Boshonti. Please, dada, my wife is with child, I said.' Boshonti's husband covered his face with his hands. Tears glinted in the yellow flame of the hurricane lamp. 'Do you want to hear what he said? You low-class people should not be allowed to reproduce if you cannot afford to feed them. Anyway, there is always the option of sending the children out begging. Can you imagine?' He wiped his face with his sleeve.

Boshonti moved around to sit near him. She smuggled her hand into his. 'It will be all right, I promise. I can work very hard.' She forced herself to smile. 'And anyway, all this is nonsense talk. By time she is born you will have a job. I can feel it.' She dropped her head towards her protruding belly. 'Won't he? Baba will definitely have a big important job.' She looked up at her husband. 'This little one will bring you good luck. In a few years we won't even remember this day. She'll grow up, go to school, get married, have her own children...'

'School fees, education, dowry, jewellery, marriage costs. Boshonti, we cannot even afford to feed this child.' He was suddenly angry. 'How you can even think of marriage and what-not? We are low-class people, Boshonti. We cannot afford even our own dreams, let alone our children's.'

Boshonti started cleaning the plates. 'Let us leave this topic for now.' She stacked the dirty crockery in a corner, ready to be washed the following morning. She felt her husband's eyes on her.

'Look at you,' he said.

Boshonti turned to face him.

'You cannot move. How you think you can keep working...'

Boshonti picked up the broom and began to sweep the floor. She was struggling with the weight of her pregnancy. Her back ached. But she didn't dare complain in this climate. Instead, she forced a charade of agility.

'And they want clothes and jewellery and this and that,' her husband continued with his monologue. 'What do they give you back? Headaches and then they are gone.'

Boshonti tried not to listen.

'And the dowry. You know what he said, that bastard? Fifty thousand – going rate for a half decent groom.'

Boshonti replaced the broom in its corner. 'Why are you paying attention to that good-for-nothing?' she challenged. 'How much did my mother pay? Tell me. I am paying my own way and so can she. The world is changing.'

'Are you saying I can't provide for you?' Boshonti's husband looked at her with the most frighteningly sad eyes she had ever seen. 'I am sorry, Boshonti. I am a poor man. I have tried to reach for joys beyond my station and now I am being punished. I should have known – a poor man can't have a wife, Boshonti. And a poor man can't have daughters.'

Boshonti's husband broke down; his body convulsed from finally speaking out loud the desperation he had been struggling against. Boshonti tried to cajole her husband out of his depression but he was not going to be persuaded and Boshonti knew she could not raise a baby by herself.

Later that night, from the cupboard in the kitchen, Boshonti's husband retrieved the parcel with the medicine he had bought in Siliguri. At first, Boshonti refused. She threatened to run to her mother and never come back; but when her husband threatened to take his own life, she could no longer hold out.

Twelve hours later, a baby girl left the world.

❋

As Boshonti nears the end of her story, I wonder about ma and bapu. I wonder if they long for me, the way Boshonti longs for her little girl.

Boshonti had finally let go, and although she did not possess the words with which to describe the meeting of my soul with hers, she did understand. And in that understanding, there was love. And there was peace.

21

The phone in Moyur's house rang just as they sat down to eat. Lily mashi answered. She nodded intently into the receiver before handing it to Moyur. 'From doctor's chambers,' she said. 'They are saying they need to change the appointment to next week.'

Moyur took the wireless handset from her. Bapu and ma slowed their chewing to concentrate on his conversation. 'So when? Same time? Okay.'

As Moyur put the phone down, three pairs of eyes threw questions at him. 'The doctor had to reschedule. Some family emergency. They have asked us to go next Friday, same time.'

'What kind of family emergency?' ma asked.

'I don't know. I didn't ask.'

'But who did you speak to?'

'I don't know, ma – probably a nurse or his practice attendant.'

'And she didn't know?'

'What does it matter?' bapu interjected. 'The good news is that I can take it easy this afternoon. What do you say?'

'Absolutely. I will go back after lunch, in any case.'

'At least finish eating in peace. Joba is there, he can manage for a couple of hours.'

He would certainly have to manage for a couple of hours. Long after bapu and ma had finished their meals, Moyur continued. Lily mashi watched him, fond recollections playing on her lips. 'Some things never change. Till this day, you are the last one, even now that you are a big man.'

'Sorry,' he grinned. 'Why don't you go and start eating.' But Lily mashi waited stubbornly until he had finished and washed his hands. The clock on the wall read two, but it had grown too old to chime. Moyur helped Lily mashi clean the table. There was no urgency to leave; Moyur's old habits had grown rusty from disuse. He was usually at the shop from morning till night and he had forgotten how to simply pass time.

Once their plates were cleared and Lily mashi started eating, Moyur drifted towards the balcony. It was the only thing he knew how to do in these still afternoons. He scanned the world: stagnant with heat, shop-fronts hidden behind shutters, stray dogs sprawled lethargically in the shade of the giant banyan, bicycles reclining against iron railings. What had he and Jonali found to entertain themselves with for hours and hours every day?

Moyur was about to go back inside when the door to the neighbouring balcony opened and Jonali appeared, a metal bucket in one hand, some clothes pegs in the other.

'Jojo.'

The bucket rattled as it hit the floor. She looked at him in surprise. 'What are you doing home?'

'What are *you* doing here?'

'Friday is a half-day for me.'

'I see. Do you college types ever do any work?'

Jonali picked up the bucket. 'Well, if you are just going to insult me...'

'So easy to wind you up. I'm sorry, okay?'

She narrowed her eyes at him.

'Really sorry,' he repeated.

'Are you going to tell me why *you* are here?' Jonali asked again.

'I was supposed to take bapu to see the doctor but the appointment got postponed.'

Jonali walked up to the edge of her balcony. She was wearing a pale pink kaftan that was a little bit see-through against the sun. 'How is your bapu?'

'Better, but he is a stubborn old man. Doesn't take his medicines when he is supposed to, keeps eating fried food. Ma has to constantly keep him in check.'

Jonali giggled. 'Sounds like you aren't holding back on the discipline front either. Your poor bapu.'

'He deserves it. He is so childish sometimes.'

'Old habits die hard, and bad habits die even harder.'

'Wise words, Jojo.'

'I mean, look at us.'

They fell silent, both gazing at the empty street. 'It's so quiet… I had forgotten how little happens here in the afternoons,' Moyur persevered.

Jonali looked at him. 'I haven't forgotten, Moyur. I am here most Friday afternoons; sometimes I come out here and sit for a few minutes.'

'Really? By yourself?'

Jonali nodded. 'What else can I do? You are never around these days. Big-shot businessman you have become.' She sighed. 'We used to spend hours together.'

He chewed his lip. 'We still can,' he said finally, hoping she would not catch the quiver in his voice. 'I don't have to go anywhere now.'

'The shop?'

'It's quiet season.'

Jonali laughed. 'Oh, so now there is quiet season, is there?'

'Haven't you heard of quiet season?'

Jonali shook her head, still laughing. 'Do you want to come over for some shorbot? It really is too hot out here. I don't know how we did it before.'

'Are you sure?'

'Of course. Come over.'

Moyur raced down the stairs towards Jonali's invitation, not bothering to check who was awake and who was asleep. He tried to subdue his heart as it jumped far, far ahead of itself; Jonali did not suspect him of harbouring mischievous boy-girl feelings, but how he wished she would. He heard the familiar flapping of her slippers against the staircase and the front door opened.

'Baba, that was fast. Come on. The house is empty today. Ma has gone for singing lessons with kakimoni.' Jonali giggled. 'In their old age they have decided to rediscover their talents.' She sneaked a glance at him as they climbed the stairs. 'You know what that means.'

Moyur hesitated. He didn't want her to think what he thought she was thinking. 'What about Shikha didi?' he asked.

'She has gone to visit her friend for the afternoon.' Jonali made quotation marks in the air around the word friend.

'Oh, like-that friend,' Moyur said.

'Hmm. I keep saying to her, Shikha didi, just tell me, but she refuses. Anyway, good for us that the house is empty, na?'

Moyur followed Jonali into the kitchen. He wanted to ask her if she had a 'like-that friend' but he kept silent.

The inside of Jonali's house was smaller than he remembered, the colours less vibrant. 'What do you want? Lemon or orange?' she asked.

'Whichever is easier.'

Jonali set about cutting and squeezing the juice from the lemons with great concentration. Her hair, open for a change, tumbled around her face, and she kept lifting her shoulder to try and move it out of the way. Moyur felt a sudden urge to touch it, pull it to one side, maybe clip it in place while she worked. But he dared not move.

'Okay, almost done.' Jonali had diluted the lemon juice with water and was stirring the sugar in, rattling the spoon around each glass with great energy. 'You have to do this or the sugar just settles at the bottom.' Once she was satisfied, she gave Moyur his glass and led him to her room.

Moyur took a sip of his shorbot. 'Delish, Jojo.'

'You like it?'

'Yes.'

Moyur sipped his drink with self-conscious determination. The room they were in – Jonali's bedroom, witness to so many of their private forays – felt a little too familiar for bringing up new ideas. But were they all that new?

'What are you thinking?' she asked.

'Oh. Umm. I was thinking about the shorbot. You must give me the recipe.'

'Liar.'

'I'm not lying.'

He felt her eyes on him, observing, evaluating.

'So, Moyur,' she said, 'you must be very happy surrounded by all those lovely saris.'

'Not a bad job, and I am good at it,' he replied.

Jonali hesitated. He willed her to ask him about his dressing up. He could see it balancing on the tip of her tongue but, like fine cobwebs, reservations had silently gathered in the disused nooks and crannies of their relationship. The next line with which to reciprocate would be to ask about her college and her education but that was in the arena of polite chit-chat in front of probing eyes. It was not what he had promised himself. This was his second chance, after his courage had failed him during pujo, and he could not afford to let her go again.

'Jonali, I have something to tell you.'

'Oh, this sounds serious,' Jonali said light-heartedly.

'No. Really. It is important.' Moyur tried to inject gravity into his words by peppering them with pauses. 'I tried to tell you once before, do you remember, during pujo?'

'I know,' she replied, 'and I was in such a rush. I still feel bad about that, Moyur. That too after all we had said about not spending any time with each other.'

'Doesn't matter. Okay, look, what I have to tell you is that...'

Jonali's face was so intense, she almost made him lose his nerve again. 'Is that,' he restarted, taking in a long hard breath, 'I think you are the most beautiful girl in the world.'

The room spun to a bashful pause around them.

'You're so silly,' Jonali replied. 'You have been saying that ever since we played rajkumar-rajkumari. Anyway, it's not true.'

'Jojo, I have to tell you something else,' Moyur continued in his sober tone. 'I am not like that any more.'

'Like what?'

'Like the old days,' he lied, 'when we used to play rajkumari games and I used to dress up. I don't do that sort of thing any more.'

At first Jonali didn't respond. Moyur tried to give her time to digest what he had said but he also felt impatient. 'So what do you think?'

When she finally spoke, Jonali did so very carefully. One after another, she asked him questions about why and when and how he had stopped. Moyur did not have satisfactory answers but he told lie after lie with such solemn sincerity that he noticed that, despite her continuing stream of questions, there was a telling coquettishness creeping into her demeanour.

As their conversation progressed they slipped, in imperceptible movements, towards each other. Moyur felt his heart pounding inside his chest. And then she pinned him in place with a doe-eyed stare that he knew belonged exclusively to him.

'Jojo?'

'Yes.'

'Will you be my girlfriend?'

Jonali smiled a delicious smile. There was no need for further explanation.

'You have no idea how long I have been imagining this,' Moyur said as he nudged towards his sweetheart. He placed his palm softly against her cheek and she tilted her face towards him. Moyur felt his arm trembling, but hoped that Jonali would not notice as he brought his lips to meet hers and for the first, momentous time, they kissed.

Part III

1994

22

All the confusion, the uncertainty, the strife evaporated in the space of one kiss.

Jonali wanted to tell everyone, and to relive the moment over and over again. Of course, telling her mother or, for that matter, anyone at home was out of the question. But Jonali knew the consternation of her family would be matched if not surpassed by the excitement of her friends. So she started with Mita and soon the news spread through college. She even told Fidel who, Mita informed her, no longer harboured any feelings for her – after all, he was fast becoming a college cricketing legend and there was no shortage of admiring damsels.

In the thrill of her situation, Jonali forgot all about Mr Mollick. So when, out of the blue, note number three arrived, inviting Jonali on an outing to New Market, her first reaction was to simply say no. But Jonali had a kind heart and she knew what he had risked. It was only right that she let him down with as much dignity as possible.

Almost a month into the new term, on the day she was going to set things straight for once and for all, Jonali took much longer than usual to get ready. From the depths of her wardrobe she dug out one of her oldest kurtas – pale brown with faint remnants of a pattern that had been scrubbed away. Her salwar was similarly mismatched and baggy. She tied her hair in a long plait and even abstained from her near religious application of kajol.

At breakfast, her mother and kakimoni both commented. 'How pretty you look,' her mother said approvingly. Jonali grunted, struggling with a dry, unappetizing rooti that wouldn't go down.

'Is that all you will eat?' her mother asked, and Jonali grimaced by way of explanation. Jonali's mother shook her head. She turned to kakimoni. 'Ever since this Miss Universe nonsense, these silly girls have lost their heads.'

Kakimoni smiled at Jonali. 'Yes, such a craze. Still, how can we blame the youngsters, it is their age for getting carried away. But I have seen women our age, Meena didi! Going mad. They want to look like sticks or what, god only knows.'

'That's true. Every day there is a new gym opening up around here.'

The two women tutted. 'We should open up an exercise business,' kakimoni said.

'Get a few yoga teachers. So lucrative it is.'

They carried on in the same vein until Jonali stood up to leave.

'When will you be back?' her mother asked.

Jonali hesitated at the top of the stairs. 'Seven maybe.'

'So late?'

'I have an extra class today,' she lied.

'All right. Study hard.'

As she disappeared into the stairwell, kakimoni's voice floated down after her: 'Such a bright girl. Always studying.'

'Let's hope that is all she is doing.'

❋

After classes that day, Jonali took the Metro from Park Street to her final meeting with Mr Mollick. The platforms were clean, spacious enough to stand without bumping into fellow commuters, and with enough room to breathe. But Jonali held her breath. She didn't want the transparent blue glow of the underground in her lungs nor the infinite blackness of those tunnels. It would have been dangerous on a day like this because she felt ordinary again and it struck her how quickly she had forgotten herself in the rush of her romance with Moyur, and how invincible she felt when he was near her.

Jonali thought again of Mr Mollick's subdued face when they had last parted and the memory turned her stomach. How she wished that she was going to meet Moyur instead. He had come to pick her up a few times after class and they had strolled blissfully together on the Maidan, eating Rollick ice-cream from one cup with two spoons. He liked vanilla, she liked strawberry. So they always had the swirly one, where the vanilla and strawberry curled around each other like two crescent moons, cream and pink. Afterwards they would tuck themselves away in a quiet corner and kiss with cold, tingly, ice-cream flavoured lips. But their meetings were not as frequent as she would have liked. Perhaps this was an impossible wish because there seemed to be no limit to how often she wanted to feel his hand on her waist, his lips against hers, and then what? If she wanted to see him a hundred times a day, a thousand times a day, could she? Would she ever?

Jonali had slept badly the night before, worrying about what she would say to Mr Mollick. Her eyes stung from lack of rest and from the dust of Chowringhee. The columns that lined the passage in front of the Grand Hotel were plastered with announcements of films, shows and rallies. Entrepreneurs jostled for space with their hillocks of T-shirts and jeans, handkerchiefs, clockwork toys, fans, replica 'Gucchi' watches and 'Channel' bags, all at knockdown prices. Normally, she would bypass these hawkers, trailing faithfully behind her mother, who knew the market inside out, straight to a handful of favoured shops housed securely in the old building. Those were the regular shopkeepers, the accountable ones, those with whom they had a rapport. Jonali's mother did not buy from the shifting masses of hawkers, but that day Jonali dawdled amongst them, examining their wares, pondering the desirability of different items. In the background, the traders incessantly announced their merchandise to passers-by. 'Nightie-T-shirt-duster-handbag-wallet, first-class, didi, dada, looking.' When they weren't busy attending to customers, they were tidying and rearranging or soliciting business, pouncing upon the most tentative displays of interest.

It was only half past two and Jonali was in no rush to reach the Princess. So she meandered through the street stalls, trying but failing to preoccupy herself with things she could buy, things she could wear.

'Jonali?'

Her heart sank at the sound of his voice.

'You are early,' he said.

Jonali felt her pulse quicken. It was not three o'clock at the Princess Bar and Restaurant. It was two-forty-five in broad daylight. Mr Mollick reached out and took her hand. 'I'm so glad to see you.'

Immediately, she retracted it. 'It's not three yet, is it?'

'Not quite.' Mr Mollick glanced at his watch. 'Shall we walk across now, or are you busy?'

'You go,' Jonali replied, reaching out to examine a small red ladybird hair slide. 'I need to buy something for my hair.'

'Let me buy it for you,' he offered.

Before she could reply, Mr Mollick and the suddenly animated stall-keeper had embarked on negotiations over the price.

'Twenty rupees, piece.'

'Twenty!'

'I buy for eighteen, sell for twenty. No profit margin.'

'So you are charging us full price?' Mr Mollick challenged.

'Come on. I don't want them that much,' Jonali said.

Sensing his advantage ebbing away, the stall-keeper started to unclip the hair slides from the string shelf in his makeshift gallery of goodies. 'How many do you want?'

'None, if you are going to rob us,' Jonali retorted.

'Didi, honestly, I am telling you, there is no profit in this business any more.'

The street where they stood haggling was getting busier. The faceless crowds of Calcutta harboured countless narrow misses. 'Let's just go,' she urged and started to walk away. Mr Mollick stared after her.

'Okay, last price. Thirty rupees for two,' he offered the stall-keeper.

'Fifteen for two,' Jonali replied, re-entering the fray.

The stall-keeper chortled. He stuck his tongue out, gently biting it with his teeth, and shook his head elaborately. 'Didi, do you want me to go out of business?'

'So what is your last price?' Mr Mollick demanded.

'Twenty-five for two.'

'Twenty for two.'

He shook his head again. Mr Mollick and Jonali made to go. They all knew the routine.

'Okay, okay. Here, take it,' he said. Mr Mollick paid him twenty rupees.

Jonali waited for him a few paces ahead. 'You know, you really shouldn't buy me things.' Immediately, she regretted saying it.

'Jonali, I am sorry if I have stepped out of line.' The packet dangled uncertainly from his fingers.

'No, don't be sorry. It's just that there was no need.'

They headed towards the restaurant, Jonali trying to maintain her distance from Mr Mollick without seeming uncivil. But then he wanted to stop en route for cigarettes.

'I'll meet you there,' she said.

'It will only take a minute.'

She nodded. There was a desperate look in his eyes, which she wanted to run from. In the handful of months that she hadn't seen him, Mr Mollick had grown even more haggard. Was it her fault? Did that make it acceptable for him to be reckless with her reputation? She had everything to lose now. He had nothing. But was that not her fault?

Mr Mollick stopped at one of the stalls at the top of the road next to Globe cinema, and Jonali stopped with him. It was the same one she went to with her mother when they got thirsty in New Market, conveniently opposite a row of tailoring shops, including her mother's favourite.

'One packet Charminar, dada,' Mr Mollick shouted at the middle-aged man who sat cross-legged behind the counter. The stall was perched on stilts, suspended several metres off the ground. On one side lay a stack of crates crammed with empty soft-drink bottles balanced precariously on top of each other; underneath the stall an anorexic bitch suckled a litter of pups.

Jonali avoided looking at the stall-keeper in case he recognized her. But perhaps she need not worry. The stall was by far the most popular on the stretch, with hundreds if not thousands of clients. Not only was it ideally located, the stock was marvellous.

No matter what was asked for, the stall-holder seemed to find it with a good rummage underneath his cavernous counter.

On this occasion, however, the search went on a little longer. The man flicked his eyes down towards Mr Mollick and Jonali. 'Charminar, you said?'

'Yes.'

He looked into his stash. 'No, we don't have it.' He turned to his assistant. 'Eyi, ja toh. Bring one packet of Charminar.'

The assistant asked Mr Mollick, 'Ten or twenty?'

'Doesn't matter.'

The assistant scrambled down the crates on his left and disappeared into the surrounding alleys.

As they waited, Mr Mollick took the opportunity to reach for Jonali again. He took her hand in his, and placed the packet with the hair slides in her palm.

'Thank you,' Jonali said. 'Mr Mollick, I have to tell you something.'

'Jonali, what is this thank you rubbish?'

She opened the packet and forced a display of appreciation for the two ladybirds poised atop the red hair slides. 'They are lovely. But I have to tell you something.'

'Put them on.' He smiled at her, a sickly, sugary smile. 'Do you want me to do it for you?'

'No, it's fine. Really, Mr Mollick. What I need to tell you is that... umm... I...'

The assistant returned just then and clambered up to his prior position. The crates rocked nervously.

'Ek packet, here you go, moshai.'

'Oh, yes.' Mr Mollick let go of the hair slides and turned to pay. Jonali took the opportunity to quickly push the ladybirds into her hair.

By the time he turned around she was done. 'Oh, you already fixed them.' He sounded so dejected that, despite her stern intentions, Jonali felt herself succumbing to guilt. Mr Mollick extracted a cigarette from his new pack. It was a risky situation to be standing next to a man smoking cigarettes in broad daylight in a place like New Market. This would be the last time, Jonali promised herself. Somehow or the other she would tell him, and then maybe she could run. She didn't have to wait for a response – she could just tell him and run. That way she would have done her duty.

'Mr Mollick, I want to tell you something. Something important.' Jonali scanned the people around them; she wanted to hasten the proceedings, to escape the relentless stares of passers-by. She knew they looked odd together. 'Mr Mollick, I am so grateful for everything you have done for me.'

'Jonali, please.' He inhaled the cigarette smoke between phrases. 'It is nothing.'

'No, you don't understand. It is something. What I have to tell you might make it something.'

'Go on.'

'Mr Mollick, I do not have any romantic interest in you.'

There, she had said it. She did not leave, though, as she had planned. She was not that kind of girl.

Mr Mollick switched his cigarette from one hand to the other.

'Oh,' he said, 'thank you for clearing that up.' That was it. There was nothing else. No recriminations, no protests, just an awkward space.

'Mr Mollick, have you got work somewhere else?'

That made him snigger so hard he choked on his cigarette, but even after he regained his composure he didn't reply.

Jonali wondered whether she should just leave. She didn't need his dismissal, but the truth is that she was at once angry and guilty: his bitterness was her doing. There was not that much left of his cigarette, so she decided to wait. If for nothing else, at least as a courtesy to a man she would never see again.

It was a fatal mistake. As Mr Mollick took his final drag, the door opposite them opened.

It just so happened that after Jonali left them sitting at the dining table that morning, her mother and kakimoni decided to spend the afternoon shopping in New Market. It just so happened that as they walked out of the tailor's shop in search of some refreshment their eyes fell upon the stall across the road. What they were not expecting was to see Jonali standing there, conversing with a lowly-looking man with a cigarette dangling from his lips.

Their eyes met. Jonali froze. Mr Mollick, unaware of the drama that was unfolding across the road, turned towards the butt to retire it well and truly into the tarmac with his heel. Jonali's mother raised her hand to cover her mouth. Her face folded inwards. Kakimoni continued to look at Jonali in disbelief.

23

In the days that followed their kiss, Moyur threw himself into his work with renewed energy. He single-handedly sold more saris than he and Joba kaku had sold together at the height of the pujo shopping madness. He also relished the thought of the story he would tell Boshonti. She was the only one he trusted with his love life and the only one who would not object. But as one week rolled into the next without any sign of Boshonti, Moyur grew impatient. After all, what is the point of good news if there is no one to share it with?

So, one evening, a handful of weeks after Jonali had become his girlfriend, as the clock struck seven, Moyur piped up, 'Joba kaku, why don't you close up today? I am not feeling too well.'

Joba kaku was busy with a customer and signalled for Moyur to wait and so he did, for a few minutes, but the customer, a well-proportioned woman both in girth and in self-importance, refused to be rushed. Moyur walked up to them. 'Madam, please excuse me one moment.' He extracted the padlocks from his bag and laid them beside Joba kaku. 'I will see you first thing tomorrow. I really don't feel well.' Before Joba kaku could protest, Moyur made his getaway.

Once outside, he summoned a taxi. Normally, he would have taken the bus, and part of him immediately regretted that he had not, because as soon as he mentioned his destination, the driver shot him a dirty smile, exposing a clutch of bent yellow teeth. He reeked of sweat and diesel. It's not what you think, you swine, Moyur wanted to say, but he kept quiet. Instead, he decided to use this opportunity to take in the city. Usually, he was one among thousands forging ahead along chance fissures of space in the manic claustrophobia of north Calcutta evenings.

As they approached the red-light district, the driver asked Moyur to guide him precisely to where he wanted to go. Moyur asked him to stop on the main road, partly because he didn't want to take the taxi all the way to Boshonti's doorstep, partly because the alleys were so narrow that even the most dextrous of drivers would have struggled to weave in and out of the warren.

Unsurprisingly, the taxi driver, when presented with a hundred-rupee note, claimed not to have change. This was not the kind of place where a young middle-class man would want to be found making too much of a fuss. An abundance of impressionable policemen patrolled the streets around Sonagachi and an accidental allegation could easily result in a messy fiasco that might cost him much more than a thirty-rupee tip.

Annoyed with the taxi driver, Moyur retreated. In any case, his mind was on other, more pressing matters. It was a little later in the day than on his last visit and he found that his audience of prostitutes was rather diminished on this occasion. In their place the streets were full of loitering men: young, old, fat, lanky, balding, greying. The assortment made him queasy and he hurried past them.

Boshonti was not expecting Moyur and he knew there was always the possibility that she might be occupied with a transaction. However, Moyur dusted the thought from his head and, to his relief, when he got to her doorstep, he found Boshonti peering into the street. She was dressed for business and he noted the flush of embarrassment with which she spotted him. 'Moyur babu! What are you doing here?'

'Sorry, Boshonti didi. I had to speak to you today. It was a must.' Suddenly confronted by how naïve he had been, Moyur averted his gaze and stared at his feet. 'Anyway, you haven't come for so long,' he mumbled. 'Why should you be the only one to decide when we meet?'

Boshonti gawped at him. 'Okay, come in. But you can't stay long.'

'No, I won't. Promise.'

They stepped inside, Boshonti leading the way. Her room was on the far side of the open courtyard they had dined in the last time.

'Close your eyes,' Boshonti instructed him in a bossy whisper.

'What?'

'Close your eyes,' she repeated. 'You can't see this. Here, give me your hand.'

Moyur protested but Boshonti was adamant and she turned to check on him every few steps. The courtyard had turned into a trading ground – it was where the men and women set their terms of business and where appetites were whet.

When they reached her room, Boshonti apologized. 'I am sorry you had to see these things, Moyur babu, you are too young. That is why I told you to come on that day only. But you will do whatever you want.'

'I didn't look, didi.'

She searched his face.

'… that much,' he confessed. 'It doesn't matter, didi. I knew, anyway.'

'Yes, Moyur babu, but there is knowing and there is knowing.' She sighed. 'Okay, come in.'

Boshonti's room was tiny, maybe six-by-six feet at a stretch. She had, over the years, managed to save up enough for a camp cot with a slim mattress. From under the bed the open mouth of a battered old suitcase protruded into the room.

They sat down on the bed. 'So, what is it?' she asked.

'You know how you said that everything would work out between Jonali and me?'

'Yes.'

'Well, I have some news and I just couldn't keep it to myself any longer, Boshonti didi. That's why I came.'

'Okay, tell me then, what is it?'

'Jonali is my girlfriend. I persuaded her.'

'Oh, Moyur babu, you don't know how happy that makes me. It is the best news I have had in weeks.' She smiled shyly. 'What did I tell you? Just remember to invite this Boshonti to your wedding. Don't forget me then.'

Moyur nodded. 'You will be the guest of honour, Boshonti didi, if ever that happens.'

'What ever and never? Of course it will happen,' Boshonti said.

'Na, it's not so easy,' he replied. 'Meena pishi wants a Brahmin boy.'

'What? Not even a Kayastha will do?'

'No, but I don't care. I'll think of something.'

'Well,' Boshonti reflected, 'you could have a runaway marriage. Romantic style.' She laughed. 'Just tell me where it is.'

'You're right, didi. Why not? Meena pishi is full of bullshit, anyway.'

'Eesh! Don't use such foul language in front of me.'

'Sorry.'

Boshonti glanced nervously at her plastic carriage clock. 'Moyur babu, can I come and see you tomorrow afternoon?'

'Fine, I'll wait for you.'

As Moyur stood to leave, a commotion broke out outside. 'Boshonti, Boshonti.' It was a woman's voice. 'Come quickly.'

They stood up at once. 'Oh, god. What now?' Boshonti muttered to herself. The scuffle seemed to be making its way determinedly towards them. Just as Boshonti reached for the door, it flew inwards.

There on her threshold stood Joba kaku, his face distorted with contempt. He looked from Moyur to Boshonti and back again to Moyur. 'Moyur baba, I cannot believe it. I was praying all the way here – let it not be true, let it not be true.'

Moyur was too startled to respond. By the time he regained his composure, Joba kaku was already striding away.

'Joba kaku, wait. We are only friends.' Moyur ran after him and grabbed his arm.

Joba kaku shook him off. 'Your bapu can decide, Moyur baba. It is in his hands. How unfortunate a man I am to have to give him such terrible news about his one and only son.' With that, he wrenched his arm free and disappeared into the night.

❁

The next day, both houses were silent except for the whispering walls and the desperate counsels of two mothers.

After Joba kaku had left him stranded and undeservedly humiliated, Moyur had come home to find bapu and ma at the dining table. Telltale streaks lined ma's cheeks. Lily mashi stood in the doorway between the kitchen and the dining room, eyes lowered to the ground. Moyur walked to the table slowly. He had run through many alternatives, but it turned out that, on this occasion, the truth was the most innocent of explanations.

'What has he got to say for himself?' ma asked bapu.

'What have you got to say for yourself, Moyur?' Bapu relayed the question, but before Moyur could answer, ma started: 'The shame. Chhi! Will I ever be able to look Joba in the face again? What must he be thinking?'

'It's not like that, ma.'

'Don't call me ma. Tell him,' she addressed bapu again, 'tell him I am no longer his mother.'

There was no point in trying to speak to ma when she was intent on melodrama, so Moyur tried bapu, and bapu listened. Moyur recounted the story of his first encounter with Boshonti, then their subsequent encounters. He embellished the truth ever so slightly here and there, pitching Boshonti as an expert dancer to add credence to their acquaintance. He told them that he had danced for her in exchange for the stories she told. After all, friendships grow on reciprocation.

When Moyur realized he was not making any headway, he told them of her profound sadness. He told them of her journey from the foothills of the Himalayas to the gritty, anonymous solace of the city, and finally the story of the baby girl that she had lost.

'The strangest part,' Moyur said, 'was that when she spoke of her sorrow it became my sorrow; it belonged to me.'

It belongs to me. And as Moyur tells his story, I become the words.

As Moyur speaks, I watch ma, I watch bapu, I examine their every breath, their every twitch, willing them to become overwhelmed, willing their hearts to fill with longing, willing them to cry, to agonize, to be reminded, to want me, to miss me, to love me.

And they do.

Bapu brimmed with tears of regret. Ma, who had already cried herself dry, sat silent with open, stagnant eyes, her face unreadable. Only Lily mashi seemed reasonably intact.

'Ma? Bapu? Do you believe me?'

Bapu nodded. 'We do, baba, we do.'

Moyur looked from one to the other. 'Say something then...'

Bapu sniffed loudly. Moyur had never seen him so distraught. Ma tried to stand but her chair slipped against the mosaic tiles and she stumbled onto the table for support. Moyur and Lily mashi rushed forward but she waved them away. Ma tried to speak but the words that formed in her mouth were so exhausted they were barely audible. She sat down and took a sip of water. Finally, she managed to garner some energy to her voice. 'This friend of yours, she will never be able to forget what she did.'

'Shh...' Bapu moved closer to ma and put his arm around her. 'Come on, Kakuli, I think you should lie down.'

'Don't touch me,' ma screeched, shrugging him off. 'Never,' she repeated to Moyur.

'It wasn't her fault,' Moyur said. 'She was forced.'

'It will always be her fault, Moyur,' ma said under her breath. 'She should have been stronger.'

'Kakuli, please,' bapu intervened and this time she surrendered, allowing him to guide her to their bedroom. Moyur's legs, which had been rigid with adrenaline, suddenly failed him and he juddered towards the floor, collapsing against the wall as he did so.

The room around him quietened except for the rising evensong of park-side crickets.

'So? This time you have really outdone yourself,' Lily mashi sneered at Moyur. 'If you were mine, I would cut my head off in shame.'

Moyur didn't have the wherewithal to continue his defence, but Lily mashi's condemnation lumped in his throat.

She carried on, 'What do you think will happen when the rest of the neighbourhood finds out?'

'They won't. Why would they?' Moyur muttered.

'Well, you better hope Joba doesn't open his mouth to anyone else.' She stuck her tongue out and shook her head to emphasize the measure of his misdemeanour. 'You should have seen him... so upset. No surprise, really, he has seen you since you were this high. He just ran into the house and blabbed in front of everyone.' Lily mashi tutted to herself. 'Still, I can't blame him. He was so upset. Now let's just hope Meena didi keeps it to herself.'

'Meena pishi? She was here?'

'Yes, poor thing. She was already upset when she came over, and then this! God only knows what she thinks now, Moyur.'

'Did she say anything?' He heard the tremor in his own voice.

'What can she say? Bechari. She has her own problems. Your Jojo – caught romancing with some lafanga in New Market.'

'Lies!' Moyur screamed.

Lily mashi backed into the kitchen. 'Such goody-goody acting...' she mumbled. 'Outside she acts like such a good girl but inside she's no better than a slum girl.'

She was not loud but she was loud enough, and Moyur jumped up from where he was sitting. 'Liar. Liar.'

She recoiled further into the kitchen. 'Get away from me, you little rascal.'

But Moyur couldn't draw himself away. 'Why are you saying these things? Why?' His eyes filled with angry tears.

Lily mashi screamed for bapu.

Moyur didn't wait for bapu to reappear. He ran down the stairs, out of the house and straight to Jonali's front door. He rang the bell three times in quick succession. There was no answer. He waited a few seconds but the seconds lengthened, as they do in times of unrest. He curled his hand into a fist and banged on the wooden door. The door shuddered. He didn't stop. Across the road, in front of Ram kaku's shop, a couple of the neighbourhood loafers leaned in to get a good look at the commotion. Finally, someone appeared on Jonali's balcony. He couldn't see who it was in the dark. 'It's me,' he said. 'I need to speak to Jojo.'

'What the hell do you think you are doing?' It was Meena pishi. 'Haven't the two of you created enough trouble for one day? Did you plot this together or something?' She made to turn away but then she stopped. 'Actually, since the day you were born, Moyur, you have been a curse on your family. And now, on ours.' She left.

Moyur stood, ashamed, winded by her scorn. It was a misunderstanding. He could not give up. 'Jojo! Jojo!' he shouted. Moyur screamed for Jonali until he tasted blood in his throat but she did not come. It seemed that Jonali no longer had either ears or heart for him. He tried to remember what Lily mashi had said about being caught with someone. He didn't believe her. But as the minutes dragged past, Moyur had no choice but to be persuaded that Lily mashi had spoken the truth. After all, how could Jonali, if she loved him, be so cruel as to let him stand outside her door, howling for her like a madman, stricken with grief? How could she not, if she loved him, fight with her mother and run down the stairs at least to find out what had really happened?

Moyur made his way home, despondent. The neighbouring balconies were filled with the usual assortment of gossipmongers.

From the corners of his eyes he saw the loafers lining the street, their numbers swollen with ranks of hastily recruited voyeurs. They managed to slip in a few heckles on his very brief walk back home. Cries of 'Eyi, hero' and 'mostaan' rang in his ears but they were meaningless. He had fallen to the very bottom.

Back home, bapu was waiting for him. The front door was open and he sat in the drawing room. As Moyur entered, bapu stood up. The pale white of the tube light cast a sallow grey shadow across his face. Moyur looked away. He took a few steps into the house and stopped. The repercussions of his actions were simply too much for Moyur to take in. His head pounded with impossible consequences. He stood silently at the threshold, wondering if perhaps he had gone too far. Maybe bapu would know. But before he could utter a word, bapu rushed over to him and gathered him up in his arms. And they stood there, wrapped in each other, understanding.

24

Jonali had known there would be consequences; it was unbecoming for a girl of her background to be discovered loitering on street corners, that too with a clerk.

Jonali's mind kept flitting back to the moment she was caught with Mr Mollick. She had hated him in an instant, and left him without a heartbeat's hesitation.

On returning home, Jonali had recounted to her mother what had happened – the mix-up with her college place, how Mr Mollick had helped her, how he had fallen for her – tastefully censoring the details of their more intimate encounters. However, what Jonali had not reckoned with was the force of her mother's disappointment.

Jonali's mother had listened as she explained, over and over again, the innocuous nature of their meeting. Then, without offering even the slightest gesture of reassurance, she had deserted her daughter to seek sanctuary in the counsel of her friend and fellow mother, Kakuli.

The news that Jonali's mother brought back from next door, however, was far more terrible than anything Jonali could have done. Soon afterwards, Moyur had come over. Jonali had heard him banging on the door like a maniac but she had nothing to say to him. It was a rancid business, this loving and longing, and Jonali had already had her fill.

Over the week that ensued, Jonali's mother took to waking every day at dawn. A routine that was normally reserved for Friday mornings morphed into a daily ritual. After completing her ablutions, her mother would settle down in the pujor ghor to pray.

The entire front wall of this room was given over to a series of altars of differing heights and materials, decorated with a bustling array of statues and picture frames: some containing images of gods and goddesses, some photos of family members who had departed this world – her parents, her in-laws, her husband. Jonali's mother would serenade each image in turn with the flame of the oil lamp in her right hand and the mellow metallic ring of the brass bell in her left. She always spent longest on her husband, dutifully paying her respects before getting down to business: chiding him for leaving her before she updated him on the latest goings-on in the household. As the years passed, the conversation had grown steadily more succinct, recrimination giving way to a brief but informative monologue. The events of the last few days, however, had reversed this trend and she found herself seeking his advice on an almost continuous basis. And her husband responded in the ways of the dead: through dreams or manipulations of circumstance.

A few days into her mother's efforts, Jonali was summoned to the pujo room and instructed to sit in front of the altars while her mother tried to secure yet more divine blessings for her daughter. Finally, she turned to Jonali.

'Jojo, you have seen me these last few days, praying endless hours for your sake.'

Jonali nodded, wary of her mother's intentions.

'Well, it seems that somebody up there has been listening.'

'Ma, really, I am telling you – nothing was going on.'

'If nothing was going on, why the need for all this secrecy? You didn't get a place in college, you had to do this, that and the other, and all of it you kept inside you? How do I know what other deceptions you are capable of?' Jonali's mother shook her head emphatically and pulled her anchol tighter around her shoulder. 'Na, no more risk taking. Thank god, I have had some very relieving news. Do you remember Mou mashi?'

Jonali squinted at her mother.

'Mou has been approached by her college batch-mate with a matrimonial proposal.'

Jonali could not believe what her mother was saying. Well, she too would rise to the occasion.

'No, ma,' Jonali cried out. 'Not marriage, please.'

Her mother stared at her. 'Do you have no shame?'

Jonali glowered at her mother. 'Never, you tell your friend. Never!'

'You will, for once in your life, do as you are told. Understand?'

'I will finish my studies. Then I'll do whatever you want.'

'Studies! Studies!' Jonali's mother turned away and muttered at the congregation of deities in front of her. 'That is what we all thought, that you will become some big-shot after college. How much money your kaku and kakimoni wasted behind you and your stubborn ideas for college education, and what were you really up to? Chhi chhi chhichhi... And that letter? How could you? Under that innocent, studious face, such duplicity.'

'Letter?' Jonali asked unsurely. 'Did Riya—'

Her mother cut her short. 'Don't bring your cousin into this. I only thank god that all this has come to light now and I can put a stop to it. Or else who knows where this would have ended.'

They sat in silence together. Jonali's mother carried on with her ministrations for a few minutes before returning to her. 'The boy's name is Suman and he is a civil engineer—'

Jonali did not let her mother finish. 'I don't care who or what he is. I am not getting married until I finish college.'

'All these years I have raised you by myself, through so much stress and strain, and this is your idea of gratitude? I can't take any more, Jojo. I want you off my hands. You are lucky that such an offer has come. If anybody finds out what all you have done…'

'I don't need an offer. I can look after myself.'

'With what? Your clerk?' Jonali's mother tried to propel herself off the floor. 'You are a disgrace.'

Jonali stood up deftly and waited for her mother to get up. 'You are the disgrace,' she said, almost spitting into her mother's face. 'At least I am trying to stand on my own two feet. You, on the other hand, have been living shamelessly, begging from kaku and kakimoni, begging your whole life. I am the one who is ashamed of you. Parasite—'

But before Jonali could go any further, her mother landed a hard slap straight across her face. And they stopped, each as stunned as the other. Jonali's mother took a step back. Jonali did not move. It was the first time her mother had hit her in years and she waited for her to apologize. But she just turned from her daughter and fled.

As the door opened and closed, Jonali caught sight of kakimoni standing in the doorway. She did not come in; Jonali did not go out. Kakimoni would probably run after her mother and comfort her.

Jonali sat stroking her cheek. It stung with her mother's alleged good intentions. Well, at least it was over now.

There are many people in this world who dream, who work hard and cling to their hopes. For most, the little dreams come true; for the blessed even the big dreams come to pass, but there are some who eventually discover that theirs is not to dream. How foolishly Jonali had hoped for college and to stand on her own two feet. Yet more foolishly she had believed that she would find true love; she had indulged in whimsical daydreams of holding hands and going to the cinema, of giggling together and plunging into fantasies that were theirs and theirs alone.

Don't give up on him, I try to tell her. He loves you. But Jonali doesn't hear me.

Why would she?

I don't even exist.

Sometimes it is only when we lose that we realize how far we were immersed and how fragile we have become because of it.

For Jonali, it was too much.

She could no longer think of Moyur because he had not just broken her dreams, he had shown himself to be someone she could never know, someone with other loves, and riddles she could not bear.

❁

Barely a month later, Meena pishi began sending out the invitations.

The one for Moyur's family she hand-delivered on a Sunday afternoon when she knew she would have the largest audience. 'What a beautiful card,' ma said and it certainly was: crafted from the finest handmade paper with luscious vermillion borders; a groom atop a painted white elephant across the front of the card, on the back, a bride leaving in a magenta and gold palanquin attended by an entourage of wailers.

Moyur left Meena pishi with ma and bapu. A month had already passed since he had seen Jonali. One more month and he might never see her again.

Time carried on its relentless march, punctuated by lapses of bitterness and vulnerability and the implicit finality of an invitation card that demanded his attention.

For Moyur, there would only be one last chance and he had to try; Meena pishi was so susceptible to misunderstandings. What if she had misread the circumstances of Jonali's liaison? What if he could persuade Jonali that his friendship with Boshonti was innocent? Ma and bapu would back him. Maybe he could take Jonali to meet Boshonti – surely then she would appreciate the truth. There were so many ifs and maybes that a future with Jonali seemed at once impossible and certain.

That evening, Moyur sat down with a pad of paper and a pen, and though he was not by any means a writer, it was the only way he could think of to reach her. Moyur wrote for two hours and eleven pages in a small, methodical hand to ensure that her task in reading it was made as easy as possible. However, he peppered the pages with crossings-out: hopeful words, propitious phrases that he felt he needed in order to be truthful but which might be seen as presumptuous without a line through them.

Moyur explained everything: Boshonti, the enduring abnormalities that he had denied, and, most of all, the overwhelming feelings he had always had for her.

Feelings that we share. After all, though she may never have known it, Jonali is my friend too. When they played together, I was playing too. When Jonali lined Moyur's eyes with kajol and put bangles on his wrists – they were also my eyes and my wrists.

But sometimes they forgot about me. And I would become the girl in the corner. Alone. Petrified that their forgetfulness might last for ever. Because, of all his worldly distractions, for Moyur, Jonali was the dearest.

❖

BB block was flanked by two bus stops, of which Jonali's was the messier, strewn with the vestiges of enthusiastic construction: leftover sand and broken bricks from the government's efforts to plug the marshland that lay underfoot, so that civilization, with its hopes, its triumphs and its anxieties, could flourish above the murk.

Moyur waited there for Jonali. He had no idea when she went to college so he arrived too early, prepared to wait until it was too late. In the background, stray dogs cavorted, rickshaw-walas departed for the school run and returned, the paan-wala rolled up half-dozen lots of betel leaves in readiness for business. Jonali did not appear.

Moyur shuffled up to the paan shop. 'A sweet one, please.' He popped it into his mouth. Anything to break the monotony of waiting.

'No work today?' the paan-wala asked.

'Yes, yes. Just waiting for something.'

The paan-wala offered Moyur his stool for a few minutes' rest. Moyur declined. It was almost time for him to go to work, anyway, so he walked the few short steps back to his bus stop, when he spotted Riya walking in his direction.

How different the two cousins looked. Riya had done a lot of growing up since the last time he had seen her, not that he saw her very often, but she seemed to have retained a forced childishness about her. She came to a halt right next to Moyur but clearly hadn't noticed him standing there.

'Riya.'

'Oh, Moyur dada. I didn't see you.'

Moyur hesitated. He couldn't remember the last time he had spoken more than two words to her, that too outside the safe company of others. Her canary-yellow top and dangling earrings grated against his mood.

'Where's Jonali? Isn't she going to college today?' He had to ask. Riya was his only option.

'At home. What's it to you?'

'I have to see her.'

Riya shrugged. 'Go and see her then. What are you waiting here for?'

'I can't. I mean, I tried but...'

'I don't understand.'

Bystanders began tuning into their exchange. Moyur lowered his voice. 'Riya, whatever you heard isn't true.'

She cocked an eyebrow. 'No? I heard the source was very reliable.'

'He misunderstood.'

'Whatever, I have to go now. My bus is here.'

A couple of state buses rattled towards them. Moyur took out the letter from his bag; he had put it in a sealed envelope that he had left unmarked. 'Riya... please can you give this letter to Jonali? Please, I beg you. I just want her to hear my side of the story before she decides.'

Riya stared at him. He couldn't read her at all. Was it contempt? Was she agreeable? When she took it from his outstretched hands he felt a weight lift from his shoulders. 'Okay,' she said, narrowing her eyes. 'I knew there was some chakkar.' She put the envelope into her handbag. 'You know she is getting married, don't you?'

'I know.'

'To a Brahmin. An engineer. A professional.'

The bus pulled up in front of them and Moyur tagged along behind her to the steps of the bus. The conductor rapped its side impatiently. 'Kankurgachi, Phoolbagan, Sealdah, Howrah. Ki dada, are you getting on the bus? If not, stand to one side.'

Moyur watched Riya swing herself onto the first step. 'Riya, will you give it to her?' he shouted. 'Do you promise?'

Riya turned to him and sighed. 'Yes, Moyur dada, I promise.'

The bus drove off, taking Riya and his letter with it.

25

The next day, the day after that, in fact, for a whole month after he gave Riya the letter, whenever he could, Moyur left the shop in Joba kaku's hands in the afternoons. Although they perhaps did not know the full truth behind his sadness, the family rallied around him.

After lunch, Moyur would retreat to the balcony, waiting for as long as his work commitments permitted. But Jonali never came. He would see her sometimes, leaving the house or returning in a rustle of shopping bags and preparation; she never looked at him, not once. The month flew past and the day of Jonali's wedding to Suman arrived in a trough of insipid winter.

Moyur came home to the suffocating smoke of hundreds of incense sticks and ma's insistence that he attend. She reminded him that his absence would raise questions, that etiquette was unforgiving, and so, despite his reluctance, Moyur went.

❉

The flat terraced roof of Jonali's house had been decorated by L.P. Das & Sons with garlands of marigolds, row upon row of flickering tooni-lights and a prominent banner advertising their services. The priest, Jonali's uncle and the bridegroom sat at the centre of a series of circles in which the guests had been arranged; the marital fire burned brightly at the heart of the proceedings.

Meena pishi stood next to Jonali. The palanquin was ready. Her bearers – distant cousin brothers – stood to attention, waiting to transport Jonali towards her new life.

Moyur waited impatiently for the action to begin. In his head he read out the letter he had written, as he had been doing every day, agonizing over whether he should have said something more or less, wondering if destiny hung in the balance of a missed word. And then he imagined her reply, written in her long lilting hand, replies of understanding or loathing or even ambivalence, but he had received nothing, and a part of him was desperate for the ceremony to begin, to alleviate the limbo that had befallen him, to declare him a bystander, forsaking her as she had forsaken him.

Jonali stooped down to touch her mother's feet. Meena pishi touched her daughter's head. Then Jonali sat on her throne and the cousins got into position. Meena pishi began the countdown: 'One, two, three... lift.' Riya sounded the shaankh and the echo of the conch shell reverberated through the hall, overwhelming the hubbub. The women in the assembly ululated, coming to a crescendo with the arrival of the bride.

Moyur tried to retreat into the audience. With each mantra, his head spun a little more. He tasted the bhang on his lips again. It had been his consolation, something to fill the hollow in his chest, to fill his mind with images of them dancing through the heavens, arms linked, dressed in saris the colour of bougainvillea. Through the haze, he saw Jonali's pretty face, done up in bridal colours, with a large red bindi and sandalwood patterns swirling across her forehead. She smiled at him. But when he smiled back, Moyur did not recognize himself.

Moyur came crashing down from the bhang-laced sky. And suddenly, in front of him, Jonali. Just the same, dressed in a sari the colour of bougainvillea, spinning through the heavens in a downward spiral. He struggled to catch his breath and the frantic hollow in his chest beat louder and louder.

He looked around nervously. Bapu nodded him a reassurance. In front, Suman continued his walk around the fire in time with the priest's chants. Jonali, her sari knotted to his kurta, followed.

Moyur took a few steps backwards and wove his way slowly down the stairs. He had done his bit for propriety.

The following afternoon, Jonali and Suman left. The whole para gathered outside Jonali's house to bid her farewell. All of Jonali's worldly possessions, a large chunk of which had been acquired in the run-up to the wedding, were packed into three large suitcases. She was still heavily laden with gold jewellery and a line of sindoor announced to the world her altered status. So established, yet so forlorn.

Moyur positioned himself safely behind a battalion of relatives. Meena pishi and Riya were clinging to Jonali, stroking her hair, her arms.

They were only going to Shyambazar. On a good day, it was barely a twenty-minute taxi ride, a little longer on the bus. As Suman's white Ambassador pulled away, they all waved vigorously. Suman sat quietly to one side, letting his bride indulge in her departure. As it turned out, it would be a long time before she would again have the pleasure of so many goodbyes.

Part IV

1995

26

'Moyur. Moyur.' Piklu was frantic.

Moyur was with a customer. 'One minute, madam.'

'Moyur, your father...' Piklu panted. 'In hospital. Your mother just telephoned.'

By the time Moyur and Joba kaku got to the cardiac ward, the worst was over. They were keeping him for observation. Thankfully, the heart attack he had suffered was small, nothing that would affect him too badly in the long run. Ma was sitting quietly beside him, hands folded, lips moving ever so slightly. A nurse pounced on bapu's arm with the blood-pressure cuff as soon as the doctor retreated.

The nurse didn't waste any time in acknowledging Moyur or Joba kaku. Instead, she gazed sternly at the dial of the blood-pressure instrument. They waited politely for her to finish. Eventually, satisfied with the reading, she let all the air hiss out of the cuff.

'140 by 100,' she announced.

'Is that all right, nurse didi?' Moyur asked.

'And who are you?'

Ma interrupted her prayers to introduce Moyur and Joba kaku to the nurse. 'And this wonderful lady has taken the best care of

your poor bapu,' she continued. 'Ma Durga has truly blessed us
by bringing her to us. Her name is Shiuli Ghosh.'

And that is how Moyur first met her.

❖

Following his heart attack, bapu returned home to an even
more austere diet and exercise regime. The fried foods that had
crept back into the family menu were now uncompromisingly
forbidden. Instead, they had boiled vegetables, lightly curried in
the finest, most health-conscious, zero-per cent fat oil available in
the market. A daily programme of morning walks and yoga was
instituted in the house, to be attended by bapu and Boss, a man
employed for the specific purpose of keeping bapu company.
Finally, as a back-up, in case these measures proved inadequate,
ma paid Shiuli, the nurse, to come to the house twice a week to
record bapu's blood pressure and to monitor his progress.

With bapu out of action, the full responsibility of the shop
fell on Moyur's head, with help from Joba kaku. The hours he
worked grew longer every day. But Moyur didn't mind. Boshonti
had ceased her visits completely and Moyur did not have it in
his heart to return to her neighbourhood. Work was his only
diversion and he welcomed it as an escape from thoughts of
Jonali.

Moyur never saw either Boss or Shiuli – they came and went
during working hours. As a result, his only encounters with them
were through ma's enthusiastic updates. Until one evening,
when he came home early to find ma and Shiuli at the dining
table, having tea and muri.

Moyur had shut the shop early as the opposition and its allies
had declared an all-Bengal bandh. Their posturing was eroding
his profit. But ma looked thrilled.

'Moyur, you are home in such good time today.'

'Yes, ma, no point risking it during the strike.' Turning to Shiuli, he said, 'Hello, nurse didi. Ma has told me how much you have been helping bapu. The whole family is indebted to you.'

'Oh, don't mention it. It is a pleasure to come to such a wonderful household. And Kakuli mashi is constantly spoiling me.'

'Oh, good.'

Ma had mentioned that Shiuli was spending more time at the house. 'That Shiuli,' she would tell Moyur, 'really a godsend. Coming to see your bapu out of the goodness of her heart. Otherwise how would we afford to have her three–four days a week?'

Shiuli addressed Moyur again, 'Mr Mitra, are you going to have some tea with us?'

'Yes, of course he will, won't you, baba? Shiuli has done so much for your father.'

Moyur couldn't refuse. The evening he had been wishing for, drenched in flights of imagination, cavorting in the secret crevices of his mind, disappeared; in its place was the prospect of a sterile evening of tea and thanking and no-mentioning with Ma and the nurse.

As it turned out, it was the first of several meetings over the course of the month – facilitated by a string of bandhs coupled with ma's elaborate excuses to get Moyur home for evening tea and snacks. On each encounter he thanked Shiuli even more profusely than the previous occasion.

But that was the extent of their conversation. As soon as their exchange showed signs of seizing, ma would deftly step in and the two women would take recourse in easy discussions about new shopping haunts and beauty parlours and the scandals of the film stars. Over the next few months, the topic of bapu's health was deposed by these other, more pressing issues. The following January, ma asked Moyur the question directly. Would he marry Shiuli? It was more of a fait accompli than an enquiry because she had already asked Shiuli whether she was prepared to marry her son. And Shiuli had agreed. Moyur seemed like a pleasant, gracious man with ambition and Shiuli had got to know him better than many others might their future husbands.

Even bapu, who rarely imposed his will on anybody else's life, told Moyur that she was a wonderful girl, the best daughter-in-law he could hope for – so clever, so caring. 'She is the perfect wife for you, Moyur. She will be out of the house, doing her job, not causing you any bother and you will not cause her any either.'

For some reason, Moyur relented. Maybe it was losing Jonali, maybe he was caught out by bapu's plea, or maybe it was just seeing ma and Shiuli chatting together for hours on end. After all, isn't marriage a union of the whole family? As for the bond between husband and wife, well, he knew better than most the caprices of love, so much more whimsical than the stable ties of family.

❋

Except that families don't come into bedrooms. Some domains are private, between husband and wife.

And as night after night fell on their marriage, Moyur found himself lying silently in their bed, keeping his body to his designated half.

Shiuli slept facing the door. Her body, wrapped in a light cotton sari, undulated in the darkness. On the other side of the bed, Moyur curled himself around a silk bolster, the soft fabric luxurious against his bare skin, transporting him into the realms of spoilt princesses. Both Shiuli and Moyur observed the unspoken divide. But there were exceptions.

After all, it is only human to crave the touch of another. And beneath even the solemnest reserve lies empathy.

That night, as Moyur fell hurriedly towards the threshold of fantasy, he was interrupted by the warm, sweet smell of jasmine. It was a scent that he was accustomed to from a distance, yet there it was, all of a sudden, surrounding him.

In the dusky palette of the midnight, Shiuli's long wavy hair tumbled, black and wild, across her shoulders and the whites of her eyes shone fiercely against her face. Her sari had unravelled to reveal an ill-fitting blouse, gaping in the middle where the hooks had come undone. As she reached out to touch Moyur's face, her breasts pressed against his chest. For a second, he allowed himself to relax into her soft, fragrant persuasion and then he retreated. Immediately, she withdrew her hand. Wrapping her sari around herself, she removed herself swiftly to her side of the bed.

From the corner of his eye, Moyur could see the to and fro of Shiuli's arm as she wiped noiseless tears from her face. They had been married three months now; night after night he had lain unmoving, feigning sleep, tentatively waiting for the rhythm of her breathing to assume the steadiness of sleep.

Shiuli's crying continued. He wanted to comfort her, to let her lean against his body, but he was too scared, teetering between an inadvertent longing for his wife and betraying Jonali.

27

For Jonali, there was no family to fall back on, except those captured in black and white.

The house in Shyambazar to which Suman brought back his new bride had come to him when his parents passed away in an accident. The house remained in a state of shock, though almost ten years had elapsed. The rooms were hollow and cold, and the memorabilia of his parents' curtailed lives rattled uncomfortably in every space they could find.

As soon as they arrived, Suman gave Jonali a guided tour of the house, which was easily one of the oldest in the para. It needed a bit of love to set it straight, but nothing beyond repair – maybe a new door, window frames, a good cleaning and some more light fittings. The interior was too dark, that was how these houses were built: to keep the sun at bay. Jonali was accustomed to bright, airy, modern houses and the dankness made her uneasy. She stopped on the stairs, which wound round to the back of the house. The roof over the front of the house was half built, leaving a gap through which the sky dropped onto the stairs.

'How do you like it?' asked Suman.

'Very beautiful,' she replied.

He guffawed. 'You can tell the truth. It is a roof over our heads but we both know it is no palace.'

Jonali blushed. 'No, no, it is a charming old house,' she said and turned towards the open sky. 'And this staircase is...' She finished the sentence with a brandish of her arms.

Suman nodded. 'Yes, it is nice. Mind you don't end up spending all day here.' He chuckled. He held out his hand and Jonali took it. It felt strange: incorrect and legitimate all at once. Her mind darted to Moyur and his treachery. She dispelled him promptly lest her thoughts cascade onto her face.

The tour of her new home culminated in the living room, where Suman directed Jonali to the biggest armchair in the room (there was only one) and insisted she close her eyes. As she waited, Jonali tentatively allowed herself the reassurance that the man she had married was not unpleasant – in fact, he might even turn out to be nice. She let her left eye open just a fraction. Suman seemed to be dusting something. She closed her eye again. He was a handsome man, possibly. Or at least he might, in the course of familiarity, acquire a dignified appearance. His shoulders were broad and set upon a tall trim frame. His eyes sat a little too close together but he had a sharp European nose to compensate, and a thin jet-black moustache.

'Okay. Ready. You can open your eyes.'

Jonali did as requested, taking in first his excitement and then the television set he was pointing at, its screen filled with black-and-white motion. 'A TV?'

'Yes, first one in the street and, until three weeks ago, the only one. Then the Ghoshes had to get one. Theirs is smaller, though.' Suman was beaming. He wiped the screen with his sleeve. 'Do you like it?'

'Yes.' Jonali hesitated, underwhelmed. 'We have one too. A colour set.'

'Oh.' Suman's smile slithered away. 'Colour set?' He turned away from her and jabbed the power switch with his finger.

Jonali stood up. 'I still love it...'

But he had already left the room, slamming the door shut.

Later that evening, Suman apologized. 'I've always had a bit of a temper,' he said, 'since I was a child. I was notorious for it in the family.' He looked at her awkwardly. 'I am much better now.'

'Don't worry, we all have our peculiarities,' Jonali reassured him.

'What are yours then?'

Jonali whirred through the options in her head – illicit affairs, lying, maybe daydreaming. She settled on daydreaming.

When Suman heard her answer, he laughed. 'What a fine wife I have procured for myself, worst flaw is daydreaming. Just remember, too much fanciful thinking and cut.' He snipped at the air in front of her with imaginary scissors.

The following day was Sunday. It was the first full day of their marriage, a day for starting-as-you-mean-to-go-on. But when she woke up, Jonali found herself alone, apart from two large portraits of her dead in-laws covering the bedroom wall. She stepped out of bed in a hurry and straightened the sheets. She tiptoed towards the stairs and perched on the top step, straining for sounds of Suman, but the house was silent.

The three suitcases Jonali had brought with her were still languishing in the hallway. So before she did anything else, she lugged them up the stairs one by one, struggling against the considerable weight of her worldly possessions.

The master bedroom had two almirahs, both full of Suman's perfectly arranged outfits. Apart from that there were shelves carved into the walls or running along them, but wherever she looked, there were things. So many useless things: magazines, old textbooks, dusters, plastic toys, chewed-up pens, empty containers of talcum powder and expired perfume bottles.

Jonali struggled to make a little space for herself, rearranging Suman's belongings with slight economy and cramming in as many of her own saris and kurtas as she could manage into just one shelf. It was a start. There was no way the remaining two-and-a-half suitcases would be accommodated, so she left them. She could ask Suman later.

In the kitchen, the dirty plates from the previous night remained stacked against the wall. There was no sink, just a tap that gushed water directly onto the green cement floor. That was how it was in these old houses. It didn't matter how wet the floors got. In fact, the water helped to keep the houses cool. Soon enough, the sun would suck it up.

Jonali selected a small saucepan and filled it with some water to boil. Then she looked around the room. One whole aspect was devoted to rows of shelves, unsurprisingly crammed with large tins, none more than half full, of rice, flour, dal, sugar, tea leaves. On another shelf, a small collection of stainless steel bowls was stacked, full of bay leaves, cardamom, turmeric, salt.

Just as she was concluding her inspection of the household provisions, the front door rattled open and Suman walked in, his arms laden with shopping. 'Hello, hello, so Sleeping Beauty has finally woken up.'

Jonali smiled at him, slightly embarrassed.

'Not to worry. I have bought some vegetables and your favourite item – your ma told me.'

'What's that then?'

'Chingri machh – the size of apples.'

'Oh, how nice!' Jonali clapped and her mouth filled with the succulent thought of tiger prawns, especially the way her mother made them, steamed in chillies and wholegrain mustard. 'You are already spoiling me.'

Suman looked triumphant. 'Well, if I can't spoil you on day one, when can I spoil you?' He deposited the bags on the kitchen floor. 'They were very expensive, but,' he added, looking pointedly in her direction. 'Very expensive.'

The water in the pan began to bubble, demanding their attention. Jonali rushed to the stove. 'Tea?'

'Yes, with milk and one sugar.' He pulled the damp fabric of his shirt away from his body. 'Okay, I am leaving the shopping. It's too hot in here. Look through it when you are ready.' Undoing his buttons, he hurried out.

Jonali poured the tea into a pair of matching cups, the only two she could find, both made from the same thick white glass with painted pink flowers, one intact, the other chipped in two places along the rim. She brought them out to the living room, where Suman had relaxed into his armchair and switched on the television. Without averting his gaze, Suman took his cup from Jonali's hand. She perched on the divan with her chipped cup and drank slowly from it.

Suman's black-and-white television had pride of place in the downstairs living room. The doilies with which he kept it so carefully decorated, she discovered, were 'Made in England' presents that his mother's second cousin who lived in London had brought on one of her trips back home. As for the rosewood cabinet on which the television stood, well, that was by far the most beautiful piece of furniture in the house. Jonali had asked Suman what he kept inside the cabinet, but he had simply winked at her.

'Suman,' Jonali began.

'Hmmm.' His eyes remained fixed on the screen.

'Where is the market?'

'Not far.'

Jonali turned to the television. Some serial or the other was on. 'Suman...'

He was too engrossed. So she concentrated on her tea. She took small sips, busying herself with the to-ing and fro-ing of her cup. As soon as she finished she stood to leave, picking up Suman's empty cup from the floor. 'Lovely tea,' he said. 'So, what were you asking?' The programme had broken into advertisements. Jonali knew nothing of the routine of the house, so she asked.

'A cleaning lady comes in three times a week to sweep and mop the floors. I pay her to do some dusting, but you know what these people are like.' He shrugged. 'Maybe now that you are here you can supervise.'

'When does she come?'

He seemed to be calculating something as he let his eyes wander over her. 'Don't worry, it won't interfere with your precious college. She comes first thing. You might have to curtail your beauty sleep, though.' He chuckled.

Jonali laughed nervously with him. Nothing could jeopardize college. Nothing. That had been a condition, a verbal contract. Her fees had come with her and were locked away in a steel box that was hers and only hers. Otherwise she would never have agreed, no matter what.

'And the cook?' she asked.

Suman almost choked on his own spittle as he exclaimed, 'What cook? I don't have the money for one hundred and one servants.' His voice grew quiet. 'I shop, you cook. We all pull our weight, fair and square. Is that all right?'

'Of course.'

'Good.'

Jonali didn't bother enquiring about the dirty dishes. As she walked back to the kitchen with the two empty cups, tears came to her eyes. For her, normality was of plenty and she had not prepared for this meanness, but perhaps she was to blame: accustomed to too much, she had insulted Suman twice already by accident. She thought back to her ambition – of standing on her own two feet. And she let out a sigh. Just one of the many that were trapped inside her.

Jonali's mood improved as she sorted through the shopping. The prawns, though not quite as large as she had envisaged, were still a reasonably-sized offering of her husband's good intentions. In return, she decided to prepare a feast for Suman. After all, marriage equals compromise, give and take. Besides, the practicalities of relationship-building consoled her. Recipes and routines were easy compared to what she had left behind.

After washing and peeling the prawns, Jonali dried her hands and placed a telephone call to her mother.

'Ma? Shikha didi?'

'Hello. Hello, Jojo.' It was Shikha didi. 'Meena didi, Riya, it's Jojo.'

'Hello, Jojo. How are you?'

'How is married life?'

'How is your husband?'

'What is the house like?'

'Who are your neighbours?'

Jonali patiently answered the same questions four times as first Shikha didi and then Riya, kakimoni and ma took the phone in turn. She ended with ma and, finally, when the questions ran out, Jonali asked her mother to give her the recipe for shorshe chingri.

'Oh, how sweet, but Jojo, do you really want to make something so difficult the first time you are cooking?'

'It's fine, ma,' she insisted. 'Just tell me.'

So Jonali's mother relayed to her the list of ingredients and how they should be prepared. In the background Jonali could hear Shikha didi and kakimoni prompting: 'Make sure she steams it for twenty minutes.' 'She should grind the mustard really well.' And so on. How excited they all were at the thought of her cooking. If only they had been as enthused about her studies.

'Okay, have you got all that?' her mother concluded. 'You want me to repeat anything?'

'No, ma,' Jonali replied heavily. 'No.'

'You will need some help with grinding the mustard seeds into a paste and chopping the chillies.'

How easily her mother assumed she would have a cook at her disposal. Suddenly Jonali wanted to end the conversation. She was irritated with her mother's queries. Her mother's concern lost its relevance somewhere along its journey down the Calcutta telephone lines. In the ration-quality surroundings of her marital home, her mother's worries were ludicrous.

It was late by the time Jonali managed to get lunch on the table. The smells of cumin and cloves, of onions browned in deep-fry oil and roasted chillies had steeped the house in temptation and tickled Suman's nostrils. He lingered beside the table as Jonali brought in the plates and glasses, the dal, rice, sheem and the masterpiece, succulent (reasonably-sized) Bay of Bengal prawns, drenched in the delicious aroma of mustard.

'Finally,' he complained. 'I thought you were going to starve me.' He looked at the food and nodded. 'Let's see what you have done.'

'I am sorry. Please sit.' Jonali took her husband's plate and served him some steaming rice.

'Dal?' she asked.

'Yes, and you can give the vegetable at the same time.'

Jonali served him. Then she served herself and sat down next to him. Suman clucked his appreciation through his first few mouthfuls. 'Daroon. Only one thing is lacking... needs a little more salt.' He stopped eating but didn't move. 'Salt,' he repeated.

'I'll get some.' Jonali returned to the kitchen and put a few teaspoons of salt on a plate. She would have to buy a little bowl for the dining table. Suman reached for it.

'Did you slice the lemon I bought?'

Jonali shook her head, disappointed. Her food was getting cold and she was hungry, but she hadn't sliced the lemon. So much preparation for an everyday meal. 'I can cut it for you now,' she said.

'No, no. Almost finished. Don't worry.' Suman smiled at her. 'Soon you will know my habits inside out.'

For the rest of his meal, Jonali remained in attendance and Suman accepted her kindness with ease. When he finished, he stood up, walked to the small green ceramic washbasin in the corner and washed his hands and mouth. Then, without any further to-do, he retired to the living room. Jonali heard the crackle of the TV screen as it yawned back to life.

Next to his used plate, Jonali's meal had become the untouched leftovers of Suman's feast. She ate, chewing each mouthful slowly, savouring her own cooking. It was the first time she had prepared so many items by herself. She had done a fantastic job. If she had made this at home, her mother would have been so proud. Jonali imagined her mother boasting, 'So tasty, so tasty. Who would have thought! And she made it all by herself, with not even a tiny bit of help.' Of course, that would not have been true – Shikha didi would have been on hand to chop the vegetables and grind the spices, not like here where she really did have to do everything herself. Jonali sighed. She promised herself that the next time she went home, she would cook for her mother – a whole meal from start to finish with a plethora of accompaniments.

Jonali was in no mood to go and sit with Suman, so she cleaned the table, washed the utensils and returned to their bedroom upstairs, where two-and-a-half suitcases of her possessions remained to be sorted. Jonali began an exploration of the bigger of the wall cupboards. It was not much more than a cavity, with sturdy cement shelves that had been constructed into the shell of the house. Perhaps that was the problem: they were indestructible racks that could cope with all manner and weight of clutter. There had probably never been any need to throw anything away. Jonali sneezed. Handling forgotten fragments of somebody else's life was a dusty business.

Carefully, she arranged the bottles, magazines and books into designated piles, then wiped the shelves down before returning them more tidily, more frugally, trying to squeeze a little room for herself on which she could arrange a little bit more of her life.

Her clothes, undergarments, books – they all fit. In the shoe box that had once housed her ramshackle collection of nail colours she arranged her lipsticks, eyeliners and two surviving bottles of nail polish. With a bit of meticulous stacking, Jonali managed to squash into two shelves all the contents of her big suitcase and most of the middle one. All that remained at the bottom of her second case was the steel box, her most crucial possession. Inside it were her tuition fees and wedding jewellery. Jonali cradled the box in her arms; she wore the tiny key as a locket around her neck. She held the key for a moment between her forefinger and thumb, before touching it to her forehead. This was the remnant of the future she had dreamed of and she would never again be so foolish as to let it slip from her mind. She kissed the key and let it come to rest against her chest, draping the folds of her sari over it.

'Jojo, Jojo... what are you doing?' Suman's voice ruptured her thoughts. Hastily, Jonali buried her box under a pile of her saris.

'Can I have a cup of tea?' Suman's voice was getting closer.

Jonali stood up. 'Coming, one minute.'

The door to the bedroom opened. 'Were you sleeping?' he asked.

'No.' Jonali pointed to the empty suitcases. 'I was just putting some of my things away.'

'Oh.'

The bedroom was not very large, and with the bed, the two almirahs, Jonali and Suman, it began to feel very crowded. Suman squeezed himself through the narrow gap between the foot of the bed and one of the almirahs and looked inside. Then he looked at his wife.

'You moved my things.'

'One shelf. Sorry. I just... I can put it all back.'

'You fit everything into one shelf?'

'No. I also used that one behind the wall.'

Suman turned very slowly and lifted the curtain Jonali was pointing to. Seconds ticked past uncomfortably while he examined her handiwork. 'Two shelves. One mine, one my parents.' His tone was flat.

Until the moment he had walked in, it had not struck Jonali that she was being impertinent. Husbands and wives. Were they not supposed to share everything? So what was a little cupboard space? What was his was hers, what was hers was... Suddenly Jonali stopped. She remembered the steel box. That was most definitely hers and only hers. 'Suman, I am so sorry. I should have asked. I'll move everything back.'

Suman did not reply immediately. He took his time, considering Jonali, watching her disproportionate apology, savouring her discomfort. She could feel his self-satisfied indignation. 'Two shelves isn't much, is it?' he said eventually.

'It's...'

'No, no, it is nothing.' Suman walked back to the cupboard and flung open the door. 'Here,' he said, reaching inside, 'take more. Have another shelf.' With a sweep of his right arm, he deposited an armful of his clothes to the floor. 'Have another. In fact, why don't you have the whole cupboard?' His voice was shrill. Shelf by shelf he emptied the entire contents of the almirah, except the one Jonali had used.

'Happy?' he said when he had finished.

Jonali did not reply.

He moved closer, until his face was just inches from hers. 'Are you happy now?' he demanded.

Well, Jonali didn't answer that question because some questions are not asked to be answered. Instead, she let Suman stalk out of the room, and once she had pieced herself together, she tidied up the mess he had made, returning his garments to their rightful places and hers to theirs.

28

In the weeks and months that followed, Jonali and Suman fell into a sort of understanding. Suman always apologized after his outbursts and it turned out that his displays of regret were as lethal as his displays of anger – if not more so.

But Suman kept his word about college; despite his bemusement he had not raised any objections. So Jonali kept herself busy. Between classes and chores, she was not left with much scope for reflection. Old friendships fell by the wayside and previous hobbies were forgotten. Her only respite came at the end of the day when Suman lounged in front of the television and she perched on the open staircase, the evening air caressing her face as she leaned against the wall. It was a pastime she shared with the women from the surrounding houses, exchanging pleasantries and neighbourhood news. Invariably, they would leave after a few minutes while Jonali lingered.

The banter across twilit skies reminded her of Moyur. The truth was that many, many things reminded her of Moyur – ambling cows with swishing tails; bicycles against lampposts; radios announcing football scores; the magenta, blue and vermillion of saris that had been hung out to dry – the list was endless. And the other truth was that she let herself be reminded, by the most trivial, most irrelevant of sights and smells, and when she could no longer bear him she would run from the open vista of the balconies and stairways into the narrow claustrophobia of the kitchen.

Outside of the banalities of running the house, Suman and Jonali had little to share. Suman had his routine and Jonali had hers. She took pains to keep their lives as separate as possible, as did he, leaving early each morning and returning progressively later at night, except when he did not return at all. So it took Jonali by surprise when she returned from college one afternoon to find the house unusually occupied, full of the familiar electric cackle of Suman's favourite pastime.

'Suman?' she called out. 'Is that you? You are home early.' She walked towards the living room. 'Suman?'

She found him slumped on the floor in a lungi and vest. As she entered, he raised his head, a shiny streak of dried saliva tracked from the corner of his mouth almost down to his chin. 'Hello, my bou.' His voice was lazy.

She rushed up to him. 'What happened? Are you all right?' Jonali struggled to remember the name of the doctor's clinic she had seen on her way to college. Dr Das, was it? She couldn't recollect his opening hours but the chamber was on the ground floor of his house. Surely he would respond in an emergency.

'I am fine. Come here.'

As she bent down she caught a whiff of his breath. The rosewood cabinet, which Suman religiously kept under lock and key, was finally open and revealed a trove of cheap whisky. He had two bottles lined up next to him – one empty, the other barely half full.

'So, tell me, what did you learn today in college?'

Jonali did not reply. She stared at him blankly.

'What, no answer?' Suman slapped his knee imprecisely. 'What a life! Try and make chit-chat with your own wife and she won't even speak.'

Jonali stood to leave. His health was intact. But before she could turn, he grabbed her wrist and pulled her back down. 'I haven't finished yet.'

Jonali's toe jammed against the foot of the divan. She suppressed a cry. 'Let go of my hand,' she said, her tone steely.

Suman dropped her hand. 'I only want a bit of your company,' he said. 'Is that too much to ask of my wife?'

Jonali sat down again.

'Thank you,' he said. They both stared at the television set. 'I was demoted today.'

'Oh.' Jonali absorbed the news with dismay, but not with surprise.

'Oh? Anything else you have to say?'

'Why?'

'Because they are bastards, plain and simple. Favouritism is going on all the time and honest hard-working people are being left by the wayside.'

Honest hard-working people, she thought, and alcoholics. 'What will happen now?'

He shrugged. 'Maybe nothing. Maybe I have to do a little polishing of somebody's backside.' He laughed vacuously. 'Would you like a drink with me?'

'No.'

'Why not?' Suman watched her again in that uncomfortable way. 'You are not always as innocent as you seem, are you?'

Jonali blushed.

'Yes, my little flower, we all have our dirty secrets.' He leaned forward and ran his finger along her chin. His nails were long

and dirty and left a slight scratch on her skin. Jonali looked away.
'Don't worry.' He leaned against the divan. 'I'll have a drink for
you then, shall I?' He lifted the bottle to his lips and tilted his
head. After he put the bottle down he said, 'I am going to be
out tonight.'

'Where?'

'Tut-tut. That is my little secret.' He smiled. 'But I have a
favour to ask from you. Nothing big, just...'

'What do you want?' She knew what was coming and she
was not prepared to give in this time.

'Only two hundred rupees.'

'No. Not again. Where is your salary this month?'

Suman laughed and pointed at the sky. 'God gives with one
hand and takes with the other.'

Jonali began to get up but Suman pulled her down again.
'It is my money that has been fattening you up these last few
months, madam... time for you to give something back. We
have landed on hard times.'

Jonali tried to shake his hand off. 'I don't have any money,'
she said, her voice low and unwavering.

Suman relaxed his grip. 'Oh, how sweetly the lies drip from
your rosy lips. Don't take me for a fool, Jonali. Not in my own
house.'

'I am telling you the truth.'

Suman lunged towards her, grasped her necklace and yanked
it from her neck.

She felt her skin smart but that ceased to matter when she
realized that Suman was holding her key in his hand.

She watched, horrified, as he swaggered to his feet, spilling
whisky on the floor. He made his way across the living room
and to the landing. Jonali tried to swipe the key from his hand
but he was already climbing the stairs. She clawed at his arms

from behind, but Suman was determined. From inside her middle suitcase, under her pile of saris, he retrieved the steel box and shook it.

'Feels heavy.' He smiled at her crookedly. 'Plenty of money you have been hoarding away.'

'That is money for college. You promised.' Jonali made for her box.

'Uh-uh-uh.' Suman raised the box and held it high above his head. 'You miserly little bitch,' he crowed, 'happily feeding off my sweat and toil, and now that we are in bit of strife it's all my money-your money.'

Suman put the key in the lock and looked at his wife. 'I'll put back what I take, promise.' He turned the key and the lid sprang open. Three terms' worth of fees, tied together in neat bundles, stared at them. 'Bah, there is enough money here to feed us for several months. And you have been hiding this?'

'It was part of the deal... for college.' Jonali could no longer contain her sadness. 'Please, Suman, put it back.'

Suman did eventually put the box back, and without completely emptying it. As a matter of fact, he took less than half of one term's fees, because he was a man who believed in compromise. And after he had taken what he needed, he returned the key to Jonali with a grateful nod and made his way out of the bedroom.

A minute later, Jonali heard the door rattle open and then shut into its ill-fitting frame.

29

'Jonali! Jonali!' Suman sounded impatient. 'God only knows where she has vanished to. Jonali, open up! Has she gone out or what?'

Jonali heard another man speak. It wasn't a voice she recognized. 'Suman, perhaps some other time, kemon? I have just arrived out of the blue. No warning, nothing.'

Suman had developed a penchant for bringing home guests, unannounced. He called it backside-polishing, and the less money he brought home the more friends he seemed to acquire.

Jonali hurried to get dressed and rushed to the door. She was slightly breathless, her sari hastily draped around her body. Jonali glanced at her husband and then smiled politely at his guest.

'Is there a problem? Where were you?' Suman put his arm around the man's shoulders. 'Please come in.'

The man hesitated but Suman deftly intercepted his retreat. 'Just one cup cha. Please come or my wife will never forgive me.'

Jonali continued on cue, 'Yes, dada, you must. Please come inside. First time you are visiting us, you must have a glass of water, if nothing else.'

Suman's guest could not resist their combined efforts. He crossed the threshold into the lightless interior and took off his leather slippers.

'Jonali, this is Sandeep dada. He is my immediate boss and a wonderful friend.' Suman smiled benignly in the direction of his guest. 'This way, please.' He showed Sandeep to the fancy armchair in the living room. The fourteen-inch black-and-white television set was, as usual, bedecked in glorious layers of crocheted doilies.

As Sandeep sat down, Suman delicately undressed the television, plugged it into the mains and switched it on. 'Shall we have some news?'

'Why not? Though it is always bad. This strike, that strike. Some poor bastard murdered by party activists. So depressing.' He shook his head. 'You know, Suman, in this country the price of everything is going up. Everything – except one thing. Want to know what that is?' He paused and sighed for maximum effect. 'Life. Human life. That is the only thing getting cheaper by the second.'

Suman nodded. 'Spoken like a true philosopher, dada.' Suman's momentary disappointment in his guest's apathy towards his television was displaced by the calibre of his pronouncement and then by the need for refreshments. He looked up at Jonali, who was standing near the door. 'Jojo, what are you standing there for? Won't you get some tea and nimki for our guest?'

Hot nimkis were Jonali's specialty. Thankfully, there was enough flour. She kneaded a handful of kalonji into the dough before rolling it out, cutting it into small squares and deep-frying it.

In the kitchen, the electric bulb had blown its fuse weeks ago and the meagre light from the candles, guarded greedily by a battalion of frenzied insects, was barely enough to cook with. Little droplets of perspiration lined Jonali's upper lip and forehead. Her hair was coated in a fine film of recycled nimki oil. She had used the same oil the night before to fry two slivers of aubergine for Suman's dinner. The nimkis were soon ready but she noted how they had shrunk. Lately, whatever she cooked seemed to shrink. Oil had grown an appetite. She lifted the lid of the flour tin again, just in case. It remained unchanged.

On a pair of thick white plates that matched the cups, she placed handfuls of nimki, carefully arranging them so the guest had the bigger diamonds. On a tray, along with the tea and nimki, she added a plate with some diced mango.

As Jonali entered the living room, Suman immediately came to her assistance, busying himself with the optimal positioning of the side table on which the refreshments were to be arranged. The contents of the tray did not go unnoticed.

'So much trouble you have gone to,' Sandeep started. 'Hot nimki, fresh mango. If you spoil me like this, I will be forever returning.' He followed this up with the obligatory chortle. Suman responded with a disproportionate laugh. Jonali wiped her hands on her sari and offered the more substantial plate to Sandeep, who grasped it in his keenness to be polite.

'Do you take sugar in your tea?' Jonali asked.

'No, not these days. My wife scolds me.' Sandeep briefly acknowledged his belly before popping a couple of nimkis into his mouth. Jonali retired to the kitchen.

Over the last several months she had come to know this kitchen intimately. She preferred its seven-by-seven feet confines in the evenings, when shadows played tricks that she could immerse herself in.

As she tidied up, Jonali's thoughts hovered around the rows of empty tins that lined the shelves. There must have been a period of plenty in the history of the house. The tins bore the imprints of struggle against overflowing stocks of grain. It was not a time Jonali had known. Since the day she had entered the house, the tins had never been more than half full and the hollow sounds of scarcity had riddled her marriage.

At about eight o'clock Jonali heard the two men approach the door, their conversation full of the niceties of a welcome goodbye. She heard Sandeep ask after her and Suman reply that she must have gone to rest. His voice was terse. Immediately, she stood up. With renewed purpose, she started inspecting the containers, removing them from their neat rows along the ledge and realigning them along the floor, their lids strewn helter skelter in a flurry of foraging. *Please let there be something, just enough for a couple of rootis.* But the metal tins that had heeded her pleas over the past few days remained resolutely unhelpful this time.

Jonali felt sick. She had not yet prepared dinner. The last of the flour had been used to make the nimki. She heard Suman walk back to the living room, then the scraping of chairs being restored to their correct position. For that, she thought, she must be grateful. He was a neat and tidy person, always returning the furniture to its rightful configuration. His cupboard was neatly arranged with piles of colour-co-ordinated pant-shirt combinations that he personally supervised the ironing of. He even took it upon himself to give the television and its doilies a daily clean with a feather duster purchased especially for this purpose. In the living room, Jonali could hear him clearing the plates and putting them on the tray. In readiness she picked up the remaining half of a cauliflower; she would have to concoct something edible from its browning florets.

Jonali began cutting the vegetable. She sat as usual on her piri with the chopping board and a plastic bowl on the floor in front of her. The sound of knife against board filled the kitchen. She couldn't hear Suman any more. So she carried on, cutting it into smaller and smaller segments, forcing the knife into the board, immersing herself in the mindlessness of her task.

When she stood up, she almost dropped the bowl. She had been so absorbed that she had failed to notice her husband waiting patiently at the entrance to the kitchen, tray in hand.

'Let me see what you are cooking.'

Reluctantly, Jonali held the cauliflower in his direction. She cursed herself for having taken so long. If only she had fried them or covered them in turmeric. Maybe in the dark he would not notice that it was withered and brown.

'What is this?' he asked.

'Phoolkopi.'

'And?'

Jonali looked at the floor. It was safest to avoid his eyes. Suman stepped forward until he was standing over her; she could smell his warm acrid breath on her neck.

'What is this?' he asked, pointing to the remaining nimki. She said nothing. 'Oye, you idiot, what is this?'

'Nimki.'

'Nimki? This is how your mother taught you to make nimki? No wonder. Idiot mother, idiot daughter.'

He laughed. He had never done that before, never laughed in the middle of one of his outbursts. Perhaps it was a good sign. Jonali risked an upward glance. She noticed the meticulous side-parting in his hair, greying strands lying obediently on either side.

'Oh ma, dekho toh, my wife has learned to look at me now. What a lucky fellow I am. The last time you looked at me like that was when we were freshly married. Oho, why are you looking away?'

Jonali stumbled as he took another step towards her, pushing her against the wall. The tray dug into her ribs.

'Hold it.'

Jonali took the tray from him but her arms were trembling. The plates rattled. She dropped the plastic bowl and the tiny pieces of cauliflower scattered across the floor.

'Now look what you have done, stupid.'

Jonali began to bend down but the plates chattered terribly and Suman stopped her. He picked a few pieces off the floor. He examined them closely, his expression impenetrable. Jonali could barely breathe. Her insides were empty, her heart clamoured against her breast, wishing he would start. It was the anticipation she could not bear.

'Is this food?' Suman screamed finally. 'Is this what you call food, idiot? Or the nimki you gave my boss? Is that food? Is it?'

He yanked her face upwards. 'Open your mouth.' Gripping her open jaw with one hand, he thrust the raw pieces of cauliflower into her mouth. 'Now eat.'

From the tray she was still holding, he picked up the remaining nimkis and pressed them against her mouth.

'Hurry up, idiot. Eat. See what poison you feed me day after day.' He bent down and scooped up the remaining cauliflower from the floor. 'Open your mouth.' Again he dragged her jaw open and thrust the dirty raw florets into her mouth. 'Swallow it. Swallow, idiot, swallow.'

He clamped her head with his left hand and, with his right, jerked her jaw open and shut, open and shut. The food turned to sludge in her mouth.

'Swallow, swallow,' he commanded.

Jonali gulped down as much as she could, but her aching throat betrayed her and the food sat in her mouth, escaping from the corners where it could.

Suddenly, Suman let go. He stepped back, behind the counter, and fell to his haunches, burrowing into the darkness. The kitchen was silent except for the unabating clatter of the plates. Slowly, Jonali put the tray down on the floor. Her view of Suman was blocked by the small cement counter but she could hear his tasteless whimpers.

Let him cry, she thought. Crocodile tears. She thought back to the first time. She had gone to comfort him afterwards – when he had started with his wailing, hugging himself, rocking back and forth like a master madman. In those days, the remorse lasted longer. But that was then.

She felt a hot trickle down her face, tears of frustration which she hastened to wipe away. In his corner, Suman continued orchestrating his repentance. Jonali stood up. She turned on the tap. The water pressure was low but it was enough. She spat out what was left in her mouth and washed her face and hands. Then she washed the plates, the cups, the tray. She swept the kitchen floor and threw the remaining florets into the bin.

As she finished off, Suman stood up and left quietly. The front door opened and closed. The house was once again empty – except for her, of course. She was always there, its constant companion.

30

Like many Bengalis, Shiuli's family were firm and demonstrative devotees of Kali. For Shiuli, worshipping at Kalighat was interwoven with the routine of life in such a way that she probably would have found it impossible to persevere in a relationship with a husband who did not participate in her visits. Shiuli insisted on this one thing, despite the obvious despondency in their marriage. Because, for her, not to have insisted would have been a binding acceptance of defeat. For Moyur, it was an opportunity to do something for his wife.

On the appointed morning, Shiuli woke him. Sunlight was just beginning to fumble through the pre-dawn precipitate, nudging the night away. Even the street dogs were yet to stir.

'Shunchho, are you listening? We must get there early. If you don't hurry, it will be too late for dorshon.' Shiuli started undoing the ties on the mosquito net.

'Yes, yes. I am almost ready,' Moyur muttered through half-sleep, still wrapped in bedsheets.

Ma had got out of bed to see them off. She was dressed in a messily-put-together sari of creamy mellow cotton that had aged into a deep and well-worn softness that melted onto fingertips. The curly grey hairs that framed her face seemed out of place, premature. As the taxi pulled away noisily, ma waved vigorously at them. The tired muscles and loose fat of her inner arm wobbled for an almost imperceptible moment longer. She looked wrong, standing by herself in the doorway, tragically hopeful for her son and daughter-in-law.

Moyur waved back until the taxi turned the corner. Then he turned towards Shiuli; she had wound down the glass and was smiling into the velvety wind as it disorganized her carefully combed hair.

The taxi made good progress, speeding turbulently down uneven roads. Every so often, the driver would have no choice but to slow down and, as the sound of the engine subsided, Moyur heard fragments of his wife's humming. He tried to piece together the tune but couldn't. He didn't interrupt her to ask. Shiuli was relaxed. She had plunged herself into the moment – an early morning taxi ride – in a way he had not seen her do before.

They approached Kalighat through a complex network of one-car-wide lanes that lay under the umbrella of the temple. Just outside the compound, priests in siren-orange robes touted for business. Shiuli's family had an established relationship with one of the senior priests, who had been forewarned of their arrival and bestowed upon them both a benevolent paan-stained grin.

'Nomoshkar, nomoshkar. Come. You must be Shiuli's husband. When did you get married? Why haven't you been to visit sooner?'

As he fired the questions in quick succession, very amiably, without expecting any response, he led the couple into the temple grounds, alternately addressing them and doling out instructions to assistants they passed along the way.

Even at six in the morning, the inner courtyard was alive with prayers and throngs of worshippers shepherded by priests. The ground was already covered in a sticky slush of water from washed feet, crushed flowers, milk, honey and tulsi leaves.

The priest guided them to a small washroom-cum-cloakroom at the edge of the courtyard. On spotting Shiuli, the woman in charge moved towards her. 'Bhalo accho, ma? Come.' She nodded politely at Moyur and reached for Shiuli to guide her through. Inside, she waited for them to remove their sandals and stored them neatly to one side so that they would not get mixed up in the clutter of the public shoe racks. Then she picked up a brass jug and poured water over their hands.

'We will be back soon, mashi,' Shiuli said as they were handed back to the priest.

'Yes, have a good dorshon.'

Moyur and Shiuli were taken straight through, up the V.I.P staircase, to the inner temple.

The goddess was as black as night, with a bright red crown, framed in a haze of incense; her eyes, deep and luminous, resonated with infinite observation. They had barely stood before her a few seconds before they were ushered along by the next batch of devotees. As they came out and went down the staircase, Moyur looked at Shiuli. She was just a few steps ahead, contented, a restful expression on her face – an unwelcome reminder to Moyur of the many things he did not do.

'Shiuli, was everything all right?' Moyur asked. 'Were you happy with the dorshon?'

'Yes, yes. We are very lucky to have Chatterjee moshai as our priest. You saw how he got us in. Otherwise we would have had no chance.'

'We'll have to come again sometime.'

Shiuli looked at him sharply. 'Do you mean that?'

'Of course.'

'Once a month?'

Once a month seemed like a lot to Moyur. 'I'll try,' he said. He should have been more enthusiastic, but he had had enough of making promises he couldn't keep.

Moyur and Shiuli headed back towards the washroom. They were unaccustomed to walking together, so they drifted in the same direction with a noncommittal togetherness.

Shiuli had just started climbing the stairs, Moyur lingering behind, when he spotted them through a parting in the crowd. Moyur stopped. He was sure it was them. He remembered vividly the thick bullish neck and ungainly walk. Beside him, the woman was wrapped tightly in a sari, the anchol drawn over her head.

'One minute,' he said to Shiuli and made his way towards them.

The man was saying something. She turned, and it was her face. It was Jonali. Moyur stumbled as he picked up pace. She had grown thin, her eyes shadowed, her cheeks angular. With just a few steps remaining, Moyur called out to them.

Suman turned and squinted in Moyur's direction as he hurried up to them.

'Moyur Mitra,' Moyur introduced himself, slightly out of breath. 'We are next door to Jonali in Salt Lake.'

'Oh, yes, of course.' Suman broke into a smile. 'You looked a little familiar. And this must be your wife.' Moyur looked back to see Shiuli hovering behind him. 'Nomoshkar, madam,' Suman acknowledged Shiuli and then turned to Jonali. 'Look, Jojo, it is your neighbour Moyur and his new wife. Aren't you going to say something?'

'So nice to see you both. How are you keeping?' Jonali gave them a perfunctory glance.

'You haven't been back home in a while, Jojo,' Moyur said. 'You have to come. Everyone misses you.' He still longed for her so much – he hadn't even realized it himself until he heard it in his voice, clear as day, clear as the bemusement in Suman's eyes. Moyur checked himself. 'You both have to come, Suman, you must meet Shiuli properly.'

Suman took over. 'Yes, of course. You know how it is. Once you get busy with everyday life, it becomes a battle in this city. Only here we have some respite at Ma Kali's feet.' He shook his head meaningfully. 'Anyway, we should be going. Jojo, say goodbye.'

A stage-managed smile scurried to and from Jonali's lips. And they were gone.

Shiuli turned to Moyur. 'That is your Jonali?'

He nodded.

Back inside the waiting room, Shiuli and Moyur sat quietly on the wooden bench while they waited for their proshad. The room was dark, all the windows were kept firmly shut during the day.

'Are you thinking of Jonali?' Shiuli asked.

Moyur did not respond.

'Do you love her?'

Moyur was taken aback by the directness of her question. He had never thought that Shiuli and Jonali would meet. Yet they had, and she had suspected, and Moyur wasn't sure how to answer. Of course he loved Jonali. He loved her very much but he couldn't tell his wife that. So he shook his head, conscious of Shiuli's unwavering examination. 'I am worried about her.'

'Why?'

Moyur wasn't sure why.

The washroom mashi re-entered the room in a hurry, her arms full with bags and bundles.

'Achha, mashi, you know that Jonali and Suman?' Moyur asked.

'Yes, yes. Very well. Why?'

'Jonali used to live next door to me before she got married. Now she never comes home. She has forgotten all her old friends and family, she is so enamoured with her husband.' Moyur tried to end with a laugh but it ran out.

'Is that so?' The woman looked at Shiuli, then back at Moyur. 'Well, they come here once a month. Very devout couple they are. She never says much, though, quiet girl. He toh, even more devout, comes once a week, first thing on Saturday morning, as soon as the gates are open.'

'At least she has married into a good family, even if she doesn't come home.'

The attendant nodded, her lips pressed tightly together. As they were leaving, she said quietly, 'She is disappearing... smaller and smaller every time I see her. One day, I wonder, will I see her at all?'

Moyur pressed yet another twenty-rupee note into her hand. 'Thank you for looking after us, mashi.'

'May Ma Kali's blessings be with you both,' she said as they left.

❁

After dropping Shiuli back home, Moyur went to the shop. Joba kaku would be there, uselessly drinking tea, newspaper in hand. Bapu had insisted that Joba kaku stay on, so Moyur tolerated him, but he held him responsible for everything and not a day went by when Moyur did not wish him gone.

As Moyur turned the corner to the Bengal Silk House, a passing bus deposited a waft of exhaust fumes onto the pavement. Moyur coughed. He didn't want to face Joba kaku. Of all days, not today. So Moyur walked past the shop to pick up a kochuri from Gupta Brothers. Then he went to collect a cup of tea from the cha-wala. Not the old man from his childhood. With his one-kettle-only capacity, he had been outdone by the younger guys. He had tried valiantly and then, one day, he just stopped coming.

The final ingredient for the morning was his newspaper. With his tea, kochuri and newspaper, Moyur entered the shop.

'Good morning, Moyur baba. How was thakur dorshon?' He was always asking questions, even now.

'Not that busy yet?' Moyur responded, examining the shop. All the saris were stored away, the white display platform undisturbed.

Moyur positioned himself across two stools, one his seat, the other his table. He ripped open the brown paper packet and prodded the kochuri until it lay open, the tasty pea filling oozing from its belly. He opened the newspaper.

Mornings were quiet, and once the stock checks and organization and ordering were done, they could rest a while and gather their energies for the evening rush. On a normal day, Moyur would have devoured the paper in detail, scouring the stories, reading every line. But today, he ended up spending more time rustling than he did reading. His mind was full of Jonali, and the truth was that he couldn't think about anything else. Time dragged its feet like never before, and lunch, when it finally came, brought a welcome break to the morning's inaction.

As Joba kaku prepared to nod off, Piklu from the telephone shop sent word for Moyur to come over – for an inter-city call.

Piklu was sitting in his plastic chair as usual, staring at the television. He nodded at Moyur and indicated the back of the shop with a jerk of his head. His assistant chuckled. Piklu told him to shut up. Moyur looked at the back of the shop and saw the familiar shape of a woman in an unmistakable chik-chik sari. Moyur rushed up to her. 'Boshonti didi?'

Boshonti looked tired. 'Moyur babu.' She reached out for him. 'Let us sit. I think this is the safest place. Do you agree?'

Moyur looked around. Piklu was absorbed in his filmi hits. His assistant, however, was perched on one leg, his back against the wall and his little finger digging around his right nostril, observing them intently.

'What are you looking at?' Moyur snapped at him.

The assistant grinned and winked at Moyur. He rocked his hips in a lewd back and forth motion before sloping off.

'Sorry, didi. Such scoundrels these days – sullying the country.'

'I miss you,' Boshonti said.

Moyur looked down. 'I am so sorry for everything that happened. I can't believe you have come back.' Moyur took her hands in his. 'Didi, can you ever forgive me?'

'Shh… It is unfortunate and fortunate both. Whatever happened happened. Some good also came of it.' She stopped for breath and Moyur noticed that she was trembling.

They found two chairs for themselves and Moyur asked Piklu to order some tea for them.

'You are still too kind, Moyur babu.' Boshonti took a sip from her clay cup. 'I heard you got married.'

Moyur shook his head in disbelief.

'Streets talk in this city, Moyur babu, the buildings, the trees, not to mention the people. Constant phish-phish. That is why I came here and didn't go to your shop.' She lowered her voice.

'This one at least you can rely on,' she said, motioning to Piklu. 'He would not notice even if Netaji visited his shop, unless by television.'

They both giggled.

'So,' she continued, 'you didn't marry your sweetheart but somebody else?'

Moyur said nothing.

Boshonti's voice grew sad. 'I saw her today.'

'Who?'

'Both of them. And I knew straight away which one was your wife and which your sweetheart. That's why I came today, Moyur babu.'

Moyur found himself floundering along the thread of her story.

'It is Wednesday, Moyur babu,' she explained.

Finally he understood. 'You were there at Kalighat? I didn't see you.'

Boshonti smiled. 'I was in the queue, Moyur babu, squashed between other ordinary people with second-class priests. We all look the same, don't we, bundled together?'

Moyur blushed. 'It's not that. I would recognize you anywhere. I was just...'

'Shh. I am teasing. I know what you are. That is why I have come today – to tell you about your sweetheart and her husband.'

Suman had started visiting the brothels long before his marriage to Jonali. He first went as a college boy, cajoled into illicit experiences by the enthusiastic heckling of his batch mates. As he passed from college to working life and his resources grew, so did his taste for sex and drink. In this, he was not unusual.

After all, a whole neighbourhood of the city subsisted on the wayward tastes of middle-class men.

Following a brief period of trial and error, Suman eventually settled on a slightly older woman – a friend of Boshonti's – who became his regular associate. He developed a fondness for her that went beyond sex. Sometimes he paid simply to spend the night on her bed.

Over the next few years, he often came to her with his ups and downs, mainly ups: news of his placements, his progress reports, his promotions. They would celebrate with the clink of tired glasses and the cheap watered-down whisky that he brought with him.

Finally the day came round, as they had both known it would, for Suman to announce his betrothal. It heralded the beginning of their separation and the evening that ensued bulged into a night of bittersweet commemoration. Thereafter, as his wedding day grew closer, Suman's patronage of his mistress dwindled until there came a time when his visits ceased completely.

Boshonti's friend lamented the end of their relationship to the other women, Boshonti amongst them. Her arrangement with Suman was a great deal more pleasurable than the pungent releases of grunting, faceless clients.

So, seven months later, when Suman made his first reappearance, although she felt a little sad for his new wife, it was swallowed up by the relief she felt for herself. It was, however, short-lived.

In the months that had passed between Suman's visits, his wedding had been the only positive thing in his life. His career had taken a turn for the worse and he was plagued by a string of disciplinary actions and an impending demotion. The problem was that when he had fallen out of the arms of his mistress, rather than falling into the arms of his new wife, he had fallen headlong into the tentacles of drink.

Gradually, his visits to the brothel gained fresh momentum until they became a regular Friday-night habit. Once or twice, he even asked Boshonti's friend for credit – but that was not a luxury she could afford. As the weeks dragged on, things continued to deteriorate. More often than not, Suman ended up spending the early hours of Saturday morning in the rat-infested alley, a sorry drunk pawing blindly for company. The girls knew him well and took pity on him. As business slowed down with the approach of dawn, they hauled him in and lay him down in the corridor.

Suman usually woke around mid-morning, brushed himself down and removed himself from the building, taking great care not to touch anything, lest he sully himself.

As her account came to its conclusion, Boshonti could see quite clearly that she had left the biggest question unanswered. 'I am sorry, I don't know anything about your sweetheart.' She leaned forward. 'Moyur babu, we women of the night only ever know one half of a story. We don't ask about the rest.' She felt obliged to continue, plugging the silence of Moyur's shock. 'Today was the first time I saw her, Moyur babu, and I only knew it was her because of your eyes telling the world that she is your sweetheart.'

Moyur stood up. Boshonti stood up too. She reached out to touch his arm, to offer some comfort, but Moyur brushed her hand away.

'Don't touch me.' He kicked the chair into a corner of the room.

Piklu turned around. 'What happened? What are you doing?'

Boshonti reached for the chair but Moyur screamed at her. 'Leave it alone,' he shouted. He picked up the chair and threw it violently against the wall. Boshonti and Piklu watched as the old infested wood splintered across the floor.

Moyur did not wait for the consequences. He pushed Piklu and the gawping assistant out of his way and disappeared into the bustle of the street.

31

In the days that followed, Moyur tried to work but he couldn't concentrate – he misheard requests, produced blue saris when asked for shades of yellow, incorrectly entered figures in the ledger, ordered incoherent quantities of stock. The situation prompted a plea from Joba kaku, followed by bapu's return to the shop.

At night, Moyur was unable to sleep and he would prowl through the hours, reliving Boshonti's story until exhaustion forced him down..

The thought of taking Riya into his confidence, maybe even Meena pishi, played briefly on his mind. After all, many months, even years had passed since *that* day. In the end, Moyur decided against them both. Time can heal most things. But not always. For Moyur, time could not diminish the consequences of that evening, nor sweeten the bitter aftertaste of Meena pishi's attempts at civility. Nor could it make him feel any less unwanted in her house.

I should know. After all, time has not healed me. There are some things too enormous even for time to cope with.

Notwithstanding his misgivings, Moyur paid a visit to his neighbours. He didn't sit down despite several requests. Instead, he emphasized his rush, enquired politely after the health and well-being of the family, and asked for Jonali's telephone number. Riya wrote it down for him, while Meena pishi gently admonished him for never bringing his wife over to see them.

Meena pishi looked thin. The veiny, transparent kind of thin of a person who might accidentally be extinguished by too much excitement. 'You don't have to wait for an invitation, Moyur.' Meena pishi paused to cough. 'Just bring Shiuli and drop in. Anytime, no need to tell us in advance,' she said, her voice a masquerade of warmth. 'I shall have to have a word with that mother of yours.'

Moyur thanked Meena pishi and Riya. He folded the piece of paper Riya had given him and tucked it into his trouser pocket. 'I should go now, but I will come back soon, I promise, with Shiuli and ma.'

As he walked away, Moyur heard footsteps behind him. 'Moyur dada, wait.'

He turned to face Riya. 'Moyur dada, I tried to phone her yesterday but the phone was out of service.'

'Oh.' Dead end. If the phone line was out of action it might be weeks before it started functioning again. 'Do you have her address?'

Riya nodded. 'Are you going to go?'

'Maybe.'

'Does Shiuli didi know?'

Moyur looked away. 'Have you heard from her recently?' he asked.

'Yes, I speak to her once every two or three weeks.'

'And?'

Abruptly, Riya sat down, almost losing her balance; her bottom hit the edge of the step and she let out a soft cry. She buried her face in her hands.

Moyur knelt beside her. 'Something is wrong, isn't it?'

Riya lifted her face and propped her forehead up with the flat of her palm. 'Moyur dada, I have to tell you something.'

'What? Is she all right?'

Riya shook her head. 'I have to tell you something and you will hate me for it. Do you remember the letter you gave me?'

'Letter?'

'The one before her wedding, the one you gave me at the bus stop and made me promise to give her.'

Moyur held his breath.

Riya started crying.

He grabbed her arm and shook it impatiently. 'Please tell me, Riya, whatever it is. Just tell me.'

'I never gave it to her… I am so sorry…' Her words melted into tears.

'What?' he said, his voice rising in disbelief. 'What do you mean? Why?'

'I never gave it to her – and now she is so unhappy.'

Moyur was staggered by her confession. This he had not been prepared for. All the while he had accepted Jonali's rejection, and the truth was that her cousin had rejected him on her behalf.

Moyur slowly lowered himself to the floor. Riya was sobbing next to him. He let her. Not one word escaped his lips. He took out the piece of paper she had given him and rooted in his pocket for a pen.

'Write down her address,' he said.

Riya took the pen. 'Moyur dada, I am so sorry. Ever since that day, I have been saying sorry to you and Jojo didi in my head. Over and over again. If you could have read my mind all these months you would have known.'

Moyur began to stand up.

'Moyur dada, wait. There is something else.' Tears began to well up in her eyes again. 'That clerk she was caught with. It was all a mistake. She told me. It was all a mix-up.'

'What kind of mix-up?'

'I can't remember exactly.'

'Try. Try harder.' Moyur raised his voice without intending to.

Riya shook her head. 'You have to ask her. You will see her, won't you, Moyur dada? She is so unhappy and I don't know...'

Moyur didn't wait to listen any further. The truth is, he couldn't bear it. He had nothing nice to say to Riya, so he ran. Down the hard mosaic stairs, across the alley, along the street, in full view of the morning, back to his house, out of breath, out of mind, he rattled the handle. And Shiuli opened the door. On her way to work.

She grimaced.

'Shiuli,' he began.

She did not say anything. She simply looked at him with such abject apathy that he could not bring himself to continue.

'No. It's nothing,' Moyur mumbled. 'Sorry. I am making you late.'

After Shiuli left, Moyur walked back to the bedroom they shared, taking the cordless handset with him. The bed was made, all the pillows stacked up in an orderly pattern: two on his side, two on hers and a bolster in between. How appropriate, Moyur thought, that even during the day their bed was arranged this way. He sat down on his side of the bed and dialled the number. There was a promising silence and then a recorded voice informed him that the number was out of service. Moyur threw the phone on the floor.

'What is going on, Moyur?' It was ma. 'What do you think you are doing?' She bent down to pick it up. 'Have you seen what you are doing to your wife? Do you ever think of anybody's feelings but your own? You selfish...'

Moyur, startled at first by ma's sudden appearance, let himself acclimatize. Then he stood up and brushed past her. Her concerns quickly became rants, and his dilemma was solved. There was no need to tell anybody what he was doing or where he was going. If they found out, they found out. There was no way he was going to create opportunities for people to meddle. Not again.

❁

Jonali's neighbourhood was a warren of alleys. The houses were old, some magnificent in their dotage, others simply clinging onto the last shreds of life before decay set in. They were of all heights and proportions, seemingly collapsing ever so slightly towards each other, casting into shade the narrow snaking streets in between. One or two houses had their front doors open and Moyur saw that behind their narrow, colourless exteriors, they were deceptively spacious, leading into open courtyards framed by rooms on all sides.

As Moyur progressed, he noticed that the majesty of these old houses was dissolving into a preponderance of rickety front doors and faded lettering. He had not really had a picture in his head of what Jonali's house would look like, but the further he walked into the disintegrating heart of the neighbourhood, he realized that this most certainly was not it.

Finally, Moyur came to the street he had been looking for. The houses along this stretch of road were perhaps the most neglected. Moyur approached each door cautiously, trying to decipher the numbering, but years of sun and rain had chipped away at the paint, leaving a despondent mishmash of strokes that had once upon a time held some meaning. Moyur hoped desperately that Jonali was at home and that she was alone. He had brought with him the usual packet of sweets but no clever excuse to accompany it. He stopped outside what he believed to be the correct house.

The sturdy iron handle looked out of place against the fragile planks of jade-coloured wood. It was barely a door: having shrunk then swollen over countless seasons, it fit the frame poorly and through the fractures in the wood, the barren landing behind it was woefully apparent. Moyur rang the bell and waited, his breathing unruly, wondering whether he should stay or leave. A couple of neighbours eyed him with lazy interest. Then he heard the flapping of her chappals.

The door opened a crack. Those almond eyes he knew so well peered at him suspiciously for a millisecond before widening with disbelief.

'You?' she said. 'What? Why?' Jonali opened the door a little further. Suddenly a look of horror spread across her face. 'Is ma okay?'

Moyur nodded. 'Jonali, everyone at home is fine. There is nothing to worry about.'

Jonali let go of the door and walked inside without indicating to Moyur what he should do. So he paused at the threshold, crossing it slowly to give Jonali time to object. Jonali perched herself upon a ledge, her head between her knees. She was wearing a full-sleeved black kurta. He noticed the outline of her spine protruding through the fabric.

'Jonali, what is the matter? I tried to phone you but the phone was out of order.' He bent down to peer at her face. 'Shall I fetch a doctor?'

With great difficulty, Jonali lifted her head. 'No, I am fine. It's just that my head spins sometimes. It's nothing.'

Moyur kneeled next to her. 'How long has this been going on? You need to see a doctor.'

Jonali waved her hand dismissively. 'Anyway, why are you here?'

'Jonali, that day... I mean, when I saw you, I...' Moyur dithered around what he had to say. He hadn't prepared, trusting that the right words would tumble out to conjure up the right sentiments.

'What is it, Moyur?' Jonali snapped, standing up. 'Why are you here?'

'I am worried about you,' he blurted out.

'I see.' She paused. 'What is it specifically that is of such concern to you, Moyur, that you suddenly decided to travel all this way?'

'Sorry, Jonali. I know you... I mean, how is everything with Suman? I... umm... I heard things about him. Maybe I'm wrong, that's completely possible, but I was just worried and...' He trailed off.

Jonali looked at him with incredulous eyes. Moyur had never seen her this way, body shaking, spittle gathered at the corners of her mouth. She might have been frightening if she were not so pathetic.

'So you have come here because you heard something or the other about my husband. What is it? Tell me. What do you know that I don't?'

Moyur hesitated.

'Please enlighten me. Suman will be back any minute. I am sure he will be delighted to hear it too.'

'He is a drunk.'

'I know.'

'And he sees prostitutes.'

Jonali sniggered. 'So, I hear, do you.'

'But I don't, Jojo. I tried to tell you what happened, before you got married. You wouldn't even look at me. So I wrote a letter and I explained everything and I gave it to Riya to give to you and she never did and now look...'

'Moyur, get out of my house.'

'What?'

Jonali didn't let him finish. 'If Suman finds you here, he will kill me. So get out of my house you... you...' Jonali didn't scream; she didn't want to draw any more attention to her visitor by disrupting the composure of the afternoon, but her eyes were cold and her nose and mouth flared with anger.

Moyur stepped back hastily. He halted at the door but Jonali opened it for him with resounding certainty and he stumbled out into the light.

Blinding, honest light. And suddenly I wonder... I quiver from the measure of my own doubt.

Is this my fault?

Is it only my longing? Was it always only mine?

❁

Jonali sat heavily on the floor. She did not know what had come over her. As her rage subsided, it left a hollow where her heart should have been. She knew Moyur had come because he cared. She knew of Suman's antics – she would be blind not to know – but as long as it kept him away from her she was willing to sacrifice her dignity. But even with the most resilient of people, there is only so much that can be endured. Jonali had had her fill of humiliation, of being disciplined, and so she snapped, pushing herself even further from the person she loved the most.

Part V
1996

32

Six months later, Meena pishi passed away. Her death took them by surprise. True, she had been getting thinner, but she had been eating less and had not complained of any other symptoms. It turned out to be a cancer that had steadily eroded her heart since the day of Jonali's marriage, fuelled by guilt and the nagging suspicion that perhaps she had manoeuvred her daughter towards a lifetime of unhappiness. Finally the time came when Meena pishi could withstand her burdens no longer.

A distraught Riya brought them the news late in the evening; ma had gone across immediately, with Moyur by her side. Ma gently stroked her friend's brow and whispered endearments into her ear – hoping that Meena pishi's life, so impalpable yet so vital, was still hovering nearby, perhaps witnessing silently over the corpse's shoulder this final outpouring of love, and hoping that her soul derived some peace from it.

As for the freedom of her soul, well, that lay in Jonali's hands. In the absence of a son, it fell upon Jonali to release her mother from this world. It was a duty she could not be seen to shirk.

On the day of Meena pishi's final rites, Moyur found himself hounding the dawn. While both houses were still deep in sleep,

Moyur stood on the balcony, wrapped in a shawl. The winter fog hung creepily low in the sky, thick with the silence of recent death. Moyur shivered. In the face of mortality, his childhood with Jonali seemed so far away. Time had played a stealthy game and now they were married, with jobs. Somehow they had started becoming the generation next in line to leave the world.

Moyur's solitude was interrupted by the sound of a taxi. So many early mornings and late nights, before and after work, he had waited for Jonali, chasing glimpses through the alternating light and shade of many a passing window. But the taxis never stopped, until that morning, when it came to a halt outside her house.

There was no one left to arrive except her, but in the pale yellow glow of the car's headlights, Moyur could not be certain. A thin woman, her sari drawn tightly around her, a small bundle across her shoulder, scurried from the car to the front door. Was it Jonali? His mind was playing tricks on him. Once upon a time he would not have doubted himself, but she was no longer the girl he had known. Her frailty turned his stomach, because of the two of them she had always been the one in control of destiny. He was the one who should have lost. Moyur walked back inside. Five minutes past five. In an hour the world would be awake. One hour.

For a few seconds, Moyur hovered near the bed. Enviously, he watched Shiuli, lying snug in her nest of warm blankets and blameless past; how peacefully she slept, the minutes rolling easily into hours. Those same minutes tormented him, one by one by one.

Moyur switched on the television in the living room. The Doordarshan logo filled the static screen. Programmes did not start till six. He turned it off again and sat down with the previous day's newspaper. He tried to read but the lines were just strings of words. His eyes wandered to the clock every few seconds until he forced himself to count at least sixty between glances.

At quarter to six, Moyur heard the creak of ma's bed. Twenty-two seconds later, her slipper slapped against the floor. At ten to six, she found him on the divan in the living room. She studied her son a little while before she spoke. 'Has she come?'

'I don't know, ma. Someone came in a taxi but I couldn't see.'

Ma responded softly, 'Moyur baba, esho. Come and eat something. Just some tea and a biscuit if nothing else. Then we will go to their house together. Come.'

Ma's concern was comforting but Moyur only managed a few sips of tea and half a Marie biscuit.

They left the house with Shiuli and bapu to follow behind. Ma led the way; in the months before Meena pishi's death, the two women had grown even closer, letting go their pride and sharing many secrets.

Riya opened the door and took Moyur and ma upstairs. In the living room, relatives and friends sat in concentric circles around Meena pishi's ashes as she rested in an urn on a bed of marigolds with incense sticks burning in front of a garlanded photo. To one side, a priest made preparations. Jonali sat next to him, engulfed by her sari, eyes transfixed on her mother's photograph. She looked even smaller than when he had gone to see her.

Riya walked round to where Jonali was sitting and told her that Moyur and ma had arrived. Jonali looked up, straight at Moyur, but it took her a few seconds to register him. When she did, her eyes flitted across his for the briefest, most impersonal of moments.

Riya caught Moyur's eye but she did not look away. Instead, she nodded her head towards Jonali, gesturing to him to go and speak to her. Moyur ignored her. The place next to Jonali was vacant. But it was not his to fill. Those rights and responsibilities had long been denied to him.

In spite of everything, though, he could not leave her stranded. Every time he set eyes on her, it seemed she disappeared a little more. When was it going to stop? Cautiously, he negotiated his way through the barricade of relatives and flowers and sat next to her. Again, she gave him a quick glance that surrendered itself to an overwhelming distance, a distance further than death. The cold of the morning returned and crept up his spine. He would have to be content just to be there, sitting close to her, taking solace in the priest's incantations.

Once the final prayers had been concluded and the food served, one by one, friends and relatives queued up to offer their condolences before leaving. When it was their turn, ma took Jonali in her arms and, for the first time that day, Jonali's lips quivered.

Ma stroked her hair. 'You are like our own daughter, Jojo. Understand? Any problem, just come to me. I promised your mother, on my life, that I would not let anything happen to you.'

Jonali's face sank deeper into ma's well-padded shoulder.

'Understood toh?'

Jonali nodded.

From behind her, Riya was signalling to Moyur to stay. Shiuli had already gone home with bapu. Moyur knew what Shiuli thought. How could he not know? Besides, her suspicions were not incorrect. Nor were they wholly correct. Because there is never only one truth. And the other truth, the one that Shiuli had not realized, was that slowly, day by day, she was seeping into him and he into her, like two metals lying side by side with the resolution of centuries.

As ma released Jonali from her embrace, Moyur stepped to one side. Ma deliberated for a second and then walked to the dining room with Riya, in earnest search of a glass of water. So they were left – Jonali and Moyur – alone again with a chasm between them, far deeper than the three years they had been apart.

Jonali pulled her sari taut around her, straining the cotton. Moyur barely trusted himself to speak for fear of stumbling over the feelings she had resurrected. He wanted to touch her and draw her into him. He wanted to become her, to flee from the rest of the world until it became inconsequential. Instead, he just stood, with the inertia of someone who is more than one person.

Jonali was the first to speak. 'Shiuli seems nice. She is very beautiful. You are a lucky man, Moyur.'

'It was arranged.'

'Oh?' She tugged at her sari again. 'But she looks so modern.' The end of her sentence dribbled out in a mumble to herself.

Moyur seized the opportunity to elaborate on ma's manipulation of their meetings and their marriage, and filled a few minutes with the details of ma's scheming. Jonali listened quietly, neither prompting nor discouraging him. So Moyur carried on until he got to the point where they were married. There he stopped. For a few seconds, Jonali remained silent.

'You don't love her, do you, Moyur?'

Moyur kept his eyes focused on the floor. The vague ruckus of chirping crickets grew into a deafening roar. A chair scraped across the floor in the next room. Moyur caught a glimpse of Riya's head peering at them and then hastily withdrawing behind the door.

Jonali sighed. 'She loves you.'

'What?'

'Shiuli loves you, Moyur, because she has no choice.'

Moyur suppressed a sigh. It was such an unfortunate accusation. Moyur had to regain his composure before continuing, 'She doesn't. I promise you, she wishes every day she hadn't married me.'

Jonali retreated towards the divan in the corner of the room. It was covered in a white sheet like everything else, in preparation for mourning. 'So,' she said, 'you are making a habit of misleading women who love you.'

Moyur remained where he was. Fragments of thought rose and fell in inarticulate pulses. Words would not come to his defence.

'What, Moyur? You weren't satisfied with just one? First the pretend dressing-up, then the prostitute, then marriage. Really! Who would have thought you would turn out like this?

Moyur took a step in her direction, desperate to erase the goings-on of the last few years, but she wouldn't let him. As she tried to avoid his reach, Jonali fell onto the divan. The sari she had been clutching so tightly around her unravelled, exposing an arm covered in a purple crisscross of welts and burns. Moyur stopped moving. It was so hideous it demanded to be seen. Jonali pulled the sari back quickly and sat stiffly on the divan. She turned towards him, her voice sour and distorted.

'Are you happy? See what you did, Moyur. Now who is abnormal?'

Before she could finish, her anger subsided and in its place entered a terrible howling sadness that he couldn't bear to listen to.

Riya and ma came rushing back.

'Ki holo? What happened?'

Riya wrapped herself around her sister and Jojo sobbed into her arms. Riya motioned to Moyur and ma to go.

❋

That night, Moyur went and stood on the balcony. He could barely see anything through the thick black fog except for the fuzzy neon halos of streetlights and the occasional lit window of a fellow insomniac.

Jonali's words kept returning to him. He replayed them again and again in his head, each time adjusting the volume, the nuances of tone, adapting her expression, giving those same few words a hundred different meanings. And then her arm – scarred and disfigured – flashed before him with its deep purple troughs and burnt craters. He couldn't bear to think of it for long. Was he the only one who had seen it? She kept herself so well-concealed, befittingly so for a daughter in mourning; his opportunistic glimpse might have been the only one, but surely Riya or kakimoni must know.

Moyur sat down on the cold floor of the balcony. He had to kneel uncomfortably, folding his limbs into submission so that his body fit. There were no stars, no moon, no dogs, no watchman. There was nothing to distract him from the unremitting cycle of his thoughts. The night was dead.

The soft, bashful sigh of the door to the neighbouring balcony brought hurtling back many long-ago memories from a time when they had been innocent. Moyur jumped up. Jonali stood opposite him. She had taken off her sari and was wearing an old salwar kameez, one of his favourites. She had been wearing it that day after Holi; the sleeve had ridden up to reveal his dirty green handprint. Her hair was untied and she almost looked like a college girl again, except for the brittleness.

'I'm glad you came,' Moyur said.

She took a long time to respond. 'I knew you would be here.' Before he could speak further she continued, 'Riya told me about the letter today.'

'I,' he began, 'I...'

'I should have listened to you, Moyur. I would say sorry but it's too late for all that now.'

A light flicked on in the distance and seconds later flicked off again, and in the glut of unconsciousness around them, they found themselves stranded, only too aware of the worlds they had come to inhabit.

'You know, you were right about Suman.'

This he really did not want to hear.

'He didn't let me finish my degree in the end.'

'I knew it.' Moyur shook his head. 'You should have left him. Immediately.'

'Left him?' She paused, digesting this idea, as if encountering it for the first time. 'I am married, Moyur, married. Where exactly would I go after leaving him? Live on whose charity? It's not that easy.'

Moyur thought of Shiuli lying dissatisfied in their bed and the resignation that filled them both. Why did he not leave? It was never that easy.

'And your arm? How did you get hurt?'

Again, she took her time. With each passing second her frailty ebbed away and she expanded little by little into the space that was rightfully hers.

'Moyur, what do you think? I'm used to it now. It's nothing. Actually, it is a lot less these days. He was under stress with something or the other. We both were.'

'Suman?'

She nodded. 'And me.'

'And you let him?'

'Yes, Moyur, I let him.' Her voice grew tight. 'I let him, just like Shiuli lets you.'

'Lets me what? You know I would never...'

'No, of course not,' she cut him short. 'But there is more than one way to hurt somebody.'

'And some more painful than others,' Moyur retorted. How dare she accuse him. She too was responsible. 'You know, it goes both ways. Maybe if you had listened to me...'

'Moyur, is that you?' Their stand-off was interrupted by ma's voice. He turned around to see her a few feet behind him. Hastily, Moyur walked towards her.

'Yes, ma. What are you doing up at this time?'

'Who are you speaking to? Is it Jojo? Riya?'

'No, ma. No one. Don't worry.'

'Why don't you speak tomorrow at a more civilized hour?'

'Yes, ma. Go to bed now. I am also going to sleep.'

Reluctantly, ma peeled back into her bedroom.

Her interference had given him a chance to calm down and he apologized to Jonali. The first rays of dawn bounced against the bleak horizon, trying to infuse the world with some light.

'What are you going to do, Jojo?'

'What can I do?'

'Come back here. Live with Riya and kakimoni.'

She laughed. 'This isn't my home any more. Anyway, I don't want to go back in time. What kind of life is that?'

'Okay, stay with us. We can manage somehow. Ma and bapu will be overjoyed. Ma knows something is wrong and it will give her peace to know that she is keeping her promise to your mother.'

Jonali stood up abruptly. In the amorphous haze of misty streetlights he once again noticed her arms, adorned with the purple criss-cross of old slashes. She caught him staring.

'I am hideous, aren't I? It's not all his handiwork, you know. I did most of it.'

'You can't go back,' Moyur whispered.

She looked at him with the emptiest eyes he had ever seen and it terrified him. In her eyes, he saw the carcass of her soul.

'It's too late now, Moyur. Far too late to stop now.'

33

Late the following morning, almost into afternoon, Moyur woke up, exhausted, from the first real sleep he had managed in several days.

'Moyur, get up.' They had barely touched each other, yet Shiuli was shaking him without inhibition, her voice condensing on his face. 'You have to do something.' As Moyur's eyes adjusted to the light, he saw an unfamiliar distress in her expression. He sat up as quickly as he could, but he was slow that day, handicapped by fatigue.

Words tumbled from Shiuli's mouth, a combination of phrases and gestures that led him to the balcony. A tired Ambassador stood outside Jonali's house. He recognized the car – it was the same one that three years ago had been bedecked in a net of flowers, strings of rajanigandha dotted with bright red rosebuds, the chariot in which Suman had whisked his new bride away, to the promise of love, honour, duty.

In the dining hall, ma was pacing up and down. Every few seconds, she picked up the telephone and started dialling and then slammed it down again.

'What shall I do? You tell me. What if I do more harm than good?'

Frantic words spilled from many lips and clogged Moyur's ears. He knelt down and retched but there was nothing except a bilious backwash. Shiuli ran away from him and his squalor. Moyur looked up. The sky was falling down in great haste. He looked at the mosaic floor. Shiuli returned with a wet towel with which she wiped his face.

'Moyur, you have to go over there. Whatever terrible things are happening, you can't just sit here. Please go.'

Her words rang in his ears. Her sincerity was unbearable. He couldn't reconcile her behaviour with the history they shared. Yet nothing but Shiuli's words and Shiuli's sincerity could keep the sky from falling down.

Moyur struggled to move. Next door, he heard raised voices: a man shouting. Riya screaming. The sound of glass shattering. And then silence.

'Please, Moyur.' Shiuli dropped her voice to a whisper but she persisted. 'Isn't she your beloved?'

Moyur stared at Shiuli, confused.

Shiuli stood up. 'If you aren't coming, I'll go by myself.'

'No, wait. I'll come.'

Moyur ached, his body and mind too weary to bear any more witness. How much he wanted to remove himself from the chaos. But that day it was Shiuli's inexplicable compassion that lifted him. Moyur surrendered to her will and, together, they ran down the stairs to Jonali's house.

Ram kaku, the corner-shopkeeper, and his assistants stood in a concerned huddle at a safe distance from the house. The neighbouring balconies were filling up as the para emerged to watch and pontificate. Raucous crows perched in linear formation along an overhead cable.

Shiuli and Moyur walked up to the door. Riya stood guard at the entrance. She looked in turn at Shiuli and then Moyur.

Then she directed her gaze straight ahead, avoiding any further eye contact.

'Her husband has come to collect her and she wants to go back,' Riya spoke in monotone.

'And?' Moyur asked.

'And what?'

'What happened?'

Riya shrugged. 'Nothing much. Marital tiff. These things happen.'

Moyur took a step back.

Shiuli remained near the door. 'Can I speak to her?'

Riya looked taken aback. 'Shiuli didi, I think it is too late now. They have finished packing and everything.' Riya was obviously struggling to remain composed. 'But thank you. So kind of you. I won't forget.'

Shiuli put her arm around Riya.

From within the house they heard the steady slaps of heavy footfall interspersed with the scuttle of a lighter step. They came out together. Jonali was embalmed in her old buttercup-yellow sari, her weekend bag tucked under her arm, eyes cast down. All that was visible was the top of her head and an elaborate streak of sindoor.

Suman walked beside her. His hand rested on the back of her neck. His fingers were taut. Kakimoni emerged behind them.

Suman looked at Riya and kakimoni. 'Okay, we must get going. I am indebted to you for looking after my wife.' He stood beside Jonali as she said goodbye to Riya and kakimoni. She did not look at anybody else. As they turned, Moyur caught a glimpse of her face. Her left cheek was bruised.

Suman scanned the people gathered outside the house. Recognizing Moyur and Shiuli, he smiled. 'You must visit us one day, mustn't they, Jojo?' He stood in front of them, eclipsing Jonali. 'But you must excuse us now.'

The driver was standing to attention, door wide open in readiness. Suman guided Jonali into the back seat. He passed her the bottle of water he had been carrying and then climbed into the front passenger seat. The driver turned the key in the ignition, once, twice. The engine started up. The para waited. The engine died. Again he tried. They heard Suman cursing the driver, cursing the key. There was no pride in the deadly silence of the neighbourhood. Each strangulated attempt grew more conspicuous than the previous one. Eventually, the door on the driver's side flung open. Suman shifted his body to the driver's seat while the driver scurried to the back of the car. He pushed as hard as he could, driven by Suman's stream of orders. Suman turned the key, flustered, aware of the hundred eyes burning into his neck.

Eventually, the driver managed to get some momentum and the car started moving slowly. The engine spluttered to life. The driver ran to get in from the passenger's side but the door was locked. Suman did not stop.

The car drove off into the distance. They watched as it carried on straight, around the first corner, along the park, and then around another bend. There were no houses or trees to block their view. So they watched until it became a speck.

Shiuli remained by Moyur's side. With unbearable sincerity, she put one hand on his arm and with the other she wiped away her own tears. Shiuli and Moyur walked back home, still apart, but that day, their conclusions were the same. In the circumstances of that morning, the details of who was whose beloved and who was not had become meaningless.

34

Moyur did not go to work that day, nor the day after. Instead, he let the routine of the rest of the house resume itself around him and took a kind of vacant solace in inactivity. It was the first time in his life that he was encountering this vortex of exhaustion, and he surrendered.

Moyur returned to the bedroom-cum-study of his childhood, which had since been converted into a guest room with re-plastered walls and handsomely framed batik paintings of ample-hipped women. A new glass cabinet took pride of place, housing an assortment of porcelain figurines, decorative plates, plaster of Paris miniatures of the Eiffel Tower and the Taj Mahal, and miscellaneous other knick-knacks that had accumulated over the years. Shelves had been reorganized, his textbooks piled high in an economical stack, the remainder of the space given over to a collection of impressive titles, chosen specifically to be admired. His desk, once at centre-stage, had been pushed into an unobtrusive corner.

In the stillness of the afternoon, Moyur approached the desk, spurred on by a stir of curiosity. The windows were shut because the room was rarely used these days and the floor was so warm his feet stuck to it as he crossed. Moyur caught a glimpse of himself in the mirrored panel of his Godrej almirah. Ma had long since reclaimed it and piled it with sheets and towels, but he still thought of it as his, as he did the room.

Moyur ran his finger along the edge of his desk, collecting fine tufts of grey dust. Cautiously, he lifted the top. The inside was teeming. Hardcover exercise books, their lined pages inflated with his own handwriting, lay higgledy-piggledy over each other; pencils of various shades, ends industriously chewed, fell into unruly rows; and a collection of rubbers and sharpeners rattled in chance pockets.

Moyur inhaled and suddenly realized he had been holding his breath. Barely daring to wonder what he had left behind, Moyur slid his hand into the depths of his past, beyond the innocent façade of books and pencils, and found a plastic bag complete with kajol and lipstick and several jewelled hair clips. All other evidence he had removed but somehow these had slipped through time.

Moyur studied the lipstick; it was a bright orange-red, not a colour he would choose for himself now. The kajol was almost at its end. He scooped up the contents of the plastic bag and retraced his steps across the room into a bygone afternoon.

Moyur kneeled in front of the almirah. He placed in front of him the lipstick, the kajol and the hair clips. Solitude cleared a space around him, and in that hiatus old fantasies gathered.

Once upon a time, we played together.

They were my eyes you adorned, Moyur, and my wrists full of bangles that jangled with yours as we spun around. How, then, this? From immense, boundless possibility to the residue of a life not even lived. It is because you keep growing up but I don't grow with you. I wish I could, but how can I?

I should have been a woman now.

In the mirror, Moyur watched himself through large, curly-lashed eyes. He picked up the kajol in one hand and with the other he gently pulled down his lower lid, but the jagged end had barely any colour left. Moyur pulled the plastic cap off the lipstick and pressed it to his mouth but the stick had grown fragile with age and broke into a smudge against the pressure of his lips. Moyur tried to fix the glittering clips in his hair but they had lost their grip and slid loosely to the floor.

In the mirror, Moyur watched himself.

Nothing belonged. Those unpainted eyes, soft uncoloured lips, the unassuming in and out of every breath through his nose and mouth, the dub-dub, dub-dub of his dance. Nothing belonged to him.

In the mirror I sit, trapped. Watching him watch me. I sit with my large curly-lashed eyes staring into his, willing him to recognize me, moving soft orange-smudged lips in whispers that might help him remember. My Moyur.

In the mirror, Moyur watched himself through large curly-lashed eyes brimming with tears, and he saw his own soul, opaque with confusion, mired in regret for Jonali, for Boshonti, for Shiuli, for incompleteness, for the flicker of another soul.

In the mirror I sit, watching him through large curly-lashed eyes brimming with tears, and I see that he is burdened. It makes me ashamed of my hunger for life. He loves me still. But it is with the love of an addict who has forgotten why. It is with a love that aches, rife with these chance precipices where we almost coalesce, where agony and ecstasy collide. My Moyur.

Once upon a time, we had thought our embrace would last an eternity, as we lay, foreheads touching, limbs entangled. How, then, this?

I turn, finally, to face my oblivion. He cannot carry me any longer, I cannot let him – he is breaking and I cannot bear to see him this way. I have been a fugitive for too long.

I wrap my arms around my twin, enveloping myself in the in and out of breath that has sustained us both. This will be the last time.

In the mirror, Moyur watched himself and suddenly the large curly-lashed eyes that looked upon his turmoil belonged to him again. An errant smile forced itself on his face, and the soft orange-smudged lips in the mirror were suddenly his own. Moyur watched himself and abundant tears tumbled down his face.

35

Moyur and Shiuli lived in a patchwork country, a place where identities were absorbed easily into one confluent whole, where empires rose and fell with greater agility than marriages could mend. Despite compassion, despite unbearable sincerities, despite the passage of time and well-meaning attempts.

Moyur found Shiuli standing quietly by herself in the late January sun of Republic Day, enveloped in a fanfare of passionate patriotism. There was no feeling in her own life; she had to borrow what she could – snippets of pleasure from passing revellers.

Moyur had known Shiuli would be on the roof. He had often seen her sneak off to it in the sundry fragments of time when she thought no one was looking, when she thought no one was noticing her golden skin turning shade by shade from gold to bronze and finally to chocolate brown. Peeping out from between her lips was a half-smoked cigarette. One of his. Not a good example to set, but Shiuli seemed to care less, ever since she had been confronted with and sobered by Jonali's situation. A new line had been drawn, but this time it was Shiuli's line, and Moyur worried because her distance was hard, and as much from herself as it was from him.

For a while, Moyur observed Shiuli. For the first time, with the eyes of a husband estranged, hoping to find a chance – a chance for what exactly, he didn't know. He could see her silent, wiry desperation as she puffed. And it aroused in him the realization that he was the trespasser in her private world.

Moyur went down a few steps. Loudly stamping up and down on the landing, he hollered, 'Shiuli, Shiuli, are you there?' In a commotion of flapping slippers, he re-climbed the stairs to the terrace.

Shiuli had entwined herself in a saffron-coloured cotton sari. She had wrapped the anchol around her head. Her red teep had become a callous sprawl across her forehead rather than a stagnant dot; she had been rubbing it.

Moyur squinted. Even in January, the concrete floor radiated bright heat. He caught sight of Shiuli's feet. She was wearing a silver anklet around each ankle but her feet were unclad.

'Shiuli, aren't your feet hot? Shall I fetch your slippers from downstairs?'

Despite his efforts, it seemed she had not noticed his arrival. At the proximity of his voice, she jumped. She dropped the cigarette behind her and stepped barefoot on the burning butt.

Then she spoke, her eyes searching Moyur's face for clues. 'No, no, Moyur. My feet are fine. They are used to this heat.' She paused for a moment and then, by way of explanation, hastily added, in unconvincing, runaway sentences, 'You know, when we were young we used to play barefoot in our backyard. Well, not in our second house because there we had grass, but in our first house. In the second house, our parents sometimes sent us to pick flowers for pujo and we weren't allowed to wear slippers. Later, they changed their minds and bought us a pair each but by then our feet were used to the heat.' She offered him her upturned soles, one at a time, to inspect the hard callus lining each surface.

'Okay, okay. Your feet are stronger than mine,' he conceded. She had never before spoken so many words to him in one breath. 'But Shiuli, surely you must be feeling hot up here.'

'No,' she replied, 'I am quite used to this.'

'Why don't you come downstairs with me? I'll ask Lily mashi to make some shorbot for us.'

Shiuli looked at him for a long time before speaking. Her silence, as always, made him uncomfortable: it was a bold, adamant silence. Finally, she said, 'Moyur, can't you just leave me in peace?'

Moyur stood like a fool, not knowing what to say next. In her eyes, he saw Jonali's reproach.

'Can we go and talk, Shiuli?'

'Maybe later, Moyur. Not just now.'

Shiuli turned away from him. She went and stood in the far corner of the terrace, under the high branches of a coconut tree.

Moyur followed her.

'Look how ripe the coconuts are,' he said.

'Moyur, you really don't have any sense at all, do you?'

Shiuli exited, leaving him alone with the hullabaloo of Republic Day.

36

Not long afterwards, Moyur and bapu returned early from work one day. Ma was installed at the table, waiting for her late afternoon tea. She acknowledged her husband and son with alarm. 'What happened?'

'Nothing, Kakuli.' Bapu winked at Moyur. 'We just thought, why not have a half day?'

'Your heart?'

'Is fine. Business was slow, that's all.'

Ma looked at Moyur and bapu suspiciously. This was not a quiet time of year. However, she did not persist.

'Ma, is Shiuli back yet?' Moyur asked.

'Na, baba, not yet, but shouldn't be long. Come and sit.' Ma yawned and her eyes, heavy with sleep, collapsed into her face. She shook her head and turned to bapu. 'Are you sure everything is all right with your heart?'

'Ekdom. First class.' He raised his voice: 'Lily, can I have a cup of tea too, please?'

Moyur left them at the table and sidled off to his bedroom. He switched on the fan and sat down gingerly on the bed, on the side that belonged to his wife. He had spent the entire morning at the back of the sari shop, conjuring images of Shiuli in his head, dressing her in different colours and styles, delving into the depths of his experience. It was the first time he had picked a sari for his wife and it was long overdue.

He had settled on a deep pink organza with a pale gold pashmina weave along the borders. He imagined himself giving it to Shiuli, and her face when she accepted it – if she accepted it. If he were lucky, she might even be pleased. Moyur sank into the bed and sighed. The debt of happiness he owed weighed heavy on his shoulders.

Moyur started pacing around the room. Outside, the sun was beginning its descent and he heard the occasional stutter of windows being pulled shut in preparation for the eventide of mosquitoes. From his pocket he took out the crumpled square of paper on which ma had written for him a day-to-day schedule of Shiuli's activities. He had no use for it any longer. He had looked at it so often he knew it by heart. Knowing Shiuli's timetable had become his routine, whether he was devising plans around her or not. When she didn't keep to her side of the schedule, he missed her. And then there were those occasions when she visited her parents and didn't come back for days. In the past, her trips had offered Moyur some reprieve from the nag of their inert marriage. But now, every day she spent elsewhere was an opportunity lost.

'Moyur, you wanted me?'

'Yes.' Moyur stood to attention at Shiuli's voice. 'Come in, please.'

Shiuli pushed aside the thick curtain that hung in the doorway. 'Ma said you were looking for me.' Her tone was flat – no excitement, no worry, no expectation.

They stood facing each other. Thankfully, the light in the room was fading fast.

'Please sit,' Moyur said. Shiuli was carrying a heavy shoulder bag. She lowered herself onto the bed and allowed her bag to slip sluggishly down her arm and to the floor.

'I brought a little present for you. It's hardly anything.' His fingers fumbled inarticulately with the zip of his bag. Shiuli said nothing so he continued, 'You might wear it. I mean, only if you like it; if you don't, I can change it.' He placed the brown paper packet in her hands. 'Let me know what you think. I have good experience, but sometimes I get it wrong just like anybody else. So please don't be offended if it's not to your taste.'

Shiuli took the sari out and opened it up to inspect the craftsmanship on the anchol and the detail on the body. 'Very nice, Moyur,' she said, cutting through his ramblings. 'This must have been expensive.'

'Do you like it?'

'It's nice,' she replied. Moyur watched as she folded the sari and placed it back in the packet. 'Thank you.'

'I'm glad it is okay. It will match well with...' Moyur stopped in mid-sentence. He had lapsed into his routine salesman patter. Shiuli allowed Moyur a few seconds to resume, and when he did not, she walked out, leaving the sari on the bed and Moyur alone with it. He wasn't sure if she had accepted the gift and whether she had liked it. Her appraisal had been worse than an outright rejection.

Moyur gathered himself and ventured into the hall. Ma and bapu were still at the dining table. 'Shiuli has just gone to bathe. Come, sit here.' Ma gestured to the empty chair in between them.

'Women are difficult to please,' bapu tried to jest but his smile was deflated.

Ma ran her fingers through Moyur's hair. 'It will take time, baba. Imagine how she feels.' She paused. 'At least you have made a start.'

There were only starts. One start after another, and Moyur found himself in a time that was too much like a memory, from before he became a man, when his chest was still susceptible to the fluttering dread of solitary Sunday afternoons and uncontrollable futures. But he knew he had to try – for Shiuli's sake, for his sake and, most of all, for Jonali's sake.

The situation was not his alone. Sadness had grown into Shiuli over the last few months. It had become part of her, woven into her muscles and bones, hiding in the nooks and crannies of her thoughts, infesting her dreams and her smiles like a slow drawn-out malignancy. It wasn't that Shiuli wanted to be sad. But she had forgotten how to live any other way. And then she had embraced Jonali.

Disappointment had become habit. Apathy had become comfortable. Safer than the unpredictability of hopes, desires, love. But for Moyur, ma and bapu, there were no alternatives. Together, they plotted a route by which Moyur might at least reach Shiuli, if not make her happy, because the need for some light had grown unbearable.

❈

The individual operations that were to follow were planned by ma. For the first time in his life, Moyur capitulated to ma's designs. She told him how to dress, the right tickets to buy, which car to book, and he listened.

On the afternoon of the play she had recommended, ma accompanied Moyur to the front room and, after settling him in post, made her way up the stairs to keep watch on the balcony. She had assured him that Shiuli would be delighted. But Moyur couldn't relax. He paced up and down the room, pausing every so often behind the front door, listening nervously for his summons. When the time came, Moyur had a slight warning. Ma's holler down the stairs preceded the turning of the door handle, but only just.

Shiuli walked slowly into the living room, her mind obviously elsewhere. She did not notice him. For the first time in their marriage, Moyur observed the fluidity with which she moved; the swish of her sari trailed a few seconds behind her body, her wavy hair was callously deranged in the mid-afternoon breeze. She was more like him than he had realized, consumed by her own priorities, wading through a private world, far away from unpalatable realities.

'Shiuli?'

She raised her eyes, startled.

'Sorry, I didn't mean to scare you,' Moyur said. The backs of his ears began to burn.

'What is it?' Shiuli asked.

'I wanted to ask you a question.'

Shiuli looked him up and down. 'Something important?'

Moyur tried to swallow his anxiety but his throat was dry.

'So, what is it then?' Shiuli enquired.

Moyur noticed her gaze fall on something behind him. He turned, just in time to catch ma's retreating back.

'Shiuli, I have some tickets to a play. I know you will like...'

Before he could speak further, Shiuli began to protest. 'No, what for? Why are you doing all this? It is not necessary, really.'

'Please come, Shiuli. It would mean a lot to all of us.'

Shiuli shook her head. She avoided looking at him.

'So you won't come?' Moyur couldn't help the peevish note in his voice and he regretted it instantly.

Shiuli stopped. 'And if I come with you, will everything be

all right?' Her voice rose, splintering at the end of her sentence. She strode past Moyur, who followed her inside.

Ma had been waiting by the stairs and heard her outburst. She and Shiuli stood opposite each other. Ma averted her eyes. 'Shiuli, it's one of your favourite plays – *Kanchanranga*.' Her inflections were timid, as though she was unsure of her right to speak.

Shiuli's posture softened instantly. 'Ma, I am sorry. I didn't know you were here.'

From behind, Moyur offered a suggestion, holding out the envelope with the tickets towards Shiuli. 'Maybe you and ma could go together.'

Ma began to shake her head in Moyur's direction but Shiuli took the tickets. 'Will you come with me, ma?'

As it happened, ma too was often plagued by the feeling that the debts of happiness she owed were vast. So now that an opportunity presented itself so readily, she could not refuse.

Ma and Shiuli returned that night in the highest of spirits – in direct contrast to how they had left. Their giggles filled the house. Attempts to hush the conversation to a whisper failed miserably and descended into laughter that bounced up the stairwell, all the way to the dining table, where they found Moyur and bapu waiting, desperate for a titbit of their togetherness. Ma and Shiuli took turns to explain the drama: the storyline, the actors, the flaws, the highlights. Their descriptions flowed effortlessly into one another's, and every few sentences, they laughed in unison. Bapu was also smiling, slipping readily into their company. Then there was Moyur. He smiled too. But it was incomplete – happy for them, wistful for himself.

The recounting tapered to a natural end and, one by one, they drifted to their beds: ma and bapu, Moyur and Shiuli. Alone in their bedroom, Moyur told Shiuli how pleased he was that she had seen the play, how fortunate that ma had accompanied her. 'After all,' he said, 'what does a shopkeeper know of culture?'

For the first time in weeks, Shiuli turned to face him. 'You should go and watch it some time. Maybe you could take bapu.'

Moyur lay silent for a moment, wondering what he might say to keep her engaged in the conversation. 'Do you know any other plays bapu might enjoy?' Bapu's possible initiation into drama felt like a topic that there was no scope of misconstruing.

'Just like that, no, I can't think of any.'

'What about ma?'

'Oh, that is easier – *Shah Jahan, Idoor Kol, Sajano Bagan.* So many options.'

'And you?'

Moyur watched her physically recoil from the question and he cursed his poor intuition. He would need to start afresh. He thought for a while.

'Shiuli, have you registered to vote?'

'Yes.'

'Who do you think will win?'

The clock in the hallway began its hourly chime. 'Moyur, it's late. Maybe we can talk about the election tomorrow.'

'Can we?'

'If you still want to.' She turned to the other side. 'Goodnight.'

Within minutes, she was asleep. Moyur lay awake. He too wanted to be untroubled, but the night stretched out before him – dark, empty time.

In the days that followed, Moyur struggled to summon the courage to approach his wife with further suggestions of how they might spend some time together. Ma and bapu were both ardently behind him and did whatever they could do shore up his confidence. In addition to researching Shiuli's tastes and bapu's extra shifts in the shop, ma also offered to speak with Shiuli on her son's behalf.

Aided by his parents' interference, Moyur persisted, and one evening, many rejections later, more than a month after he had given her the sari, Shiuli agreed to go on an outing with her husband.

❁

The amusement park they chose was busy, the air heady with excited chatter and the expectation of merriments beyond rides and popcorn. Sprawling spaces were comfortably filled: there were families, groups of friends (high-school and college escapees) who looked as though they had been lounging around for hours, and then there were couples. They all had their niches: chugging rides for families, speeding rides for the youth and for the romantic twosomes of the city there was the boating area with its stable of multi-coloured pedallos and abundant opportunities to impress.

As the evening grew thick and pleasant around them, Moyur contemplated the best way to approach his wife. With growing resignation, he noted how utterly fascinated Shiuli was by the other visitors, absorbed in the atmosphere. She had no space for him.

As they ambled past the various rides, he intermittently suggested they try one or the other. To most, Shiuli replied with a yes-no that meant nothing.

Until they got to the Twister. Giant bucket seats spun round on a huge flat wheel, each bucket rotating on its own central axis. Shiuli stopped to watch and Moyur fell in line behind her. They caught glimpses of faces as they momentarily flicked into view before tilt-a-whirling into screeches of laughter. They looked so happy, so hopelessly trapped in exhilaration, with open laughing mouths and streaming eyes. Reflexively, Shiuli turned to Moyur and smiled, forgetting for a moment who he was. Before she could compose herself, Moyur set off in the direction of the ticket counter. 'Wait there. I am coming.'

The ride was a great success. For the first time in their married life, Shiuli was alive; she screamed with excitement as the ride spun a web of magic around them both, and, for a seldom moment in their married life, they were with each other. Where they went next mattered more, but whatever happened there would always remain – this one time.

Part VI
1998

37

Moyur woke up with a jolt in the calm austerity of the night. He realized over the next few seconds that he had been sleeping, and gratitude washed over him for the rock solid reality that follows a troubling dream. While his eyes adjusted to the pale amber glow from Shiuli's night lamp, he concentrated on the steadiness of her sleep and the one-minded revolutions of the ceiling fan.

Moyur turned towards his wife. The pregnancy had changed her life. When she first brought up the subject, Moyur had been reluctant, worried that he might fail a child as thoroughly as he had failed his mother, his wife, Jonali. As the pregnancy progressed, however, and Shiuli blossomed, he became convinced that the decision was sound: he could not be entrusted to provide her with happiness; it was entirely appropriate, then, that it be delegated to somebody else. So here she was, seven months pregnant, her womb full, resting on the mattress, her arm draped across her body protectively.

Moyur yawned and slid back onto his pillow. 'Ghoom parani mashi pishi…' he recited in his head. It wouldn't be long before he would sing the lullaby to his baby. They might fall asleep together, the little one in his lap or hers. The three of them connected, at least for the sake of the child. Moyur smiled to himself, drowsy enough for everything to seem possible. He glanced again at Shiuli as she slept, unaware. The possibilities were his alone. For Shiuli there was the baby. Only the baby.

Just as he found himself finally closing off from the world, Moyur was startled by the sound of car engines. He waited for the noise to pass and retreat into the distance, on its way to becoming someone else's drama. But it persisted. Moyur slipped out of bed, unable to ignore the urgency at his doorstep. He tucked the mosquito net carefully under the mattress. It was never advisable to be bitten, especially for Shiuli in her current condition.

Moyur stooped down and stroked Shiuli's belly through the blue nylon mesh. She stirred but did not wake. Moyur kissed his fingers and deposited his affection with a lingering caress of his wife's bump. Then he hurried to the balcony.

A mini motorcade of cars and jeeps had come to a jittery rest next door. Only one was unmarked. The others were emblazoned with the insignia of the West Bengal Police, roof-mounted lights announced steady flashes of red on the dark road.

From the upstairs window, light streamed into the black sky. A police officer in khaki pant-shirt-cap paced up and down the upstairs room, wringing his hands, speaking animatedly to someone. Moyur squinted. He could just about catch the black-and-grey mishmash of a person's head. Another car pulled up and a policeman emerged, he had the hurried shuffle of junior rank. The front door must have been open; he proceeded directly into the house. A minute later, Moyur watched him deferentially pass on some information to his senior officer, the one in the window, who stopped his pacing to listen. The next moment they both sat down, side by side, their backs to him. Moyur debated with himself whether he should go across. It might help to have a man around. Often it did, when dealing with police officers or, for that matter, officers in general, from all walks of life. But before he could decide, they were retreating to the door.

Then Moyur caught sight of Riya. She walked behind the two officers, shepherding them towards the exit.

For a few moments there was nothing to see. Moyur imagined them saying their goodbyes, their don't worrys, see you tomorrows – whatever it was that policemen said in these circumstances. Moyur heard the scuffle of the men's footsteps as they exited. The window upstairs remained empty. He looked down again. The officers were shaking their heads and muttering something. It filled Moyur with unease. He couldn't imagine what might have happened to bring them here when, suddenly, he thought of Jonali. Moyur recoiled from his vista. Of course.

How could he not have thought of her sooner? Possibilities lined up in his head and ordered themselves into nasty sequences that made him sick with panic. It could only be her. He would have to go over and find out. He had to. One by one, the car engines revved to life; tyres crunched against the bitty, gravely tarmac. Then silence.

Moyur looked once more at the window and, in one of those opportune splinters of time, caught the unsteady retreat of the woman who would always be his sweetheart. She was propped up on either side by Riya and kakimoni. Moyur collapsed against the wall of the balcony.

The following morning, the neighbourhood woke up to scandal.

Page 5 of *The Statesman:*

A twenty-nine-year-old man was found dead on the rail tracks outside Howrah last night. The body has been identified as

Mr Suman Mukherjee, a resident of Shyambazar. A suicide note has been found and the death is not being treated as suspicious. He leaves behind his widow.

Shiuli was the first to suggest they go across – they, meaning Moyur and ma. She herself refused to go in case she created more upset in a house that already had its fair share. Bapu also stayed behind, partly because he wanted to keep Shiuli company, and partly because he understood that at certain times the balance between too many well-wishers and too few is a fine one.

Riya and kakimoni received Moyur and ma with sorrowful shakes of their heads.

'Moyur dada,' Riya said, 'we don't know what to do with her. She won't eat, she won't sleep, she won't talk.' Riya's voice broke. Kakimoni put her arm around her daughter.

There was no option but to lament at that moment, so kakimoni took over where Riya left off. 'We are so grateful she is alive. Poor girl. Who would have thought he would be so disturbed? Such a tragedy, such a tragedy. What more is there to say?'

'Can we see her?' ma asked.

'Yes, yes,' kakimoni replied, 'but she hasn't uttered a word since she arrived.'

'And her health otherwise?' Moyur asked.

Kakimoni lowered her voice. 'There is nothing left of her. While we ate here so greedily, the poor girl starved.'

'Kakimoni,' Moyur reprimanded, 'you didn't know.'

Kakimoni wiped her eyes on her sari. 'She didn't ask, Moyur, not once – for help, for money, nothing. You know we would have done anything, given anything if she had only asked. And her arms, Moyur... I haven't even looked anywhere else. I can't bear it. I can't.' Kakimoni tried to suppress a gasp. 'If Meena didi were alive today, I wouldn't be able to look her in the eye. I have let her down, utterly and completely.'

'Come, come, nobody knew. He was such an eligible groom. This is what is called the tomfoolery of fate. Whatever is written is written.' Ma stroked kakimoni's arm, trying to comfort her. But her eyes flashed with turmoil and the practised words of resignation struggled to camouflage her outrage. 'What an animal he was... less than an animal. I mean, how? How dare he do this?' ma muttered.

'Let him rot in hell,' Riya said.

'Shh, Riya. Leave it to god to decide,' said kakimoni.

Riya and kakimoni led ma and Moyur inside. Jonali was sitting on her bed in her old bedroom, her knees square beneath her chin, her sari a shroud around her, her body an assortment of bones and skin. Her blouse was full-sleeved despite the heat. Her face had grown so gaunt it could have belonged to someone else, and in her eyes was a thousand-mile stare that saw nothing.

'Jojo, look who is here to see you. Who are they?' Kakimoni spoke to her as if to a child.

Jonali didn't flicker. She said nothing. She didn't look. Moyur sat next to her. 'Jonali? Jojo?' She didn't move. Ma went and sat on the other side of Jonali and drew her close. Jonali's body moved like a cardboard cutout, wordlessly compliant.

Shikha didi brought cups of tea for everyone except Jonali, for whom there was a bowl of Horlicks with a spoon. Kakimoni made to take the bowl from Shikha didi but ma intercepted, 'Let me. Give it here, Shikha.'

As ma took the bowl, Shikha didi repositioned Jonali with Moyur's support.

'Come on, Jojo, time to eat something,' Shikha didi murmured softly into her ear.

Ma picked up a spoonful of Horlicks and blew on it. She raised it to Jonali's lips. 'Come on, Jojo, open your mouth.'

Jonali parted her lips and let the liquid trickle down her throat. It was painfully slow. Between each spoonful, ma blew on the hot surface of the drink and Shikha didi and the others gave a little chorus of encouragement. They all concentrated on the first few mouthfuls, willing Jonali to eat. When the back and forth of the spoon reached a steady tempo, they took up the pressing issue of what had happened.

Well, nobody knew the full story. The police reckoned that Suman had suffered a series of demotions as his affair with alcohol consumed him. Ultimately, it cost him his livelihood. According to the policemen, he had been fired a week ago.

'We knew something was wrong,' kakimoni said. 'We knew the day she came to Meena didi's cremation. That is what is called a mother's love. That is why she died, to bring Jojo back – and what did we do? Nothing. Even when that bastard came and misbehaved under our roof, what did we do?'

'Shhh.' The Horlicks was almost finished. Ma put the bowl down. 'Our poor little girl. How much you have suffered.' She hugged Jonali and kissed her repeatedly on her forehead, perhaps trying to make some headway into the weeks and months of her life that Jonali had gone without affection. 'Husband–wife relations are so complicated,' ma said, shaking her head. 'What could you have done? Would she have listened?'

Kakimoni sighed. 'We did try. But not hard enough.'

'How were you to know it was this bad?'

They sat silently, each in their own private reflections, until Riya abruptly slammed her cup against its saucer. 'But Kakuli mashi, there is a limit, isn't there? I mean, how much do you have to know before you know?' Riya stood up, clumsy with rage, and fled from the room.

Shortly afterwards, Moyur got up too. He wanted to cradle Jonali in his arms, or just stroke her hair soothingly, but he too felt ashamed – for having done nothing to save her. Wasn't she his beloved? That is what Shiuli had called her: his beloved. Was this the way to treat a beloved?

❋

The first week of Jonali's return crawled past. Every day, ma visited Jonali and Moyur accompanied her. Jonali remained as resolutely lost as on the day she had arrived. However, the patient bowls of Horlicks progressed to bowls of rice and dal. Little by little, her body was gaining strength, even if her mind remained remote.

Slowly, word of Jonali's condition spread; the shock of her tragedy began to seep from her personal experience into the collective experience and indignation of the para. She was one of them, after all; her happiness was their happiness, her breakdown also theirs. A steady trickle of visitors filled her days. The circle widened. Bapu visited. Lily mashi visited. But Shiuli remained hesitant for many days. Until, one day, ma managed to persuade her that her misgivings were unwarranted.

That afternoon, Jonali saw them walk in together, Kakuli mashi and another woman. At first, she strained to place her, and then she remembered – Moyur's wife, Shiuli. Different this time: she was pregnant, alive. As the two women walked in, Jonali turned away. Looking at Shiuli hurt her eyes. There was too much brightness in her.

'Jonali?'

She couldn't reply.

'Jonali, you probably don't remember me. I live next door,' Shiuli said.

'Jonali, this is Shiuli,' Kakuli mashi said. 'She is like a daughter to me. Just like you are.'

Kakuli mashi and Shiuli sat next to Jonali on the divan.

Kakuli mashi continued her introduction, 'Shiuli is about your age. How old are you, Shiuli?'

'Twenty-six.'

'Almost. And she is a nurse. That is how we met her.'

Kakuli mashi nattered on, industriously dispelling silences with alternating tales first of Shiuli's talents and then Jonali's, until she was summoned by kakimoni.

Kakuli mashi turned towards the door and then stopped suddenly to look back at the two women she was deserting. 'I am coming in a minute, okay?' She scurried out, leaving Jonali alone with Shiuli.

Inadvertent companions, the two women sat side by side, Moyur's wife and Moyur's sweetheart. Once upon a time, Jonali had believed that Moyur would never get married, but in the years that she had been away, Moyur had grown more and more normal. Soon, he would be a father.

Inside her, the baby must have kicked. Shiuli placed her hand reflexively on her bump and cooed. Jonali let her eyes drift across Shiuli's arm as she followed the gentle sound, all the way to her full round belly, watching as Moyur's wife cradled the child that they would share.

Shiuli looked up to find Jonali gazing in her direction and, without hesitating, asked her if she would like to feel the child. Jonali did not reply. Instead, she turned away.

The truth was that Jonali was full of an immense desire to feel the baby move. She needed to remember life and immerse herself in the irrational optimism of beginnings, but she stopped herself. Because the child was Moyur's.

Ma and kakimoni entered with tea and lemon shorbot.

'So, have you two spoken?' ma asked.

'Not yet, but maybe soon,' said Shiuli.

The women began sipping their tea. Kakimoni sat next to Jonali on her divan and was about to help her with her drink when Jonali took the glass from her. There was a momentary silence before the women forced themselves back to normality.

Kakimoni still kept her hand lightly under the glass and when Jonali had finished, she put it back on the tray. 'Jojo, such a strong girl you are.' Kakimoni's eyes glistened. 'Your ma would have been so proud.' She turned to Shiuli. 'You must come again. See, this is the first time. It happened because of you. I am grateful, so grateful.'

'Kakimoni, please. It is all her own doing. I was fortunate enough to be here.' Shiuli looked at Jonali.

The women stayed in the room a little longer. Their discussions moved from the mundane explorations of soap-opera storylines to the unscrupulous lives of politicians. Then to the topic of Moyur's and Shiuli's baby.

'So, how many weeks left?' kakimoni asked.

'Seven weeks.'

'Coming close.' Kakimoni smiled. 'Is your mother-in-law spoiling you? If not, tell me, and I will have a word with her.'

'Ma has not stopped spoiling me since the day we met,' Shiuli replied.

'Yes, you are lucky to have such a wonderful mother-in-law,' kakimoni agreed.

'Oof, enough of this nonsense,' Kakuli mashi protested.

'I wonder if it is a boy or girl,' kakimoni remarked.

'No!' Kakuli mashi replied with an abruptness that took the little gathering by surprise. 'No,' she continued, confronted suddenly by an array of expectant eyes. 'What does it matter so long as the baby is healthy?'

'Of course, Kakuli di.' Kakimoni took a moment to gather herself before trying to soothe her guest. 'I was not suggesting otherwise.'

What about her recipe for making a thousand sons? Far away in the echoes of a distant childhood, Jonali remembered Moyur saying something about his mother's formula for boys. She never wanted girls, did she? Or was that somebody else? She exited her thoughts – they became tiresome so quickly.

As evening drew upon them, the women stood up to leave. Kakimoni exacted a promise from Shiuli that she would return. She was off work now anyway, and it would be good for Jonali to mingle with other girls her own age.

That night, as Moyur and Shiuli lay together, Shiuli told him of what had passed between her and Jonali. 'She is so frail, isn't she?' Shiuli concluded.

Moyur felt uncomfortable speaking about Jonali to Shiuli. It was as though they were trespassing on a relationship that was sacrosanct.

He nodded silently.

But that was just the beginning. Questions tumbled from Shiuli's lips in haste and they were met with reticence. Some of her queries Moyur did not want to answer, some he could not. But Shiuli would not stop. She kept probing, asking him about Jonali. She had never before wanted to know anything about their childhood but now she filled the night with questions: what they did together, what games they played, how often, in which house, were they sweethearts when they were children? When Moyur refused to answer the final question, Shiuli persevered.

'But everyone knows,' she said, 'that childhood sweethearts are inconsequential.'

When Moyur still didn't answer, she sat up in bed and began to sob.

'Please stop, Shiuli,' he begged.

But Shiuli could not stop. The restraint she had so carefully balanced over the previous months dissolved in the face of this final betrayal. 'Tell me the truth.' That was all she wanted.

So he told her. Everything.

❋

Over the next few days, both Moyur and Shiuli continued to visit Jonali – separately. But by the vagaries of time and circumstance, it was Shiuli who ended up being Jonali's more constant companion.

Slowly, irrepressibly, life began its pilgrimage back into Jonali's body. She started to dress herself, to eat, to listen, to speak. And it seemed that perhaps this resurgence was linked in some way to her proximity to the new life that was taking shape in Shiuli's belly.

Despite her initial refusal, on every visit, Jonali would gaze longingly at Shiuli's bump. Every day Shiuli would invite Jonali to feel her child and every day Jonali would refuse. Then one day, with over a fortnight behind them, she nervously acquiesced. Shiuli took Jonali's hand and placed it on her abdomen.

Jonali's touch was ever so slight. Shiuli placed her hand on top of hers and pressed it into her body. 'There. She kicked. Did you feel her?'

Jonali nodded, and as she did so, a smile ruptured the sadness on her face.

'Isn't she beautiful?' Shiuli continued. 'She always knows when we are talking about her, you know. She is such a cheeky little thing.'

'She'll be a right monkey,' Jonali whispered, struggling with her words.

'Yes, she will be – a right little monkey. Won't you, baby? Did you hear what your mashi just said?'

Jonali lowered herself onto the floor. 'Have you thought of any names?'

Shiuli looked mischievously at the ceiling. 'Well, if it is a girl we think we are going to call her Moyna. Moyna – like the bird.'

'That's a pretty name.'

'You like it?'

Jonali nodded.

'And if it's a boy.' Shiuli hesitated for a second. 'Shall I tell you a secret?'

Inspite of herself, Jonali nodded.

'It's definitely a girl, I can feel it, a mother's intuition – but don't tell anyone else. Promise?'

'Promise. I am very good at keeping secrets. Ask Mo...' Jonali didn't finish.

It was so long ago that she sometimes wondered whether she had blurred the boundaries of reality.

Sensing her retreat, Shiuli intervened, 'Do you want to talk to her?'

'Really? Okay, but what am I going to say?'

'Anything.' Shiuli looked at Jonali. Jonali felt her skin prickle. 'She likes it when I sing to her.' Shiuli turned to her belly. 'Eyi, Moyna shona, your mashi wants to speak to you. Isn't that exciting?' She stroked her belly.

Jonali approached with delight and leaned her head against Shiuli's body. 'I can hear her heartbeat,' she whispered.

Shiuli nodded.

'Moyna, Moyna,' Jonali called out her name very softly.

The baby girl inside Shiuli kicked gently against her mother. She was so happy, so cherished.

38

Over the next few days, Jonali found herself confronted by a battalion of words, charging to reacquaint themselves with the roll of her tongue and flow of her lips. She began slowly, gingerly pronouncing sounds that after weeks of silence had fallen into misuse, but the words kept coming. Relentless thoughts she had tried to suppress now demanded articulation and, little by little, Jonali spilled her story to kakimoni, to Riya, to Kakuli mashi, but most of all to Shiuli, because Shiuli had the most time to spare and because when she did, Jonali liked to tell the story to them both: she would tell it to Shiuli and then whisper it to the little girl inside her. But there were other reasons too. For instance, Shiuli had the most delicate fingers of them all, and when Jonali spoke, Shiuli would wipe away her pain with a touch as soft as a feather on her broken skin. Shiuli had the most compassion, and the most beguiling sincerity.

Late one morning, the two women sat together. They had interrupted their conversation to sip from cups of rapidly cooling tea. The regular banter between kakimoni and Shikha didi about the cooking and cleaning and washing and ironing filled their ears. It was a comforting babble, a blanket within which Jonali could wrap herself against memories of her barren marriage. Of course, blankets may not be perfect and in this one there were defects – threads that had come undone, holes, absences where Jonali's mother's voice should have been.

'Jonali, can I ask you something?'

'Yes.'

'Well,' she began. Shiuli did not continue into a question. She proceeded instead into an explanation, a preamble intended to convince Jonali of her response before she had even heard the question. Jonali listened.

Shiuli was right to have taken this longwinded tack because what she was asking of her was not going to be easy and Jonali did not want to incite her past, one that might easily drive her back into madness. But, with little assurances, Shiuli persuaded her that it would be different. They would go together – just Shiuli, the little one inside her and Jonali, early in the morning. They would pray and eat proshad and be blessed.

Two days later, kakimoni, Kakuli mashi and Moyur waved the two women off. They had all been concerned. 'Are you sure?' and 'Just by yourselves?' and 'Let me come with you.' There had been much interjecting and insisting but in the end Shiuli had her way, because the wisdom in her way was obvious to them all.

Jonali and Shiuli arrived at a temple alive with the sounds of prayer and preparation. Outside Kalighat, Chatterjee moshai was waiting for them with the diligence of a man proud to have been entrusted with a responsibility beyond his station. As soon as he spotted her, he rushed up to them with his paan-stained smile. And there was something else. Jonali had seen it before. That sort of smile. But where? And she remembered. Her mother's face on the day of her wedding, wearing a tender, bitter smile, full of concern and affection for a girl who had once been so little and had since grown so big: a wife, a mother.

'Come, come.' The priest shepherded them along. Two of his assistants walked on either side as they headed inside.

The waiting room was as busy as ever, with shoes and handbags spilling from the racks and jostling under the benches. But the old mashi had been replaced by a new woman. 'Gone for holidays to her village,' the priest explained, anticipating the question, 'but she will be back, not to worry.'

In most ways, Shiuli's pregnancy probably made it easier for her to gain access to the goddess because the goddess is also a mother and the mother is revered. Jonali followed closely in Shiuli's footsteps, up the V.I.P stairs. She too felt protected from the masses by the baby inside Shiuli's belly and by the assistant priests, who had formed a dutiful barricade against the sudden surges of people. But what of the surges of shadows?

In the trail of Jonali's footfall, Suman followed, slipping through the entourage of priests. The last time she had come, he had been with her. Towards the end he had taken to drinking every day, even when they were due to go to the temple. He had embarrassed her in front of the priests, slurring his words, instructing her prayers. And afterwards, when they returned home, he had hit her for not being devoted enough.

Jonali shuddered. Around her, men, women and children prayed and their prayers overflowed with the goodness of the moment. How long does goodness last? In the chants and supplications of wholesome men and women, Jonali saw many shadows and they frightened her. Did nobody else see?

In front of her, the corridor was clear; Shiuli and Chatterjee moshai were striding towards the goddess and the gap between them and her was widening. Jonali felt herself slip; suddenly the ties that were holding her in place began to unravel. A sea of black swelled up around her and Suman reached for her.

'Jonali? Are you okay? Almost there.'

It was Shiuli's soft hand that grabbed hers, not Suman's. Light returned to her eyes and Jonali saw the priest waiting for them ahead. He signalled for them to hurry. Shiuli had come back for her.

'Come,' Shiuli said, 'let's hold hands.'

Jonali clung to her. Even though it was inconvenient and their arms suffered from differing paces and unwieldy corners, Jonali did not let go. Not until they reached the inner sanctum and orbited, one behind the other. Bells rang out, priests chanted and prayers filled the air. And then they arrived in front of Ma Kali, black as night, darker than darkness, destroyer of shadows...

❀

Jonali and Shiuli emerged only a few minutes later to find the temple in a state of commotion. The queue of worshippers was snaking twice around the courtyard and it was difficult to tell who was coming and who was going. Shiuli's priest led them to one side; his assistants had disappeared.

'From here we will be fine, Chatterjee moshai. Thank you for looking after us,' Shiuli said.

'Yes, thank you,' Jonali added.

'Not at all. I should be thanking you. Achha, are you sure you will be fine?'

Shiuli reassured the elderly priest and paid him. As he walked away, Shiuli took Jonali's hand again. 'Was everything all right?'

Jonali nodded.

'Time to go home?'

Jonali smiled. Yes, shadows had been cast and destroyed, but she was tired and it was definitely time to go home.

The two women headed towards the exit, swathed in a crowd of people. It was difficult, despite their best intentions, not to step on unfortunate feet or knock handbags off shoulders. These were the minor hazards that were to be expected and were, on the whole, borne with good grace. There were exceptions, of course, usually when a minor trample became something more. So it was with dismay that Jonali registered the ripping sound of a sari behind her, caught somehow in a compromising position under the small but sharp heel of her sandal. The woman behind almost collided into her.

'Oooh. Gone.'

Jonali and Shiuli stopped and turned around. 'Let's see. Let's see,' Shiuli said, trying hopelessly to bend. Jonali crouched down. The sari was a bright pink synthetic one with chik-chik motifs that glinted in the morning sun. Jonali could see the gash where her shoe had caught the fabric; the material was probably quite old, allowing the slightest pinch to wear into a fissure. Hopefully it wouldn't be too expensive to replace.

Jonali straightened up. 'So sorry. It was an accident.'

The woman was looking at Shiuli intently. At the sound of Jonali's voice, she shifted her gaze. A gaze full of recognition.

'Didi?' Jonali started again, confused.

The woman did not reply. She was a little odd-looking for a temple-goer: her teep too ornate for the occasion, her bangles a little too shiny and her hair, though enviably long and thick, arranged in a plait that might have been more appropriate on someone twenty years younger. When she opened her mouth to speak, Jonali noted her neat and clean teeth and large pink gums, out of kilter with the rest of her get-up.

'Yes. Big tear in my sari. Big tear,' the woman said distractedly. She turned to Shiuli. 'You are going to be a mother soon?'

Shiuli nodded and grinned. 'Few weeks left, didi.'

'It is a great honour,' the woman said, 'to give life.' There was something about the way she spoke, an extreme tenderness in the way she asked if she could place her hand on Shiuli's bump, that mesmerized both Shiuli and Jonali.

'A girl?' the woman asked.

Shiuli nodded. 'How do you know?'

The woman smiled. 'Something good should come from old age, no?'

The woman asked Shiuli's permission before kneeling down. She placed her head against Shiuli's belly and listened. 'Dub-dub, dub-dub,' she mouthed.

And suddenly it felt as though the entire courtyard was resonating with the sound of my heartbeat.

The woman stood up. 'Have you thought of a name?' she asked.

Shiuli wrapped her arms around her belly. 'What? Shall I tell her? Ki?' She paused as though waiting for her baby to speak. Then she looked up with a cheeky smile. 'Okay, didi. Her name is Moyna.'

'Moyna, like the bird?'

Both Shiuli and Jonali nodded.

'Such a beautiful name, isn't it?' Jonali said.

'It matches Moyur,' Shiuli whispered.

To their astonishment, the woman's eyes filled with water, with tears that seemed neither sad nor joyful. Puzzled, Jonali searched for clues but this woman was impossible. The tears flowed freely now and all Jonali could fathom was that they were the tears of someone who was overwhelmed.

Jonali and Shiuli waited patiently for her to regain her composure and when she did, Jonali once again raised the issue of her sari.

'Let me pay for it, didi. It is my fault that you have to get a new one.'

But the woman was adamant in her refusal.

'No. What use does an old woman like me have for new saris?' She shook her head and folded her hands together in the direction of the temple. 'Thanks to Ma Kali, I have seen you today. The goddess protects her daughters and she is inside you, inside your Moyna.'

'At least accept some money,' Shiuli said.

'No, no.'

It was a strange convention: the three of them in the courtyard in Kalighat. Shiuli was too ready, too eager to share her child with everyone, Jonali mused, but she quickly set aside her misgivings. For, hadn't Shiuli shared her baby with her, of all people?

'I am leaving this city,' the woman said. 'Time for this poor woman to go back home.'

'Where is that?'

'Somewhere far, near the clouds... You take the toy train from Siliguri. You know it?'

Shiuli shook her head.

The woman laughed. 'Too far for big suitcases full of new saris,' she said.

Shiuli looked unconvinced but she relented.

'Don't worry, madam. Ma Kali understands. You tearing my sari is nothing. You have brought me so much peace. I thank Ma Kali that I heard your baby, your Moyna. Now I can go home.'

'Okay, well if you are sure,' Jonali intervened. 'I think it is time for us to make a move.'

'Yes, of course, of course. And me, time to go back to my village, back to my mother.'

The woman turned and walked away from them and the chik-chik of her pink sari glinted gleefully as she moved. 'Moyur,

Moyna, Moyna, Moyur. The peacock and the starling.' Her incomprehensible mumbles floated back towards them but she did not look back, not once.

Shiuli turned to Jonali and gave her a little shrug. 'Strange.'

'Strange,' Jonali agreed. 'Moyna is a beautiful name.'

'Isn't it? I wonder if she will sing, if she will dance.'

The two women drifted back into the business of the temple and then slowly made their way home.

39

Exactly two weeks later, halfway through a humdrum everyday morning, Shiuli and Jonali sat together, singing to Moyna as she kicked happily inside her belly, when Shiuli let out a howl. She clutched her abdomen tightly as a wave of pain ripped through her. A flush of blood stained her sari.

'Oh, my god, my god. What is happening? Jonali, go quickly, get ma.'

Jonali ran as quickly as she could out of the room. The family was already heading towards the room. 'Jojo, what happened?'

'Blood.'

'Riya, go and call your Kakuli mashi. Jojo, call an ambulance.'

Kakimoni rushed in to find Shiuli hunched over her belly. 'Ambulance is on its way, Shiuli.'

'It will be all right, won't it, kakimoni?'

'Of course it will.' Kakimoni allowed herself a false laugh. 'How long have women been having babies?'

'I have never wanted anything, have I, kakimoni?' As the pain relented a little, Shiuli found herself in the middle of a hopelessness she had all but forgotten. 'Except this little one. I love her so much. Surely she won't be taken from me.'

Kakimoni stroked her forehead. 'No way. They perform miracles these days.'

Ma arrived immediately. The ambulance arrived. Ma and Shiuli travelled together. Jonali, Riya and kakimoni followed in a taxi.

Bapu and Moyur had been telephoned to come directly to the hospital. They were waiting by the time the women arrived.

❁

The long hospital corridor winding down to the maternity wing was silent except for the creaking of tired wheels. Shiuli lay semi-recumbent on the stretcher, clutching her belly as the porters pushed her along and a nurse chattered incessant words of distraction. Moyur walked beside her; the rest of the family followed as best they could.

The End

Calcutta 1998

I am soaring now. Soaring through skies as bright as my heart is abundant.

I see the woman who is my mother struggling with my birth and I look to the goddess who cradles us. And I know we will both be all right, whether in this life or the next.

Once, long ago, you reached for me; we had only chance moments of joy. But now our nights spill over with a moon so piercingly bright that even shadows shine.

The time has come for me to reclaim my soul. The time has come for me to dance my own dances. For stolen dances to be returned.

Acknowledgements

I would like to begin by remembering Didama for the time and energy with which she introduced me to books and for the many wonderful stories with which she filled my childhood. I would also like to remember Thammi and Jetthumoni, a lover of fine arts, who would have been so proud.

I am fortunate to be surrounded by a big, warm and loving family, all of whom have in some way or other journeyed with me through the ups and downs of writing this first novel and sending it out into the world.

I would like to thank my parents for the immense love and light with which they always surround us. I would like to thank Keith and Catherine Bullock for their love and comradeship. I would like to thank my uncles and aunts, in particular Moni jetthu, Mishti kaku, Chhoto kaku and Sumit mesho for their insightful comments, enthusiasm and endless support. And a special thanks to Shilpi for her editorial suggestions as well as her thoughtfulness in all aspects of my writing endeavours.

Back when I first conceived of this novel, I never imagined that I would find myself at this point. For carrying me along on the path to becoming a writer, I would like to thank my tutors, Harriet Gilbert in particular, and my fellow students at City

University, London, from whom I learned so much more than I had anticipated.

I would also like to express my gratitude to Stephen Lansdown for saving me from my own punctuation, and to my wonderful friends and colleagues who have generously shared in my excitement for this book.

I am extremely grateful to my agent Caroline Hardman and her colleagues at Christopher Little Literary Agency for their unfaltering belief and efforts in bringing this novel to fruition.

I would also like to give special thanks to the team at HarperCollins India, particularly Neelini Sarkar for embracing the story and for the consideration with which she has nurtured it through its final stages.

There are three people, in particular, to whom I owe the biggest debt of gratitude.

With all my love and affection, I thank my brother, Saswata, for being by my side during the two hardest years of my life when most of this book was written, for valiantly showing up when it mattered the most, and for making us laugh away our 'croglinks'.

For reading and re-reading the drafts I have produced, for editorial suggestions, and the many discussions we have had as this book has evolved, for loving Moyna and Moyur as much as I do and for the complete joy with which she shares my moments, with all my heart, I thank my sister, Sohini.

I am immensely fortunate to have you both.

And finally my husband, Marc, without whom this novel would not have been written. Thank you for pointing me in the right direction, for encouraging me, and for believing in my writing more than I did. Thank you also for the rooftop conversations and endless cups of tea, and for driving thousands of miles up and down the country so that I could have my dream. I love you.